About the [Author]

Cindi Myers beca[me a writer in] eighth grade wh[en she wrote a] torrid historical roman[ce and passed the manuscri]pt around among friends. Fa[me was hers;] the English teacher confiscated th[e book. S]ince then, Cindi has written more than fifty [publishe]d novels. Her historical and contemporary roman[ce]s and women's fiction have garnered praise from reviewers and readers alike.

Jo Leigh has written over fifty books for Mills & Boon since 1994. She's a triple *RITA* finalist and was part of the Mills & Boon Blaze launch. She also teaches story structure in workshops across the country. Jo lives in Utah. If you X, come X her at @Jo_Leigh, or find out the latest news at tumblr.com/blog/joleighwrites/

With over 2.1 million copies published in over twenty-one countries, **Sarah M. Anderson** has published over fifty books. Sarah's book *A Man of Privilege* won an *RT Book Reviews* 2012 Reviewers' Choice Best Book Award. *The Nanny Plan* was a 2016 *RITA* winner for Best Contemporary: Short and *Seduction on His Terms* won the 2020 Bookseller's Best Award for Short Contemporary. She lives in rural Illinois with her family, her rescue dogs, and a collection of oversized tea mugs.

Romance On Duty

March 2025
Irresistible Sparks

April 2025
Love in Action

May 2025
Undercover Passion

June 2025
In Pursuit of Love

Romance On Duty:
Undercover Passion

CINDI MYERS

JO LEIGH

SARAH M. ANDERSON

MILLS & BOON

All rights reserved including the right of reproduction in whole or in part in any form. This edition is published by arrangement with Harlequin Enterprises ULC.

This is a work of fiction. Names, characters, places, locations and incidents are purely fictional and bear no relationship to any real life individuals, living or dead, or to any actual places, business establishments, locations, events or incidents. Any resemblance is entirely coincidental.

This book is sold subject to the condition that it shall not, by way of trade or otherwise, be lent, resold, hired out or otherwise circulated without the prior consent of the publisher in any form of binding or cover other than that in which it is published and without a similar condition including this condition being imposed on the subsequent purchaser.

® and ™ are trademarks owned and used by the trademark owner and/or its licensee. Trademarks marked with ® are registered with the United Kingdom Patent Office and/or the Office for Harmonisation in the Internal Market and in other countries.

First Published in Great Britain 2025
by Mills & Boon, an imprint of HarperCollins*Publishers* Ltd
1 London Bridge Street, London, SE1 9GF

www.harpercollins.co.uk

HarperCollins*Publishers*
Macken House, 39/40 Mayor Street Upper,
Dublin 1, D01 C9W8, Ireland

Romance on Duty: Undercover Passion © 2025 Harlequin Enterprises ULC.

Running Out of Time © 2020 Harlequin Enterprises ULC
Lying in Bed © 2013 Jolie Kramer
Pride and Pregnancy © 2017 Sarah M. Anderson

Special thanks and acknowledgment are given to Cindi Myers for her contribution to the *Tactical Crime Division* series.

ISBN: 978-0-263-41733-3

This book contains FSC™ certified paper and other controlled sources to ensure responsible forest management.

For more information visit: www.harpercollins.co.uk/green

Printed and Bound in the UK using 100% Renewable Electricity
at CPI Group (UK) Ltd, Croydon, CR0 4YY

RUNNING OUT OF TIME

CINDI MYERS

Prologue

Who knew death could be so satisfying?

Half the people in town had gathered, watching police—every cop in the county from the looks of it—mill about while the paramedics wheeled out the gurney, the body on it covered by a sheet. Whispering, like the rush of wind through catalpa trees, rose from the crowd as people speculated on the identity of the person under the sheet. Mayville, West Virginia, population 2,000, was small enough that almost everyone knew everyone else.

But they didn't know each other. Not really. They didn't know what people were really capable of doing.

This was the third death in as many days. No one felt safe anymore. Things they had taken for granted—something they had trusted—had turned deadly. Eat too much chili at lunch? Pop a Stroud's Stomach Soother. Stress have your guts in a knot? Stroud's Stomach Soothers to the rescue. Safe and Natural—Our Promise to You. It said so right on the label.

Not so safe now.

A woman broke into sobs. Tammy somebody, who worked on the factory floor. "How can this be happening?" she wailed. "This used to be such a safe place."

Two other women moved in to comfort Tammy. The men around them shuffled their feet and stared at the ground, their expressions grim. Fear hung in the air like diesel exhaust, a choking poison that threatened to kill the town.

The killer had done that. One person had brought a town—a whole region, even—to its knees.

What a rush to have that kind of power. Seeing the body on the gurney sparked an idea. The perfect way to solve problems.

Chapter One

"We've got another tough case on our hands." Jill Pembroke, director of the FBI's tactical crime division, surveyed her team from the head of the conference table in the Bureau's Knoxville headquarters. "One that requires a great deal of discretion."

Something in the director's tone made Agent Laura Smith sharpen her focus. Pembroke, with her well-cut silver hair and feminine suit, might be mistaken for a high society grandmother, but she was as hard-nosed as they came, and not prone to exaggeration. That she reminded her team of the need for discretion pointed to something out of the ordinary.

The door to the conference room opened and a man slipped in. Tall and rangy, Agent Jace Cantrell moved with the grace of an athlete. He nodded to the director and eased into the empty seat next to Laura. No apology for being late. Typical. Laura slid her chair over a couple of inches. Cantrell was one of those men who always seemed to take up more than his share of the available space.

"We're going to be investigating product tampering at Stroud Pharmaceuticals in Mayville, West Virginia." Director Pembroke stepped aside to reveal a slide showing a squat factory building set well back on landscaped grounds.

"The antacid poisonings." Agent Ana Ramirez spoke from her seat directly across from Laura. She tucked a strand of dark hair into the twist at the nape of her neck, polished nails glinting in the overhead light. "That story has been all over the news."

"Do the locals not want the FBI horning in?" Agent Davis Rogers—the only member of the team not wearing the regulation suit—sat back in his chair beside Ramirez, looking every bit the army ranger he had once been. "Is that why the extra discretion?"

"No, the local police are happy to turn this over to us," Pembroke said. She advanced to the next slide, a listing of the deaths—six so far, with two additional people hospitalized—attributed to Stroud's Stomach Soothers, a natural, organic remedy that claimed a significant share of the market as an alternative to traditional antacids. "This hasn't been released to the public, but the poison in the contaminated tablets was ricin."

Laura would have sworn the temperature in the air-conditioned room dropped five degrees. "Any suggestion of a link to terrorism?" Hostage negotiator Evan Duran, bearded and brooding, spoke from the end of the table. "Anybody claiming credit for the deaths?"

Pembroke shook her head. "At this point, we aren't assuming anything. Obviously, we want to avoid panicking the public."

"The public is already panicked," Rowan Cooper, the team's local liaison, said. "People have been organizing boycotts of all Stroud products." She absently twisted a lock of her jet-black hair, brow furrowed. "We'll need a strategy for managing the public's response."

"The facility where the Stomach Soothers were manufactured has been closed for the time being and the product is being pulled from store shelves," Pembroke said. "But another facility in town, which manufactures other items, remains open, and the company has reduced hours and reassigned as many employees as possible to the single plant. The company, the town, even the state officials, are very anxious to downplay this tragedy and get Stroud up and running full-speed as soon as possible."

"Why do that?" Kane Bradshaw, Agent-at-Large, said. Laura hadn't noticed him until now, seated as he was behind her and apart from the rest, almost in the shadows. Kane always looked as if he'd just rushed in from an overnight surveillance, all wind-blown hair and shadowed eyes. The fact that he was here spoke to the gravity of this case. While always on hand when the team needed him, he wasn't much on office decorum.

"Jobs." Cantrell's voice, deep and a little rough, like a man who smoked two packs a day, sent a shiver through Laura. He didn't smoke, but maybe he once had. "Stroud Pharmaceuticals is one of the biggest employers in Boone County," he continued. "The coal mines are shutting down, and there isn't a lot of other industry. Stroud has been a savior to the community. They—and the officials they elected—are going to do everything in their power to keep the company running and redeem its reputation."

"Even covering up murder?" Laura asked.

Cantrell turned to her, his gaze cool. "I doubt they want to cover it up, but they'll definitely downplay it and keep it quiet."

"They want us to help, but they don't want us to be obvious." The youngest member of the team, computer specialist Hendrick Maynard, jiggled his knee as he spoke. A genius who looked younger than his twenty-six years, Maynard never sat still.

"Precisely." Director Pembroke advanced to another slide of a small town—tree-shaded streets lined with modest homes, some worse for wear. A water tower in the distance displayed the word *Mayville* in faded green paint. "Agents Smith and Cantrell, you are to pose as a married couple and take jobs at the Stroud factory. Investigations so far point to the poisonings having originated from within the plant itself, so your job is to identify possible suspects and investigate. Agent Rogers, you'll be in town as well..."

Laura didn't hear the rest of the director's assignments. She was focused on trying to breathe and holding back her cry of protest. She and Cantrell? As a couple? The idea was ridiculous. He was rough, undisciplined, arrogant, scornful...

"You look like you just ate a bug." Cantrell leaned toward her, bringing with him the disconcerting aroma of cinnamon. His gravelly voice abraded her nerves. "Don't think I'm any more excited about this than you are."

"Do you have a comment, Agent Cantrell?" Pembroke asked.

He straightened. "I think Agent Smith is going to stick out like a sore thumb in Mayville. Everything about her screams blue blood as well as law enforcement."

"I've worked undercover before." Laura bristled. She didn't care what Cantrell thought of her, but to imply she wasn't capable of doing her job—

"I'm sure Agent Smith will adapt," Pembroke said. "Smitty, you'll be working as assistant to the plant director, Parker Stroud, son of company owners Steve and Donna Stroud. This should give you access to personnel files, as well as financial records and other information you might find useful. Agent Cantrell, you'll be on the manufacturing floor."

Where he'd fit right in, Laura thought. Cantrell had the Southern drawl and casual attitude of the classic regular-guy down pat.

"Our profiler, Dr. Melinda Larsen, will assist with evaluating suspects," Pembroke continued. "She'll be available to travel to Mayville if necessary. Agent Maynard is on call for research and anything else you need. Agent Rogers and

Agent Ramirez will be the FBI's official representatives in the area and will be on location as backup."

Davis Rogers cracked his knuckles. "Happy to help."

"Smitty, you and Cantrell will need to report immediately to the support center for your background documents and everything you'll need to start your assignment. You'll depart for Mayville tomorrow. Rogers and Ramirez will be a few hours ahead of you." She surveyed the team again, then nodded, as if satisfied with what she saw. "Any questions?"

There were none. The team knew how to launch a new op and hit the ground running. "Then get to work." Pembroke dismissed them.

Laura pushed back her chair and started to stand. "Agent Smith, a word, please," Pembroke said.

Self-conscious over being singled out, Laura kept her eyes on the table as the others left. Cantrell stood and slid a stick of gum into his mouth, then leaned over her chair. "Later," he said, with a cinnamon-scented grin.

When she and the director were alone, Pembroke sat beside her. "I know you're not happy about this assignment," the director said.

"I never said—" Laura began.

"You didn't have to say it." Pembroke smiled. "Your dislike of Agent Cantrell is clear, but he's very good at his job, and he has a connection to this region that makes him ideal for this assignment."

"Is he from Mayville?" Laura asked.

"He's from a small town in Tennessee. A town very similar in many ways to Mayville. He has an insight into the culture of the area that could prove very useful. I'm counting on you to rein in some of his more unorthodox tendencies."

Great. She was on this job to babysit.

"I also think this assignment will be good for you,"

Pembroke said. "You're very dedicated and skilled. You pay attention to details. Those are the skills this assignment requires. But you'll also need to make friends among the locals and attune yourself to the overall atmosphere. I know you prefer to work alone, so this assignment will help you build your skills at relying on others for help and information."

"I work with this team every day," Laura protested.

Pembroke nodded. "You do, but you also can be a bit... aloof. I believe it's this tendency to hold yourself a bit apart that's behind Agent Cantrell's belief that you'll have trouble fitting in at the factory. I'm counting on you to prove him wrong."

Laura did her best to hide any response to this criticism, though the director's words stung. So what if she wasn't one to hang out with her fellow agents after work or discuss her private life with them? She preferred to keep her personal and business lives separate, but that didn't mean she was as cold as Pembroke made her sound. "I'll do my best," she said.

"You always do." Pembroke rose, signaling an end to the meeting.

Laura rose also and was gathering her coffee cup and notebook when the door opened and a slim young man entered. "Sorry to interrupt, Director," he said. "But there's a call for you. It's urgent."

Pembroke nodded and walked to the phone in the corner of the room. Laura moved toward the door. She had just opened it when the director called to her. "Smitty, wait."

Laura turned. As the director continued to listen to whoever was on the other end of the line, some of the color drained from her face. "Yes," Pembroke said. "We'll get right on it." She hung up the phone, her expression grave.

"What is it?" Laura asked. "What's wrong?"

"That was West Virginia State Police Office. They've

just learned that at least a dozen bottles of potentially tainted Stomach Soothers are unaccounted for."

"You mean consumers didn't turn them in?"

Pembroke shook her head. "According to the company's records, these bottles were never sent to stores. They're missing from the factory. They might have been stolen."

"Or the person who planted the ricin in the product originally has stashed them, maybe waiting until things calm down to release them again," Laura said. Like a deadly bomb the killer could set off to wreak havoc whenever he wanted.

Chapter Two

Driving down Main Street in Mayville, West Virginia, on Sunday afternoon gave Jace an itchy feeling between his shoulder blades, as if someone had slapped a target back there and he was bracing for the first shot. He had never been here before, but he already knew what he'd find: a mix of aching beauty in blooming azaleas and stately homes side-by-side with the despair of lost glory and opportunities passed by. Closed storefronts, weedy lots, and idle men and women paired with groups of laughing children, flourishing gardens and rolling fields.

He'd grown up in a place like this. His family—his parents and sister—still lived there. Whenever he visited, he couldn't wait to leave, smothered by all the problems he couldn't fix.

"It's not like I thought it would be," Smitty said.

He glanced at her strapped into the passenger seat of the ten-year-old mustard-colored Chevy pickup. Her blond hair, normally twisted back in a bun, hung loose around her shoulders, the no-name jeans and peasant top making her look younger and softer. More accessible.

He focused on the street once more. A man would be a fool to think there was anything soft or vulnerable about Agent Smith, especially where Jace was concerned. She didn't exactly curl her lip in disgust when he approached, but the expression was implied.

"What do you mean?" he asked, slowing the truck to allow an elderly couple—her with a walker, him with a cane—to cross the street.

"It's so quiet," she said. "It doesn't look like a place where violence has made national headlines. I expected more press, and people milling around."

He slid a fresh stick of cinnamon gum into his mouth from the pack that rested on the dash and then gave the truck some gas. "I imagine the powers that be are tamping down any hint of panic," he said. "From the media reports, the politicians are downplaying the poisonings as an attempted terrorist attack that has already been stopped."

"What about the dozen potentially poisoned bottles that are unaccounted for?"

"They haven't released that information to the press and they're counting on us to find them before anyone else dies."

She shuddered. "If someone else does die, the politicians will be pointing their fingers at us."

"If that bothers you, you should be in another line of work."

She stiffened, just as he had known she would. "I take a great deal of pride in the work the Bureau does," she said. "As should you."

"But I don't waste time worrying about what a bunch of pencil pushers and pontificators think of me," he said.

"Except those are the people who sign the bills that ultimately pay your salary," she said.

"They need people like me more than I need people like them." He glanced at her. "If you remember that, it makes the job a lot easier."

"Easier to cut corners and ignore the regulations, you mean."

He grinned. "That, too."

She made a noise in her throat almost like a growl. Kind

of sexy, but if he told her that, she would rightly blow a gasket. Smitty was the poster child for "wound too tight."

"We need to figure out who has it in for the Strouds," he said.

"You think that's what's behind this?" she asked. "Destroy their reputation by sabotaging their most popular product?"

"Don't you?"

She didn't answer right away, staring out at the passing scenery—a park with a bronze statue of a coal miner in overalls and hard hat, lunch bucket in one hand, a pick over his shoulder. Jace's father could have been the model for that statue, before he got sick.

"Maybe the goal isn't to destroy the Strouds," Smitty said. "You said yourself the town depends on the company for jobs. Maybe someone has a grudge against Mayville. And there's always the possibility that the target was one of the people who died, and everyone else is just a way to muddy the waters."

"Maybe," he said. "Whoever it is isn't being subtle. Ricin isn't like putting a little rat poison in someone's soup and hoping you used enough to do the job. It only takes a few grains of ricin to kill."

"Maybe we'll know more after we visit the factory."

"Rogers is supposed to brief us later today, after he and Ramirez meet with the local cops. Meanwhile, we have to move in." The back of the truck held everything a down-on-their-luck young couple might deem worth transporting to a new home—clothes, kitchen items, a television, and an antique chest of drawers that was someone's idea of a family heirloom. The Bureau's support center was known for its attention to detail. They had also supplied identification for Jason and Laura Lovejoy—a surname Jace was certain was someone's idea of a joke. The rental they were moving into was supposed to be furnished with everything else they'd need.

He turned the truck onto an unpaved side street identified by a leaning green sign as Lover's Lane.

"You have got to be kidding me." Smitty sneered at the sign.

"It's probably just the first suitable place they found to rent," Jace said. He watched the addresses on the mailboxes at the end of each drive and turned into the rutted lane at the very end of the street. The trailer was a rectangular white metal box with faded blue metal shutters, set well back from the road in the shade of a catalpa tree, the large heart-shaped leaves a brilliant green, the faded orchid-like blossoms littering the ground around the tree.

"Not what I was expecting." Smitty ground out the words through clenched teeth.

"It fits the profile," Jace said, shutting off the truck's engine. "We're broke newlyweds, remember? Besides, it's at the end of the road, with no close neighbors to spy on us."

Smitty got out of the truck, and he followed her up a two-foot-wide crushed gravel path to a porch, apparently made of old pallets, at the front of the trailer. She climbed the steps, inserted the key in the lock and shoved open the door.

They stood frozen for a moment, taking in the dark wood paneling, avocado-green carpet, and faux-leather sofa and matching recliner, complete with duct tape patches. The room smelled faintly of stale cigarette smoke. Smitty made a strangled sound, took a step forward and did a slow turn. "At least it looks clean." Her eyes met his. "I've never lived in a trailer before."

He had, but he wasn't going to share that with her. "Let's unload the truck," he said, and moved back outside.

She didn't immediately follow. He lowered the tailgate of the truck and pulled out a square cardboard box labeled

KITCHEN. By the time he'd made it up the walkway with this burden, Smitty was waiting for him on the porch. "We have a problem," she said.

"What is it?" Jace moved past her and carried the box to the kitchen table, a metal and Formica relic from the 1960s. A hipster might have deemed it charmingly vintage, while his parents had discarded theirs years ago as a piece of junk.

"There's only one bed," Smitty said.

"The rental agreement said two bedrooms." The document, complete with their own expertly forged signatures, had been included with all their other paperwork.

"There are two bedrooms, but only one bed," she said. The faint worry lines on her high forehead deepened.

He shrugged. "So we'll get another bed tomorrow."

"What are we going to do tonight?"

"I guess you can either share the bed with me or sleep on the couch." He gave her a wolfish grin—primarily because he knew it would get a rise out of her.

Sure enough, her cheeks turned rosy and sparks all but snapped from her blue eyes. "Why should you get the bed?" she demanded.

Because we're equal colleagues and any other time you'd be insulted at being treated with deference because you're a woman. "Because I'm bigger and taller. You fit the couch better. Of course, I'm always willing to share."

She twisted the plain gold band on the ring finger of her left hand. He wondered if she would take it off and throw it at him. "That is no way to speak to a fellow agent," she said.

"No. But it's how I might speak to my wife."

She was saved from having to think of a retort by the crunch of tires on gravel. They both turned to watch a silver Honda creep up the drive and stop behind the truck. Agent Davis Rogers unfolded his tall frame from the driver's seat and stood, hands on hips, studying the trailer. Sun burnished the dark brown skin of his bare arms and glinted on the steel frames of his Wayfarers.

Smitty moved ahead of Jace to greet Rogers at the door. "This looks like a cozy little love nest," Rogers said.

"Where are you staying?" Smitty asked.

He tucked the sunglasses into the neck of his pale blue polo shirt. "The Magnolia Inn on the other side of town."

Jace was pretty sure the Magnolia Inn was a few stars down from wherever Smitty was used to staying, but he'd have bet she would have traded places with Rogers in a heartbeat.

"I'll help you unload the rest of your stuff and we'll talk," Rogers said.

It didn't take long for the three of them to move the assorted boxes and bags into the trailer. While Smitty opened windows, Jace made coffee, then they gathered around the kitchen table. "Ramirez and I met with the local police department," Rogers said. "They seem pretty competent and did a good initial investigation, given their limited resources. As we already know, they think the Stomach Soother poisoning was done prior to the safety seals being applied. There was no sign of tampering with the packaging in the bottles they've been able to recover."

One of Jace's goals working on the factory floor was to determine who might have tampered with the product, and how. "What about the missing bottles?" he asked.

"Stroud's computer system assigns a bar code to every bottle at the plant," Rogers said. "Those bar codes are matched to shipments that go to each store. If someone uses a store loyalty card when they make a purchase, they can even tie a specific bottle to a specific customer. They were able to recall most of the suspect medication that way. These twelve bottles, however, never went to a store or made it to a consumer. They disappeared shortly after they were filled."

"What do you mean, disappeared?" Smitty asked.

"They show up on the records as having been manufactured," Rogers said. "There's no trace of them after that."

"Does that happen often?" she asked. "Maybe employees help themselves?"

"The potential has to be there," Jace said. "But with these jobs, if you're even suspected of stealing, you're out on the street. And I'll bet they have cameras on the factory floor."

Rogers nodded. "The local cops say if the Strouds have ever had trouble with employees lifting product, they've handled it themselves."

"What do the Strouds say?" Smitty asked.

"Ramirez is talking to Donna Stroud right now. She's also making sure everything is set for you two to show up tomorrow as the newest employees of Stroud Pharmaceuticals." He grinned. "Better you than me."

BALLOONS, FLOWERS AND a couple of stuffed animals decorated a section of chain link fence in front of the headquarters of Stroud Pharmaceuticals. A stiff breeze rattled the ends of a ribbon bow tied to a vase of wilting daisies as Agent Ana Sofia Ramirez walked past. She stopped to study the display. The flowers lay in front of a hand-lettered sign on white poster board. "We'll never forget you, Gini," it read.

Virginia Elgin, chief financial officer of Stroud Pharmaceuticals, had been the third person to die after using the contaminated Stomach Soothers. The bottle, found in her desk, had been traced to a local grocery store, as had the bottles that contained the tablets that had killed Herbert Baker and Gail Benito, the first two victims. The other five victims, three of whom had died, had purchased their

Stomach Soothers from two different stores in a county directly east of Mayville.

Would the missing bottles turn up on yet another store's shelves, or in the medicine cabinet of the next victim? Were they merely lost in the system, or stashed on a shelf in the killer's closet, waiting to stir up a new panic?

Donna Stroud was a middle-aged woman with dyed black hair in a sensible cut, dressed for business even on a Sunday afternoon in flat shoes and the type of pantsuit that had never been in or out of fashion. She greeted Ana with a firm handshake. "Thank you for coming, Agent Ramirez. My husband and I are anxious to do anything we can to get to the bottom of this tragedy. I appreciate you meeting with me on a Sunday. I hate to upset the staff any more than I have to."

"We appreciate your cooperation," Ana said.

"I've reviewed all the information you gave local and state law enforcement," she continued when she was seated in front of Donna's desk, a scarred oak model whose surface was obscured by towers of precariously leaning paperwork. "When did you discover that some of the product in the batch in question was unaccounted for?"

"My son brought it to my attention yesterday afternoon. I notified the state police right away."

"That would be Parker Stroud, the plant manager?"

"Yes. He was in charge of verifying the inventory reports and noticed the discrepancy. Everyone is putting in overtime, trying to determine how this could have happened."

"Has anything like this ever happened before—inventory going missing?"

"No!"

Ana didn't hide her skepticism. "You've never had an employee decide to, say, help herself to a box of something?"

"No." Donna leaned across the desk toward Ana. "We

have a zero-tolerance policy for that sort of thing. Employees and their belongings are subject to search at any time, and we have closed-circuit TV monitoring all parts of the factory. Beyond that, we're very careful about who we hire. We screen potential employees thoroughly, train them well, and I'm proud to say we have an industry-high retention rate. We have employees who have worked for Stroud for twenty years."

"So you don't have anyone you suspect might be responsible for contaminating the Stomach Soother tablets?"

"No one."

Donna Stroud looked Ana in the eye when she spoke. She was clearly weary, and frightened. But Ana didn't think she was lying. "We're hoping our agents here at the facility will be able to spot irregularities you may not have noticed," Ana said. "We appreciate your willingness to allow us access."

Donna sat back. "It's not as if I have much choice, is it? But I'd like to be allowed to inform Parker about what's going on. After all, one of the agents will be working under him, and the other will be right in his office."

"No." Ana spoke as firmly as she could. "It's imperative that as few people know about this operation as possible. If you'll remember, that was part of the agreement we reached that allows you to keep the rest of your facility still operating. If you don't feel you can uphold that agreement…" She let the words hang, an implied threat.

The lines around Donna's mouth tightened. "I understand."

Ana stood. "The Lovejoys will be here for orientation at 8:00 a.m. tomorrow." She handed over a business card. "If you think of anything that might be helpful to the investigation, or spot anything suspicious, don't hesitate to call me. That's my direct number and I'll answer anytime, day or night."

Donna stood also, weariness bowing her shoulders. "Thank you, Agent Ramirez," she said. "I hope you can get to the bottom of this quickly. Then we can at least begin to get back to normal."

She escorted Ana out of her office. They passed a side door marked V. Elgin, CFO. Ana stopped. Donna followed her gaze to the door. "As horrible as all of this is, it's even more horrible, losing Gini," she said, her voice tight with emotion.

"I understand she died here, at the office?" Ana asked.

Donna nodded. "She came back from lunch and was working in there, with the door closed. One of the admins went in to discuss the agenda for an upcoming meeting and found her." She put a hand to her mouth. "We thought at first it might have been a heart attack. She suffered from chronic heartburn and we thought maybe it was something more serious after all." She cleared her throat. "When they told us it was the Stomach Soothers, we couldn't believe it."

"What do you know about ricin, Mrs. Stroud?" Ana asked.

"They—well, the local police chief—told us that was what was in the Stomach Soother tablets. I know it's deadly... Maybe something terrorists have used elsewhere? Do you think this was done by terrorists?"

"We haven't reached any conclusions at this point. I won't take up any more of your time." She left the office, aware of Donna and several other women watching her walk away. She felt sorry for them, ordinary people caught in such a nightmare. But she wouldn't let her pity get in the way of doing her job. The most likely scenario involved someone inside the factory contaminating those tablets, which meant the Strouds and everyone who worked for them were potential suspects.

As she turned onto the sidewalk, she noticed a man standing in front of the makeshift memorial. He was young, early-to midtwenties, wearing new-looking jeans and a blue dress shirt unbuttoned and untucked over a gray T-shirt. She stopped and studied him. He looked out of place. Lost.

A trio of women, possibly factory workers on the weekend shift returning from a lunch break, approached. Ana caught their eye. "Who is that man?" she asked.

The oldest of the trio, an African American woman in her forties, glanced toward the memorial, and her expression changed to one of sorrow. "That's Miss Gini's boy, Leo."

"Gini Elgin?" Ana clarified.

A very pale woman with hair the color of carrots nodded. "He's real tore up about his mama's passing."

The third woman, brown-haired and freckled, made a face. "It's terrible about Miss Gini, but that Leo always was a little odd."

"What do you mean, odd?" Ana asked. Leo had moved closer to the memorial now, actually standing on some of the flowers, head bowed, hands shoved in the front pockets of his jeans.

"Just, odd," the woman said.

"Not friendly," the older woman said. "Real quiet. Now, Miss Gini was as friendly as could be, and not what you'd call quiet."

The others nodded. Then, as a group, they moved on. Ana continued down the sidewalk. When she was about ten feet from the memorial, Leo Elgin leaned down and snatched up the vase of flowers and hurled it over the fence. It smashed on the concrete on the other side, sending glass and petals flying. Then he turned and ran away, with the awkward gait of someone who doesn't run often. He didn't look at Ana as he passed, but she had a clear view of his face, his expression one of agony, tears streaming down his cheeks.

Chapter Three

Laura spent most of her first night in Mayville tossing and turning and deeply resenting Jace for sleeping so soundly. She could hear him snoring in the next room. After she finally managed to doze off she overslept, awoke in a panic and charged into the trailer's single bathroom to find a shirtless Cantrell, face half-covered in shaving cream, a straight razor in one hand.

Even half-asleep, she was impressed, both with the way he wielded the razor over his cheekbones and the impressive abs and pecs revealed in the anemic bathroom light. Stammering, she backed out of the room, his laughter trailing her all the way to the kitchen.

By the time he emerged from the bathroom, she was halfway through her first mug of coffee and had managed to rein in her racing heart. She ignored him and went to take her turn in the steamy shower, unsettled by the knowledge that he had been in here only moments before—naked. Then she was even more disturbed by the idea that he could hear her in here and might at this very moment be imagining *her* naked.

Clearly, she hadn't had nearly enough sleep. She and Cantrell were both professionals. She did not fantasize about her coworkers as a rule, so why should she assume he did? Then she remembered his wolfish grin when they had argued over the bed and bit back a groan.

When she returned to the kitchen, he shoved something wrapped in a paper towel in her hand. "We have to go now or we'll be late for our first day," he said.

"What is this?" She stared at the warm bundle in her hand.

"Fried egg sandwich."

"I don't eat fried foods." Her usual breakfast was a cup of yogurt or a piece of toast.

"Today you do." He handed her her purse. "Let's go. I'll drive and you can eat in the truck."

The sandwich was delicious, though she was aware of him watching her eat, which made her feel self-conscious and awkward. Then again, everything about this assignment was awkward.

The next hour passed in a blur. Laura suffered through an orientation that consisted of a ten-minute film about the history of Stroud Pharmaceuticals, a fifteen-minute drill on safety procedures and thirty minutes signing paperwork with her new fake name. Finally, she was directed to her new office, where she was greeted by a slender young man with thinning hair, oversized ears and a sour expression.

"Are you the new admin?" Parker Stroud, her new boss, asked.

"Yes, Laura Lovejoy." Laura offered her hand. He stared at it until she put it back down at her side.

"Great. Can you start by getting me some coffee?" He moved past her toward his office. "Two sugars," he called over his shoulder.

She retrieved the coffee from the machine in the adjacent break room and carried it in to him. Stroud was seated behind his desk, staring at a computer screen. He accepted the coffee and looked her up and down. "My mother said she hired you for this position," he announced. "What happened to Cheryl, the girl who was here before?"

The "girl" was fifty-five years old and had been temporarily relocated to work in the accounting department. "I'm not sure," Laura responded.

"No offense to you, but I'm thirty-four years old. I don't need my mother to pick out my secretary—excuse me, administrative assistant." He sipped the coffee, gaze lingering on her chest in a way that made her bristle. "Though I have to say, you're a lot better looking than Cheryl. And you know how to make a decent cup of coffee. So we'll see how it goes."

"Yes, sir." She tried to appear neutral in front of him, though inside, she seethed.

"Well, don't just stand there. Go back to your desk." He waved her away. "If I need you, I'll call you."

She returned to her desk and studied the row of old-fashioned filing cabinets along one wall. She'd investigate their contents under the pretense of organizing her workspace or something. Later, she'd attempt to hack into the firm's personnel and financial records. She could contact Maynard for help if she needed it.

She tucked a strand of hair behind her ear. She wasn't used to wearing it down at work, and it felt in the way. But the support office had deemed her usual chignon too sophisticated for the role she was playing.

She opened the top drawer of the first cabinet and stared at a row of filés, each labeled with a month and a year. A quick flip through the first file revealed production records for the two manufacturing plants—one of which had produced all of the Stomach Soothers sold by Stroud's, the other responsible for herbal throat lozenges, a sleep aid and a preparation for teething infants.

"It's a little early in the day to be looking for an insomnia cure."

She hadn't heard the door to Parker's office open, and his voice right behind her startled her. She choked off a gasp, returned the file and shut the drawer, then turned to him with a smile firmly in place. "Did you need something, Mr. Stroud?"

"Call me Parker. Mr. Stroud is my father." He nodded toward the filing cabinets. "Every bit of this data is in our computer system, but my father insists on hard copy records. Just one of the many examples of how my parents are keeping this company from realizing its full potential."

"Surely you'll be in charge of the company one day," she said.

"Thinking you'll be moving up in the world if you stick with me?" he asked. "Don't hold your breath. My folks have made it clear they don't intend to let go of the reins for years to come. Though why they'd even want it now, I don't know."

"You mean, because of what happened with the Stomach Soothers?"

"Yeah, what else do you think I mean?"

She widened her eyes, feigning ignorance, hoping she wasn't overacting.

Apparently, Parker bought it. He rolled his eyes. "Go down to accounting and tell them I need last month's financials ASAP. And don't let them give you any nonsense about this whole business with the Stomach Soothers disrupting workflow. That isn't the only product we make and people have wallowed enough."

"Yes, sir." The way he said the words sounded rehearsed, as if he'd been practicing a tough-guy act in front of a mirror. Maybe that was how he thought a hard-nosed CEO should behave.

She hurried out of the office, but slowed as soon as she turned the corner. Now was as good a time as any to familiarize herself with the layout of the building. She strolled the halls, opening and closing doors, locating the men's and women's restrooms, an empty classroom, a larger meeting room and the janitor's supply closet.

"Can I help you with something?" A round-faced young woman with a halo of brown curls, a sheaf of papers clutched to her chest, approached as Laura shut the door to the supply closet.

"I'm looking for the accounting department," Laura said.

"I'll show you." The woman motioned for Laura to follow, then set off down the hall, high heels clicking like castanets on the polished tile floor. "Ask for Angela," she said, indicating a frosted glass door, then turned and tap-tapped away.

Angela proved to be a middle-aged woman with flawless brown skin whose desktop was dominated by an oversized computer monitor. "Mr. Stroud needs the April financial reports," Laura said. "Parker Stroud," she clarified.

Angela frowned. "Today is the third. Those reports aren't compiled until the tenth. He knows that. And now you know it, so don't bother me again."

"Did he send me here to bother you to give me a hard time because I'm new, or does he do this every month?" Laura asked.

Angela's frown eased some. "Probably a little of both. Don't let him get to you. He's really okay, just a little tightly wound, I guess. A lot different from his mom and dad, that's for sure."

"I'd think everyone would be a little extra tense right now," Laura said.

"You got that right." She held out her hand. "Let's start over. My name is Angela Dupree. Welcome to Stroud Pharmaceuticals."

Laura took the hand, which was warm, smooth and beautifully manicured. "I'm Laura Lovejoy. I'm the new administrative assistant to Parker Stroud."

"This is a good place to work, despite the recent troubles," Angela said.

"Scary to think about the poisoning." Laura leaned toward Angela and lowered her voice. "I heard a reporter say the police think someone who worked at the plant must have put the poison in those bottles. Who would do such a horrible thing?"

"Nobody I know," Angela said. "And I think the reporters are wrong. I know it's a cliché to say a workplace is like a family, but we really are here at Stroud. No one has any reason to want to hurt people like that."

"That does make me feel a little better," Laura said. "Thanks."

"It was nice meeting you, but we both need to get back to work."

"Yes, ma'am."

Laura started to turn away, but Angela stopped her. "Laura?"

"Yes?"

"It would probably be a good idea if you didn't go around talking about the poisonings and such," she said. "People are pretty upset and it's not the best way to make a good impression."

"Gotcha. Thanks."

Laura wasn't worried about the kind of impression she made, except that getting people to like her might help her do her job. Had Angela warned her off because she was really trying to be helpful, or because she knew people here had things they wanted to hide?

"Who is that woman in with Angela?" Merry Winger craned her head around the edge of her computer screen to look toward the office. She had a view of a woman's slim back, long blond hair in graceful curls, slim-fit khaki trousers, low beige heels and a light blue shirt.

"That's Parker's new admin." Jerri Dunn followed Merry's gaze toward the office door. "She's a cutie, isn't she?"

"I didn't know they'd filled that position." Merry tried to hide her disappointment.

"Yeah, I think the job was only posted a week ago, but I guess they wanted to fill the spot quick."

Merry had put in for that position. It would have been ideal—she and Parker working together, seeing each other every day, not just a few times a month. He had an office with a locking door and a big desk—the fun they could have had in there. "You'd think they would choose someone from inside the company," she said.

"I gave up second-guessing decisions around here a long time ago," Jerri said.

Merry waited until the blonde left, then stood. "I'm going to the ladies'," she said.

She bypassed the ladies' room and headed for Parker's office. The blonde looked up from her desk when Merry entered. She was pretty enough, though kind of skinny and flat-chested. "Hello. May I help you?" she asked.

"I need to see Parker."

Merry started to walk past the desk, but the blonde stood. "Let me see if Mr. Stroud is available. What is your name?"

"Merry Winger. That's Merry, with two *r*'s and an *e*. Like *merry* Christmas." She wanted to make sure this woman knew exactly who she was. "And I'm sure Parker will want to see me."

"I'll let him know you're here." She knocked on Parker's door and, when he said "Enter," she slipped inside, leaving Merry to cool her heels in the outer office. He had better not refuse to see her. Not after all she'd done for him. Done with him.

The door opened and Parker followed the blonde out. "Merry, come in." He gestured toward the office. No smile of welcome, but then, Parker wasn't much for gestures of affection.

Parker shut the door behind them, but didn't move toward his desk. "What do you want?" he asked, keeping his voice low.

She pressed her palm against his chest and gave him a warm smile. "Maybe I just wanted to see you."

She stood on tiptoe and tried to kiss him, but he turned away. "I told you, not at work," he said.

She pouted. "Why not at work? Are you ashamed of me?"

"Of course not." He patted her shoulder. "But there are rules about executives dating workers. If anyone found out, we'd have to quit seeing each other and I don't want that, do you?"

If he married her, she wouldn't have to be an employee here anymore and that would solve the whole problem, but she knew better than to bring that up. Parker was the type of man who liked to think of things himself. "You're so considerate of me and my reputation," she said instead. "It's one of the things I love about you."

"Thanks for being so understanding. Now you'd better get back to work."

He urged her toward the door, but she resisted. She nodded toward the outer office. "Who is she?"

"The new girl?" He frowned. "I don't know. Someone my mom hired."

"You don't even get to pick out your own admin?"

"She's just a body behind a desk. I don't really care."

"I was hoping to get that job," she said. "Did you know I applied?"

"No, but it's just as well you didn't get it."

"Why not? Wouldn't you like having me around all the time?"

"I think it would be too distracting—for both of us." There was definite heat in his eyes now. A thrill shot through her. Whenever she started to worry he was getting tired of her, he always did something to quell her doubts. He really did care, he just had to be careful, given his position and all. She needed to be patient. When the time was right, they'd be together forever.

She left the office, even smiling at the new admin as she passed her desk. The blonde might look down her nose at Merry now, but she'd be singing a different tune when Merry was Mrs. Parker Stroud. By then, Parker would be running the whole business. And Merry would be running Parker.

LAURA WAITED UNTIL Merry and Parker were in Parker's office, then she moved to the door and pressed her ear to the gap between the door and the frame. A few moments later, she moved away. So Parker was fooling around with one of the office staff. That didn't strike her as a motive for mass poisoning. But she filed the information away as one more facet of the picture she was assembling of the company and its inner workings.

Promptly at five o'clock, Parker Stroud exited his office. "Go home," he told Laura. "No hanging around hoping for overtime."

"Good evening to you, too," she said.

He frowned and moved on.

She was searching Parker's desk a few minutes later when Cantrell strolled in. Jace. She needed to get used to thinking of him as Jace, so she wouldn't slip and address him as Cantrell, blowing their cover. Dressed in gray coveralls with his name in red script on the pocket, he still carried himself with a swagger. He was chewing gum—not smacking, but the muscles of his jaw bunched in a way she found distracting. He leaned on the doorjamb and watched her rifle through the desk drawers and peer under the blotter. "Find anything interesting?" he asked.

"Nothing." She shut the last drawer and moved toward him. "What about you?"

"I'm getting a feel for how this place operates. I can tell you, things aren't as watertight as the Strouds think. I'll fill you in at home. Let's get out of here."

They crossed the parking lot in a crowd of other workers leaving for the day. Heat billowed out of the cab of the truck when she opened the door, and she slid in carefully to avoid burning the back of her legs. Jace climbed into the driver's seat. "I'm starved," he said as he cranked the engine. "What's for dinner?"

"Why are you asking me?"

"I made breakfast. And lunch. It's your turn to cook."

Lunch had been a ham-and-cheese sandwich. With mayonnaise, which she hated. She had pulled out the cheese and eaten it with the apple and fig cookies, which had been surprisingly good. Her stomach grumbled at the memory. "Let's get takeout."

"Then your choices are pizza or barbecue."

They opted for barbecue, which was moist, smoky, spicy and some of the best food she had ever eaten.

"Director Pembroke says you grew up in a place like this," she said, wiping sauce from her fingers with a paper napkin.

"Yeah."

"What was that like?"

"What do you want me to say? It was okay, until it wasn't."

"I'm just asking. Trying to be friendly."

Some of the tension went out of his shoulders. "Sorry. I grew up in Hatcher, Tennessee, which is a whole lot like Mayville. My mom and dad and sister still live there. My dad has had some health problems, so transferring to the Knoxville office means I can be around to help out more."

"I'm sorry to hear about your dad." She set aside the

wadded-up napkin. "What's wrong with him? If you don't mind my asking."

"He has mesothelioma. A lung disease coal miners get from inhaling asbestos underground." He spoke very matter-of-factly, but his eyes wouldn't meet hers, as if he was afraid of revealing too much emotion.

"That must be rough," she said.

He shrugged. "What about you? Where did you grow up?"

"All over. My dad was in the military."

"That explains a lot."

"What do you mean by that?"

"Your 'don't color outside the lines' attitude. No offense. The military just ingrains that in you. I know. I was in the army for six years."

"You saw action?"

"Too much action. Fallujah. Baghdad, Kamdesh. It's how I ended up with the Bureau. They were recruiting military types."

She never would have described him as a "military type." "Davis Rogers came out of the military," she said.

"Yeah. He and I have compared notes. How did you end up with the feds?"

"I have a degree in forensic accounting from George Washington University, so it seemed like a good fit."

"Of course."

He spoke as if he had her all figured out. "What does that mean?" she demanded.

"You're a number cruncher. The whole coloring in the lines thing again. Don't get your back up. It's a useful skill. It'll probably be a big help with this case."

She forced herself to relax. They were never going to be able to work together if she took offense at everything he said. "You think money is behind the poisonings?"

"I think money has a lot to do with everything. And Stroud Pharmaceuticals is a multimillion-dollar concern."

"You said things in the factory aren't as secure as the Strouds like to portray. What did you find out?"

"I'll want to verify this, but apparently, the facility where the Stomach Soothers were manufactured is identical to this one. The surveillance cameras are focused on the production area, but not the break rooms or hallways or restrooms. I think it would have been possible for someone working with their back to the camera to slip the poison into a batch of the tablets before the bottles were sealed."

"What about the missing bottles of Stomach Soothers?"

"I haven't figured that out yet, but it's early days. Anything suspicious in the front offices?"

She shook her head. "Parker Stroud is apparently involved with one of the women who works in the offices, Merry Winger."

"What's Stroud like?"

She made a face. "Full of himself. Disdainful. Kind of a jerk, but as far as I can tell, competent. I got the impression he resents that his parents don't want to retire and turn the whole business over to him, but he was very clear that he stands to inherit one day, so I can't see a motive for him to destroy the company's reputation by poisoning their most popular product."

"We should dig into the personnel files, see if anyone has a grudge, maybe because they were passed over for a promotion or something."

She nodded and was about to ask him more about how the factory was set up when an ear-piercing siren shrieked. All over the restaurant, chairs were shoved back and people stood. "Fire alarm," a man said as he hurried past.

Another man pressed his cell phone to his ear. "It's at the plant," he said.

"Stroud's?" Laura asked.

The man nodded, then broke into a jog toward the parking lot. Jace threw some money on the table, and he and Laura joined the others leaving the restaurant. As he started the truck, both their cell phones rang.

"It's not a fire," he said, phone pressed to his ear.

"No." Ana Ramirez had just informed Laura of the reason for the alarm. "Someone planted a bomb at Stroud Pharmaceuticals."

Chapter Four

Yellow crime-scene tape flapped in a hot wind that carried the acrid scents of burning plastic and ash. Ana stood with Rogers just outside the tape, surveying what had once been a side entrance to Stroud Pharmaceutical Headquarters. The steel door, now grotesquely twisted, lay on the buckled sidewalk in front of a scorched hole rimmed by jagged brick. The windows on either side of the door had shattered and buckled. The area swarmed with fire and law enforcement personnel while farther back, dozens of Stroud employees and townspeople crowded against police barriers.

Rowan Cooper, the team's liaison officer, stepped through the wreckage of the doorway. A tall, slender woman with long black hair, Rowan was skilled at soothing ruffled feathers and persuading even the most reluctant law enforcement officers to cooperate with the FBI. She spotted Ana and Rogers and started toward them, followed by a stocky man with a gray buzz cut and heavy jowls. "This is Special Agent Terry Armand, ATF," Rowan said. "Terry, this is Special Agents Ana Sofia Ramirez and Davis Rogers."

They shook hands with the Alcohol, Tobacco, Firearms and Explosives agent. "What can you tell us about the explosion?" Rogers asked.

"Everything I can tell you is preliminary, but it looks

like the explosive was wired to the door lock. Inserting a key in the lock set the trigger, and a few seconds later—enough time for someone to step inside—it went off. The bomb itself was a fairly simple pipe bomb. The damage is pretty typical." He glanced back toward the doorway.

"Would whoever planted that bomb need access to the interior of the area?" Rogers asked.

Armand nodded. "Oh yes. As best as we can determine at this preliminary stage, the bomb itself was located just inside the door."

"Whose key set off the explosion?" Ana asked.

"Lydia Green, forty-four," Rowan said. "She'd worked at Stroud for three years as an independent commercial cleaning service."

"I talked to a few people who said that door is kept locked and generally only used after hours," Armand said. "The plant is only running one shift right now, and that ended at five. Otherwise, many more people might have been injured."

"Was that intentional or coincidental?" Rogers wondered. "We need to find out who had keys to that door."

"Here's the person who can tell us," Ana said.

They turned to watch Donna Stroud make her way through the crowd. She was still dressed in a boxy pantsuit and low heels. Only her red-rimmed eyes and pale face betrayed her distress. She hurried to join Ana, Rogers and the others on the sidewalk. "What is going on here?" she asked. "I thought you were here to help, and now this happens."

"Mrs. Stroud, have you or your husband or son received any threats?" Rogers asked. "Anyone trying to intimidate or coerce you?"

"If there was anything like that, I would have told you," she said. "We've been as cooperative as we know how to be." She looked back toward the ravaged doorway, her face a mask of pain. "Did the same person do this who poisoned the Stomach Soother tablets?"

"We don't know," Ana said. "Do you think there's a connection?"

"I don't know what to think." She shook her head. "They told me Lydia was killed. She has three children. What is going to happen to them now? What is going to happen to all of us?"

"Mrs. Stroud, where is your husband?" Ana asked. "Is he still out of town?"

The haunted look in her eyes increased. "My husband isn't well," she said.

Before Ana could ascertain the nature of his illness, a young man in jeans and a golf shirt elbowed his way through the crowd and jogged up to them. "I just heard the news," he said, putting his arm around the woman.

"My son, Parker Stroud," Donna said. "These are Agents Ramirez and Rogers, from the FBI." She frowned at Rowan and Terry. "I'm sorry, I don't know these people."

"It doesn't matter." Parker waved away the introductions and scowled at Rogers. "If you're the FBI, what are you doing to put a stop to this persecution of my family?"

"So you feel these attacks are personal?" Rogers asked. "Aimed directly at your family?"

"What else am I supposed to think?" Parker asked. "The Stroud family is Stroud Pharmaceuticals. This is clearly an attempt to destroy our reputation and our livelihood."

"Who has a key to that door?" Ana asked.

Donna took in a deep breath and moved out of her son's embrace. "I do, of course. Parker. Angela Dupree in accounting. Merry Winger, the accounting admin. Gini Elgin before she died. And of course, Lydia had a key so she could come in and clean." She pressed her lips tightly together.

"Was this Mrs. Green's usual time to enter the building to clean?" Ana asked.

"No." Donna paused and took a deep breath. "Most of the time, Lydia came in the morning, before the other employees reported for work. I like to get an early start myself, so I often saw her then. But this morning she reminded me that she was due to leave on vacation tomorrow, and would I mind if she cleaned tonight, so she could get an early start."

"How many people knew about this change of schedule?" Rogers asked.

"I'm not sure," Donna said. "I didn't mention it to anyone, but Lydia might have."

"What about Mr. Stroud?" Ana asked. "Does he have a key to that door?"

Donna exchanged a telling look with her son. "My father isn't well," he said.

"How exactly is he unwell?" Rogers asked.

"My husband suffers from early-onset dementia," Donna said.

"He's not able to participate fully in the business anymore," Parker said. "I do what I can to help my mother, though I could do more if she'd let me."

"I'm still capable of running this company," Donna said.

"What happened to Gini's key after she died?" Ana asked.

Donna's face clouded. "I don't know. I've been meaning to ask her son for it, but with so much else going on…" Her voice trailed away.

"Whoever set up that bomb knew only certain people had the key to that entrance," Ana said. "It's possible one of those people was the target."

"That's too big a coincidence," Parker said. "This has to be related to the tampering with the Stomach Soothers."

"Then who do you think is targeting the company?" Ana asked. "Do you have a rival who would wish you harm? A disgruntled former employee? Or perhaps a personal enemy?"

"We don't have any of those things," Donna said. "This has to be random. Some kind of terrorist."

"Whoever did this, it's your job to find out and put a stop to it," Parker said.

"We fully intend to do so," Ana said. "And if you have any suspicions about anyone, be sure to share them with us."

"You might start by interviewing the Lovejoys. They just started work today and now this happens. That's a pretty odd coincidence, don't you think?"

Ana followed his gaze across the parking lot, to where Jace and Laura stood with a group of other employees. "I really don't think the Lovejoys had anything to do with this," Donna said.

"No, that's a good idea," Rogers said. "We'll be sure to talk to them. Is there anyone else you can think of who might be angry with you personally, or with the company in general?"

Donna stared at the ground but said nothing.

"There isn't anyone," Parker said.

"Gini Elgin's son was very upset when I spoke with him yesterday," Donna said. "He blames us for his mother's death. But he certainly didn't poison Gini. I think it was mostly grief talking. I remember him from when he and Parker went to school together, and he was always such a nice young man. Gini was very proud of him and I know her death has devastated him."

"What is his name?" Rogers took out his phone to make a note.

"Leo Elgin," Parker said. "But he didn't have anything to do with this. You're wasting your time with him."

"Have you spoken to him since he came back to town?" Donna asked her son.

"I haven't had time," Parker said. "I've been too busy trying to keep this company going."

"I think it would mean a lot to him if you touched base," Donna said.

Parker shook his head but made no reply.

"Is there a location near here we can use to interview people?" Ana asked.

"Can't you do that at the police station?" Parker asked.

"It would be easier if we had someplace closer." Ana said. "Since we'll need to talk to all your employees. It's possible one of them saw or heard something unusual."

"There's a conference room at the back of the production plant across the parking lot," Donna said. "We use it sometimes for training. If there's anything else you need, let us know."

"Thank you," Rogers said. "We'll start with the Lovejoys. Agent Cooper, would you bring them to us, please?"

Rowan left to fetch Cantrell and Smitty. Donna turned away. Instead of following her, Parker moved closer to Ana. "If you learn anything, come to me first," he said. "My mother doesn't need any more stress right now. My father is a lot worse off than she wants to admit. That, along with everything else that has happened with the business, has her at her breaking point. I've been trying to persuade her to turn everything over to me, but she just can't give up that control."

"We'll share information with you as we are able," Ana said. But Donna Stroud was still president of Stroud Pharmaceuticals, and would be informed as well.

LAURA AND JACE kept up the pretense of not knowing Rogers, Ramirez and Rowan Cooper until they were all in the back conference room, which, as a precaution, the ATF had swept with bomb-sniffing dogs, and Rogers had checked for listening devices. Jace dropped into the chair across from Ramirez. "Before you ask, we haven't found out anything so far."

"Parker Stroud thinks you two are suspicious," Ramirez said.

"Both of us?" Laura glanced at Jace. "I'm surprised he even knows we're a couple."

"You said he didn't strike you as incompetent," Jace said.

"Did you know Steve Stroud is suffering from dementia?" Rogers asked.

"No." It annoyed Laura that that information had escaped her. "Though it explains why Parker thinks his parents should turn the business over to him now."

"Does he resent his mother's stubbornness enough to try to sabotage the business?" Jace asked.

"Why undermine his own inheritance?" Laura asked. "I think we'd be better off focusing on anyone who has a grudge against the company or the Strouds personally."

"It's possible the bombings and the medication tampering are the work of two different entities," Ramirez said.

"That makes the most sense to me," Jace said. "Poison and bombing are two very different modes of attack. For one thing, the poisoning took out a number of random individuals. The bombing seems more focused."

"Only a handful of people had a key to that door," Rogers said. "The bomb was set to go off when someone inserted their key into the lock."

"But the bomb was planted inside the building," Ramirez said. "Someone would need access to the area on the other side of the door—and time to plant the bomb, probably after everyone left for the day."

"There was only an hour between end of shift and the time of the explosion," Jace said. "They'd need fifteen or twenty minutes at least to be sure the office was empty. We should find out who stayed late that day."

"Or who came back after everyone left," Laura said. "Is there a security camera at that entrance?"

"There was," Rowan said. "It was destroyed in the blast, but maybe the tech guys can pull something off of it."

"Donna mentioned that Gini Elgin's son, Leo, is blaming Stroud Pharmaceuticals for his mother's death," Rogers said. "He could have used Gini's key to let himself into the building after everyone left."

"I saw him here at the factory yesterday," Ramirez said. "At that makeshift memorial on the corner of the property. He smashed a vase full of flowers and looked pretty upset."

"We'll definitely be talking to him." Rogers braced his hands on the back of a chair and leaned toward them. "Ramirez, Cooper and I are going to be talking to every employee over the next few days. But we're counting on you two to figure out what they aren't telling us. Somebody associated with this place has secrets. We learn those, we'll be closer to finding our killer or killers."

THE DAY AFTER the bombing, the factory operated as usual. Jace's job was to monitor a machine that boxed up herbal throat lozenges—twelve bottles of lozenges to each box. He pulled out any boxes that unfolded crookedly or didn't contain twelve bottles. Mistakes didn't happen often, and he had plenty of time to observe the workers around him who monitored various other aspects of the packaging process. Since all the poisoned Stomach Soothers, as well as the missing bottles, were from a single lot, manufactured on a single day, he suspected someone had intercepted the bottles before they were sealed, introduced the ricin in the form of a fine powder that had clung to the tablets, then put the bottles back into the assembly line to proceed to packaging.

How to do that, though, without being noticed?

The woman who was training him, Barb Falk, stopped

by two hours into his shift. A stocky middle-aged woman with bleached hair pulled back in a ponytail and sharp blue eyes that didn't appear to miss anything, she was affable and talkative. "How's it going?" she asked.

"No problems so far," he said.

"Yeah, things run pretty smoothly around here," she said. "It can make the job boring at times but be thankful for the boredom. I worked at a place before this where the machinery was always breaking down. We were constantly playing catch-up. Better to sit back and have nothing to do than to constantly be scrambling to do the impossible."

"I can't help thinking about that tragedy with the Stomach Soothers," Jace said. "I heard on a news report that the FBI thinks someone tampered with the tablets before they even left the factory, but I don't see any way that's even possible."

"I guess anything is possible if you try hard enough," she said.

"Being a trainer, you probably know every part of the manufacturing process," Jace said. "How do you think it was done?"

She shook her head. "I don't even go there," she said. "Even if it could be done, why would anyone do it? These are good jobs, hard to come by. Most people who get them really appreciate them." Her eyes met his, her expression daring him to disagree.

"I hear you," he said. "My wife and I feel lucky, getting hired on here. I just hate to think of anyone trying to do something like that, messing everything up for the rest of us."

"If anyone had, they'd be out of here before they knew what hit them," she said.

"Has anyone been fired recently?" he asked.

Her eyes narrowed. "I don't see how that concerns you.

Now come on, let's head over to the box sealer. You'll like that one—you actually have to operate the cutter."

He spent the next two hours pressing down on a lever to cut the tape that sealed the top of each box. Not any more exciting than his previous position, but it did require the use of one hand.

He thought about heading upstairs and seeing if Laura wanted to have lunch with him, then thought better of it. Lunch was his best opportunity to interact with his fellow factory workers. While Laura played the role of his wife well enough in public, he didn't sense she relished acting the part more often than necessary.

Still, she wasn't as bad as he had feared she would be. After the first day, she made no complaints about living in a house trailer or giving up her designer clothing. He hadn't been surprised to learn she was a military brat with an accounting degree, but when she had talked about her background he had glimpsed the geeky girl who never lived in one place long enough to make fast friends.

She was an intriguing combination of prickly and soft. It was like she couldn't allow herself to enjoy life. He'd seen that in the military—people so scared of losing control, they clung to the regulations like a lifeline. Do what you're told and you'll be safe.

Except you were never safe. Not really. Obey all the rules and an IED could still take you out when you were crossing the street. Eat all the right things, do all the right things, and cancer could still show up one day when you least expected it. People like Laura clung to the illusion of control instead of surrendering to the reality that they had none.

She would no doubt be horrified to know he had thought of her that way for even one moment. Smiling to himself at her imagined reaction, he collected his lunch from his locker and made his way to the break room. He sat at a table with some coworkers he recognized, opened the lunch bag and studied the contents. Laura had insisted on making lunch this morning. He had another ham sandwich but with mustard, not mayonnaise, and lettuce, tomato, onion—and was that *cucumber* on top? Instead of chips, he had carrots and celery sticks.

"You don't look too happy with your lunch." The man to his left, whose coveralls identified him as Ed, said.

"My wife's trying to get me to eat healthier." He picked the cucumber slices off the sandwich and set them aside. At least Laura had packed Oreos. For all her love of vegetables, she had a sweet tooth.

"She's the new admin in the office, right?" Phyllis, across from him, asked. "The pretty blonde."

Jace nodded. "Yeah, we were really lucky to both get jobs here. I heard these jobs were hard to come by."

"You came along at the right time," Phyllis said. "They needed someone to fill Benny Cagle's position."

"What happened to Benny Cagle?" Jace took a bite of the ham sandwich. It wasn't bad, but it would have been better with mayo.

"He got fired." Ed crunched down on a grape.

"Why'd he get fired?" Jace asked.

"He had a problem with drugs," Phyllis said. "Heroin."

"I heard it was meth," said a woman down the table.

"No, it was heroin," Phyllis said.

"When was he fired?" Jace asked.

"Oh, I guess it was a couple weeks ago now," Ed said.

"He kept showing up late for work—or not showing up at all," Phyllis said. "Everybody saw it coming, but you can't really talk to someone under the influence, can you?" She shrugged.

"Is he still here in town?" Jace asked.

"I heard he went to live with his sister in Vicksburg," Phyllis said.

"You play softball?" Ed asked Jace.

"Not in a long time," Jace said. "Why?"

"We got a coed team through the local rec league," Ed said. "You look like you could handle a bat."

"I'll think about it. Thanks." Though, with any luck, he'd be long gone by the time the season was in full swing.

Laura was waiting by the truck when Jace emerged into the parking lot later that afternoon. A soft breeze stirred her hair and fluttered the ruffles along the neck of her blouse. Jace faltered a little, struck by how pretty she looked. Not like the no-nonsense fed he'd come to know.

She spotted him and sent him an annoyed look. He started walking again, not hurrying. She never liked to wait. "How was your day?" he asked as he clicked the key fob to unlock the truck.

She opened the door and swung inside. "I got the name of an employee who was fired just a week ago," she said.

"Yeah. Benny Cagle." He started the truck and turned the air-conditioning up to full.

"Oh. You knew?" There was no hiding her disappointment.

"Some of my coworkers were talking about him at lunch today," Jace said. "They said he got canned for drugs—heroin or meth."

"The official file says he was fired for failing to show up for work and chronic tardiness," she said.

"Easier to prove than drugs," Jace said. "Probably looks better to insurance companies, too." He glanced at her. "Somebody said he's in Vicksburg, living with his sister."

"We need to make sure he didn't come back to town and plant a bomb," she said.

They spent the rest of the drive to their trailer debating the best way to investigate Cagle. As Jace turned into the driveway, Laura fell silent. Two big cardboard boxes leaned against the steps of the trailer. "What is that?" she asked, tense with wariness.

"That's your new bed." He climbed out of the truck and she followed.

"You ordered a bed delivered?" she asked, eyeing the boxes.

"Sure. Why not?" He examined the boxes then tapped the larger one. "This is the frame." He tapped the other box. "And this is the mattress." She was still frowning, so he added, "You needed a bed. We don't have time to shop."

She met his gaze, her expression softer. "Thank you," she said. "That was very thoughtful of you."

He looked away. She didn't have to act like he'd donated a kidney. "If you'll make dinner, I'll put all this together," he said, gesturing toward the boxes.

Dinner was pasta and chicken in some kind of sauce, which was good, and steamed broccoli—not his favorite, but he ate it because he was hungry. "The pasta is good," he said when they were done.

"It's lemon pepper chicken. I don't cook often," she said. "But I can cook."

"I never said you couldn't." He stood and helped clear the table, then touched her shoulder and turned her toward the door to the rest of the house. "Come see your new bed."

He'd chosen a simple metal frame, antique-looking, and one of those foam mattresses that expanded as soon as you unboxed it. Laura walked around it, surveying it from every angle, then sat on the edge of the mattress.

"How is it?" he asked, immediately annoyed that he cared what she thought.

"Better than the couch."

"That's all you can say?" He sat beside her and gave a little bounce. "Feels pretty good to me. Better than what I've got."

Then he saw the smile tugging at the corner of her

mouth. She'd been playing him for sure. She burst out laughing. "It's great, Jace. Thanks."

She looked so pretty when she smiled. Approachable. He leaned toward her, the flowers-and-vanilla scent of her swirling around him. Their eyes met and her lips parted. So inviting…

His phone rang, and they both jumped to their feet. Heart pounding, he fumbled for the phone, avoiding her eyes. What had almost happened there? Whatever it was, it wasn't going to happen again. "Hello," he barked into the phone.

"I'm sending you a report on Leo Elgin," Rogers said. "He's somebody we definitely want to take a closer look at."

"Why?" Jace asked.

"You'll see." Rogers ended the call.

Jace stuffed the phone back in his coveralls. "That was Rogers. He said…"

"I heard." Laura headed for the living room and Jace followed. By the time he reached her, she had her laptop up and running and was accessing the report. "This says Leo Elgin is employed by a firm in Nashville that makes sophisticated security systems for businesses and high-end homes," she said.

"That might give him the skill to create a bomb like the one that went off at the factory. The bomb itself was simple, but the trigger required a little sophistication," Jace said.

"Oh."

The single syllable was freighted with meaning—awe, dismay, interest. "What is it?" he asked and moved in beside her, shoulders brushing.

"Leo Elgin had some trouble in high school," she said. Her eyes met his, reflecting both fear and anger. "He was jailed briefly for giving a bomb to a teacher."

Chapter Five

Six for six.

The three words, bold print in a twenty-point font, stood out on the torn piece of printer paper. "It was in a plain envelope, addressed to me, in this morning's mail." Donna Stroud spoke calmly, only her tightly clenched hands betraying her agitation.

Ana examined the envelope, which she had already placed in a clear evidence pouch. It bore a local postmark, no return address, and had been mailed the day before. The paper that accompanied it looked like plain copy paper, torn in half. "What do you think it means?" Ana asked.

The vertical line between Donna's eyebrows deepened. "Six people died from the tainted Stomach Soothers," she said. "But I don't know what 'six for six' means."

"We'll see if we can get any fingerprints or other evidence from this." Ana slipped the evidence envelopes into her jacket. "Did anyone else in the office see this?"

"Merry Winger puts the mail on my desk, so she probably saw it. She collects it from the mailroom about nine thirty each morning. Someone in the mailroom would have seen it when they sorted it."

"Where can I find Merry?"

"Her desk is just to the left of the door to the outer office. She's the pretty blonde."

Merry was indeed a pretty blonde, all bouncy curls and

dramatic eye makeup, including spider-like fake eyelashes. "May I help you?" she asked when Ana approached her desk.

Ana showed her identification. "Do you remember putting this on Mrs. Stroud's desk this morning?" she asked.

Merry leaned forward and studied the envelope in its clear evidence pouch. She wrinkled her nose. "It might have been in with the other mail, but I don't really notice." She sat back and shrugged.

"What's your routine for handling the mail?" Ana asked.

"I go down the hall to the mailroom about nine thirty and collect whatever is in the boxes for this office. Dennis, the mail clerk, sorts everything after the carrier delivers it. I distribute everything for this office. Mrs. Stroud usually has the biggest stack. It used to be Mr. Stroud, but now that he's retired, Mrs. S gets everything that isn't addressed to accounting or personnel or a specific person."

"So you would have sorted this letter into the stack to go to Mrs. Stroud?"

"Well, yeah, but I just toss anything that isn't for anyone else into her pile. I don't stop and read anything or pay much attention." She leaned forward again, eyes bright with interest. "Why? Is that letter from the bomber?"

"Why do you think it might be from the bomber?" Ana asked.

"Well, duh! You're from the FBI, and you've got that envelope all sealed up in that pouch. If it was junk mail you wouldn't treat it that way."

"We don't know who the letter is from," Ana said. "I'm trying to find out."

"Sorry, I can't help you," Merry said.

"If you think of anything, let me know." Ana handed her card to the young woman and headed to the mail room, where Dennis told her he hadn't noticed anything unusual about the letter either.

Back at the situation room at the local police department that she and Rogers were using as their workspace, Rogers examined the letter and envelope. "'Six for six,'" he said. "A reference to the six people who were killed by the poisoned Stomach Soothers?"

"Donna Stroud thinks so." Ana studied the three words. "Maybe the bomber is saying he—or she—plans to kill six people in retaliation for the six who died."

"Kill as in set more bombs?"

"We don't know, do we?" She sank into one of the rolling desk chairs the local police had provided them. "People are poisoned and someone responds by planting a bomb. Where's the logic in that?"

"It makes sense to the bomber—our job is to get into his head and figure out how."

"Leo Elgin made it clear he blamed the Strouds for killing his mother," Ana said. "He has the skills to build a bomb and a history of making a bomb threat. It shows us he thinks of a bomb as a weapon."

Rogers nodded. "It's past time we talked to Leo."

"THE BOMB I gave Mrs. Pepper wasn't real," Leo said. "It was just a bunch of highway flares taped together and wired to a clock. Anyone with sense would have seen right away it was a fake. Which was the whole point, because Mrs. Pepper didn't have any sense."

Leo Elgin stared across the table at Ana, deep shadows beneath his eyes like smudges of soot, his hair falling listlessly across his pale forehead. He wore the same T-shirt and jeans he had had on when she had seen him at the memorial Sunday outside the Stroud plant, and the sour smell of his body odor hung in the air around him.

"Why did you give your teacher a fake bomb?" Ana asked.

"Because she was an idiot and I wanted to prove it. She

freaked out about a bomb that looked like something out of a cartoon."

"But you were the one who got into trouble." Rogers moved from where he had been leaning against the wall to loom over Elgin, his muscular bulk making the young man look even smaller. "You were expelled from school." The school district had eventually dropped the charges and Leo had been released from jail. It had taken some serious digging to uncover the incident.

Leo jutted out his lower lip like a pouting adolescent. "I hated the place anyway. It was full of idiots."

"Was Parker Stroud an idiot?" Rogers asked.

Something flickered across Leo's face—confusion? Fear? "Parker was okay," he said.

Ana leaned toward him. "Were you and Parker friends?" she asked.

"No, we weren't friends."

"But you knew him."

His nostrils flared as he blew out a breath. "We had, like, thirty people in our whole class. Everybody knew everybody. But it's not like we hung out or anything."

"Why didn't the school press charges against you?" Ana asked.

"Haven't you been listening? It wasn't a real bomb."

"You can be charged for threatening someone, even if your threat isn't real," Rogers said. "With all the incidents of school violence, how did you ever think you'd get away with such a stupid stunt?"

Leo flinched at the word "stupid," as if Rogers had slapped him. "People around here knew me. They knew I wasn't dangerous."

"Your mother worked for the Strouds," Ana said. "Maybe the Strouds put in a good word for you. After all, their business is the biggest employer in town. They probably had a lot of influence."

Leo's scowl turned ugly. "I didn't need the Strouds to pull any strings for me."

"Do you blame the Strouds for your mother's death?" Rogers asked.

A flash of anger this time. Leo sat up straighter. "They're responsible. The medication they make killed her. If they had any kind of quality control this wouldn't have happened."

"Your mother died." Rogers's voice was flat. Cold. "You held the Strouds responsible. So you decided to make them pay."

A sharp jerk of his head, left to right. "They'll pay," he said. "I've already talked to a lawyer. She thinks I have a good case."

"A bomb is quicker," Rogers said.

Leo's face twisted. "Look, I wouldn't do that. I knew Lydia. She was a nice person." His voice broke. "She and my mom were friends." He covered his eyes with one hand.

Rogers braced his hands on the table next to Leo. "We're going to search your mother's house, your car, and your apartment and office in Nashville," he said. "If you made that bomb, we're going to find out."

"Go ahead and look." Leo lowered his hand. "You won't find anything."

"How long do you plan to stay in Mayville?" Ana asked.

"Why? Are you going to tell me not to leave town?"

"Answer the question," Rogers said. "How long do you plan to be in town?"

Leo slumped in the chair. "I don't know. The...the service for my mother is Saturday, but then I need to decide what to do with the house and... I don't know. I can't really think of anything right now."

"When do you have to be back at work at Integrated Security?" Ana asked.

"I took a leave of absence. My boss said I could come

back when I'm ready." His eyes met hers. The anguish in them was like a raw wound. "She was all I had—my mother. It was just her and me, all those years. I don't know what I'm going to do without her."

Rogers moved away, toward the door. "You can go now, but we'll be in touch," he said.

When he was gone, Ana and Rogers moved to the room next door, where Smitty and Cantrell had been observing through the one-way glass. "Good call on asking about Parker Stroud," Cantrell said. "That got a reaction from him."

"It was a reaction," Rogers agreed. "I just don't know what it means."

"His grief was real," Ana said. "I think he's seriously depressed."

"I agree," Rogers said. "But that just gives him more of a motivation for wanting to harm the Strouds."

"Do you think the Strouds really persuaded the school not to press charges over that fake bomb?" Smitty asked.

Rogers shrugged. "It makes sense. His mother was a key employee, close to the same age as the Strouds. She probably went to them for help and they leaned on the school to get them to agree to not press charges, provided Leo transferred to another school."

"His mom sent him to a military academy for a year," Ana said, referring to her notes.

"That didn't come cheap," Cantrell said. "I wouldn't be surprised if the Strouds paid for that, too."

"If he owes the Strouds so much, why blame them for his mother's death?" Smitty asked.

"Maybe because he owes them so much," Cantrell said. "Obligation carries its own weight."

"You heard him," Rogers said. "Everyone at school was an idiot. His teacher was an idiot. Elgin thinks he's the smartest man in the room, whatever the room."

"Maybe he thinks he's smart enough to get away with planting a real bomb at the Stroud factory," Cantrell said.

"That bomb wasn't planted at a factory entrance," Smitty said. "It was wired to a door only office personnel used. Only a few people had a key that would trigger the detonation."

"Which brings us back to the Strouds," Ana said. "Donna, Steve and Parker all have keys."

"And Leo probably has Gini Elgin's key," Smitty said.

"The local police already searched her house," Rogers said. "They didn't find the key, or any bomb-making materials."

"We need to monitor his phone and computer usage," Cantrell said. "If he built that bomb, he had to get the materials from somewhere."

"Did his mother have a storage unit anywhere near here?" Smitty asked. "Maybe he's keeping the materials there."

"We haven't found anything yet," Rogers said. He pointed to Cantrell. "I'll see about getting permission to bug his place and monitor his computer."

"Let me know when you're ready," Cantrell said. He was the team's specialist in electronic surveillance.

"Have you two come up with anything yet?" Rogers asked.

Smitty shook her head. "Not yet."

"We checked out the fired employee, Benny Cagle," Ana said. "He was in jail in Vicksburg, Mississippi, where he had been living with his sister, when the bombing occurred."

"Had been since before the Stomach Soother tablets were poisoned," Rogers said.

"Do we think the crimes are related?" Smitty asked. "Are we looking for one person or two?"

"Seems a big coincidence to have two crimes like this

centered around one small-town business, so close together," Cantrell said.

"But two very different crimes," Smitty said. "So maybe two different people with similar motivations."

"What's the motivation?" Rogers asked.

"I don't know yet." She shook her head. "We need to dig deeper with the Strouds. Maybe they're hiding something."

"Everybody is hiding something," Cantrell said. "The question is whether their secrets are relevant to our investigation."

They tossed around more theories for a few minutes, then the meeting broke up. Ana and Smitty headed for the ladies' room. "How are things going with you and Jace?" Ana asked when she and Smitty were washing their hands at the row of sinks.

Smitty grimaced. "It's okay. At least I'm not sleeping on the couch anymore."

"Oh?" Ana didn't even try to hide her surprise.

Smitty flushed. "I mean, I have a bed now. There was only one when we moved in, and Jace took it."

"How gentlemanly of him."

Smitty waved aside the comment. "He's a lot taller than I am, so it made sense to stick me with the couch. I got the best revenge, though. My new bed is supposedly a lot more comfortable than the old one he's sleeping on."

Ana dug a tube of lipstick from her bag. "Things are going okay, then. Better than you expected?"

"Yeah. I guess so." Smitty combed her fingers through her long hair.

"For what it's worth, you two look good together." Ana studied her fellow agent in the mirror. "Like a real couple."

"Who would have guessed we were such good actors?" But Smitty's cheeks were still pink, and there was a brightness in her eyes Ana hadn't seen before. Ana smiled. She liked Smitty. She was a good agent, but maybe a little too tightly wound sometimes. Cantrell might change that.

"What are you smiling about?" Rogers asked when Ana rejoined him.

"I was thinking Smitty and Cantrell might make a good couple."

"No way! Those two are like oil and water. I'm surprised they've been able to live in that trailer for more than one night without coming to blows."

"They're professionals." But they were human, too. The job was only one aspect of their lives. She thought of her fiancé, Benning Reeves, and his two children. The four of them would soon be a family. Knowing that added meaning to her work.

"Cantrell and Smitty will both be glad when this case is over," Rogers said.

Maybe, Ana thought. And maybe she was being overly romantic, seeing a match for those two. But stranger things had happened in this line of work.

JACE PUT A hand at Laura's back as they walked across the parking lot from the police station. She forced herself not to shrug it off. It was the kind of gesture a husband might make to his wife and fit their cover. Truth be told, she didn't really want to shrug him off. The weight of his hand was warm and pleasant—almost comforting. "Some of the guys at the plant were telling me about a lake south of town," he said. "We should check it out."

"Why? Does it have something to do with the case?"

"I just thought it would be someplace nice to see. You know, to relax."

They reached the truck, he unlocked it, and they climbed in.

"All right." Though she felt anything but relaxed around this man. She was so hyperaware of him—of his bulk filling the driver's seat of the truck, the muscles in his forearm tensing as he shifted gears, the sweet scent of the cinnamon gum he chewed.

"Why do you always chew gum?" she asked.

He glanced at her. "Does it bother you?"

She shrugged. "I just wondered."

"I quit smoking six months ago. I guess you could say I traded a nicotine habit for a gum habit."

"Good for you."

"Yeah, well, I still miss it. It's just damned inconvenient when I'm working. Did you ever smoke?"

She shook her head.

"Yeah, I should have guessed."

"What is that supposed to mean?"

"You're like those girls I knew in high school—the ones who didn't drink or smoke or swear or skip school or so much as jaywalk. They always looked perfect and spoke perfect and acted perfect."

"And you didn't want anything to do with them," she said.

"Oh no. You've got it all wrong." He shook his head. "Those girls were untouchable. And I wanted so bad to touch them, to make them feel. To help them discover the bad girl I knew had to be hiding inside that pristine shell."

The rich velvet of his voice and the teasing words sent a quiver through her, low in the belly. She had been one of those girls, the ones too afraid to ever break the rules. He was the kind of boy she would have shunned, too terrified of the things he might make her feel.

She was a woman now, one with enough experience that men like him no longer frightened her. Or so she told herself.

Neither of them spoke on the rest of the drive to the lake. Laura leaned back in the seat and closed her eyes, reviewing the interview with Leo Elgin, trying to sort out where his evidence fit with everything else they knew about this case.

The silver-blue expanse of the lake reflected the pines that crowded the shore on three sides, with a rough sand beach bordered by picnic tables nearest the lot where they parked. Only half a dozen other vehicles shared space in the big lot. "They must get crowds here on the weekends, with a parking lot this size," Laura observed as she and Jace climbed out of the pickup truck.

"I'll bet a lot of high school kids come here at night to make out and party," Jace said. "At least, that's what I would have done."

Yes, Jace had probably been many a father's worst nightmare in high school. "Did you ever do that?" he asked. "Sneak out to the park and party with your friends—or make out with your boyfriend, music playing low on the radio, the moon shining down?"

He made it sound so carefree and romantic. "My father was a lieutenant colonel," she said. "And we usually lived on base."

"So no guy had the guts to risk sneaking around with you," Jace said.

"I guess." She wouldn't admit to Jace that she was the one who hadn't had the courage to defy her father.

They took a path that circled the lake. The earthy smell of sun-warmed weeds and lake water mingled with the heavier perfume of honeysuckle. Laura breathed in deeply, feeling some of the tension of the day easing from her shoulders. "This was a good idea," she said. "It's relaxing."

"It's the water," he said. "I read a study that says water relaxes us because it syncs up with our brain waves or something."

She laughed. "That's your scientific explanation—or something?"

He shrugged. "I don't have to understand why being

around water eases stress. I'm just glad it does." He scooped a rock from the shore and sent it skipping across the glassy surface of the water—one, two, three, four times, concentric circles spreading out and colliding to form mesmerizing patterns. He moved with the grace of a boy—and the bunching muscles and sinewy strength of a man. Being with him made Laura so much more aware of herself not only as a fellow agent, but also as a woman.

What was wrong with her? she wondered. She had worked with other men before, and she had never been attracted to any of them. Maybe that was because she always put the job first and didn't allow herself to focus on anything else.

Why was being with Jace so different?

"When I was a kid, for four or five years in a row, we went to a lake house on vacation," Jace said, as they continued on the path. "The place was just a little cabin, nothing fancy at all, but we loved it. We fished and paddled around in a canoe or swam off the dock. In the evenings, my dad would build a fire and we'd roast hot dogs or cook burgers in packets of foil, or even fish we'd caught. Looking back, I realize that for my folks, it was probably a really cheap vacation, but my sister and I loved it so much. I think we would have chosen that little lake house over a big amusement park. At least I know I would have."

"My parents sent me to a girl's camp in upstate New York one summer," Laura said. "Two weeks in a cabin with six other girls and six hundred spiders. I got poison ivy the third day, made a lanyard that was all knots, and almost shot my bunkmate in the head during archery practice."

"Good times," Jace said, and she laughed—a full belly laugh she couldn't keep back.

"Let's just say my first experience camping didn't make me want to try again," she said.

"I bet you'd be good at it now," he said.

"What makes you think that?" She genuinely wanted to know.

"Because you're not a whiner. And you're practical. You assess what needs to be done and you do it. Those are great strengths for camping."

"Who knew camping was so much like an investigation?" Their eyes met and her heart stuttered in its rhythm. When Jace looked at her, she felt as if he was really seeing her—all of her. She didn't like feeling so exposed, even if the heat behind his look told her he liked what he saw.

He was the first to look away, however. He frowned over her shoulder. "Isn't that Parker Stroud?" he asked.

She turned, moving slowly, as if she was merely brushing something from her shoulder, and glanced across the parking lot. Parker Stroud, dressed casually in jeans and a blue polo shirt, a West Virginia Mountaineers ball cap tugged down on his forehead, was striding away from a sleek black pickup truck. "That's him," she said.

"Let's go see what he's up to."

Keeping a line of trees between themselves and Parker, they trailed him to a fishing pier that jutted thirty feet out into the lake. He stood, looking out over the water, hands clasped behind his back. "He's waiting for someone," Laura said.

"Maybe he comes out here to look at the water because it's relaxing," Jace said.

"Then why doesn't he look more relaxed?"

Parker turned to glance toward the parking lot. Jace and Laura shrank further into the shadows as a slight figure in jeans and a gray hoodie slouched across the lot toward the pier. Laura studied the new arrival. Something about him was very familiar. "I think that's Leo Elgin," she whispered.

"Maybe," Jace said. "He changed clothes."

"He had time to do that."

The two men stood a couple of feet apart, Parker with his arms crossed tightly over his chest, Leo with his hands on his hips. Jace and Laura were too far away to hear the conversation, but the men's postures and expressions didn't appear friendly. Parker started shaking his head emphatically, and then Leo abruptly turned and fled.

Laura moved back through the trees toward the parking lot, following Leo, while Jace stayed to watch Parker. But by the time she reached the parking lot, all she could see was a pair of taillights receding into the distance.

Her cell phone buzzed and she read the text from Jace letting her know Parker was headed her way. She took cover behind a van and watched while Parker stalked to his truck, got in and drove off.

Jace jogged up to Laura. "Anything else happen?" he asked.

"Leo drove out of here before I could even get his plate number," she said. "The way he raced out of here, I'd say he was pretty upset."

"Leo blames the Strouds for killing his mother," Jace said. "Maybe he followed Parker here to have it out with him about that."

"Parker manages the manufacturing facilities at Stroud," Laura said. "So Leo may see him as being most responsible for the poisoned Stomach Soother tablets."

"It's not illegal to have a conversation," Jace said. "And they've never denied knowing each other."

"No." She turned back toward their truck. "But I think this wasn't a chance meeting. I think Parker was waiting for Leo."

"We need to find out what they were talking about," Jace said. "But we need to do it without blowing our cover."

"I'll see what I can get out of Parker," she said. Though, considering Stroud's generally surly attitude, that wouldn't be an easy task.

Chapter Six

Parker Stroud didn't appear in his office until almost noon the next day. He strode past Laura's desk without a glance in her direction and shut his door firmly behind him. Laura decided to wait to pass on the half-dozen messages that had come in his absence—two of them from his mother, who hadn't sounded too happy that her son hadn't shown up for work yet.

Ten minutes later, Laura's phone lit up. "I need hard copies of all the quality control reports for the first quarter," he said, and hung up before she could reply.

Since she had spent the morning continuing her search through the files, both online and off, Laura had no trouble locating the reports, though she wondered why Parker didn't pull them up on his computer. She spent the next half hour printing and collating the reports, which were submitted twice a week. Scanning the documents as she worked, she saw nothing that raised alarms. Stroud Pharmaceuticals had apparently been meticulous about maintaining quality control. So how had the ricin gotten into those tablets?

She knocked on Parker's door and, when he barked "Come in," slipped inside.

"Here are the reports," she said, laying the papers on his blotter. "And your messages." She added the stack of While You Were Out slips.

He grunted, focused on the screen of his desktop computer. After a moment, he finally looked at her. "What do you want?" he asked.

I want to know what you and Leo Elgin were talking about last night, she thought, but said, "Do you need anything else?"

"When I need something from you, I'll ask."

Yeah, getting anything out of this guy was going to be tough. She turned to go. "Laura?"

She stopped and faced him. "Yes?"

"What did the FBI ask you yesterday?"

"If we knew anything about the explosion. We didn't."

"You can't blame them for being suspicious. You and your husband are the only new people around here."

"I guess you knew the woman who was killed?"

The lines around his eyes tightened. "Yes."

"I always thought it would be nice, growing up in a small town where you knew everyone," she said. "But when something like this happens, I guess it makes it harder."

"Yes."

"Do you have any idea who planted that bomb?" she asked. "Who would want to do something so horrible?"

"No. Why are you so interested, anyway?"

"It's such a horrible thing. Especially after the poisonings."

"Maybe you don't want to work at such a horrible place. If you keep asking so many nosy questions, I think that could be arranged."

She backed out of the room, biting her lip to keep from making an angry retort. The phone rang as she was crossing to her desk. "Hello again, Laura." Donna Stroud had a pleasant voice, though Laura didn't miss the weariness underlying her words. "Has Parker made it in yet?"

"Yes ma'am. He came in a little while ago."

"Put me through to him, please."

Laura transferred the call. She debated listening in on the conversation, but before she could pick up the receiver again, Parker's voice sounded through the door, loud and clear. "I'm taking care of it, Mother. I'm not some idiot you have to micromanage... I put in plenty of hours for this company. If I want to come in late one morning, I can."

The receiver slammed down and seconds later Laura's intercom sounded. "Get me hard copies of the first quarter production reports."

"For which factory?"

"All of them!"

She hung up the phone and frowned at Parker's closed door. Was he trying to inundate her with busywork? Why would he need all these reports?

Unless, maybe, he wanted to share them with someone else—someone he couldn't merely forward computer links to.

JACE WAS WORKING the filling line today, monitoring the machinery that was calibrated to inject exactly .70 milliliters of solution into each bottle of Stroud's Soothing Eye Drops. No one spoke to him as he worked, or even looked at him directly, though he could feel the furtive glances of his coworkers. Word had probably gotten around that the FBI had questioned the new guy, and they were all wondering if he was responsible for the bomb that had killed Lydia Green.

Jace pretended not to notice the cold shoulder and concentrated on studying the manufacturing process, trying to spot the weak points in the system, where the poisoner might have introduced the ricin without being seen.

Even with the investigation to occupy his mind, the work was beyond boring. How did his coworkers stand it? He was all too aware that if he had stayed in his hometown, this would have been his lot. It was either that or the coal mines. Or the military. The army had been his ticket out—that and the education the army had paid for. Most of the people he had graduated high school with had opted to stay close to home and take what had looked like good jobs to them. Now the mines were shutting down and half the factories were shipping jobs overseas.

His sister's husband had been laid off so many times he had stopped looking for work.

Jobs like the one Jace was doing now were coveted in a place like Mayville. He had a hard time believing an employee would do anything to jeopardize them, but experience had taught him that people's motives for wrongdoing weren't always logical.

The time arrived for his mandatory break and he headed for the coffee machine. The quartet of fellow workers already in the break room ignored him as he entered, continuing their conversation. "I saw Leo at Bundy's Place night before last," an older man with a pockmarked face said.

"What were you doing at Bundy's Place?" a redhead with pink glasses asked.

"Hey, they have a great happy hour," the man said.

"Tonight is catfish night," a second man said. "There'll be a full house."

"Do you think Leo will be there?" a woman with her hair in braids asked. "I'd like to see him, and tell him how sorry I was about his mom."

"The bartender is a friend of mine," the first man said. "He told me Leo has been there every night. Drowning his sorrows, I guess."

"Miss Gini wouldn't be happy about that," Pink Glasses said.

"She wouldn't be happy about a lot of things that are happening around here lately."

The conversation ended as Barb entered the room.

Her gaze slid over the group, then fixed on Jace. "Well?" she asked.

Jace tossed his half-drunk coffee into the trash. "Well, what?"

"Well, did you have anything to do with that bomb?"

The others stared at him, mixed fear and anger on their grim faces.

"No," Jace said. "My wife and I came here to work, not to cause trouble."

"The FBI didn't arrest you," Pink Glasses said. "I guess if they thought you were guilty, you wouldn't be here now."

"Maybe the feds are watching, gathering evidence," Pockmarked Face said.

"They won't find any evidence against me," Jace said. "And why would I want to bomb the place where I'd only worked a day? I didn't even know the poor woman who died."

"Some people are just mean," the woman with the braids said.

Jace couldn't argue with that statement. He had met plenty of mean people in his life. But even mean people usually had a motive behind their meanness. It might be a misguided or completely unfounded motive, but in their minds it justified their meanness. Figuring out the motives behind the sabotage of Stroud Pharmaceuticals would go a long way toward finding the person responsible.

By the end of his shift, a few people had loosened up around Jace. But he was no closer to figuring out how the ricin had gotten into those tablets.

He was waiting for Laura at the truck when she emerged from the front offices. "How did it go?" he asked.

"Parker was in a foul mood," she said. "He didn't come in until noon, and then he spent the rest of the day keeping me running with busywork. I couldn't find any way to bring up Leo's name, much less the meeting at the park. What about you?"

"At least some of my coworkers no longer think I'm the mad bomber." He started the truck, the old engine rumbling roughly to life. "Let's go out tonight."

She blinked. "What? Why?"

"We're going out. To a place called Bundy's. I hear they have good catfish."

She wrinkled her nose. "Let me guess—it's fried."

"Of course."

She turned her head to gaze out the window. "I don't know if I want to go."

Did that translate to *I don't want to eat fried fish*, or *I don't want to go anywhere with you*? Probably both. Too bad. She was stuck with him for the duration. "You do want to go," he said. "It's where Leo Elgin has been drowning his sorrows every night this week."

She whipped her head back around. "Catfish it is, then."

BUNDY'S PLACE WAS a tin-roofed, windowless barn of a building at the intersection of two county roads five miles out of Mayville. Ancient oaks shaded the building, and the bass thump from a three-piece band reverberated across the parking lot which, by the time Laura and Jace arrived, was packed with cars and pickup trucks.

The smell of beer and frying fish perfumed the air as they stepped inside. They found a table with a view of the bar and Jace went to get drinks. He came back with two beers.

The beer was so cold it made her teeth hurt, but it tasted refreshing. She scanned the crowd, spotting several familiar faces from the plant. "I don't see Leo," she said.

"It's early yet." A waitress arrived to take their order and the tables around them began to fill. A few minutes later, their server returned, bearing two baskets full of catfish, fries and coleslaw. Laura stared at the food, suddenly ravenous. "Go ahead," Jace said. "It won't bite back."

The fish was tender and meaty, the cornmeal coating crispy and spicy, and not at all greasy. She didn't know when she had eaten something so delicious.

The band, which had taken a break, began playing again, an upbeat country song she recognized from the radio. Jace shoved back his chair and stood. "Let's dance," he said.

"We're supposed to be here spying on Leo Elgin," she reminded him.

"He hasn't shown up yet." He leaned over and tugged on her hand. "Shame to waste the evening."

She let him lead her onto the already crowded dance floor. She couldn't remember the last time she had danced, but Jace made it easy, guiding her through steps she thought she had forgotten, and even leading her through a few new moves. It was a heady feeling, being twirled around the dance floor by a capable partner.

The music changed to a slow ballad. Laura turned to leave the dance floor, but Jace pulled her close. He looked into her eyes, one brow quirked in silent question. *Why not?*

She settled against him. Being so close to him felt dangerous—and thrilling. She let herself enjoy the feel of his arm encircling her lightly, his hand clasping hers. The music was slow and dreamy. Sexy. She closed her eyes, feeling the music wash over her, breathing in the hint of cinnamon that always clung to him and leaning into his embrace. When she opened her eyes, he was looking at her, a raw longing in his gaze that made her breath catch and her heart beast faster. She tried to look away, only to shift her gaze to his lips, the pull of them impossible to resist. The song ended and she let the kiss come, his mouth firm and insistent, her body pressed against his.

A loud whistle, followed by laughter, broke the spell.

She stared up at Jace, who looked amused now, and heat flooded her cheeks. Backing away, she hurried off the dance floor to the ladies' room, where she sat in a stall, trying to catch her breath and pull herself together. She and Jace were supposed to be working together. They were professionals, yet they had just behaved very unprofessionally.

You're human, a small voice inside of her whispered—one she didn't listen to very often. She wasn't going to listen to it now.

When she was feeling more composed, she emerged from the stall, washed her hands and studied her face in the scratched mirror. She looked the same as always—a little pale, maybe, but calm. Competent. Not the type of woman who would get involved with a coworker on an assignment.

But what did that kind of woman look like, anyway?

She left the ladies' room, almost colliding with a man in the hallway. He mumbled an apology and brushed past, head down, but not before she had gotten a good look at him. She hurried back to their table, where Jace was accepting an order of two fresh beers from their waitress.

"You didn't have to run off," he said as she settled into the chair beside him. "But hey, I'm sorry if—"

She waved away the apology and leaned toward him, keeping her voice low. "I just saw Leo Elgin," she said.

"Where?"

"He was headed into the men's room." She swiveled in her chair to get a view of the hallway that led to the restrooms.

"There he is," Jace said as Leo merged with the crowd, moving toward the bar. Jace tapped her shoulder. "You go talk to him."

Laura made her way to the bar, hanging back until the chair next to Leo was vacated. She slipped up beside him and when he glanced her way, she stuck out her hand. "Hi,

I'm Laura," she said. "I'm new in town. Are you from around here?"

He looked down at his drink. "I'm not exactly good company right now. Maybe you should find someone else to talk to."

"Oh, what's wrong?" She leaned toward him. "If you want to talk about it, people tell me I'm a good listener. Sometimes it helps to get things off your chest, you know?"

"Talking won't help this." He took a long pull of his beer. "My mother died a week ago. She was murdered."

Laura gasped. "That's horrible! Who killed her? Do they know?"

He studied her, eyes narrowed. "She was one of the people who died after taking poisoned Stroud's Stomach Soother tablets."

"I'm so sorry." Laura lightly touched his shoulder. "That is just horrible. I heard about that on TV. Actually, I just went to work at Stroud. I wasn't so sure about the job, after what happened with those Stomach Soothers and everything, but I really needed the money, you know?"

"You work in the plant?" Leo asked.

"No, I'm in the office. I'm Parker Stroud's secretary."

Leo's eyes widened and he set his beer down with a thump. "Do you know Mr. Stroud?" Laura asked.

He looked away. "I know him a little."

"I'll admit, as a boss he's a little intimidating."

"Parker is all right. He's pretty torn up about what happened."

"Oh? You've spoken to him recently?"

"No. I just… I just know he's that kind of guy."

"I think if I was in your place, the Strouds wouldn't be my favorite people right now," she said. "I mean, aren't they supposed to have safety rules and stuff to keep that kind of thing from happening?"

"Yeah, but Parker's mom and dad really run the place.

They won't let him modernize the way he wants. He thinks he could have prevented this."

That was interesting. Were things really more lax than she and Jace suspected? Was Parker asking for all the safety and production reports in order to make a case for changes?

"Fight!" A roar rose up from the crowd behind them and she and Leo turned in time to see a chair sail through the air and crash against a pillar. Two men were grappling, rolling on the floor, fists flying.

"Jace!" Laura screamed the name as she recognized one of the men on the floor—who currently had blood streaming down his face.

Chapter Seven

Jace knew trouble was headed his way the minute he saw the look in the man's eye. He just didn't have enough time to get out of the way. "Are you Jace Lovejoy?" the man—six-foot-four with eighteen-inch biceps—asked.

"Who's asking?" Jace stood, hands on the table, out where the man could see them.

"My name is Shay Green and my aunt was Lydia Green. Somebody told me the cops think you planted that bomb that killed her."

"I had nothing to do with that bomb," Jace said. "And I'm sorry about your—"

But he never finished the sentence. Green's fist was already headed his way. Jace ducked, and flipped the table at Green, throwing him off balance long enough for Jace to step up and land a blow that should have ended the fight before it started.

But Green—hyped-up on grief and adrenaline and the alcohol that came off of him in fumes—hadn't gotten the memo. He momentarily staggered under the force of the blow, then charged at Jace like an enraged bull.

The next thing Jace knew, he was on the floor with blood streaming from his nose and Green straddling his chest. Someone else tried to pull Green off of him and Jace took advantage of the distraction to squirm out from under him and knee him in the chin. Green's howl hurt his ears and he dove at Jace again.

They rolled across the floor, into tables, dodging people's feet. Jace would be on top, then Green. A circle of spectators had formed around them by the time they got to their feet again, grappling in the clumsy way of two evenly matched fighters, neither of whom would give an inch.

"The cops are on their way!" someone shouted, and Jace swore under his breath. He didn't want to have to explain this to the local police and risk blowing his cover. He shoved Green back. "You got the wrong guy!" he yelled. "Leave me alone."

In answer, Green punched him in the gut. Jace doubled over, fighting for breath, vision going gray. Two men dragged Green back, and Jace felt a hand on his back. He whirled, fist raised, to face Laura. She wrapped both hands around his arm and dragged him toward the edge of the crowd. "Come on," she said. "We've got to get out of here."

He didn't try to resist, but let her lead him through the crowd and out a side door to the parking lot. He was dazed and bleeding, and only when he felt her hand digging in his pants pocket did he wake up. "What are you doing?" he asked.

"I need the keys to the truck."

He pushed her hand away and fished out the keys. "Come on," she said, taking the keys and grabbing hold of his arm again.

They turned out of the parking lot just as the first patrol car turned in. Jace leaned back in the seat, eyes closed, trying not to think about how much his face hurt. "What was that all about?" Laura asked.

"He said he was Lydia Green's nephew." Jace's voice sounded thick and unfamiliar. "He was drunk and had it in his head that I was responsible for the bomb that killed his aunt."

"But a fight? What were you thinking? What if you had had to draw your weapon?"

Jace was very aware of the gun holstered out of sight at his ankle. "I wouldn't have shot the guy."

"What if he had threatened you with a gun?" she asked.

"That didn't happen. He used his fists." He gingerly touched his nose and winced. "He could have broken my nose."

She braked hard, throwing him forward against the seat belt. "Do we need to go to the doctor? The hospital?"

"I don't think my nose is broken. I just need to get back to the trailer and clean up." He shifted to dig a handkerchief from his pocket and pressed it to his still-bleeding nose. "What did you find out from Elgin?"

"He says Parker's parents are preventing Parker from modernizing the factory. I got the impression he blames Donna and Steve, but not Parker, for what happened to his mother."

"The two of them didn't look all that friendly when we saw them at the lake yesterday."

"No, and Leo didn't really talk about Parker as if they were best buddies. But he did talk as if he knew him well—as if maybe they had been closer once." She had detected a note of regret in Leo's voice when he spoke about Parker.

"Maybe Leo was confronting Parker about Leo's mother's death and he was angry Parker wasn't pressing his parents to do more," Jace said.

"Or maybe there's no way we'll ever know what they talked about unless they tell us." Laura turned the truck into the rutted drive to the trailer. She parked and climbed out, but Jace was slower to join her. He moved stiffly, as if in pain. "What's wrong?" she asked. "Did he hurt more than your nose?"

"I'm still feeling a couple of those punches." Jace tried to straighten, but grimaced and remained bent over.

Laura took his arm. "Come on. I think there's a first aid kit in the closet."

"Nothing a stiff whiskey and a good night's sleep won't cure."

She wanted to lecture him on the stupidity of fighting. If things had turned ugly and he'd had to pull his weapon to defend himself, their cover would have been blown and the operation aborted. Not to mention, he could have been seriously injured, and she'd have been without a partner. While Jace went into the bathroom to wash off as much blood as possible, she rummaged through shelves until she found the first aid kit. When he emerged, water still dripping from the ends of his hair, purpling bruises already forming beneath both eyes, she had an assortment of bandages and ointments laid out on the kitchen table.

"Are you sure your nose isn't broken?" she asked, eyeing him critically.

"I'm sure." He squeezed the tip between his thumb and forefinger, wincing as he did so. "I couldn't stand that if it was. But he did bang it up pretty good."

"At least put some antibiotic ointment on that cut on your lip and the one on your chin," she said. "He must have been wearing a big ring or something."

"Everything about the dude was big."

"I hope he doesn't decide to come after you again."

"I'm touched that you're so concerned for me," he said as he dabbed ointment onto his chin.

"I'm concerned for me. We live together."

His eyes met hers, and she felt that flare of heat again, the spark that seemed to ignite every time they were alone together. "About that kiss on the dance floor," he began.

"I don't want to talk about that kiss."

"We need to talk about the kiss." He reached out and captured her hand in his.

"It shouldn't have happened," she said, trying, and failing, to pull away from him. "It was a momentary lapse of judgment."

"I think it was the natural reaction of a man and a woman who are attracted to each other."

"We are work partners. Gender shouldn't figure into it."

"We're human beings, not robots. Gender is part of what makes us who we are." He rubbed his thumb across her knuckles, sending a current of sensation through her, like an electrical charge. "I'm pretty happy about that right now."

She jerked her hand away from him. "We have a job to do," she said. "We can't make this about us."

He straightened in his chair. "I respect your feelings, even though I think you're wrong. If you really believe the only way to handle this is to keep things strictly business between us, then I'll do that."

She forced herself to look him in the eye again. "I have to know that I can trust you," she said.

His expression hardened. "I never have and I never will force myself on a woman. You don't have to worry about anything like that."

"I didn't mean…" But what had she meant? Maybe it wasn't Jace she couldn't trust but herself when she was around him. He made her forget the woman she needed to be in favor of a wilder, more out-of-control version of herself. Losing herself that way felt more dangerous than any criminal she had ever faced.

Laura drove to work the next morning while Jace, his face an ugly mass of bruises, sat hunched over in the passenger seat. "Maybe you should have called in sick," she said.

"Everyone will have heard about the fight by now. If I don't show up for work, they'll think Green got the best of me."

"It looks to me like he did," she said.

He glared at her, which only made her grin. Grumpy Jace was certainly easier to handle than easygoing Jace, who always seemed to find a way to glide past her doubts and hesitations.

That wasn't quite a fair assessment, of course. True to his word, he hadn't so much as brushed up against her this morning, keeping a very respectful and businesslike distance between them and coming to the breakfast table this morning fully and properly dressed.

What did it say about her that she had spent half the meal picturing him without his shirt anyway?

She was on her way to her office when Donna Stroud intercepted her. "Laura, I was hoping I'd catch you," she said. "Could I speak with you in my office for a minute?"

Laura followed the older woman into her office. Donna settled heavily into the chair behind her desk. She looked as if she had aged in the last week, the lines around her eyes and on either side of her mouth deepened. "Is something wrong?" Laura asked.

"I'm hoping you can tell me if you've made any progress in this case," Donna said.

"I don't have anything I can share with you at this time," Laura said. They had one suspect for the bombing and nothing for the poisoning, and things were moving agonizingly slow. "Investigations like this take time," she continued. "There's a lot of evidence to sift through and people to question." Even then, sometimes a lucky break was as critical as good detective work. She was sure they had the latter in this case, but they needed the former.

"I feel as if my life is on hold, waiting for the other shoe to drop," Donna said. "First the poisoned Stomach Soothers, then the bombing—what next? Why is someone out to destroy me and my family?"

"Right now, we don't have anything to show that the same person committed both crimes," Laura said. "It could be that the bombing was done to retaliate for the poisoned stomach medication."

"Who would do something like that?"

"People who are grieving sometimes react drastically," Laura said, thinking of Lydia Green's nephew and Jace's bruised face. "That doesn't at all excuse what was done, but it does give us motivation and an idea of where to look."

"You're thinking of Leo Elgin, aren't you?" Donna shook her head. "I've known Leo since he was a little boy. A smart, quiet boy. I can't imagine him killing someone—a wonderful woman like Lydia Green. Especially not when he's grieving his mother's death."

"We're looking at a lot of different people and motives," Laura said. "That was just one example."

The door to Donna's office opened and an attractive man with thick silver hair entered. He smiled at Laura. "I'm sorry, dear. I didn't mean to interrupt."

Donna half rose from her chair. "I didn't know you were coming in today."

"Oh, I thought I should come in and check on things." He moved into the room, then looked at Laura again. "It's good to see you. It's been a while, hasn't it?"

"Steve, this is—" Donna began.

"Oh, I know who it is." The man—Laura realized it must be Steve Stroud—waved away the interruption. "I'm not likely to forget our future daughter-in-law, am I?"

"Steve, this is Laura Lovejoy. She's Parker's new administrative assistant, not his fiancée." Donna's voice was firm. "Parker and Kathleen split up almost two years ago."

Steve's face clouded. "They did? I guess... I guess it just slipped my mind." He offered Laura a sheepish smile. "You do look a lot like her. A very pretty young woman." He turned back to his wife. "Is Parker here?"

"I don't know," Donna said. "He's been coming in late some mornings."

"That's all right." Steve's expression remained benign. "The boy works too hard. Always burning the midnight oil, working late."

Donna and Laura exchanged glances. Certainly since Laura had been here, Parker had not worked late. "Why don't you go into your office?" Donna suggested. "I'll send some reports in that I need you to review."

He looked relieved. "Of course I'll review them for you," he said. "I did always have more patience for that sort of thing than you do."

"Go on and I'll send them over in a minute," Donna said.

She waited until her husband had entered his office and shut the door behind him before she dropped into her chair once more. "I'm sorry about that," she said. "He's not supposed to drive, but sometimes he gets away from the caretaker I've hired and heads down here. I'll have to call the caretaker and find out what happened." She glanced toward the office door. "And as you can see, he's not always well-oriented to time and place. He mixes up the past and present and simply doesn't remember other things."

"Who was Kathleen?" Laura asked.

"A young woman Parker dated for a time. They were engaged for a little over six months. Then she broke off the relationship and moved away."

"Where is she now? Do you know?"

"The last I heard, she was living in Washington, DC."

"I'll need her full name and address so we can check." At Donna's astonished look, she added, "She probably had nothing to do with any of this, but we need to check out anyone who has had a relationship with the family." Maybe things between Parker and Kathleen hadn't been so amicable.

"All right," Donna said. "I'll get that information for you."

"All this must be very stressful for you," Laura said.

"It is. But there's nothing to do but carry on."

"Parker mentioned that he had tried to persuade you to let him take on more of the day-to-day operation of the business," Laura said.

"He has." Her expression hardened. "I know that my son is not really your boss, at least not for the long term, but I still don't feel right discussing him with you this way."

"I'm only interested if it pertains to the case," Laura said. Not precisely true. She had a human curiosity to know more about the man she worked with every day. But she was professional enough not to give in to that curiosity.

"Then let's just say that I don't think Parker is ready for the responsibility of running this business," Donna said. "Especially not in this time of crisis." She stood again. "If you'll excuse me, I need to get some sort of paperwork to keep Steve occupied, before he decides to wander into the factory and cause trouble."

Laura left the office, pondering the dynamic between husband and wife. What would that be like, to watch the person you had vowed to love for better or worse slipping away right before your eyes?

When she reached her office, Laura was surprised to find Merry seated behind her desk. "Can I help you?" Laura asked, moving past the woman to stow her purse in the filing cabinet.

"I'm just waiting for Parker to come in." Merry swiveled back and forth in Laura's chair. "You're late."

"I stopped to talk with Mrs. Stroud."

"What would she want with you?"

Laura didn't bother answering the question. "I'll tell Parker you stopped by when he gets in," she said. "Right now, I have work I need to do."

Merry made no move to leave, swiveling back and forth

in the chair, a smirk on her face. "I think I'll wait here for Parker to get in."

"I don't care what you do, but you need to get out of my chair." Laura glared at the woman. She wasn't above yanking Merry out of the chair by her ponytail, but she hoped they could resolve this in a more adult fashion.

"I like this chair," Merry said. "It's more comfortable than mine."

Laura was debating her next move when the door behind them opened and Parker came in. "Good morning, Parker!" Merry called.

Parker looked from Laura to Merry. "What are you doing here?" he asked.

Merry vacated the chair at last and hurried around the desk. "I stopped by to say good morning," she said.

"Good morning," he said, then disappeared into his office and shut the door.

Merry stared at the closed door, looking close to tears. Laura settled into the chair behind her desk and booted up her computer.

"He doesn't like you," Merry said.

Laura looked up and Merry stalked over to the desk. "Parker was never like this when Cheryl worked for him. Having to work with you has put him in a bad mood."

Laura shrugged. "If you say so."

Merry leaned over the desk, both hands planted on its surface. "What are you doing here, anyway?"

"I'm trying to work." Laura turned back to her computer.

"Everyone thinks it's strange that you and your husband showed up here out of nowhere and the next day that bomb goes off. You're not even from here and you move into one of the top jobs at the company. We all think you're up to something."

"I'm not up to anything," Laura said.

"I think you are," Merry said. "And I'm going to find out what it is." She whirled and hurried away, reminding Laura of a defiant child. Her last words might as well have been, *I'm telling!*

"THE WARRANT CAME through to allow us to bug Leo Elgin's house," Jace said after dinner that evening. Laura had made tacos, so he was supposed to be cleaning up, though he lingered at the table over a glass of iced tea. His bruises looked worse than ever, though she had to admit the rugged look added an air of danger that suited him. "We'll go in tomorrow, during his mom's memorial service."

"What's your plan?" she asked. Jace always had a plan for these things. His aptitude for legal breaking and entering was one of the reasons he had been recruited for the tactical crime division.

"We're going in as caterers for the reception after the service."

"Leo is paying caterers for a reception?" He hadn't struck Laura as someone who would go to that much trouble.

"Stroud Pharmaceuticals arranged it all," he said. "Donna Stroud insisted."

"Ah." Laura nodded. "And we insisted that Donna Stroud insist."

"Ramirez might have encouraged her a little, but she doesn't know that we're going in or what we'll be doing."

"Of course not." She sighed. "What do you need me to do?"

He studied her across the table. "You need to get a wig," he said. "Something mousy. And a maid's uniform."

"I hope this isn't going where I think it's going," she said.

"Get your mind out of the gutter, Smitty," he said. "I'm

not talking about a *French* maid. Frankly, we need to drab you down so you're less noticeable."

"Since when am I noticeable?" She stared at him. "I'm a federal agent. I know how to blend in."

"You know how to blend in when you're wearing your black suit with your hair in a bun. But here in Mayville—trust me, you stand out."

"What do you mean, I stand out?"

He grinned. "Do you know how many men have come up to me and said something about the hot new blonde in Parker's office?"

She flushed. "What did you say?"

"I told them, yeah, that's my wife, so hands off."

Her expression must have conveyed her annoyance. "Hey, it's what they expect," he said. "Don't take it personally."

How could she not take it personally? On one hand, it bothered her to know men at the plant had been talking about her. On the other hand, she melted a little at the thought of Jace warning them off—as if he really did care.

"Headquarters is sending over a package tomorrow morning," he said. "It should have everything we need, including the disguises I asked for."

"Good. Because I think if I go shopping for a wig in Mayville, it's going to spark rumors."

His grin was positively wicked. "Then you could tell them you were just trying to liven things up in the bedroom."

She threw her spoon at him, but he caught it in the air and laughed. "What's your disguise?" she asked.

"Glasses, earring and fake tattoos."

She frowned. "Someone could recognize you."

"Trust me, they won't."

She slept fitfully that night, anxiety over the next day's job mingling with wild dreams of Jace—Jace kissing her, touching her, then leaving her, guaranteeing she awoke tired and out of sorts.

The promised box from headquarters arrived at nine thirty. The memorial service for Gini Elgin was due to begin at eleven. Jace figured they would have about an hour to get in and out before the real caterers showed up, followed by Leo and the other mourners. They each retired to their rooms to get ready.

The black pants, white shirt and gray apron were definitely on the drab side, Laura decided as she studied what she could see of herself in the dresser mirror. The wig—a mousy brown bob with thick bangs—also did little to draw attention to herself. She added the white Keds that had also been in the box, secured her weapon in its harness beneath the apron, and called it good.

She met up with Jace in the kitchen, where he was examining the electronics that had also been packed in their box. Laura stared at his transformation. He wore black pants and a tight black T-shirt that clung to his biceps and abs, showing off details she hadn't noticed before—mainly, that Jace Cantrell had put in his share of time in the gym. Below the short sleeves of the tee he'd added full-sleeve tattoos—a vividly colored tapestry of birds, fish, serpents and at least one skull. A gold hoop glinted at one ear, and he'd shaved his scruff into a soul patch.

"Is this your idea of drabbing down and not standing out?" she asked, trying—and failing—to tear her eyes away from him.

"I'm going for the opposite effect," he said. "If anyone does see me, they'll remember the body art. Once we're done with the job, I'll remove the sleeves and the earring, shave off the soul patch and essentially, vanish."

At ten forty-five, they left the trailer. At a warehouse on the other end of town they traded the pickup for a panel van, Bread and Butter Caterers stenciled on the side. Jace drove past the church where Gini's service was being held. The parking lot was full and more parked cars lined either side of the street. From there, it was only five blocks to Gini's house, where Leo was staying. The cottage sat well back from the road in a grove of mature trees. Roses climbed trellises on either side of the front door, their scent heavy in the humid air.

They headed for the front door, carrying two plastic totes that to any passerby would look like supplies for the catered reception. Laura blocked the view from the road while Jace made quick work of the front door lock, which didn't even have a dead bolt. Then they were in.

Gini Elgin had favored hominess over haute couture in her furnishings, a sagging sofa with faded floral cushions sharing space in the living room with a scuffed maple coffee table, an armchair upholstered in gold velvet, and a braided rug in shades of brown and gold. Dust filmed every flat surface, and Laura wondered if Leo had even been in here since his return.

The dining room and a small home office had the same air of disuse and abandonment. Only the kitchen looked lived-in, with a stained coffee cup in the sink and an open box of cereal on the counter. Jace went to the brick-like cordless phone in its charging station on one end of the counter. "I'll start here," he said. "Set out the food, and then see if you can find his bedroom."

Laura unpacked a tray of finger sandwiches and another of cookies and set them on the kitchen island. The real caterers would bring more food later. She and Jace had carried these two trays as part of their cover.

She turned her attention to the search for Leo's bedroom. Though she knew the house was empty, she moved cautiously down the hall, as wary of leaving evidence behind as of surprising an unforeseen occupant of the house. The first door she reached led to a bathroom with avocado-green tiles and an old-fashioned claw-foot tub. A blue bath towel hung crookedly on the towel bar by the tub, and a man's shaving kit balanced on the edge of the sink.

Leo's bedroom was next door—a child's room with a single unmade bed draped in a blue corduroy spread, posters for decades-old baseball players on the walls. Old athletic trophies shared space on a bookshelf with paperback thrillers and computer software manuals. A small desk in the corner held a laptop computer and a phone charger, minus the phone. Dirty dishes and fast food wrappers crowded the nightstand.

"This his room?" Jace looked in the doorway.

"Yeah." Laura stepped aside to let him get to the desk. "Pretty depressing. I think he's probably been spending most of his time in here."

"Makes our job easier." Jace assessed the room, then picked up the bedside lamp and examined it. "I'll put one bug here, another on the desk," he said. "It's overkill, but we've got the hardware, so why not use it?"

While he worked, Laura searched the bookcase, closet and dresser drawers. She felt under the mattress, looked behind the curtains and shone a flashlight into the heating vents, looking for any secret stash. The local police had already searched the house once and hadn't found anything linking Leo to the explosion at Stroud Pharmaceuticals, but it never hurt to give everything a second going-over.

"If he did plant that bomb, I think he made the device somewhere else," Jace said.

"Where else?" Laura asked. "This place doesn't even have a garage, just that little shed out back, and the report from the search team says it's full of gardening tools."

"A storage unit, maybe. An abandoned barn? There are probably a few of those around here."

"Maybe we'll hear something that will give us a better idea." She watched him fit the tiny listening device into the base of a stapler that sat on one corner of the desk, then snap the bottom of the stapler back in place.

She hugged her arms across her chest. "Let's get out of here," she said. "This place gives me the creeps."

He stowed his tools and they headed toward the door. One step into the hallway, Jace froze.

"What's wrong? Why did you stop?" She shoved at his back, then went cold all over as she recognized the sound of the front door opening, and someone coming inside.

Chapter Eight

Laura's anxiety radiated around her and through Jace. He reached back, grabbed her hand and squeezed.

"I'm okay," she whispered.

He released her hand and moved forward, stopping at the end of the hallway as Leo rounded the corner toward them. The younger man, face pale and eyes reddened, stared at them. "Who are you?" he demanded, his voice shaky.

"We're from the caterer." Jace extended a hand and Leo automatically took it. "We weren't expecting anyone so soon."

Leo dropped Jace's hand, and his gaze shifted away. "I... I needed to get out of there," he said.

"We're very sorry for your loss." Laura adopted a Southern accent and prayed Leo wouldn't see past her disguise to the woman who had chatted him up at the bar last night.

"What were you doing back there?" Leo looked past them, toward the back of the house.

"We like to check that the bathroom is ready for guests," Laura said.

Leo scowled. "It took two of you to do that?"

She didn't miss a beat. "There was a spider in the sink. I asked Jeff to kill it for me."

Great improvisation, Jace thought, though Laura didn't strike him as the type to freak out over a spider. In fact, the only time he'd ever seen her lose her cool was when he kissed her. She'd all but melted in his arms, making him believe that even if she resisted the idea of getting involved with him, she wanted him.

Now was not the time to be thinking about that, he reminded himself.

"You need to leave," Leo said.

"We won't be much longer," Jace said. "We just need to arrange a few things."

"No! I don't want you here." Leo's voice rose, his eyes wild. "It's bad enough I have to put up with all these people coming over after the funeral. You can at least leave me alone for now."

"All right." Laura took Jace's arm. "We can finish later."

They moved past him toward the kitchen, but paused in the hallway to listen as he made his way down the hall and shut the door to his room behind him. "Let's go," Laura said.

They left the food, grabbed up both totes and headed out the front door. Jace started the van, drove around the corner and parked behind a deserted office complex.

He texted Rogers that they were out, then leaned his head back against the seat and let out a breath, waiting for his racing heart to slow. As operations went, he had been in tighter spots. Still, it was unnerving when the surveillance subject found you in his house.

"Why did he leave his own mother's funeral scarcely twenty minutes into the service?" Laura asked.

"Funerals are hard for a lot of people," Jace said. "Maybe it got to him and he just wanted to be alone."

"Maybe." She swiveled toward him. "Drive back around to where we can get a good look at the house."

"All right." He started the engine again and drove around the block, parking at the end of the street, where they had a clear view of Leo's driveway and front door.

They had scarcely parked when a white Chevy sedan turned onto the street.

Laura gasped as the sedan passed, the driver never even glancing in their direction. "That's Merry Winger," she said.

"Remind me who she is."

"She's Parker Stroud's girlfriend."

Merry turned into the Elgins' driveway, got out and walked up to the door. She was a pretty blonde in a neat navy-blue miniskirt and a sleeveless white blouse, and very tall white heels. She rang the bell and a moment later, Leo answered the door.

"He doesn't look happy to see her," Laura said. She had pulled a pair of binoculars from the backpack at her feet and was studying the couple. As she said this, Leo stepped aside to let Merry in, and shut the door behind her.

Laura lowered the glasses. "How did you know he was going to meet someone?" Jace asked.

"It was just a hunch." She continued to stare toward the door. "But what is Parker's girlfriend doing meeting Leo Elgin in secret?"

"We don't know that it's secret."

"He left his mother's funeral to meet up with her. That's pretty secretive, if you ask me." She leaned forward, as if that would help her see through the closed door. "And where is Parker?"

"Maybe Leo and Merry have a thing on the side?" Jace speculated. "Or they were a couple before and now that he's back in town she's trying to renew the acquaintance?"

The door opened and Merry emerged. Head down, she hurried to her car, then drove away. Laura sat back in her seat. "She wasn't in there long enough to do anything," she said.

"He didn't even walk her to the door," Jace said. "So maybe they're not having an affair. Or maybe she came on to him and he turned her down."

Laura stowed the binoculars again. "Let's head back to the trailer. Maybe your recording devices will pick up something useful."

"He hasn't had a single phone call in the last twenty-four hours," Rogers said when Jace checked in with him Sunday afternoon. "No visitors since the reception after the funeral, and all of those conversations are variations of either condolences over the loss of his mother, or questions about what he plans to do next."

"What does he plan to do next?" Jace asked.

"He doesn't know. That's the answer he gave everyone, and if they tried to press, he either changed the subject or clammed up entirely."

"What about Merry Winger—the woman who showed up right after Laura and I left? What did they talk about?"

"She delivered something," Rogers said. "Here. Let me play you the recording."

> Sound of door opening.
> Leo: What do you want?
> Merry: I brought you this.
> Leo: You'd better go.
> Merry: Not until you tell me what's going on.
> Leo: Unintelligible mumble.
> Merry: No. You men are all alike. You think I'm stupid and I'm not.
> Leo: You need to go now.
> Long pause. High heels clicking on hardwood. Slamming door.

"Any idea what she brought him?" Jace asked.

"It could have been a sympathy card or a cake or plastic explosives," Rogers said. "We can't tell from his reaction."

"Merry works in the Stroud offices with Laura. Let's

see what she can find out. In the meantime, we need eyes on Leo."

"We don't have enough people to babysit him full time," Rogers said. "At this point we don't have any proof he's even worth watching. It was a stretch getting the okay to bug his place."

"I'll watch him after my shift at the factory," Jace said.

"When will you sleep?"

"When he does. You can keep an eye on him while I'm at the factory."

"I have other work to do," Rogers said.

"When you have a free moment," Jace said. "Just for a few days."

Rogers grunted, which Jace chose to take as agreement. "What do you think we're going to find out?" Rogers asked.

"Who he's seeing, where he's going. If he assembled that explosive, he did it somewhere other than his mother's house."

"I'm willing to try for a few days," Rogers said. "But I'm not convinced we're not wasting our time."

Jace ended the call and looked up to find Laura studying him. "You're going to surveil Leo?" she asked.

"Merry brought him something yesterday. From the tone of their conversation, I don't think she was the person he was expecting to see, and he got rid of her as fast as he could."

"What did she bring him?"

"We don't know. The bugs haven't picked up any other suspicious conversations."

"So, if he left the funeral to meet someone, they either didn't show, or they sent Merry instead," Laura said.

"That's what I'm thinking."

"Maybe Parker sent her." The frown lines on Laura's

forehead deepened. "I got the impression if he said jump, she'd ask, how high?"

"Talk to her. See what you can find out."

"I'll try, but I'm not her favorite person. Apparently, she applied to be Parker's admin before I stepped in and took the job."

"Yeah, but it sounds to me like she wants to keep an eye on Parker. Maybe you can offer to be her spy."

Laura stared at him. "You really think she wants to keep tabs on him? I thought she wanted to be closer to him."

He shrugged. "Hey, I never claimed to be an expert on relationships. But I'm betting Parker wouldn't have picked her for the job. Most men don't like the woman they're involved with always looking over their shoulder."

He couldn't begin to decipher the look she shot him, though he would describe it as somewhere between disgust and incredulity. He started to reassure her that he knew she wasn't the type to get all up in his business, but bit back the words. He and Laura weren't "involved." Never mind that he couldn't be in the same room with her without being hyperaware of her: of her soft scent, her softer skin, and the hard shell around her emotions that he ached to break through.

"I'll see what I can do," she said. "What's your next move?"

He grabbed a backpack with binoculars, camera, water and snacks off the floor beside his chair. "I'm going to keep an eye on Leo. Don't wait up."

THE FIRST THING Laura noticed when she arrived at Stroud Pharmaceuticals on Monday was that the damage to the side door to the executive offices had been repaired, the police tape removed, and the sidewalk replaced, and everything sported a new coat of paint. A crew must have worked all weekend to effect the transformation.

Once inside, however, she noted people still avoided the area. Whether out of superstition or real fear, she couldn't tell. Her coworkers' reactions to her were still subdued, but she pretended not to notice. Maybe in their shoes, she'd be suspicious of the new couple, too. She didn't need to be best friends with any of these people in order to do her job.

She detoured to the break room and fetched two cups of coffee and two doughnuts from the open box on the table, then headed for Merry's desk. The younger woman looked up as Laura approached, eyes narrowed. "What do you want?" she asked.

"I need your advice." Laura set a cup of coffee and a doughnut in front of Merry, then slid a chair close to her desk.

Merry clearly hadn't expected this. "What kind of advice?" she asked, still wary.

"I want to do a good job," Laura said. "But Mr. Stroud—Parker—doesn't seem very happy with my performance. I figure you're the person who knows him best, so I thought maybe you could give me some tips on how to get on his good side."

"Why should I help you do the job I wanted?" Merry asked. "The job I still want?"

"I thought maybe I could do you a favor, too." Laura focused on stirring a packet of sugar into her coffee. "I know you and Parker have to be discreet about your relationship, what with working together and everything. I can make it easier for you to get in to see him, and I can make sure you have all the access you want."

"I can see Parker anytime." Merry tossed her head. "I don't need your help."

"I can run interference if anyone tries to interrupt you," Laura said. "And I can give you his schedule so you know when he's free."

"Why would you want to help me?" Merry asked.

"Because I need your help to do my job," Laura said. "And because Parker is always in a better mood after he's talked to you." The last part was a blatant lie, but she was counting on Merry wanting to believe it.

Merry relaxed a little. "I can give you a few pointers for dealing with him," she said. "But I can't promise they'll help. It could be he just doesn't like you." Her smirk said clearly that she didn't blame Parker.

"I'm grateful for any advice you can give me," Laura said, keeping her face straight.

Merry took a bite of doughnut and chewed, looking thoughtful. "I can't believe I'm even suggesting this to you, of all people," she said after she had swallowed. "But Parker likes women who keep themselves up. He'd probably like it if you dressed a little sexier—you know, shorter skirts and lower necklines."

Fat chance of that happening, but Laura nodded, her expression neutral. "Anything else?"

"He likes it when I compliment him. You know, some men need women to build up their egos."

Did she really believe that? "But you're his girlfriend," Laura said. "I'm just his assistant."

"Well, yeah." Merry shrugged. "I don't know what to tell you. Maybe smile more or have a better attitude. If he's grumpy around you, you must be doing something wrong."

Or maybe he's just a jerk, Laura thought. "I'll keep that in mind." She stood. "Thanks."

"Just remember—you owe me."

"I'll remember." She started to turn away, but hesitated. "Hey, did you go to Gini Elgin's services Saturday?" she asked.

"Yes. Why do you care?"

"I just wondered. I drove by the church and it looked like there were a lot of people there."

"Yeah, there was a big crowd."

"I guess you went with Parker, huh?"

"Well, yeah, though we had to pretend we weren't together when his parents were around." Merry rolled her eyes. "It's so silly, but Parker says I just have to be patient. All this fuss about the poisoned medication and the bomb is slowing everything down."

"I'm sure your patience will pay off," Laura said. "How was Gini's son—Leo?"

Confusion clouded Merry's eyes. "How do you know Leo?"

"I met him in town. He seemed really torn up about his mom's death."

"Yeah. They were close."

"Do you know him well?" Laura asked.

Merry wrinkled her nose. "No."

"I thought somebody told me the two of you used to date."

Merry laughed. "Me and Leo? Get out of here! Somebody was pulling your leg. He's definitely not my type." She shook her head, emphatic.

"I guess I misheard." Laura stepped away. "I'd better get to work. I'll talk to you later." She headed to her office, reviewing the conversation with Merry. She didn't think Merry was lying about her relationship with Leo. Gini's son wasn't handsome, wealthy, powerful or charming—all things Merry appeared to value. If she wasn't in a relationship with him, she must have gone to see him on Parker's behalf.

Parker was already in the office when Laura arrived. He turned from her desk. "Where have you been?" he demanded.

Laura moved around the desk and slid into her chair. "I was talking to Merry."

"About what?"

"About you." She looked him in the eye. One of her

early trainers had stressed the importance of sticking to the truth whenever possible. "I was asking her how I could do a better job for you."

"As if Merry would know anything about that," he scoffed.

"She's your girlfriend, isn't she?"

He frowned. "I guess she told you that."

"Yes. Why? Is it a big secret?"

"It isn't appropriate for me to be dating an employee of the company." He tapped his index finger on the papers in her in-box. "So don't mention it to anyone."

"Your secret is safe with me." She smiled and he took a step back. Before he could escape to his office, she asked, "How was the service for Gini Elgin? I drove by there Saturday and it looked like a big crowd."

"Gini had a lot of friends," Parker said. "She'll be missed."

"How's your friend Leo?"

"I don't imagine he's doing very well, considering his mother was killed."

"Do the police have any suspects yet?" she asked.

"I don't think so. We'll probably never know who did something so horrible." He turned away. "Block off the rest of my morning. I have a meeting with my mother." Not waiting for an answer, he left the office.

She settled behind her desk. She hadn't learned anything new from her questioning of Merry and Parker. Not that she had expected them to spill their secrets to the nosy new employee, but the lack of progress in the case frustrated her.

The door opened and Merry sauntered in. "I want to see Parker," she said, and headed for his office.

"He's not here," Laura said. "He said he had a meeting with his mother."

Merry pouted. "He really ought to be in charge of this place, not her." She sank into the chair across from Laura's desk. "Honestly, she treats him like a child. When we're married, things are going to be different. I'm not going to let her run over him this way."

Laura opened her mouth to ask what Merry intended to say to Mrs. Stroud when the building shuddered, and a deafening roar surrounded them. Both women dropped to their knees on the floor as pictures, coffee cups and a vase of flowers slid to the floor and shattered. As the concussion subsided, screams rose to take its place. Laura was on her feet and running, Merry at her heels.

"What happened?" The younger woman screamed as people, some bleeding, others showered with debris, raced past them, out of the building.

Laura shoved her way through the crowd, toward the source of the commotion. "I think there was another bomb," she said, more to herself than to Merry. Why had she been too late to stop it?

Chapter Nine

The man and woman looked up when Ana tapped on the partially open door to the hospital room. "Mrs. Stroud? We need to ask you and your son some questions."

Donna Stroud, her face washed of color except for the purple half moons beneath her eyes, pressed her lips together tightly and nodded. Parker, on his back in the hospital bed, white bandaging swathing his forehead, said nothing, though his gaze bored into Ana and Rogers as they entered the small room, which smelled of antiseptic and dry-erase marker. "How are you feeling, Mr. Stroud?" Ana asked.

"About like I would expect a person to feel who's been blown up." He pressed a button by his side to raise the head of the bed. "They tell me I have a concussion and contusions, which is medical talk for being beaten half to death."

"Where were you when the blast occurred?" Rogers asked.

"I was standing just outside the door to my mother's office. I was about to go in."

"Did you know Ms. Dupree was in the office?" Rogers asked.

"No. I didn't know anyone was in there."

"This is so horrible." Donna spoke in a hoarse voice, just above a whisper. "Angela wasn't just an employee. She was a friend." She swallowed hard. "I can't believe she's gone."

"Do you know why Ms. Dupree was in your office yesterday morning?" Ana asked.

Donna shook her head. "I don't know. But it wouldn't have been unusual for her to stop by and say hello. We often chatted at work."

"Ms. Dupree's assistant, Shania Merritt, said her boss was bringing some pay raise authorizations for you to okay," Ana said.

Donna nodded. "That sounds right."

"Why weren't you in the office, Mrs. Stroud?" Rogers asked. "Wouldn't you usually be there at that time of morning?"

"Yes, but…" She glanced at Parker. "My husband isn't well."

"Is this to do with his dementia, or something else?" Ana asked.

Donna looked pained. "Steve is forgetful, although most days he manages fine. But sometimes, he's frustrated by his inability to remember and gets confused. Then he becomes angry and we argue. Yesterday morning he was especially combative and I stayed home to try to calm him down."

"What was he being combative about?" Ana asked.

"He had gotten it into his head that Parker was negotiating to sell the business to a competitor and he insisted we should fire Parker." She shook her head. "It's utter nonsense, of course, but once he gets an idea like this into his head, there's no reasoning with him."

"Where would he get such an idea?" Rogers asked.

"There's no basis in reality for these delusions," Parker said. "It's a symptom of his disease. He could see something on TV or dream something and believe it's real."

"What were you doing outside your mother's office, Mr. Stroud?" Rogers asked. "Wouldn't you normally be in your own office at that time?"

"I wanted to speak to my mother about the production

schedule for next month. As the factory manager, I often consult with her."

"Your assistant, Ms. Lovejoy, told us you told her you had a meeting scheduled with your mother," Ana said. "She was told to leave your calendar clear for the whole morning because of this meeting."

"Yes, that's right."

Ana turned to Donna. "We didn't see any notice on your calendar of such a meeting, Mrs. Stroud."

"My son doesn't have to make an appointment to consult with me."

"So this wasn't a prescheduled meeting?" Rogers asked.

"No," Parker said. "If Ms. Lovejoy thought that, she was mistaken."

Or perhaps Parker had wanted Laura to think the meeting had been scheduled earlier, for whatever reason. Ana turned her attention to Donna again. The woman seemed to have aged five years since their first meeting a week ago. "I know you've answered this question before, but we need to ask again," she said. "Can you think of anyone who might wish to harm you?"

"Are you suggesting my mother was the target for this madman?" Parker asked.

"The bomb was in her office, we think under her desk," Rogers said. "It was designed to trigger when she opened her bottom desk drawer." He looked to Donna, who had blanched even paler. "We were told that drawer is where you keep a box of tissues and some other personal items."

She nodded. "I don't know of anyone who would…" She wet her lips. "Who would want to kill me?"

Parker struggled to sit up in bed. "You're upsetting my mother. Don't you think she's been through enough?"

"Why would Angela open that drawer?" Ana asked. "Do you know?"

"I… I can guess."

They waited as Donna stared at her fingers laced together in her lap. When she looked up, her eyes were desolate. "Angela was recently diagnosed with breast cancer. She was due to have surgery, then chemotherapy the week after. I was the only person she told. We had cried together over the news. I can guess that if she came to talk to me yesterday, she was going to let me know her treatment schedule. We would have cried again. When she didn't find me there, maybe she got teary-eyed. She knew I kept tissues in that drawer, so she might have opened it, intending to pull herself together before she went back into the outer office."

"Did you see anyone suspicious in or around the office that day or the day before?" Rogers asked Parker.

"No."

"Mrs. Stroud? Did you see anything or anyone suspicious?"

Donna shook her head. "No."

"Have you received any threatening letters or phone calls?" Ana asked.

"Only the one letter I gave you—the 'six for six' message. Nothing else."

"Are you going to find the person who did this?" Parker asked. "Because you're not doing a very good job so far."

Ana ignored the dig. In his place, she would probably have been frustrated by the lack of progress in the case, too. Civilians expected law enforcement to solve crimes quickly, in the space of a few days. Building a case and finding the guilty party usually took much longer. "Have you considered closing the plant temporarily?" she asked Donna.

"Out of the question," Parker said.

Donna's answer was less strident. "We have a hundred employees and their families who depend on us," she said. "We can't shut them out. As it is, we had to temporarily lay off fifty people when we shut down the plant that made the Stomach Soothers."

"We need you to find whoever is doing this so we can put this tragedy behind us," Parker said.

"This case is our top priority," Rogers said. A nurse entered the room and he moved toward the door. "We may need to talk to you again."

He and Ana moved into the hallway. He waited until they had reached their rental car before he spoke. "What do you think?"

"I think someone has targeted these people," she said.

"Leo Elgin?"

"Maybe. Has your surveillance turned up anything on him?" He and Jace had been trading off watching Leo during daylight hours.

"No. The plant is closed today, so Jace is watching Elgin. If he doesn't turn up anything, we need to focus on someone else."

"Who?"

"We're going to look at everyone who had access to that office," Rogers said.

"Donna Stroud had access," Ana said. "And she was conveniently not there this morning."

"Do you think she killed two of her employees and sabotaged her own product?"

"I think we both know criminals who have done stranger things."

He nodded. "Let's look closer at her and see if we can find out."

"And let's talk to that competitor Steve Stroud accused Parker of negotiating with. Maybe someone is angling to get Stroud Pharmaceuticals at a bargain price."

"Good idea." One more item on the long list of threads to pull in this case. This was the tedious part of working a case—following leads that went nowhere, talking to people who might or might not have something to hide and trying to put all the information together to form a picture that led to the guilty party. It took hours of effort and focus, but that, more than bravery or cunning, was what solved most cases. It was one reason the bureau hired as many accountants as military types. Brains counted more than brawn more often than not.

Four to go.

Merry had placed the envelope on the top of the pile of mail Tuesday morning, and pointed it out to Donna when she delivered it. "It looks like the other letter, doesn't it?" she asked, leaning in close, so that Donna caught the scent of her perfume—floral and delicate, if applied with a heavy hand. "The one the FBI was so concerned about."

Donna stared at the plain white envelope, with her name in dark block letters, no title, and the address for Stroud Pharmaceuticals. "Aren't you going to open it?" Merry asked.

"I think I should call the police," Donna said. "Or maybe Agent Ramirez. I have her card in my desk somewhere." But she made no move to search for it, fixated on the envelope.

"What if it's a solicitation from the local funeral home or something?" Merry asked. "I mean, really?" She plucked the envelope from the stack of mail and slid one pink-polished nail beneath the flap.

"You'll destroy fingerprints," Donna protested.

Merry shook her head. "Every criminal knows to wear gloves." She flicked open the envelope flap and dumped the contents onto the desk. The half sheet of copy paper lay crookedly on the blotter, twenty-point type exclaiming, *Four to go!*

Donna gasped and swayed.

"Mrs. Stroud, you've gone all pale." Merry took her

arm and eased her back in her chair. "You sit there and take deep breaths. You've had a shock." She left, then returned with a cup of water from the cooler in the corner. "Drink this."

Donna drank and began to feel a little steadier. "Thank you." She glanced at the words on the paper and suppressed a shudder, then opened her desk drawer and took out Ana Ramirez's card. "I'd better telephone for someone to deal with this."

"What does that mean?" Merry asked. "'Four to go'?"

"I don't know," Donna lied. Though she knew very well what it meant. Six people had died from taking poisoned Stomach Soothers. Two people had perished in the two bombings at Stroud Pharmaceuticals. Four more deaths before the score would be even, in the bomber's twisted logic.

JACE WAS NUMB with boredom after three nights of tailing Leo Elgin, but he forced himself to stick with the surveillance. The man might be the dullest person Jace had ever met, but that didn't mean he wasn't up to no good.

Though, as far as Jace could tell from the bugs he'd placed in the house, Leo wasn't up to anything but sitting in front of his computer playing hundreds of rounds of solitaire. He received no visitors or phone calls, and the only person he attempted to call was Parker Stroud. The afternoon after the bomb exploded that killed Angela Dupree, Leo tried to call Parker, who was in the hospital, six times. Parker never answered, though that wasn't too surprising, given that he was injured. Leo left only one message. "This is Leo. What's going on over there?"

Jace slumped in a van with the logo of a fake pest control company, parked on the street with a clear view of Elgin's house. Times like these, he missed smoking the most, even though smoking while on surveillance was forbidden—the scent of smoke might attract attention. Still, he missed how smoking gave him something to do with his hands and something to focus on besides his own breathing.

Movement in the house, followed by the sound of a door opening and closing. Jace sat up straighter. It sounded as if Leo had left the house, but Jace saw no movement near the front door. Had Leo gone out the back? Jace got out of the van and, walking purposefully, he marched down the sidewalk. When he reached Leo's house, he ducked down the side, into a screen of shrubbery between Leo's house and the neighbor's. He reached the backyard in time to see Leo unlock the door to a wooden shed in the back corner. With a sagging roof and sides almost devoid of paint, the shed looked on the verge of collapse.

Jace shoved further into the screen of bushes, gritting his teeth as thorns raked his arms and face. He could hear movement from inside the shed—something heavy being shoved around. He headed toward the back of the little building, hoping for a window or a missing board that would allow him to see inside. But instead of an opening, he discovered the back of the shed was all but covered by a five-foot mound of dirt and sod, as if the shed had been built into the side of a hill.

But this was no hill. Jace had seen a similar structure at his grandparents' farm. At some point the Elgins, or whoever had owned the property before them, had built an old-fashioned root cellar. Rather than digging out a space underground, they had built up the earth around the shed. Somewhere inside there was probably a door leading into the storage area within the mound of dirt.

The FBI had searched the Elgin property, but would they have recognized the root cellar?

Jace retreated the way he had come, and walked back to his van. He called Rogers. "The people who searched the Elgin home. Did they look in the root cellar?" he asked.

"Let me check." A moment later Rogers was on the line again. "There's no mention of a root cellar."

"It's at the back of that old shed, built into a mound of earth," Jace said. "They need to check it."

"We're not going to get another warrant," Rogers said. "We've already had complaints that we're harassing the locals and not finding anything."

"There's something going on in that shed," Jace said. "Leo is in there now. I could hear him moving stuff around."

"Maybe he's finally clearing out his mother's property."

"He's been calling Parker Stroud, leaving cryptic messages. Something is going on."

"Find proof then. You haven't got enough to go on."

Jace ended the call and sat back. He'd find the proof. He punched in another number.

Laura answered on the second ring. "Hello?"

"Don't wait up. I'll be working all night."

"What is it? Have you found something?"

"Maybe."

"What is it?"

"I don't know yet, but I need to hang around here tonight. I'll talk to you later."

He started to hang up, but her voice stopped him. "Jace?"

"Yeah?"

"Be careful."

She ended the call. He sat with the phone in his hand, an unsettling tremor in his chest. It was the kind of thing anyone might say to another person. But Laura wasn't just any other person, and when she had told him to be careful, she had sounded as if she really cared.

LAURA TUCKED HER phone back into her pocket. Why had she said that to Jace—"be careful"—as if she were his mother or his wife or something? She should have been demanding he tell her what he was up to. After all, they were partners in this investigation.

She pulled out her phone and hit Redial. "Yeah?" Jace answered.

"What is going on?" she asked. "What are you doing?"

"You don't want to know."

She gripped the phone harder. "Tell me."

"I think Leo is up to something in the old garden shed behind his house—or rather, in the attached root cellar."

"And?" There had to be an *and*.

"I'm going to wait until after dark and sneak in there and look around."

"You don't have a warrant." If he had a warrant, he wouldn't have hesitated to tell her. "Not only is what you're proposing illegal, nothing you find could be used in evidence. You'll compromise the whole case." This was just like him, wanting to take shortcuts, thinking the rules didn't apply to him. He'd gotten away with this kind of thing before now because he had good results, but this time he was going too far.

"I'm not compromising the case." His voice was calm, as if they'd been discussing what to eat for dinner. "I know how to get in and out without leaving a trace, and I won't touch anything. I just want to see if my hunch is right. Then I'll be able to get a warrant."

"How will you get a warrant if you don't reveal what you find in there?" she asked.

"I'll say I saw Leo do something suspicious, or carrying a suspicious object." She swore she could almost *hear* his sly grin. "It won't take much. I can be very persuasive."

"But you'd be lying!" She didn't even try to keep the horror from her voice. "You'd be manufacturing evidence."

"I wouldn't be manufacturing anything. I'll only speak to what I will know is in that root cellar."

"It's still a lie."

"A very small one, and for a good cause."

That's probably what every corrupt agent or politician or businessperson said when they started. But little lies led to big ones. And big lies led to the corruption of the whole situation. "Jace, don't do this," she said, unable to keep the pleading from her voice.

"Why not?" he asked.

"Because you're better than this."

He was silent so long she thought he had hung up. "Jace?" she asked.

"I'm here." He blew out a breath. "I need to get in there and look around," he said. "If Leo is responsible for those bombs, he's killed two people already. We can't let him kill anyone else."

"No." She felt her convictions wavering. Was Jace right, that the ends—stopping a murderer—justified the means? But then, where did she draw the line? "You can't lie to get the warrant," she said.

"Let me go in and see what I find," he said. "Maybe I'm wrong and I'm wasting our time. At least then we'll know we need to focus on someone beside Leo."

"All right."

"Right. Gotta go."

"Jace?"

"What?"

"Be careful."

THE ELGIN HOUSE was located in an older neighborhood on the edge of town. Most of the houses looked to have been built in the seventies or eighties and were occupied by older couples. By midnight, every house on the block was silent and dark. Leo had turned off the last light in his place an hour before and hadn't moved since.

Jace, dressed in jeans and a black hoodie, slipped out of the van and made his way along the side of the yard to the back, not in the bushes this time, but alongside them, concealed by deepest shadow. The night air was still and humid, like furnace exhaust, without a hint of coolness. Within five minutes, he was sweating in the heavy sweatshirt.

The shed and root cellar hunched in the back corner of the yard, looking even more decrepit in the washed-out light of a quarter moon. Jace checked the windows on that side of the house for any sign of movement, but found none. Heart pounding, he stepped into the moonlight and walked over to the door.

Using his body as a shield, he trained the beam of a small penlight on the lock, a hefty padlock, so shiny it couldn't have been on here long. The lock was threaded through a rusty hasp—but the hasp was fashioned with new screws. *What are you so concerned about locking up in here, Leo?* Jace wondered. He'd have to check the records to see if this lock had been here when the FBI conducted their warranted search.

He studied the lock a moment, then took out a set of picks and went to work. The standard commercial lock popped open in less than two minutes. Jace lifted the hasp, opened the door, then hung the lock in place and slipped inside.

The shed smelled of mildew and weed killer. The penlight revealed a shovel, rake and hoe on nails along the far wall. Bags of potting soil and several five-gallon buckets crammed with wood scraps and bits of rusty metal crowded the floor. A leaning metal shelf against the side wall held flower pots, bags of fertilizer and enough weed killing concoctions to poison half the town. If one of them had been found in the Stomach Soothers, Jace would have been suspicious Leo had decided to take out his own mother.

The root cellar was on the other side of the back wall. Jace played his light over the rough wood siding, looking for any kind of opening. It couldn't be obvious or the previous searchers would have found it right away. They would have found most hidden doors as well, so this had to be something especially clever.

A big copper pot, the kind once used for boiling clothing over an outside fire, took up most of the back corner of the shed, filled with tangled fishing gear and an old tarp. Recalling the noises he had heard when Leo first entered the shed, of something heavy being moved, Jace dragged the pot out of the way and shone his light into the corner.

Nothing looked out of the ordinary. The weathered boards of the shed appeared firmly nailed in place. One rusting nail stuck out of the wood a scant quarter inch. When Jace tugged at the nail, it didn't move. But when he grasped the nail like a handle and attempted to pull it, the whole section of siding slid toward him, and a wave of cooler air washed over him, smelling of machine oil and damp.

He stilled, ears straining for any sound, but all remained silent. He stepped around the pot and ducked into the opening. The root cellar was not large, perhaps five feet deep and seven feet wide, like a large closet, the ceiling so low he had to hunch to keep from brushing the top of his head against the chicken wire that had been used as a frame to support the sod laid over it. A wooden work bench took up most of the space, with a small drill press, scales, and various hand tools littering its top. Cardboard apple boxes filled the space beneath the bench. Jace nudged the lid off one box and let out a soft whistle as he played his light across the collection of wire, fuses, blasting caps, and a hefty bundle of dynamite.

The other boxes contained metal pipes, and some electronics he thought must be part of timing mechanisms. If the bomb-making materials matched those used in the Stroud explosions, there was enough evidence here to put

Leo away for a very long time. He switched off the light and backed out of the root cellar. He had just shoved the copper pot back into place and was moving toward the door when the clank of the padlock against the hasp and a soft curse made his heart stop beating.

He had just enough time to dive into the front corner and pull a tarp over his head before the door opened and Leo stepped inside.

Chapter Ten

Jace couldn't see through the tarp, which smelled of mud and decay. He crouched beneath it, one hand on the gun at his hip, his body tensed to spring if Leo discovered his hiding place. But Leo's footsteps moved away, toward the back corner. The copper pot scraped across the floor, a faint sliding sound announced the opening of the secret door, and something rattled on or beneath the workbench.

Jace risked rearranging the tarp so that he could peer from beneath it. Leo had switched on a light—maybe a battery-operated lantern—inside the root cellar, and its yellow glow illuminated the back of the shed as well. Jace had a limited view of a space just to the right of the secret door. He could hear Leo moving around in there, jostling boxes, rearranging tools. Unable to sleep, had he decided to build another bomb?

Seconds later, Leo emerged from the root cellar, carrying one of the apple boxes. He exited the shed, footsteps retreating across the yard. Jace's ears rang in the silence that followed. He remained still, counting to one hundred, giving Leo time to return to the house. He waited for the sound of the door opening and closing, but it didn't come. Instead, just as he was debating throwing off the tarp and making his way back to his van, a car started somewhere very nearby. Was Leo leaving the house, taking the apple box somewhere?

But instead of growing fainter as Leo drove away, the roar of the car's engine grew louder, until the vehicle was idling right outside the shed door. Then the engine died, the car door slammed, and Leo was inside the shed once more. He retrieved a second box from the root cellar, carried it to the car, then returned a third time.

Jace shifted beneath the tarp. He couldn't risk leaving his hiding place. But he couldn't let Leo move his bomb-making operation out of the shed without trying to stop him. He eased his phone from his pocket and tapped out a text to Laura: SOS I NEED YOU HERE ASAP.

ADRENALINE SURGED THROUGH Laura as she read Jace's text. She traded the shorts she was wearing for jeans, pulled on her weapon harness and boots, and grabbed a big flashlight that could double as a truncheon. In the truck, she called Ramirez. Though she had probably been asleep at this late hour, Ana sounded alert. "What's going on?" she asked.

"I just got a text from Jace," Laura said. "He's at Leo's place and it sounds like he's in trouble."

"What was he doing at Leo's at this hour?"

"He said something about a shed in the backyard. He'd seen suspicious activity around it." She didn't want to get Jace in trouble with the complete truth, and she didn't want to jeopardize their case.

"We'll be right there," Ramirez said.

Laura pushed the truck hard across town through the darkened streets, mind racing. Jace had planned to search the shed behind Leo's house. Had Leo surprised him? Had Leo shot him? Pain squeezed her chest at the thought, and she pressed harder on the gas, hands white-knuckled on the steering wheel.

She turned onto Leo's street and spotted Jace's van right away. She parked behind it, then ran to Leo's house. She drew her weapon and, keeping to the darkest shadows, she headed for the backyard, where Jace had said the shed was located.

She spotted the car first, the driver's door and the trunk open, spilling light onto the weedy space in front of a leaning wooden shed. She froze as someone emerged from the shed. Leo, carrying a cardboard box.

A car passed in front of the house. Leo didn't even look up. He stowed the box in the trunk of the car and returned to the shed. Her phone vibrated and she pulled it from her pocket and glanced at the screen. Where are you? From Ramirez.

North side of the property, toward the back. Leo is at the shed.

Moments later, two dark shapes moved toward her. She waited until they were almost on her before she whispered, "Over here."

Ramirez moved in close behind her, followed by Rogers. "What's going on?" Ramirez asked.

"Leo's moving something out of that shed."

"Any sign of Jace?"

Laura shook her head. She could try to text him, but what if he wasn't in a position to answer her?

Leo emerged from the shed again with another box. "What's he got?" Rogers asked.

"I think we should find out," Laura said. She pulled the big Maglite from her belt, aimed it toward Leo and pressed the on switch.

"FBI!" Rogers shouted. "Drop the box and put your hands in the air."

Leo dropped the box and looked around wildly. "Put your hands up!" Rogers ordered, his voice booming.

Leo tentatively stretched his hands up. Ramirez and Rogers raced forward. Laura hung back, keeping the light trained on Leo and her face in the shadows. If possible, she and Jace needed to protect their cover.

While Ramirez and Rogers dealt with Leo, she slipped past them into the shed. "Jace?" she called.

"I'm over here."

She turned toward the sound of his voice as he emerged from beneath a brown tarp. Something loosened in her chest as he moved toward her, no sign of blood or injury, only a smear of dirt across one cheek. "Where's Leo?" he asked, looking toward the open shed door.

"Rogers and Ramirez have him. What's going on?"

He switched on a penlight and shone the beam on an opening in the far wall. "There's a workshop in there full of bomb-making materials," he said. "Or there was, until Leo started moving them out."

"Leo is the bomber?" The knowledge didn't surprise her, but it did disappoint her. Leo had seemed more pathetic than evil to her. Yet he had murdered two people.

Ramirez joined them in the shed. "Rogers has Leo cuffed in our vehicle and the local police are on their way," she said.

"What was in those boxes?" Laura asked.

"Electronics, wiring, fuses and explosives," Jace said. "Everything you'd need to make a bomb. Lots of bombs, I'd guess."

"Has Leo said anything?" Jace asked.

"Only that he didn't kill anyone. Then he asked for his lawyer and shut up." Ramirez shrugged. "We'll get the whole story, eventually." She looked Jace up and down. "You okay?"

"Yeah." He gestured toward the shed. "I saw Leo in here moving around and got curious. I came to get a closer look, then got trapped when he started moving in and out. I texted Laura for help."

"He didn't resist," Ramirez said. "I don't even think he

was armed. We'll wrap things up here. You two should go before your cover is blown."

They headed back toward the truck and the van. "You could have arrested him yourself," Laura said. "Why did you call me? To preserve your cover?"

"That, and to make sure there were plenty of witnesses to catch him red-handed with those bomb-making supplies." He grinned. "I wouldn't want anyone to accuse me of taking short cuts and jeopardizing the case."

She wanted to give him a good shove. She also wanted to throw her arms around him and tell him how glad she was that he was safe. Instead, she moved away from him, toward her truck, before she let emotion get the better of her.

"I DIDN'T KILL ANYONE." Leo Elgin, in an orange jumpsuit with PRISONER in large white letters stenciled across the front and back, sat across the table from Ana and Rogers at the Mayville Police Department, his wrists and ankles shackled, his court-appointed attorney on one side of him, a police officer on the other.

"Leo, we can match materials we found in your workshop to both the bombs that exploded at Stroud Pharmaceuticals," Ana said. "The bombs that killed Lydia Green and Angela Dupree."

"Did Angela or Lydia put that poison in the Stomach Soothers?" Leo asked, more desperate than defiant. "The poison that killed my mother?"

"Is that what you think?" Ana leaned across the table toward him. "That Lydia and Angela killed your mother, so you planted the bombs to kill them?"

"Did they?"

"We haven't found anything to link either of them to the poisoned medication," Rogers said.

Leo buried his face in his hands and began to sob.

"My client is clearly distraught," said the attorney, a motherly woman in her midfifties, with silver curls and tortoise-shell bifocals. "He has nothing else to say to you at this time."

Ana and Rogers rose. "We have more questions for you, Leo," Ana said. "We know you made those bombs. That makes you guilty of murder, whether you put them at the plant or not. If you didn't, as you say, kill Lydia and Angela, then who did?"

She followed Rogers from the room. The chief of police, Gary Simonson, met them at the end of the hall. "Did you get anything out of him?" he asked.

Rogers shook his head. "But Leo made those bombs. I don't have any doubt about that."

"But did he plant them at the factory?" Ana asked.

"Maybe." Rogers rubbed his jaw, stubble rasping against his palm. Like Ana, he had had only a couple of hours of sleep in the past two days, and his eyes looked sunken in his handsome face. "Probably. He had his mother's key and pass to get in. She had worked there for years, so he probably knew his way around."

"But who poisoned the medication?" Ana asked. "Was it really Lydia and Angela?"

"Is that what he's saying?" Simonson asked. "That he killed those women because they poisoned his mother?"

"We'll take a closer look at them, but nothing in the backgrounds of any of the Stroud employees points to a motive for the poisonings," Rogers said. "Both Angela and Lydia had worked for Stroud for years, with good reports. They didn't have so much as a traffic ticket on their records."

"He asked us if they put the poison in the Stomach Soothers," Ana said. "As if he wanted us to confirm what he thought." She frowned. "Though really, he sounded unsure. And he kept insisting he didn't kill anyone."

"The bombs he made killed them," Rogers said. "That makes him a murderer."

"You and I know that, but maybe Leo wasn't clear on that," she said. "Maybe he made the bombs for someone else to use. Or he thought they would be used for some other purpose." The more she considered Leo's words and reactions, the more this idea fit.

Her phone rang. She checked the display. "It's Maynard," she said. "I'd better take it."

She moved down the hall, leaving Rogers with the police chief. "Hey Hendrick," she answered the call from the team's technology expert. "What have you got for me?"

"I've been through all the video you sent from Stroud Pharmaceuticals' security cameras. All of it," he emphasized. "Three weeks' worth of footage, inside and out."

"And?" She pressed the phone more tightly to her ear.

"There were hundreds of people going in and out of that place, but all of them were either employees, vendors, or family members of employees. My team was able to identify every single person on those feeds."

"Great job." She tried to put more enthusiasm into her voice than she felt. "Anything significant?"

"The only thing significant is who *isn't* there," Hendrick said.

Her stomach churned. "Who isn't there?"

"Leo Elgin isn't there. Not inside the buildings. Not outside the buildings. We've got good footage of the areas around both bombing sites and Leo was never there."

Rogers joined her. She met his questioning gaze and shook her head. "Thanks, Hendrick," she said, and ended the call.

"Leo Elgin isn't in any of the security footage from Stroud," she said. "He may have made those two bombs, but he didn't plant them."

"So he has an accomplice who works for Stroud?" Rogers asked.

"He must have. But who?"

"There's only a couple of people we know he's met with since he got back in town," Rogers said. "Let's get Parker Stroud in here and talk to him."

Chapter Eleven

At work Wednesday, Parker, still sporting a few bruises but otherwise seemingly unhurt, asked Laura for more reports. "Why are you looking at everything from the first quarter?" she asked when she delivered the first batch to his desk.

"Not that it's any of your business, but I'm working on a new design that will make us even more efficient and productive."

"I heard there might be another bomb," she said. "Do you think that's true?"

His eyes narrowed. "Who told you that?"

She shrugged. "I just heard some people talk."

"Haven't you heard talk is cheap?"

"But do you think there could be another bomb?"

"I don't know. Maybe."

"But why?"

"Because someone is out to destroy this business and my family." She heard no anger behind his words, only bleak resignation. "Now get out of here and leave me to work in peace."

She left and remained at her desk the rest of the morning, having finally hacked into Stroud Pharmaceuticals' financial records for the past two quarters. On the surface the reports were competent, but the deeper she dug, the messier things got. Was Virginia Elgin that incompetent, or had someone conveniently deleted chunks of data from the files?

Parker wasn't at his desk when Ramirez and Rogers arrived after lunch and asked to speak to him. "He stepped away half an hour ago," Laura said. "He didn't tell me where he was going."

"Any idea where we should look?" Rogers asked.

"Let me see if I can find him," she said, and hurried away. Better she should go roaming through the plant than two known federal agents, who would raise alarms and have everyone competing to come up with ever-wilder explanations for their presence.

When the coffee room and his mother's office showed no signs of Parker, she headed for the factory floor and found him with Jace, of all people, discussing a malfunction with the fill machine. Jace gave her a warm smile. "Hey, sweetheart," he said.

She ignored him and focused on Parker. "There are two FBI agents here who want to talk to you," she said.

He masked his alarm so quickly she might not have noticed if she hadn't been watching for it. "Tell them I'm unavailable," he said.

"I can't do that," she protested. "They're the FBI."

"And I don't have time to talk to them. Tell them you couldn't find me. You don't know where I am." He turned to Jace. "That goes for you, too," he said.

"Yes, sir." Jace met Laura's gaze, one eyebrow raised in question.

"Yes, sir," she said, and turned away.

Back at the office, she found Ramirez and Rogers still standing. "He's on the factory floor," she said. "Packaging. But my guess is he'll be headed for the parking lot soon. If you hurry, you can catch him."

Ten minutes later, Ramirez and Rogers followed Parker back into the office. He headed for his private sanctum without a glance in Laura's direction. Ramirez nodded at her and followed Parker and Rogers, but she left the door open a scant half inch.

Laura moved to the door. "Why were you running away from us?" Rogers asked.

"I wasn't running," Parker said. "I had an appointment to meet our regional sales manager. If you want to speak with me, you can schedule a meeting with my secretary."

"This can't wait," Rogers said. "We want to talk to you about your relationship with Leo Elgin."

"I don't know what you're talking about." Parker's voice was forceful and sure. He was a good bluffer. But not good enough.

"You know Leo Elgin," Ramirez said.

"Yes." Parker's chair creaked. "His mother worked for us before her tragic death. And Leo and I went to the same high school."

"The two of you are friends," Ramirez said.

"We're acquaintances. And what difference does that make, anyway? I know a lot of people."

"Leo Elgin was arrested early this morning, and charged with manufacturing the explosive devices that killed Lydia Green and Angela Dupree," Rogers said.

Silence, then Ramirez's voice. "Mr. Stroud? Are you all right?"

When Parker finally spoke, his voice had lost all its energy and defiance. "Leo planted those bombs here? But why?"

"Why don't you take a moment to pull yourself together," Ramirez said. She moved to the doorway. "Mr. Stroud needs some water," she said.

Laura filled a paper cup from a dispenser across the room and brought it to her. "What happened?" she asked, her voice low.

"The news of Leo's arrest clearly shocked him," Ramirez said. "I thought he was going to pass out."

She moved into Parker's office once more, still leaving the door ajar. "Mr. Stroud, how well did you know Ms. Green and Ms. Dupree?" Rogers asked.

"They were family friends as well as employees, but my mother knows—knew—both of them better than I did." Parker paused, perhaps to sip water, then added, "I'm still upset about their deaths. Such a waste."

"Do you know of any reason either woman might have wanted to sabotage the Stomach Soothers?" Rogers asked. "Could they have put the poison in the tablets?"

"Angela and Lydia?"

"One or both of them," Ramirez said.

"No! Why would they? They were good women. Lydia taught Sunday school. Angela and my mother were best friends. Besides all that, neither of them came near the factory operations. I don't see when or how they could have introduced the poison into the tablets." Another pause. "Are you suggesting Leo planted the bombs to kill those women because he believed they were responsible for Gini's death?"

"We're exploring a number of possible motives," Rogers said. "Right now, we want to know more about your dealings with Leo Elgin."

"I didn't have any dealings with Leo."

"We have witnesses who have seen you together on at least two occasions recently," Rogers said.

Parker's voice remained calm. Reasonable. "We've run into each other a couple of times since he returned to town and I've offered my condolences, that's all."

"What about the money you gave him?" Rogers asked.

"What money?" Parker's voice was sharp, with a hint of outrage.

"The money you had your girlfriend, Merry Winger, deliver to Leo last Saturday," Rogers said. "The day of Gini Elgin's memorial service. Ms. Winger says you asked her to leave the service, drive to the Elgin home, and give an envelope of money to Leo Elgin."

"My family wanted to contribute to the funeral costs. Leo was too proud to take the money when I originally offered it, but I thought if Merry delivered it he would accept it, and I was right."

"You were already paying for the catering for the reception after the service," Ramirez said.

"Yes, but we wanted to do more," Parker said. "Gini was a beloved, long-time employee of Stroud Pharmaceuticals and while we didn't cause her death, we feel terrible that one of our products was the instrument of her demise."

The instrument of her demise? Really? Laura wondered if he had practiced delivering that line.

"What do you think you're doing?"

She turned to find Merry in the doorway. "Two FBI agents are in there questioning Parker," Laura said, keeping her voice low.

Merry's eyes widened and she hurried to join Laura by Parker's door. "What does the FBI want with Parker?" she whispered.

Laura led her back to the desk. "They asked about the money you delivered to Leo Elgin the day of the funeral," she said.

Merry scowled. "What does that have to do with anything?"

"Why did you leave Gini's funeral to deliver that money to Leo?" Laura asked.

"Parker asked me to do it." She dropped into the chair in front of the desk. "He begged me to do it, really. Finally, he agreed to buy me a pair of diamond earrings if I would do it for him." She fingered the glittering earrings at her lobes.

Laura leaned back against the front of the desk. "But

why did he want you to go to Leo's during the funeral?" she asked.

"He said he didn't want to embarrass Leo." She looked toward the office door. "What did Parker say when the feds asked him about the envelope?"

"He said the money was to help pay for Gini's funeral."

Merry raised her hands, clearly exasperated. "Why couldn't Parker tell me that? He just said to give the envelope to Leo and not to ask more questions. He didn't even tell me it was full of money—to find that out, I had to peek."

"What did you think when you saw the money?" Laura asked.

"I was worried Parker was buying drugs off Leo or something."

"How much money was it?"

"A lot. There was a thick stack of hundred-dollar bills."

Laura crossed her arms over her chest. "Would a funeral cost that much?"

"I don't know. I never had to pay for one. But I've always heard how expensive they are."

"Do you think Parker is doing drugs?" Laura asked.

"Well, no," Merry said. "I mean, when we go out he hardly ever has more than one beer. He doesn't smoke, either." She smiled. "It's one of the things I like about him. He doesn't really have any bad habits. If you ask him, he'll say his only vice is that he works too hard."

Laura hadn't seen much evidence of that, considering how often her boss came in late or left early. "Why would Parker give Leo money for his mother's funeral?" she asked.

"Because he felt terrible about Gini's death. He really did. I was with him when he got the news that she died. He went paper white and I thought he might pass out. He kept saying 'no, no, no.' I didn't know he was that close to

Gini, but she had worked here a long time, so I guess he thought of her like an aunt."

Or maybe Parker had paid Leo to keep quiet about something. Or to stop publicly blaming Stroud Pharmaceuticals for his mother's death. The bad publicity surrounding the poisonings had hurt the business and though there were signs of things improving, it would take a long time to fully recover from this. Paying for the funeral might be an acceptable way to buy Leo's silence and cooperation.

The door to Parker's office opened and Parker, Ramirez and Rogers emerged. "If you think of anything else that might help us in our investigation, please call," Ramirez said.

Parker said nothing, and when Rogers and Ramirez were gone, Merry rushed to his side. "What did they want?" she asked.

"They've arrested Leo in connection with the two bombings here at the plant," Parker said. He looked older, the lines around his eyes and mouth deeper, his skin tinged with an unhealthy pallor.

"Leo planted those bombs!" Merry's voice rose. "Leo, who wouldn't say boo to a fly?"

"They think he was working with someone here at the plant," Parker said. "Someone who helped him gain access."

"But why?" Merry asked. "I mean, his mother dies, so he's going to take out two more random people? That doesn't even make sense."

"Grief can do strange things to people." Parker fixed Merry with a chilly gaze. "Can you think of anyone here who might be helping Leo?"

"No! Why are you looking at me that way?" She put a hand to her chest. "I certainly didn't help him. I think he's creepy."

"You just said he was harmless," Laura said.

"Well, yeah. Harmless, but creepy. As far as I know, he doesn't even have friends. At least, not here."

"They asked a lot of questions about the money I gave Leo." Parker's expression grew more frigid. "What were you doing, talking to the FBI about me?"

Merry took a step back. "They questioned me. I couldn't not answer their questions, could I? I mean, they're the FBI!"

"You should have kept your mouth shut."

"Parker, I—"

He put a hand on her shoulder and steered her to the door. "You need to go now." He opened the door, pushed her into the hallway, then shut the door in her face.

She left and Laura moved back to her desk. "I know you were listening at the door," Parker said.

"I was curious what they wanted with you."

"Are those the two who interviewed you and your husband?"

"Yes."

"Did they ask you if you knew Leo?"

"No."

"Don't worry, they probably will. They're not making any progress in the case, so they're grasping at straws." He started out of the office.

"Where are you going?" she asked. When he glared at her, she added, "In case anyone is looking for you."

"I'm going back to work. You should do the same."

He had been gone less than a minute when the phone on Laura's desk rang. "Hello?" she answered.

"I just saw Ramirez and Rogers leave," Jace said. "What happened up there?"

"They questioned Parker."

"And?"

She glanced toward the open door and lowered her voice. "Apparently, the envelope Merry delivered to Leo the day of his mother's funeral was full of hundred-dollar bills, from Parker."

Jace whistled. "What was the money for?"

"Parker says it was to pay for Gini's funeral. He had Merry deliver it during the service to avoid embarrassing Leo."

"Do you believe him?"

"I don't know. What does Leo say about what happened?"

"Leo isn't talking."

"Maybe we should make a deal with him—the name of his partner for a lighter sentence or reduction of charges."

"He's responsible for the deaths of two people." Jace sounded outraged. "And we caught him red-handed with the bomb-making materials. We're not going to make any deals with him."

"Maybe we should. In case there's another bomb."

"He's not going to be making any more bombs in prison," Jace said.

"There was a lot of material in that root cellar," Laura said. "Enough for a dozen more bombs. What if he made more than two to begin with? What if there's another one out there, ready to go off any minute now?"

Chapter Twelve

"We're not getting anywhere with Elgin." Rogers's frustration threaded his voice. "He's scared, and we're trying to use that to get him to cooperate, but so far he hasn't given us anything."

Jace tucked the phone under his chin and began turning the burgers that sizzled on the grill in the shade of the catalpa tree behind the trailer. "Did you get anything out of Parker Stroud this morning?"

"He's hiding something, but a lot of people are," Rogers said. "Maybe the money he gave Elgin really was for Gini's funeral. Right now we can't prove it wasn't."

"Laura thinks Elgin might have built more than the two bombs. There was enough material in that root cellar for that."

"Maybe. We're working on tracking all his movements for the last month. You know this isn't a fast process."

Right. But sometimes the Bureau was too methodical for Jace's taste. While they dotted all the *i*'s and crossed all the *t*'s, someone else could get hurt—or killed.

He ended the call and thought about going into the house to find Laura. But that would mean leaving the burgers to possibly burn. Instead, he took his phone out again and texted her. Heard from D. Come out here for update and dinner.

Five long minutes passed before the back door opened

and Laura stepped out, balancing a stack of plates and silverware and a tray of condiments. She wore shorts that showed off smooth, toned legs and he had to force himself not to stare. Fortunately, she was too focused on her task to notice his reaction. "What did Rogers say?" she asked and set her burden on the picnic table near the grill.

"They're not getting anything out of Elgin."

She settled at the picnic table. "If a suspect won't talk to us, it's usually because they're more afraid of someone else than they are of us," she said.

They had changed out of their work clothes into shorts and T-shirts, and it was surprisingly pleasant in the shaded backyard, almost relaxing, except for the case that nagged at them. Jace topped the burgers with cheese and waited for it to melt. "Who's he afraid of? His partner?"

"That would be my guess," she said.

He slid the burgers onto a plate and joined her at the table. Guesses were fine for steering the investigation in a likely direction, but what they needed now was proof. He didn't have to point that out to Laura. She had been with the Bureau longer than he had, and she seemed much more comfortable with the way they worked. He admired her smarts and dedication, if not her play-by-the-rules attitude.

"I've found something worth looking into," she said.

The way she delivered this news—oh so casual—had him on high alert. "What did you find?"

"I've been digging through Parker Stroud's financial records." She spread mustard on her burger and arranged lettuce and tomato.

Jace sat across from her and focused on his own burger. "What did you find?"

"I found a secret bank account, under the name Steven Parker. With a balance of $10 million."

Jace whistled. "Where did Parker get $10 million to stash away?"

"I wondered that, too," she said. "The money began showing up about two years ago—a few thousand here, ten thousand there. But the pace of deposits has really accelerated in the past six months."

"That doesn't sound like an inheritance or a lucky investment," Jace said.

"No. And here's something else even more interesting." She picked up her burger. "The money isn't just going in. It's going out, to the tune of two payments of $50,000 each over the past two weeks."

"Is he buying up property or other investments?" Jace asked.

"Let me give you another clue. The first payment was made three days after the first victim was poisoned by Stomach Soothers. Two days after Gini Elgin died."

Their eyes met, a look of triumph lighting hers. "You think someone is blackmailing Parker because he poisoned the Stomach Soothers," Jace said.

"I think it would be a good idea to ask him, don't you?"

Jace glanced at his plate. "Can I finish my burger first? I mean, he's not likely to run, is he?"

"He's at a Rotary Club meeting, of all things, tonight. And he's supposed to be at work in the morning. I haven't seen any sign of him wanting to run. So I think we're good. I'll pass this info on to Ramirez and Rogers and let them handle it."

"That's great work," Jace said.

Her cheeks went a shade pinker, until she took a big bite and chewed, looking thoughtful. With her hair down around her shoulders and no makeup, she looked young and soft. Not weak, but...touchable.

She took a long sip from a bottle of a local microbrew and sighed. "It would fit so neatly if we found out Parker had planted the poison in those tablets and was setting off these bombs," she said. "But he's given every indication that he's desperate to keep the business going—so why do something like planting poison in the company's top product? It's going to take years to recover from the bad press. And from what I can tell from looking at the company financials, there's a very real risk they won't pull out."

"See anything alarming in the company books?" Jace asked.

"Only that they're a mess. Gini Elgin may have been a wonderful person, but she kept terrible records. It would require months of close work to straighten out completely. I've only been able to look at them in my spare time."

"I agree that Parker doesn't have a good motive for the poisoning," Jace said. "So where does that leave us?"

"I don't think Angela or Lydia did it," she said. "There's no motive and even less opportunity. They both worked in the offices, not on the factory floor. And I don't think Leo did it."

"Maybe he didn't do it intending to kill his mother," Jace said. "Her death was an accident."

Laura shook her head. "Leo was in Nashville when the poisonings began. He hadn't been back to Mayville in four months."

"That we know of. It's only a six-hour drive, and only a couple hours on a plane. He could be here and back in well under a day."

"I still don't think he did it."

"Then who did?"

She set aside her partially eaten burger. "Maybe we've been looking at this all wrong," she said. "Maybe the poisoning didn't have anything to do with Stroud. Maybe some nutso contaminated the pills after they were placed on store shelves—like the Tylenol case."

In Chicago in 1982, someone had removed bottles of Tylenol from store shelves and contaminated the pills with potassium cyanide. Seven people had died, and requirements for tamper-resistant packaging had been instituted as a result.

"We haven't found any evidence of tampering with the safety seals on the bottles of Stomach Soothers or the boxes containing the bottles," Jace said. "The forensic people examined every container they could get their hands on with X-rays. And how do we account for the missing bottles? They never made it from the factory to a store."

"Which brings us back to the idea that someone working in the factory slipped the ricin into the bottles during the packaging process?" She picked up her burger and took another bite.

"That person might be Elgin's partner," Jace said. "The one who planted the bomb. But what's the motive?"

"To destroy the company? Or maybe the Stroud family?"

"It seems like if you had an enemy who hated you that much, you'd know about it," Jace said. "And the Strouds insist they have no idea who is doing this."

"People lie," Laura said.

"They do, but we ought to be able to spot the lies."

They fell into silence, finishing their burgers and beer, letting the late afternoon stillness wash over them, a hot breeze fluttering their paper napkins and stirring the ends of Laura's hair. They were seated across from each other, not touching, yet the moment felt intimate. She pushed her empty plate away and sat back. "I like it here a lot more than I thought I would," she said, glancing around the weedy backyard, with its scraggly line of bright yellow daylilies along the fence and the arching branches of oak and catalpa providing shade.

"It has a way of getting to you," he said. "Life here moves at a slower pace, the people are a little less guarded, the landscape is so lush." He felt the pull of settling into old routines, and he couldn't say he liked it.

"How is your family?"

The question caught him off guard. He shrugged. "They're my family." He kept in touch by phone, but he hadn't let anyone know he was working so nearby. "Like all families, they do things that I love and things that drive me crazy."

She leaned toward him, elbows on the picnic table. "Like what?"

He shook his head. "They don't understand why I ever left home. Ambition isn't something they admire. It's just another word for 'getting above yourself.' They judge me for my choices, but if I do the same to them I must think I'm better than them." He shrugged. "I can't change them. I don't try anymore, and maybe that's a good thing. What about your family?"

"There's just my dad. My mom died when I was ten."

"That's rough. Do you have any brothers and sisters?"

She shook her head. "And no close family. We moved a lot, so my dad and I relied on each other."

"Still, it must have been hard, always being the new kid."

She sat up straighter. "It taught me to adapt, to learn how to fit in."

He studied her a moment. Maybe it was that second beer loosening his tongue—or maybe he just wanted to risk being honest with her. "I think it taught you to keep your distance, to not get too involved."

She frowned. He held up a hand and said, "Don't look at me that way. I didn't say there was necessarily anything wrong with that."

"You think I'm cold." Pain clouded her blue eyes. "It's all right. You wouldn't be the first to say so."

"Oh, you ought to know by now that I don't think you're cold." He moved around the table and slid onto the bench beside her. She watched him, wary, but didn't resist when he pulled her into his arms and kissed her.

You shouldn't be kissing him. It isn't professional. It isn't part of your mission.

Shut up. I'm not a robot. I have a life outside the mission. Laura shut her eyes, shutting out the nagging voice inside of herself—a voice that too often sounded like her father—and surrendered to the pure pleasure of kissing Jace. The pressure of his lips on hers sent sparks of awareness dancing along her nerves, awakening desires that had lain dormant too long. She leaned into his embrace, done with fighting her attraction to him.

When she finally pulled away, the heated longing in his eyes made her toes curl. "What are you thinking?" he asked.

"That we should take this inside." She stood and tugged him to his feet. Grinning now, he let her lead him into the house. When the door was closed behind them, she kissed him again, his back against the wall, his hunger matching her own.

His skin smelled of pine and soap, and the faint whiff of the barbecue smoke. He tasted of salt and cinnamon as she traced her tongue along his jaw. He groaned when she nipped at his throat, and slid his hands around to cup her bottom and snug her more firmly against him. Oh, yes—those shorts of his didn't leave any doubt how he felt about her. She smiled up at him. "Want to try out my new bed?"

"I thought you'd never ask."

She hurried through the awkwardness of shedding her clothes, sneaking looks as he took off his shorts, shirt and underwear, her heart speeding up in appreciation for his naked body. She had seen him a few times in the gym at headquarters, but she'd never admired him with the same interest before. He had plenty of sexy muscles to go with the brains and bravery that had attracted her in the first place.

They crawled into bed and moved into each other's arms, a sigh escaping her as she pressed her body to his. His hands slid up her thighs, calluses dragging on her smooth skin. The heat of his fingers pressed into her soft flesh and delved into the wetness between her legs.

She moaned, the sound muffled by the liquid heat of his tongue tangling with her own. He dipped his head to kiss her naked breasts—butterfly touches of his lips over and around the swelling flesh, then latching on to her sensitive, distended nipple, sucking hard, the pulling sensation reaching all the way to her groin, where she tightened around his plunging finger.

He stretched out beside her, kissing her deeply while his hands caressed, stroking her breasts and tracing the curve of her hips and stomach, never lingering too long at any one place. She arched toward him, anxious with need. "Shh," he soothed. "We don't have to hurry." He patted her stomach. "I'll be right back," he said, then rose and padded out of the room.

Curious, she propped herself on her elbow and enjoyed the view of him leaving the room. When he returned holding a condom packet aloft, she laughed and opened her arms to welcome him back.

The sight of him sheathing himself left her breathless. He levered himself over her, and she raised her knees and spread her legs to allow him access, but he only smiled and slid down her body, his tongue tracing the curve of her breasts, the ridges of her ribs and the hollow of her navel. By the time he plunged his tongue into her wet channel, she was quivering with need, half-mad with lust. She buried her fingers in his hair as he stroked her clit with his tongue.

"What do you want?" he whispered, his voice rough, as if he was fighting for control.

"I want you." Her voice rose at the last word, as he levered himself over her and entered her, his fingers digging into her bottom. The sensation of him filling her, stretching her, moving inside her, made her dizzy. "Don't stop," she gasped. "Please don't stop."

"I won't stop. I promise I won't stop."

He drove hard, but held her so gently, his fingers stroking, caressing, even as his hips pumped. She slid her hands around to cup his ass, marveling at the feel of his muscles contracting and relaxing with each powerful thrust.

He slipped his hand between them and began to fondle her clit, each deft move sending the tension within her coiling tighter. He kissed the soft flesh at the base of her throat. "I want to make it good for you," he murmured. "So good."

She sensed him holding back, waiting for her. When her climax overtook her, he swallowed her cries, then mingled them with his own as his release shuddered through them both.

MUCH LATER, THE dull buzz of Jace's phone vibrating across the bedside table pulled him from sleep. Eyes half-open, he groped for the device and swiped to answer it. "Hello?"

"Jace, it's Ramirez." The tension in Ramirez's voice snapped him awake. He swung his legs up to sit on the side of the bed as Laura propped herself up beside him.

"What's happened?" he asked.

"There's been another explosion at Stroud Pharmaceuticals," she said. "It's bad. That's all I know. Just...bad."

Chapter Thirteen

The chaos at Stroud Pharmaceuticals overflowed into the streets, so that blocks away, Jace maneuvered the truck through crowds of people, some openly weeping, others agitated or merely excited to know what was happening. The strobe of the light bars atop police cruisers looked garish against the soft pink and orange of sunrise.

He parked three blocks from the Stroud compound, unable to go farther, and he and Laura walked the rest of the way, joining a parade of Stroud employees headed in that direction. "I swear I heard the bomb go off," said a woman named Janice, who worked in packaging. "I had just let the dog out and I heard it. I thought it was someone hunting."

Police and county sheriff's vehicles formed a barricade at the entrance to the factory and offices. Media trucks ringed the area, satellite dishes pointed to the sky. Jace thought he spotted Rogers talking to one of the cops, and then he was swallowed up in the confusion. "I heard Mr. Stroud—Mr. Steve—is dead," Barb Falk said.

"Mr. Parker is in the hospital," Phyllis Neighbors added, blotting tears from her eyes with her index fingers.

"This is so awful," a woman Jace didn't know said. "It just keeps happening. I'm too afraid to go back in there again. Not with some nut job trying to blow up everybody."

"There's Donna." Laura tugged at Jace's sleeve and he followed her gaze to where Donna Stroud, dressed in a navy pantsuit, stood surrounded by reporters, microphones and recorders all but obscuring her face.

Jace and Laura shoved forward, ignoring the grumbling of those they displaced, until they reached the ring of reporters.

Donna Stroud's face looked drained of blood, and her voice was strained. "We will stop production for the next few days out of respect for my husband, and to protect the safety of our employees," she said.

"Do you have any idea who did this?"

"What about the suspect the police have in custody? Do they have the wrong man?"

"Why hasn't the FBI stopped this?" The reporters fired questions at the dazed woman.

"Why haven't we stopped this?" Laura muttered. Anguish haunted her gaze and anger weighted her words. "I knew there were more bombs out there. We should have insisted they close the factory."

She kept her voice low, barely audible even to Jace, but still he put his arm around her and turned her away from the reporters. "We could have insisted the Strouds close the plant, but everyone from the state legislator to local officials to the Strouds themselves would have refused," he said.

"They don't have any choice now," she said. She scanned the crowd. "Most of the employees are probably too frightened to return to work."

"Let me through. I have to talk to Donna. I have to find out about Parker."

The crowd parted and Merry, wet hair straggling around her shoulders, eyes swollen from crying, staggered forward. She clutched at Laura's shoulder. "I was in the shower when a friend called to tell me what had happened," she half sobbed. "Parker's in the hospital, but when I went down there, they wouldn't let me see him!"

Her voice rose in a wail that attracted the attention of the reporters and Donna.

Laura took the distraught young woman's arm and led her away. Jace followed, shielding them from the curious stares of those around them. "When was the last time you saw Parker?" Laura asked.

Merry sniffed. "He spent the night at my place," she said. "But he left really early this morning. His mom called about some problem with Parker's dad. He had to leave to deal with that."

"What was the problem?" Jace asked.

"I don't know. He just said he had to go deal with his dad."

"What time was this?" Laura asked.

"Early. About five o'clock." She yawned. "I went back to bed. That was the last I heard until my friend Margo called me about seven." Her face crumpled again. "She said Parker was hurt in the explosion, but no one at the hospital will tell me anything."

"Merry, pull yourself together. Parker is going to be all right." Donna Stroud moved in and put her arm around the weeping woman. "He had surgery to remove some shrapnel from his legs, but he's going to be okay."

"What happened?" Laura asked. "Merry said Parker left early this morning to help his dad?"

The lines around Donna's eyes deepened. "I woke up early this morning and Steve wasn't in bed. I realized what had woken me was the garage door opening and closing. He does that sometimes, gets restless and goes for a drive. No matter how well I think I hide the car keys, he always seems to find them."

"Where does he go?" Jace asked.

Guilt pinched her features. "Often, he comes here, to his office. That's why I called Parker. He's better at reasoning with his dad, persuading him to return home. But apparently when they got here..." She covered her mouth with one hand, choking back a sob.

"Is there anything I can do to help?" Laura asked. Something in her voice made Jace think she wasn't asking merely as a way of finding out more information, but out of genuine concern for Mrs. Stroud.

"I may need you to retrieve some reports and things from Parker's office later," Donna said. "Though I know that isn't really your job."

"For now, it is my job," Laura said, with a warning glance at Merry.

Merry seemed not to have even heard. She clutched Donna's arm. "Mrs. Stroud, was there a note?" she asked.

"I don't think now is the time to talk about that," Donna said.

Merry frowned at Jace and Laura. "Don't tell me you haven't heard about the notes from the bomber. I thought everyone knew about them by now."

"We have heard some rumors," Laura said.

Donna sighed, then reached into her pocket and took out a crumpled envelope. "This was on my desk when I got in this morning."

Jace took the envelope, handling it carefully. It was different from the others in that this one had no stamp or postmark. "What does the note inside say?" Jace asked.

"It says 'three down, three more soon.'" Donna took the note from him and returned it to her pocket. "I'll give this to Agent Ramirez or Agent Rogers when I see them," she said. "But for now, I need to focus on handling the plant closure and taking care of my family. And I need to deal with these reporters." She turned away, head up, shoulders back, a woman prepared to do battle.

"How long is the plant going to be closed?" Merry asked.

Jace had almost forgotten Merry. Now she inserted herself between him and Laura, tears and hair both drying in the early morning heat. The crowd around them had thinned somewhat, many employees drifting back to their homes or vehicles, or gathering at the far end of the parking lot to watch from a distance.

"I guess they'll keep the plant closed until they figure out who's responsible for the bombs," he said.

"They arrested Leo," Merry said. "I thought he's the one who did this. It's no secret he blames the Strouds for killing his mother."

"Leo was in jail when this bomb exploded," Jace said.

"Maybe he planted it before he was arrested."

"Maybe." None of the other explosives had been equipped with a timing mechanism, but maybe this one was different.

"I'm going to tell Donna she needs to call the hospital and let me in to see Parker," Merry said, and started after the older woman.

Laura moved in close to Jace once more. "We need to get to the hospital and talk to Parker," she said.

"How are we going to do that without blowing our cover?" he asked.

"I'm his admin. I'll say how concerned I am for him and is there anything I can do to help his mother at this difficult time."

He put his arm around her. "Has anyone ever told you you'd make a good secret agent?"

She made a face, but didn't move away. The public display of affection fit with their cover, but Jace hoped there was more than that to her desire to be close to him.

THEY HEARD PARKER long before they reached his room, his voice reverberating down the hospital corridor. "I told you I need something stronger for this pain. You need to get hold of that doctor now. I don't want to hear any more of your lame excuses."

"I see the explosion didn't do anything to dampen his charm," Jace said.

"At least he's awake and lucid enough," Laura said. They halted outside Parker's door as a young black man in blue scrubs hurried into the hallway. He scarcely glanced at them as he headed toward the nurse's station. Laura tapped on the door.

"Come in!" Parker barked.

Laura pushed open the door. "Mr. Stroud, it's me, Laura. My husband is with me."

Parker, his hair uncombed and day-old stubble softening the line of his jaw, looked younger and slightly vulnerable. Or maybe it was the faded hospital gown and network of tubes and monitors that added to his air of helplessness. "How did you get in here?" he asked. "I told them no visitors."

"No one said anything to us," Laura said. Security clearly wasn't a priority at this small hospital. Jace had popped the lock on the outside door leading to the stairway at the end of this hall and they had been able to stroll in, bypassing the nurse's station and any other authority figures. "Is there anything I can do for you?" Laura asked, approaching the bed.

"You can find my doctor and tell him I need something stronger for pain than aspirin."

"What happened?" Laura asked. "Your mother said she sent you to look for your father."

"So you've been talking to her." His expression softened. "How is she?"

"She's staying tough," Jace said. "In shock, I think, but handling the press."

"She announced she's shutting down the factory until

the police catch who did this," Laura said. "I was sorry to hear about your father."

"The stupid old fool." There was no heat behind the words. Parker slumped against the pillows. "He likes to sneak away and come to the office. It doesn't hurt anything. He types up memos or prints out reports. He doesn't even know what day it is much of the time, but he's harmless. But Mom worries, so I agreed to go get him and bring him home."

He fell silent and they waited, the silence punctuated by the beep of monitors and the whirring of the automatic blood pressure cuff.

"What happened?" Laura prompted.

"I saw his car in the parking lot, and then I spotted him going into the building," Parker said. "I followed him and he was just unlocking the door to his office when I reached him. I called out his name and he turned to me. Then everything just disintegrated." His face crumpled. "He was smiling, like he was so happy to see me."

Laura plucked a tissue from the box by the bed and passed it to him. They waited while he wept. When he had pulled himself together, Jace asked, "Did you see anything else when you got to the plant this morning? Any other cars in the lot, or anyone hanging around?"

Parker grimaced. "You sound like a cop."

"I'm curious. Who wouldn't be?"

"I didn't see anyone," Parker said. "It was early and most people were still in bed. I only passed one car on the way to the plant, and that was Phil Dorsey, on his way to open the café for breakfast."

"Merry said you were with her last night," Laura said.

"So you talked to her already," Parker said.

"She was at the plant," Laura said. "She was upset that hospital personnel wouldn't let her see you."

"I couldn't deal with her distress right now."

"But you were with her last night?" Jace asked.

"I was." He laughed, a bitter sound. "Don't ever play poker, Laura dear. Your opinion of me shows all too clearly."

Only because I wasn't trying to hide it, she thought.

"You think I'm taking advantage of the poor girl, stringing her along and taking what I want. Believe me, she's getting what she wants, too."

"What does she want?" Laura asked.

"Money. The status of being associated with my name. It may not mean much to you, but in this town, the Strouds are about as big as they get."

"Merry believes you're going to marry her," Laura said.

"I've never proposed. She doesn't have a ring."

But you haven't told her it will never happen. "Were you with Merry all night?" Jace asked.

"Yes. Though that's none of your business."

The door opened and an older woman in a skirt and blouse, a stethoscope around her neck, entered. "Mr. Stroud, I understand you're experiencing some pain."

"It's about time you got here. And yes, I'm experiencing pain. A lot of it."

Laura and Jace took that as their cue to leave. She waited until they were in the truck before she spoke. "He's terrified," she said. "That's what's behind his bluster."

"He was lucky he wasn't killed," Jace said. "His father was. That's enough to terrify anyone."

"I was almost sure he was Leo's partner," she said. The two of them had been seen together several times, and Parker was so circumspect about their relationship."

"But now you're not so sure?" Jace prompted.

"No. Why would he kill his father and risk his own life?"

"If he killed his father, he'd be more likely to inherit the business sooner," Jace said. "He hasn't made a secret of wanting his mother to turn everything over to him. And there are those rumors that he's been talking about selling to a competitor."

"But poisoning the best-selling product you make and blowing up people aren't going to get you a good price for the business," Laura said. She shifted to angle toward Jace. "And Parker couldn't count on his father going to the office this morning."

"Maybe he had the explosive with him and saw his chance," Jace said.

She took out her phone and pulled up Ramirez's number. "We stopped by the hospital and spoke to Parker," she said after her colleague had answered. "He says the bomb exploded when his dad started to open his office door."

"That sounds right," Ramirez said. "The explosives expert says this was like the others, wired to go off when a door opened."

"So no timer?" Laura asked.

"No timer," Ramirez said. "And nothing to say when the bomb was put there. Donna Stroud says no one has been in her husband's office all week. After he was diagnosed with dementia and stopped working, she moved out anything that pertained to active business. She left a computer and some older files to keep him calm on the days when he did venture into the office."

"Did she say how often Steve came in to work?" Laura asked.

"Every week to ten days he would slip away from her or his minder and come down there."

"So Steve Stroud was the intended target?" Laura asked.

"It looks that way."

"What does Leo say?"

"We haven't talked to him, but we will soon."

"I've been looking into Parker's financials and I found

some things you need to know," Laura said. She filled Ramirez in on the secret bank account and the possible blackmail.

"When did you find this out?" Ramirez asked.

"Last night." She felt a stab of guilt as she remembered her initial resolve to contact her fellow agent right away, a resolve that had faded as soon as she was in Jace's arms.

"Steve Stroud's death tells us this was definitely aimed at the Stroud family, not just the factory," Ramirez said. "That's the angle we'll be hitting hard going forward."

"Anything else we should know?" Laura asked.

"The girlfriend, Ms. Winger, was here causing a scene. She corralled a bunch of reporters and told them it was the FBI's fault that her fiancé was at death's door."

"She won't be the last person to say that," Laura said.

"I didn't join the Bureau because I wanted to be popular, did you?" Ramirez asked.

"No," Laura said, and ended the call.

"I caught most of that," Jace said. "Sounds like Merry was grabbing the spotlight while she could."

"If she keeps this up, everyone except Parker is going to think of her as his fiancé." Laura tucked her phone into the pocket of her jeans.

"That may be what she's hoping for," Jace said. "Where to now?"

"Let's go back to the trailer and I'll make breakfast," she said. "Let's review what we know and brainstorm." Maybe together they could figure out the right angle of approach.

"All right." He took the next left turn and headed back toward the trailer. Away from the Stroud factory, the town looked almost normal, only the occasional media van out of place in the everyday bustle downtown. This was the atmosphere Jace had grown up in, a small town where everyone knew everyone else, so different from the string of army bases, all different yet all the same, that had made up Laura's world back then.

"Why did you join the FBI?" she asked after a moment.

"I needed a job after I came out of the military and hunting down bad guys sounded interesting. Why did you join?"

"My father suggested it." She cleared her throat. "He knew someone who knew someone—next thing I knew, I had an interview."

"Was there something else you wanted to do instead?"

"I thought about going to vet school." At his look of surprise, she added, "I like animals."

"But you don't have a pet. Do you?"

"No. This job makes it tough. But I'd like to, one day." A dog would be great, though a cat might be easier, at least at first.

"If you could go back and do things over, would you become a veterinarian?" he asked.

"No. I like this work. And I'm good at it. I'm probably a better agent than I would have been a vet."

"I was intimidated about working with you, you know?"

She stared at him. "You're kidding."

"It's the truth. I checked your record. Commendation after commendation. You have future Special Agent in Charge written all over you. Next to you, I'm a total slacker."

She cleared her throat. "I wouldn't call you a slacker." She'd checked up on him, too. He'd been a key figure in a number of high-profile investigations, but he had also been reprimanded a handful of times for crossing the line and breaking the rules. At the time, she had resented him for taking short cuts. Now, part of her envied his willingness to take risks.

"You're not as uptight as I feared," he said.

There hadn't been anything uptight about her last night.

She squirmed at the memory. "I believe in playing by the rules," she said. "They're there to protect everyone. But I can see there are times when intent is as important as the letter of the law." Her father would groan if he heard such rationalization. He had raised her to walk a straight line and never question authority. But she wasn't a soldier on a battlefield. She was a civilian, involved in a different kind of battle, where the enemy was rarely obvious or even visible.

Chapter Fourteen

Merry kept an eye on Laura and Jace until they had gotten into their truck and driven away. Something wasn't right about those two, the way they had just showed up in town, not knowing anybody, and now they were up in everybody's business, asking all those questions like they had a right to know the answers. She hadn't missed the way they had cozied up to Donna Stroud, either, all sympathetic and helpful. They might have fooled the old woman into trusting them, but Merry was going to be keeping an eye on them.

Most of the reporters were drifting away now. Getting their attention had been a smart move. Now everyone would know how concerned she was for Parker and his family. How close she was to them. She spotted Donna trying to slip away and picked up her pace to intercept her. "Donna, wait!" she called.

Donna turned, the blank expression in her eyes like a slap to Merry. Parker's mother didn't even recognize her. "Have you heard how Parker is doing?" she asked. "I've been so worried." Maybe she should have said something about Steve first, but no, Parker needed their concern now. She stopped beside Donna. Merry couldn't believe the woman had gone to the trouble to put on a suit before coming down to face everyone. As if her image as a businesswoman was more important than this tragedy. "I wanted to visit Parker in the hospital, but they wouldn't let me in to see him," Merry said. "Maybe you could talk to them about that."

Donna was frowning now. "Merry, isn't it?" She didn't wait for confirmation. "Parker had surgery and is going to be all right but he needs his rest. I appreciate your concern, except it would be better if you didn't visit."

"Well, of course we don't want just anyone bothering him," Merry said. "But I'm a little different, don't you think? I mean, Parker and I are practically engaged."

"But since you aren't engaged yet, we're limiting visitation to immediate family."

Who was this "we"? And who was this witch to say who her son—a grown man—could see or not see? "Parker was with me last night," she said. "I think he'd want to see me."

Donna didn't say anything, merely looked right through her. Merry glared at her. "Parker hates you," she said. "Did you know that? He's a grown man, but you treat him like he's a fourteen-year-old. He'd do a great job of managing this business, but you'd rather leave a loony old man in charge than trust your own son."

Two spots of bright pink bloomed on Donna's cheeks, against her otherwise paper-white skin. "You have no right to talk to me that way," she said. "You need to leave now."

"I'll leave," Merry said. "But you won't get rid of me that easily. When Parker and I are married, just remember—I'm the one who'll be picking out your nursing home."

She felt Donna's stare like daggers in her back as she headed across the parking lot. That woman had better watch her step. Merry could make a lot more trouble for her than she could begin to imagine.

"How is a man supposed to get some rest if people keep interrupting me?" Parker Stroud raged from his hospital bed. "I told the nurse no visitors!"

"We need to talk to you now," Ana said.

Rogers followed and shut the door behind them. "What is this about?" Jace asked.

"We know about the blackmail." Ana kept her voice low. Conversational.

Parker visibly flinched. "What did you say?"

"We know about the money you paid out to your blackmailer—$100,000 so far." She shifted on the bed to face him more directly. "Of course, that's just a drop in the bucket compared to the balance in your Steven Parker account, but at this pace, it won't be long before you're all but bankrupt."

"I... I don't know what you're talking about." But all color had drained from his face and his heart monitor beat a rapid tattoo. As good as a lie detector, Ana thought.

"You do," Rogers said. "Someone is extorting money from you. Why is that? Is it because you put that poison in the Stomach Soothers?"

Parker swallowed and regained some of his composure. "You're just making wild accusations," he said. "You can't prove anything."

"But we will," Ana said. "We'll find out who those payments were to, and we'll trace the poison, too."

"Get out of here," he ordered. "This is harassment."

Ana stood. "We'll leave. But we're going to be watching you closely. Don't do anything foolish."

BACK AT THE TRAILER, Jace made a fresh pot of coffee while Laura tore off a big piece of parchment paper from the roll in the pantry and pinned it to the pantry door, across from the kitchen table. She unearthed a couple of markers. She welcomed the opportunity to focus on the case, to prove, if only to herself, that she and Jace could still work well together even after they had become intimate. She had always been very disciplined about keeping her personal and business lives separate. The line was fuzzier with Jace, but she intended to try to keep it clear. "Sit down and let's review what we know about this case," she said.

Chuckling, Jace pulled out a chair and dropped into it. He sipped his coffee, a half smile teasing his lips.

"What's so amusing?" Laura asked.

"Like I said, you're a future Special Agent in Charge."

He probably meant that as an insult, but she refused to take it that way. "Do you want to stand up here and write?" she asked. "Because you can."

"Oh, no. You're much better at this than I am." He sipped his coffee. "It's a good idea," he added. "Let's get to it."

She uncapped the marker and turned to the paper. "Let's start with the timeline." She wrote "May 1. First victims of poisoned Stomach Soothers."

"Go back further," Jace said. "To April 29. That's when that particular lot of medication was manufactured. It was shipped the next day."

"That's good to know." She added in this information, then listed the other known deaths. "Gini Elgin died May 2," she said. "As far as we know, that's what brings Leo into the case."

"As far as we know," Jace said.

She wrote "May 6—first bombing at Stroud Pharmaceuticals," then added in the dates of the other bombings, along with the fatalities from each.

"All the bombs were in the executive offices," Jace said. "All places Donna Stroud was most likely to have been— the door she used when she arrived early at the office, the door to her office, and the door to her husband's office."

"She said she didn't use her husband's office," Laura said.

"But I'll bet she went in there sometimes. She was more likely to do so than anyone else."

"Donna Stroud was the most likely target," Laura said. "Why?"

"With her husband incapacitated, she's in charge of the business," Jace said.

"Who stands to gain with her out of the picture?" Laura asked. "A rival?"

"Her son would take over the business if she died or couldn't continue to manage it," Jace said.

"Anyone else?"

"We'll have to find out if anyone else inherits," Jace said.

"Merry would benefit if she married Parker," Laura said.

"I don't think Parker has any intention of marrying her," Jace said. "And unless she's a lot dimmer than she looks, she knows it."

Laura studied the paper a moment. "Let's talk about the poisoning for a minute. That's the first tragedy, and maybe it triggered everything else. Could it have been an accident? Something gone wrong in the manufacturing process? All the ingredients in the product are natural, right? Ricin is natural, too. It's from the castor bean plant. Maybe someone mistook it for something else."

"Ricin is deadly," Jace said. "It's not something people have just lying around. It certainly isn't used in anything Stroud makes. And only a few bottles of Stomach Soothers were found to be contaminated—less than a dozen. If the ricin was mistakenly used in a whole batch of product, we would have found hundreds of bottles that were contaminated."

"Which brings us back to who had the opportunity to insert the poison in those bottles, and why?"

"There were eight people on the manufacturing line the day those packages were processed." Jace ticked the names off on his fingers. "All of them are long-time employees who are still with the company. We've checked them and nothing stands out or suggests a motive for sabotage."

"Parker Stroud runs the plant and would have easy access to all parts of the manufacturing process," Laura said.

"So would his mother," Jace said. "And his father, too."

Laura frowned. "Would Steve Stroud have put ricin in those bottles of pills? Why?"

"Let's find out where he was, just to be sure," Jace said. "I looked up the report on the security footage for that day. It doesn't cover the whole line, but it does show that Donna and Parker Stroud were both on the production floor, along with Gini Elgin and Merry Winger."

"Merry was there? And Gini?"

"Merry brought lunch to Parker. Gini came down to talk to him."

Laura added this information to the paper, then backed up to stand beside Jace. "Parker still has the best motive and opportunity for all the crimes," she said. "Maybe he had set the bomb for his mother and his father getting there first was an accident. Trying to save his father, Parker was hurt, which tends to direct our suspicions away from him."

"I want to talk to Merry again," Jace said. "I think she knows something she isn't telling us."

"Something about Parker?" Laura asked.

"She's hiding something. I just haven't figured out what yet."

"PARKER IS HURT? Mr. Stroud dead?" Leo clutched his head and moaned. "That wasn't supposed to happen."

"What was supposed to happen, Leo?" Rogers slapped both palms on the table and leaned over the younger man. "We know you made those bombs. Another person is dead and one badly injured because of you. If you want this to stop, you have to tell us who has the other explosives, so we can stop them."

Leo moaned and rocked in his chair. Ana sat beside him. "I know you didn't mean for this to happen," she said, her voice soft.

He shook his head. "No."

"Maybe you just thought the bombs would frighten people," Ana said. "You wanted to make them listen."

His answering groan could have been a yes.

Ana put a hand on his arm. "How many bombs did you make?" she asked.

"Six." Another long moan.

Ana locked eyes with Rogers, her alarm evident. Three people had died in the first three explosions. How many more would die if three more bombs were let loose?

"Who did you give the bombs to?" Ana asked.

He shook his head. "I can't tell you."

Rogers leaned forward again, but Ana waved him away. "Why can't you tell us?" she asked.

"Because I promised." He raised his head, his face a mask of anguish. "I swore on my mother's grave."

"I think your mother would want you to help us and stop the killing," Ana said.

"Is Parker going to be all right?"

"He had to have surgery to remove some shrapnel," Rogers said. "He should recover, though he'll probably have scars the rest of his life."

Leo's lips trembled, and he struggled for control. "Parker tried to make things right after my mother died," he said. "I didn't want to listen to him, but he never stopped reaching out. We were friends in school. He never shut me out the way some people did. The way his mother did."

"How did Donna Stroud shut you out?" Ana asked.

Anger hardened his features, making him look older. "I went to see her and she refused to talk to me. She shut the door in my face."

"I'll bet that made you angry," Rogers said. "If I were

in your position, I might have wanted to do something to hurt her."

Leo didn't confirm or deny this.

"You made the bombs," Rogers continued. "Six of them. Why six?"

"I only made one to begin with. It wasn't supposed to kill anyone. Just frighten them."

"So you put the first bomb at Stroud Pharmaceuticals," Rogers said. "The one that killed Lydia Green?"

"No! I wouldn't do that. I told you, I liked Lydia."

"So you made the first bomb," Rogers said. "Then you made more?"

"Leo, you didn't put those bombs at the Stroud offices, did you?" Ana asked.

"No! I didn't. I didn't have anything to do with that."

"But you know who did put them there," Ana said. "We need to know who that person is so that we can stop them before they hurt someone else."

Leo shook his head.

Rogers leaned over Leo, his face very close, his eyes fierce. "Three bombs have exploded, Leo. Three people have died. How many more bombs are going to kill how many more people before you tell us the truth?"

"I can't tell you." He shoved back his chair and stood, Rogers and Ana rising to their feet also. "I don't want to talk anymore," Leo said. "I want to see my lawyer."

Ana and Rogers's eyes locked again. "We'll call your lawyer," Rogers said. "She'll tell you it's in your best interest to talk to us."

He led the way out of the room, as two officers entered to escort Leo back to his cell. "He's going to break," Rogers said.

"Yes," Ana agreed. "But will he tell us in time to prevent more people dying?"

MERRY LIVED IN a pale gray cottage in a neighborhood of older homes, many in the process of being renovated. Flowers crowded the beds alongside the front fence and either side of the walkway leading to the front door—ruffled hollyhocks in every shade of pink, orange daylilies like upturned bells, red and yellow and white zinnias and snapdragons filling every gap like dropped candies. "What do you two want?" Merry asked when she answered the door.

"We wanted to make sure you're okay," Laura said.

"Why wouldn't I be okay?"

"Your fiancé is in the hospital," Laura said. "Did you get to see him?"

"No." Merry stepped onto the porch and pulled the door shut behind her. "We can talk out here." She led the way into the garden. "I tried to see him and this sour-faced nurse told me only family was allowed to visit. Then I asked Donna to talk to her and she had the nerve to tell me that until Parker and I are officially engaged, I'm not family." She snapped a fading flower from one of the hollyhocks and crushed it in her hand.

"That was harsh," Jace said.

"Oh, I wasn't surprised." Merry snatched another wilting flower head and flung it into the grass. "She's as cold as they come. She's made Parker's life miserable. He's an intelligent man with lots of great ideas for the business, yet she treats him like a stupid boy."

"Merry, you're probably closer to Parker than anyone," Jace said. "Do you have any idea who might want to hurt him or his family?"

Merry stopped and looked him in the eye. "Why are you so interested?" she demanded.

"With the factory closed, we don't have jobs," Laura said. "The police and FBI aren't getting anywhere finding the person who planted those bombs, so we figure we might as well try to solve the case ourselves."

"We haven't got anything better to do," Jace said. "Maybe, being amateurs, we'll get lucky." He winked at Laura, who quickly looked away, biting the inside of her cheek to keep from laughing.

Merry returned to dead-heading spent flowers. "If you ask me, the cops ought to be taking a closer look at Donna."

"Donna Stroud?" Laura asked.

Merry nodded. "I already told you she's cold. She probably set those bombs herself to get rid of her loony husband. She had to be paying out a fortune to have people watch him while she's working."

"But what about Angela Dupree and Lydia Green?" Laura asked. "Why would she want to kill them?"

"I don't know. Maybe Angela was too needy. Maybe the cleaner found something incriminating in the trash can and was blackmailing her?"

"Do you think Parker could have set those bombs?" Laura asked. "Maybe because he resented the way his mother treated him? He wants to be in charge of the business."

"Parker?" Merry laughed. "Parker could never kill anyone. He doesn't have the nerve." She brushed her hands on the thighs of her denim shorts. "Parker likes to complain, but he doesn't have the guts to do something like that."

"Who would you say does have the guts?" Jace asked.

Merry smiled. "His mother, but you already know that. I can't think of anyone else." She faced them, hands on her hips. "Now let me ask you a question—what are you really up to?"

Laura kept her expression bland. "What do you mean? We're trying to solve this crime so we can get our jobs back."

"I mean, what are you doing in Mayville? You don't

have relatives here. You didn't know anyone here before you showed up out of the blue. This isn't some garden spot everyone wants to come to. You must have had a reason."

Laura searched for a plausible answer. She was usually good at thinking on her feet but right now she was struggling.

"My family is in Hatcher, just across the border in Tennessee," Jace said. "We wanted to be close to them, but not too close. Anyway, there aren't any jobs in Hatcher. There are here."

Merry looked disappointed. "That's the truth?"

"What were you expecting, Merry?" Laura asked. "We came for the jobs. As you pointed out, there's no other reason to be here."

"You get on so well with Donna Stroud, I thought maybe you had some connection to the family."

Jace laughed. "That's rich. So, what are we, the poor relations thrilled about living in a crappy trailer and working in their factory?"

Merry smiled. "I guess it is a little silly." The smile faded. "And I guess it shows how much Donna hates me. She'd rather hire a stranger to be her son's admin than give me the job."

"Some women are very protective of their sons," Laura said. Though she felt a pinch of sympathy for Merry. She had painted a not very attractive picture of Donna Stroud.

"Let us know if you hear anything interesting and we'll do the same," Jace said. He took Laura's arm. "We'll get out of your hair now."

Arm in arm, they left the yard. When Merry and her cottage were no longer visible, Laura relaxed a little. "Do you still think she's hiding something?"

"I don't know. But we'd better let Ramirez and Rogers know they should take a closer look at Donna Stroud."

"Yeah." They hadn't considered Donna as a suspect

before now because she seemed to be the person with the most to lose in all these crimes. But what if she had even more to gain?

"For what it's worth, my mom would be thrilled to know I'd taken up with you," Jace said.

The statement, or rather, the idea that he had been thinking of her in relation to his family, startled her. "Would she really? Why?"

"You're smart. Beautiful. Not afraid to get in my face when you think I screw up. My mom would appreciate all of that."

The idea was flattering, but when she considered her father's likely reaction to Jace, the fleeting satisfaction vanished. "My dad is harder to read."

"I'm betting I dealt with plenty like him in the army. Proud, strong and loyal. Also by the book and unbending. He'd hate my guts. At least until I won him over." He grinned, surprising a laugh from her. "What? You don't think I could win him over?"

She shook her head, unable to speak. Jace had won her over, and not that long ago she would have said that was impossible. "I'm not worried about my dad." She took his hand. "My dad taught me to make my own decisions, so my opinion is the only one that really counts."

"What is your opinion?" He tried to keep his voice light, but she heard the tension in his words.

"You're more complicated than I thought," she said. "I like complicated."

"We have that in common." He squeezed her hand, sending a thrill through her. She could get used to this, but she didn't trust the feeling. As an agent, she was confident in her ability to evaluate a situation and stay on top of a case. But when it came to romance, she was a rank amateur, and she didn't like her odds of succeeding.

The fourth bomb exploded at two o'clock the next morning, on Merry Winger's front porch. No one was injured, but the explosion sent a wave of terror through the town. Before, the Strouds had clearly been the target of the bomber. Now, it seemed, almost anyone could be a victim.

The poisonings had frightened people, but to avoid that danger, all you had to do was avoid taking Stomach Soothers—or all Stroud products if you were extra cautious.

But a bomb—how did you avoid a bomb? How did you live with that kind of fear?

Chapter Fifteen

"Where were you last night from approximately 8 p.m. until 6 a.m.?"

Donna Stroud, pale and disheveled, didn't look like herself without her suit and makeup. The local police had visited her home a little after seven that morning, and found her dressed in faded pink cotton trousers and a Smoky Mountains National Park T-shirt. To Ana, she scarcely resembled the competent professional she had met with her first day in town.

"Where was I last night?" Confusion clouded Donna's blue eyes. "Why is that important?"

"Please answer the question," Ana said. She and Rogers and Captain Simonson, of the Mayville Police Department, sat across the table from Donna and her lawyer, Adam Sepulveda, a local attorney who, after blustering a few feeble protests, had remained silent, occasionally fidgeting in his chair or tugging at his tie.

"I was at the hospital, visiting my son, until almost eight," Donna said. "Then I went home."

"Was anyone at home with you?" Ana asked.

"No."

"Did you talk to anyone on the phone, or speak to a neighbor? Is there anyone who can confirm that you were home last night?"

Donna sat up straighter, a little life coming back into

her face. "I told you I was there and I don't lie. There isn't any other proof, but I don't see why you need it."

"What's your relationship with Merry Winger?" Rogers asked.

Donna's eyebrows rose, disappearing beneath her fringe of short bangs. "Merry works in the administrative offices of Stroud Pharmaceuticals. She is also involved with my son."

"Involved?" Ana thought this was an interesting word choice.

"I know he sleeps with her and buys her gifts, but I've rarely seen them out together, and he's never brought her to our house, so I wouldn't call her his girlfriend."

"You don't like her," Rogers said.

"She wouldn't be my first choice for my son, but most people learn best by making their own mistakes."

"You think Merry is a mistake?" Ana asked.

"Time will tell." She spread her hands flat on the table in front of her. "What is this about? Has something happened to that girl?"

"Why do you think something happened to her?" Rogers asked. "What would have happened?"

"You asked me where I was last night. That tells me you're trying to establish my alibi. Then you ask me about Merry, a young woman I scarcely know. I don't have to be an amateur detective to put the two ideas together. Did something happen to her?"

"Merry is fine," Ana said. "But a bomb exploded on her front porch this morning."

Donna stared, mouth slack and eyes wide. She made a low sound in the back of her throat, and Ana was afraid for a moment that the older woman was having a heart attack or stroke. Ana touched her arm and Donna stared at her, then gradually came back to herself. She wet her lips. "Was it…was it like the others?" she asked.

"It was similar," Rogers said.

In fact, the bomb was identical to the other three, set to go off when the front door was opened, as Merry would have done when she went out to work in her flower garden or to get into her car, parked at the curb. Instead, the bomb had exploded when her neighbor had driven by on his way to work, in a custom pickup with oversized tires, rumbling exhaust and throbbing bass that shook the windows of every house as it passed.

"The bomb exploded accidentally," Ana said. "No one was hurt, but if Merry had opened her front door, she would have been killed, or very badly injured."

Donna covered her mouth with her hand and tears filled her eyes.

"Did you put that explosive device on Merry Winger's front porch?" Rogers asked.

"No! I would never do something like that. Not to anyone, ever!"

"My client is a law-abiding pillar of the community who has never had so much as a traffic ticket," the lawyer said. "I strongly object to this line of questioning."

"You're not in court," Rogers said. He turned his attention back to Donna. "Do you have any idea who might have put that bomb on Merry's front porch?"

"No. I swear if I did, I would tell you. I want this to stop."

"Mrs. Stroud, the first explosion at Stroud Pharmaceuticals, on May 6, was wired to a side door used only by personnel who had a key," Rogers said. "You yourself stated that you were usually the first person at the office each morning, and that you always entered via that door. Several people have confirmed this."

"Yes."

"Yet the morning the bomb exploded, you were not the

first to arrive at the building. Instead, Lydia Green opened that door and was killed."

"I was dealing with my husband. He was agitated and I had to calm him down before I came to work."

"The second explosive device was wired to the door of your office," Rogers continued. When it exploded, it killed Angela Dupree. Again, you were late for work that day, something several people have stated was highly unusual."

"My husband isn't at his best in the mornings."

"The third explosion, the one that killed your husband and injured your son, was wired to your husband's office door," Rogers said. "Everyone we spoke with said that you and your husband were the only people who entered that office since your husband's retirement, but he was there only occasionally. You were the mostly likely target of that explosive device and yet once again, you escaped injury."

"What are you implying?" Donna asked.

"We've reviewed the incorporation papers for Stroud Pharmaceuticals," Ana said. "As written, your husband has primary authority over the business until his death. No provision was made in the case of his disability by illness or injury. While you were acting administrator, you had no real authority to expand or sell the business. Your ability to borrow money for the business was also limited. Your husband's death frees you to make those kind of decisions."

"I did not kill my husband," Donna said, her voice trembling. She gripped the edge of the table. "I didn't kill anyone."

"Mrs. Stroud has lost her husband." The lawyer stood. "Her own life has been threatened several times. For you to suggest—"

"Someone connected with Stroud Pharmaceuticals is planting these bombs and killing people," Rogers said. "It's our job to take a hard look at everyone who had motive and opportunity. Mrs. Stroud had both."

"I didn't do it," Donna said. "I swear." She bent her head and began to weep, shoulders shaking.

Ana turned away. Though she wasn't convinced of Donna's innocence, she felt sorry for this woman who had lost so much.

"We can continue this interview later," Rogers said.

"I demand that you release my client at once," the lawyer said.

"She's free to go," Rogers said. "But we're continuing our investigation."

Ana walked with Rogers to the observation room where Smitty and Cantrell waited with Rowan, who had returned to Mayville last night. "How long do you think it's going to be before a story shows up in the local paper about how the FBI is bullying the newly widowed patron saint of Mayville?" Rowan asked.

Rogers dropped into the chair at the end of the table. "You tell me—how long?"

"I'd say about twenty-four hours. That lawyer had the look of someone who will hurry to get the press on his client's side."

"Then he's smarter than I gave him credit for," Rogers said. "You and I both know we're not here to win friends. And right now, Donna Stroud had the most to gain from getting rid of her husband, the chief financial officer who maybe had too tight a hold on the company purse strings, and her son's lover whom she didn't approve of."

"She also had the most to lose," Smitty said. "Her husband, her best friend, and the reputation of the business she devoted most of her adult life to."

"Do you think she's innocent?" Ana asked.

Smitty tucked her long hair behind one ear. "I'm not saying she's innocent or guilty," she said. "I just think it's good to keep all the evidence in mind, not just the parts that fit one theory."

That was vintage by-the-book Smitty. Rogers glared at her. He and Smitty had clashed more than once over her penchant for telling others how to do their jobs.

Ana shifted her gaze to Cantrell. Of all the team members, he and Smitty had locked horns the most, and she expected him to come to Rogers's defense. Instead, he leaned back in his chair, relaxed. "The trouble with this case is, every one of our suspects has just as good reasons he or she isn't responsible for these crimes as anyone else," he said.

"That just tells me we need more evidence," Rogers said. "We get the right information, we'll find the right person."

"Did the locals uncover anything useful at Merry's house?" Smitty asked.

"We gave it a good going over and didn't find anything," Chief Simonson said.

"Merry says she worked in her garden until about eight last night," Rogers said. "She went in, ate a sandwich and watched TV in her bedroom until ten thirty, then went to bed. She never heard anyone outside and she didn't see anything suspicious."

"Her bedroom is at the back of the house," Simonson said. "If she had the television on, she probably wouldn't hear anyone up front. She doesn't have a dog to alert her to a stranger's presence."

"All the other explosives have been at the Stroud plant," Ana said. "Why target Merry with this one?"

"Because someone—Donna Stroud, or maybe Parker Stroud—wants to get rid of her," Cantrell said.

"Or because the bomber thinks Merry knows something, and is afraid she'll tell," Smitty said.

"Parker was in the hospital last night," Simonson said. "He's supposed to be discharged this morning."

"What about Leo?" Rogers asked.

"He's still locked up tight. And he hasn't had any visitors or talked to anyone but his lawyer, who is still advising him not to talk to law enforcement."

"Has anyone told him about this latest bombing?" Smitty asked.

"I don't think so," the captain said.

"Tell him, and let us know his reaction," Rogers said.

The door to the conference room opened and a young woman stuck her head in. "I'm sorry to disturb you, Chief, but you're needed up front. We have a, um, situation."

"What kind of situation?" Simonson asked, already on his feet.

"Parker Stroud is up front, demanding to see you."

Ana and Rogers followed the captain down the hall to the police department lobby, where Parker Stroud looked as enraged as a man can when he's leaning on crutches and dressed in sweat pants, rubber sandals and an untucked dress shirt. When he spotted the captain, he lurched forward. "Are you out of your mind?" he shouted. "Arresting my mother? Hasn't the woman suffered enough without you digging your knife in?"

"Your mother is not under arrest," the captain said. "She agreed to answer some questions for us and you should find her at home now."

Parker spotted Ana and Rogers. "You're behind this," he said. "You can't find anyone else to pin this on, so you go after a helpless old woman."

Ana doubted Donna would thank her son for referring to her as either helpless or old. "Gathering evidence in a case like this requires asking lots of questions," she said. "We can't afford to omit anyone who might have the answers we need."

"My mother doesn't know anything." He leaned more heavily on his crutches, his face gray beneath the scruff of beard. "And she's the person someone is obviously trying to kill."

"And you have no idea who that person might be?" Rogers asked.

"No." Parker shook his head.

"What about Merry?" Ana asked.

He frowned. "What about her?"

"A bomb exploded on her front porch early this morning," Rogers said.

"Oh God." He wiped his face with his hand. "Is she—"

"She's fine," Ana said. "She was inside when it happened. No one was hurt. You hadn't heard?"

"I was just released from the hospital. No one there said anything. Where is she now?"

"I believe she's home," the captain said. "The damage was only to the porch and the front room."

"I should probably go see her," Parker said.

"You don't sound very enthusiastic," Rogers said.

"Yeah, well, I've been trying to find a way to break things off with her."

"You don't think she'll take it well?" Ana asked.

He grimaced. "Let's put it this way—if Merry gets her hand on one of those bombs, she'll probably gladly launch it at me."

Chapter Sixteen

"What are we missing?" Laura stared at the sheets of parchment she had taped to the pantry door, each filled with the notes she and Jace had made about the case. For the last hour, they had been going over everything on those pages, searching for a clue they had previously overlooked. Lists of victims, suspects, timelines, data, and other details that might or might not help solve the crimes crowded the paper, written in Laura's neat block printing.

She stabbed a finger at Steve Stroud's name. "We should have talked to him," she said. "He accused Parker of negotiating to sell the business to a competitor. What if that was true? And he kept insisting on sneaking off to his office—maybe because he knew something shady was going on there. Now we'll never have a chance to hear what he might have told us."

"He had dementia." Jace slouched in a kitchen chair, legs stretched out in front of him, hands shoved deep in the pockets of his jeans. "We didn't question him because he wasn't a reliable witness."

"We should have tried," she said. "A mistake like that could cost us this case. It may have already cost lives." The idea that Steve might still be alive if she had acted faster or done a better job nagged at her.

"Beating yourself up over this isn't going to help." Jace stood and walked to her. "Let's give it a rest." He put his arms around her and drew her close. "Tomorrow morning we'll be fresher. Maybe we'll see something new."

She leaned against him, drawing strength from the power of his arms around her. She had always resisted the idea of dating within the Bureau, believing it wise to keep her work life and the rest of her life strictly separate. But there was something to be said for being with someone who understood how consuming the job could be, and the emotional as well as the physical toll the work could take.

He brushed his lips across her temple, then her cheek, then he found her mouth and kissed her deeply, until she was breathless, her whole body humming with desire. He danced his fingers down her bare arms, sending tremors of pleasure through her. He grasped her hips and she arched toward him, weak-kneed with wanting.

"I think we should go to bed now," he said, his voice rough. "Though I'm tempted to take you right there on the table."

His impatience sent a fresh heat through her. She had a vision of plates and papers flying as he laid her back on the table. "Too messy," she said, breathless. "Too…hard."

"I thought you liked it hard." He rocked forward, letting her feel how ready he was for her.

She responded by cupping his fly, smiling as he hissed out a breath through his teeth. Still holding him, she started backing toward the bedroom, thrilling to the naked desire in his eyes as he followed her.

She was more sure of herself with him this time, a little more bold. After they undressed, when he took the condom from the box by the bed, she claimed the little packet, pushed him back on the mattress, and sheathed him while he watched, reaching for her when she straddled him.

They made love at a leisurely pace, watching each other as they moved, not saying much, but so intensely in the moment words hardly seemed necessary. He let her take the lead, responding to her guidance with a skill that kept her on edge for a long time before she came.

Afterward, she lay in his arms, spent and satisfied. "No more bombs tonight," he murmured, pulling the blankets over her shoulders. "I feel too good to move for at least the next eight hours."

She tried to think of a reply, but drifted to sleep before the words came to her.

Then she was in a house full of dark rooms, running from some unseen pursuer, barefoot and panicked, up steep flights of stairs and down long, narrow hallways. She stopped at the door at the end of the hallway, but it refused to open, no matter how hard she pulled on the knob or shoved at the swollen frame. Meanwhile, her pursuer came closer, his footsteps heavy on the bare wooden floors, his dark silhouette filling her with terror.

"Laura, wake up. It's all right. It's only a dream."

She came to with the sensation of landing hard on the floor, though she was safe in bed, Jace holding her to him. "It's okay." He smoothed her hair back from her face and kissed her forehead. "You're safe," he said.

"I dreamed someone was chasing me," she said. "And I couldn't get away. The door was locked and I couldn't escape."

"It doesn't take Freud to figure out that one," he said. "You're pursued by the case you can't solve." He pulled her closer. "Don't be so hard on yourself. You're doing all you can. We all are."

She nodded, but she didn't believe him. Yes, everyone on the team was working hard, but was it hard enough? Was she letting her personal life—her relationship with Jace—distract her from the job? Her father's voice echoed in her head: *Duty before self. Service to your country demands no less.* That was the life he had lived, reminding her whenever she whined about not seeing him enough that he had a whole company of soldiers who depended on him, and she was just one little girl.

"No more bad dreams," Jace said, rubbing her shoulder. "I'm here with you."

Her eyes stung, and she closed her eyes to hold back the tears, breathed in deeply his clean, masculine scent, and fell asleep in his arms, not dreaming, not afraid, not alone.

JACE WOKE AT first light and slipped out of bed without waking Laura. He went into the kitchen and started coffee, then stood at the back window and watched the sunrise filter through the trees. The world looked so peaceful this time of day. Even in the worst of the fighting in Afghanistan there had been a kind of peace at sunrise, as if everything was pausing, taking a deep breath before the next bad thing happened.

The rich aroma of coffee drifted to him and he turned to pull a mug from the cabinet. The sound of water running told him Laura was awake, and he took down a second mug for her, then smiled to himself. He had begun this assignment thinking it might be difficult to pretend to be married to her. Instead, he had fallen into the role so easily it frightened him sometimes. She was so fierce, and prickly, strong yet sensitive. He felt protective of her, though he was aware she didn't really need him at all. She wasn't his type—he liked simple women who didn't demand a lot from him. Laura was complicated, the type of woman with high standards he had no hope of meeting.

Yet here they were together, and it felt good. It felt right. He swallowed coffee, almost burning his tongue, glad of the pain to clear some of the sentimental fog from his head. Being with Laura right now was great, but he'd be a fool to think they had a future together. Sooner or later the lust would wear off and they'd go back to being two people with different ways of looking at the world.

Laura shuffled into the kitchen, damp hair curling around her face. "Good morning," he said, and filled a mug with coffee and handed it to her.

"Thanks." She closed her eyes and drank deeply, then sighed. "I've been thinking about the case," she said.

And here I was hoping you were thinking about me. But he didn't say it—the words were too close to the truth. "Did you come up with any new angles?" he asked instead.

"Whoever Leo made those bombs for, it's someone who knew he had the ability to make them," she said. "Someone he cares enough about to risk breaking the law for. Someone he won't give up, even to save himself."

Leo didn't have siblings or children of his own. "A lover?" Jace asked.

"I think so." Laura sipped more coffee.

"Man or woman?" Jace asked.

"It could be either," she said. "We need to dig deeper."

"He's not that old," Jace said. "I can't think he would have had that many serious relationships."

"We should start with high school," she said. "He went to school here in town and sometimes young relationships are extra intense. Maybe he reconnected when he came back here following his mother's death. His old flame saw the chance to even some scores with the Strouds."

"You're thinking someone who works at the plant?" Jace asked. "All the evidence points that way."

"Right. So we go to the school, ask questions, check the yearbook. He was the mad bomber, so he has that reputation to build on, even if the bomb he made back then wasn't real." She set her cup aside and straightened. "It's your turn to make breakfast while I get dressed. Then we can visit the high school."

And that was that. No good morning kiss. Nothing about

last night. The ardent lover of last night replaced by all-business Special Agent Smith.

Complicated.

MAYVILLE HIGH SCHOOL—Home of the Mayville Wild Cats!—had the institutional appearance shared by schools and prisons, the former usually with a large sports complex nearby, the latter encircled with razor wire. On this late-spring Saturday, the campus was nearly deserted, and their steps echoed as they crossed the empty parking lot to the front entrance.

"Were you a jock in high school?" Laura asked. "Quarterback of the football team, basketball star?"

"Tight end," he said. "And I played baseball, not basketball. Pitcher." In those days, he had dreamed of going pro, but he'd never had that kind of talent. "Let me guess, you were valedictorian."

She stared. "How did you know?"

"How could you not be?" He held open the door to the front office. Principal Mike Caldwell had agreed to meet them here.

The burly man with the gray crew cut who emerged from a back office to greet them reminded Jace of every drill sergeant he had ever met. Caldwell shook both their hands, examined their IDs, then ushered them into his office. "I'm guessing this has something to do with that mess over at Stroud," he said, settling his big frame behind a desk almost obscured by neat stacks of papers. "How can I help?"

"We're trying to find out more about a former student," Laura said. "Leo Elgin."

"I heard you'd arrested him. I suppose you heard about that whole mad bomber fiasco. It wasn't a real bomb, just a hotheaded kid being stupid."

"Did you know Leo?" Laura asked.

"Oh, I knew him. I coached football and track and taught civics. I had Leo in one of my classes."

"What was he like?" Jace asked. "Other than hot-headed."

"He was smart. Too smart for his own good. What I mean is kids like that get bored, then they get into trouble, like that fake bomb thing." He leaned forward, hands clasped on the desk. "Leo had a beef with the teacher he'd given the thing to. She'd marked him down on an exam for getting an answer wrong. Something to do with a higher mathematical theory. Turns out, Leo was right and she was wrong, but he never forgave her for the mistake."

"So he held grudges?" Laura asked.

"Yes, I'd say so."

"Was he popular?" Jace asked. "Who were his friends?"

"He was popular enough. Not in the most popular crowd, but most people seemed to like him. He had a reputation as a kind of a rebel and some kids admire that."

"Any girlfriends?" Jace asked.

Caldwell nodded. "He was surprisingly popular with the girls. I don't remember him being involved with anyone in particular, but he had quite a few female admirers, considering he wasn't athletic or all that good-looking."

"Can you think of anyone he dated who still lives in the area?" Jace asked. "Anyone who works at Stroud?"

Caldwell rubbed his chin. "I can't, really," he said.

"Do you have yearbooks from when Leo was a student here?" Laura asked. "We'd like to look at them."

"I do." He rolled his chair to the bookcase that filled most of the back wall, selected four thick volumes, then rolled over to the desk and slid them to Laura.

"*The Beacon*," Jace read the name on the cover of the top volume.

Caldwell stood. "I've got to attend a graduation rehearsal this afternoon, but you're welcome to use my office to look at those."

"Thanks," Jace said. "But we might want to take one or more of them with us."

"Just promise to return them, please. We have a complete set dating back to 1926 and I'd hate to break up the collection."

"Sure thing. We'll give you a receipt."

Laura was already engrossed in the first volume by the time Jace pulled the truck into the driveway of the trailer. "The index has a list of every student by class," she said. "Start there and see how many names ring a bell. Later, we can compare them with the employee list from Stroud."

In the next hour they found the names of a dozen former students who now worked at Stroud, including Parker Stroud. They looked at Leo's picture. He stared into the camera directly, an approximation of a sneer curling his lip. "Tell me the truth," Jace said. "Would he have done it for you when you were a high school girl?"

She shrugged. "Hard to say. I liked smart guys. And there's something about a bad boy." Laughter danced in her eyes and he fought the urge to lean over and kiss her.

Instead, he shut the book. "There are pictures in here of Leo with groups of kids, but nothing that says 'big romance' to me."

"To me, either." She studied the stack of books and shook her head. "I don't think there's anything here. We need to try college."

"He attended West Virginia University," Jace said. "That's about three hours from here."

Laura shoved back her chair and rose. "Then it's time for a road trip."

Chapter Seventeen

Merry logged on to her online bank account Saturday morning and smiled to herself when she saw the balance. Parker was so generous. Too bad things weren't going to work out the way she had hoped. But a smart woman knew when to cut her losses.

She signed out of the bank's website and clicked over to the travel page she had bookmarked. Where should she take her dream vacation?

Her phone rang. Annoyed at the interruption, she checked the display. Why was Donna Stroud calling her? Maybe all the bad press had guilted the Strouds into offering to pay the employees who'd been put out of work by the sudden plant closure. It wasn't like the family couldn't afford it. "Hello?" Merry injected an extra note of pleasantness into her voice.

"Merry, it's Donna Stroud."

Had the woman never heard of caller ID? "Hello, Mrs. Stroud. How are you doing?"

"I'm as well as can be expected. I called because I've decided to operate Stroud Pharmaceuticals out of my home office until the plant reopens. I'll need you to report there for work at nine Monday morning. You know where that is, don't you?"

Did she know where that was—really! The Strouds only owned the biggest house in town, a white-columned monstrosity straight out of *Gone with the Wind*. "I can't come in Monday," Merry said.

"Why not?" Donna asked.

"I have two weeks' time off due. While the plant is closed, I decided to take a vacation."

"I really need you to put that on hold until this situation is resolved," Donna said. "I know it's a sacrifice, but it's necessary for the future health of the company."

Merry didn't give a fig about the company. "I'm sorry, but I've already booked my tickets." She hit the Purchase Reservation button.

"How long will you be gone?" Donna asked.

"I'm not sure." She had purchased a one-way ticket.

"Merry, I can't allow this," Donna said. "You should have talked to me before you made your plans."

"Excuse me, but you're not my mother. I don't need your permission to take a vacation."

"There's no need to take that attitude. I'm simply saying I expect every team member to contribute one-hundred percent during this crisis."

"Then I guess I'm no longer a part of the team." Elation surged through her. She only wished she could see Donna's face.

"What did you say?" Donna asked.

"I said I quit. I'm going on vacation." She ended the call and tossed the phone on the desk. Then she hit Print and turned to collect the reservation confirmation from the printer behind her. A one-way ticket to Brazil.

She had always wanted to see Rio.

THE SECURITY FIRM Donna Stroud had hired to patrol the closed campus of Stroud Pharmaceuticals hesitated only a moment when Merry presented them with a letter on Donna Stroud's personal stationery, authorizing Merry Winger to access the executive offices for the purpose of retrieving some important documents. "This won't take long," Merry reassured the guard when he told her she could go on in. She already had all the papers she needed. This visit was merely so the guard would remember her and verify she had indeed been there.

She unlocked the door and went first to the executive offices. She rifled through all the desks, scoring about forty dollars in miscellaneous coins and bills and a hidden stash of pain pills—you never knew when those might come in handy.

In Donna Stroud's desk she found a file conveniently labeled FBI. Curious, she flipped through it, a thrill rushing through her as she found the employment paperwork for Laura Lovejoy—real name, Laura Smith. Or rather, Special Agent Laura Smith.

Parker's new admin was a spy! So, apparently, was her husband, whose name wasn't Lovejoy either, but Jason Cantrell. Now wasn't that interesting?

Merry returned the file to the drawer, spent a few more minutes in Donna's office, then hurried down the hall to Parker's office.

She felt under Parker's center desk drawer and found the little lever that released the catch on a second, thinner drawer. She already had a copy of the bank book inside the drawer, but why not retrieve the original, as long as she was here? She smiled at the small black book, and at Parker's fondness for paper trails. She slid the book into her purse, then left the office with only a small pang of regret. She would have enjoyed being Mrs. Parker Stroud. Parker wasn't bad-looking, was a decent lover, and his money and name would have eased any dissatisfaction she might have experienced down the road. But maybe she was destined for better things.

She waved to the guard and drove out of the lot, then picked up her phone and hit the button to dial the number she had already typed in. "Hello?" Laura Lovejoy sounded annoyed.

"I need to see you right away," Merry said. "It's really important."

"We're on our way out of town," Laura said. "Maybe later—"

"Not later. Now." Merry was the one calling the shots here. "I've found out something important about Parker that the FBI needs to know."

"Then why are you calling me?" Laura asked.

"Because I know who you are, Agent Smith. And we need to talk now."

"Fine." The word was clipped. Impatient. "Where do you want to meet?"

"I'll come to you. Don't worry, I know the address."

Ten minutes later, she turned onto the rutted dirt road that led to the single-wide trailer set back under the trees. Jace and Laura stood on the porch and watched Merry climb out of her car. "The feds couldn't find any better place to put you up than this dump?" Merry asked as she made her way up the graveled path that led to the bottom of the steps.

Jace opened the front door wider. "Come in, Merry."

"How did you find out our identities?" Laura asked as she followed Merry into the living room.

"Because I'm smart." She sat in the recliner and looked up at them. They took up positions on either end of the sofa. "Are you two really married, or is that part of the play-acting, too?" Merry asked.

"What did you want to talk to us about?" Jace asked.

She reached for her purse and both agents tensed. "Don't worry, I'm not pulling a gun," Merry said. She took out the bank book and tossed it to Laura. "Take a look at that."

Laura flipped through the book, then handed it to Jace. "Where did you get that?"

"I found it in Parker's desk," Merry said. "Just now, when I went to pick up some papers for Mrs. Stroud." If they bothered to check with Donna, the old woman would deny sending Merry on such an errand, but Merry was counting on the cops to be so anxious to get their hands on Parker, they wouldn't bother to check her story until she was long gone to Rio.

"Thank you for bringing this to us," Laura said. "We'll certainly look into it."

She didn't even act surprised. Which meant the FBI already knew about Parker's secret account. Disappointing. But all wasn't lost. "Don't you want to know what it means?"

"What do you think it means?" Jace asked.

Merry adopted a sad face. Sad, and a little terrified. "I think Parker is the one who poisoned the Stomach Soothers. Looking back, it all makes sense now."

Another exchange of looks between the two. "Tell us what you know," Jace said.

She bit her lip, as if reluctant to get Parker—the man she loved—into trouble. Then she nodded. She had to do the right thing, even if it cost her her future happiness. "I think Parker was embezzling money from his family's company," she said. "He put the proceeds into that secret account. But Gini Elgin, the chief financial officer, must have noticed something was off. I overheard her confronting him on the factory floor one day. I caught the words 'the money isn't right.' That night, Parker was so furious. He wouldn't tell me why, but he did say that Gini was poking her nose where it didn't belong. The next day, I caught him in the herb garden."

"The herb garden?" Laura was wearing her annoyed look again. Merry wanted to laugh.

"It's a garden in front of the Stroud plant, with examples of all the plants Evangeline Stroud, the company founder, used in her original herbal remedies. There are paths and a gazebo and little markers identifying everything. I helped with some of the plantings, since I have a green thumb."

"What was the significance of Parker being in the garden?" Jace asked.

"First of all, he never went there," Merry said. "He used to tease me about my interest in gardening. But he was there that day, so I paid closer attention, to see what he was doing. That's when I noticed he was standing right next to the castor plant. You know about castor plants, right?"

"Ricin is derived from castor beans," Laura said.

Merry nodded. "That didn't register with me until much later, but I think now he poisoned those tablets in order to kill Gini without anyone suspecting him. As plant manager, he had plenty of opportunity to slip the poison into the pills and substitute that bottle for the one she always kept in her desk. Everyone knew she took the Stomach Soothers all the time."

"This is really important," Jace said. "Do you know if Parker has any more ricin? Or more contaminated pills?"

Why hadn't she thought of this? The idea scared her a little. "I don't know," she said. "I haven't seen any in his home or office."

"When did you start blackmailing him?" Jace asked, just as smooth as if he'd been asking how she took her coffee.

But Merry didn't even blink. "Blackmail?" she asked.

"You went to Parker, told him what you knew, and he paid you $50,000 a week," Laura said.

Merry laughed. "I wish. But seriously, I didn't need to blackmail Parker. We were going to get married. He's so generous, buying me anything I want, and everything he had was going to be mine."

"You're using the past tense," Jace said. "Is the wedding off?"

Tears stung her eyes. She was really good at this acting stuff, wasn't she? "I can't marry a man who murdered six people," she said. "I love Parker, but he needs help. And what if my life is in danger because I told you?" She jumped up and turned as if to leave.

Jace took her arm. Not roughly, but there was muscle behind his grip. "Calm down," he said. "Sit down and tell us what you know about the bombs."

She sat, taking the opportunity to regroup. "I don't know anything about the bombs," she said.

"Do you think Parker set them?" Laura asked.

"I don't know what to think." She stared at her lap, then lifted her head to meet Laura's gaze. "I would have said Parker would never do something like that, but he and Leo have been friends for years, and then when that bomb exploded at my house…"

"You thought Parker was trying to kill you?" Jace asked.

"I thought maybe he saw me the day he was in the garden, and he was afraid I'd tell someone." She buried her face in her hands. "Now I'm terrified. You have to do something." This time when she stood, no one tried to stop her.

"We can take you into protective custody," Laura said. "Keep you safe."

"No. I don't want that!" She softened her voice. "I'll be okay. Just keep me posted, okay?" She paused at the door. "And I promise not to tell anybody you're agents," she said.

"We will be in touch." Laura put her hand over Merry's on the doorknob. "We'll be checking and if we find out you blackmailed Parker, we will arrest you."

Merry glared, then shoved past Laura and out the door. Let them look. Parker wasn't the only one with a secret account, and even if the feds found that bank, Merry had already moved the funds to an even more secure location. Tomorrow she'd be on her way to Brazil, out of their reach forever.

Chapter Eighteen

Sunday morning, Laura felt more like herself again, dressed in her own clothes. She patted her chignon, every hair in place, and buttoned the middle button of her suit jacket, then went to meet Jace in the living room of the trailer. With luck, by this time tomorrow they'd both be back in their own apartments in Knoxville.

Jace had donned a suit for this occasion as well, though he had yet to put on the jacket. His gaze swept over her as she entered the room, and she wondered if he was comparing her current look to the clothing she had worn while posing as a struggling newlywed.

Or maybe he was just remembering how she looked naked.

"Are you ready to do this?" he asked.

"I've been looking forward to it."

Driving to arrest someone in a beat-up mustard-colored pickup didn't have the same panache as arriving in a black sedan, but at least Parker Stroud wouldn't be overly alarmed when he saw them pull up to his house.

The two police cruisers and Ramirez and Rogers's sedan might set off a few alarm bells, of course, but, since they would have the house surrounded, Laura wasn't expecting Parker to give them much trouble.

As it was, they had to wait on the front steps of his house for several minutes and ring the bell three times before

Parker, hobbling on crutches, answered the door. "What are you doing here?" he demanded, scowling.

Laura opened the folder with her credentials and held them at eye level. "Parker Stroud, I'm arresting you for the murders of Virginia Elgin, Herbert Baker, Gail Benito…" She read off all the names of the people who had died after ingesting the tainted Stomach Soothers. She might have added the names of those who had died in the bombings—including Parker's own father—but the team was still building that case.

As she spoke, Parker's jaw went slack and all color drained from his face. When she had finished reciting the charges, Jace stepped forward. "Turn around and put your hands behind your back," he said, relieving Parker of his crutches and steadying him as he did so.

"There must be some mistake." Parker's voice was thin and reedy, more frightened boy than murderous man.

"Turn around, Mr. Stroud." Jace continued to steady him, alert for any attempt to fight back.

He turned, but looked back at Laura as Jace cuffed him. "I want my lawyer," he said.

"You can contact him when we get to the station." Local police would process and hold Parker until he could be transported to a federal facility. "You have the right to remain silent…"

She recited the Miranda warning, but she doubted if much was registering. Two police cars, along with Ramirez and Rogers, had arrived before Parker snapped out of his daze. "Hey!" he called as Laura was moving away, having handed him over to two officers for transport to the station. "What are you doing arresting me? You're my secretary."

"I have a lot of talents," she said, and walked back to the truck.

Jace fell into step beside her. "That's you," he said. "Multitalented." Somehow, he managed to imbue the words with a sexy heat that melted a few synapses. She shot him a stern look, which he met with a wicked grin that turned up the heat another notch.

While the local cops processed Parker, Laura and Ramirez joined Rogers in searching Parker's home. The four-bedroom, five-bath home featured a media room, billiard table, walk-in closets, and a pool and spa. One of the bedrooms was being used as a home office and they started the search there, donning gloves and methodically combing through every drawer, opening every book, and feeling behind every painting.

Laura found the flash drive, tucked in the toe of a pair of dress shoes at the back of the master bedroom closet. She connected it to the laptop from the office and smiled as rows of figures populated the screen.

"What are we looking at?" Jace leaned over her shoulder and studied the images.

"I'm pretty sure these are the missing financials from Stroud Pharmaceuticals," she said. She pointed to a column of red figures. "These are all the places the income and expenses don't match up. My guess is Gini Elgin spotted these and connected the missing money to Parker. That's probably what they were arguing about that day on the factory floor, and why he decided to kill her."

"Why keep these files?" he asked. "Why not destroy them?"

"Sooner or later, the company would be due for an audit. Missing data gets flagged and that would be a real problem. So I think he planned to use this file as a basis for reconstructing the data to paint a more favorable financial picture. Especially if he planned to partner with a competitor, or even sell the business outright."

"Steve Stroud was telling the truth," Jace said. "Even if no one believed him."

"Maybe that's why Parker planted that bomb in his

dad's office," she said. "He couldn't risk someone—like the FBI—finally paying attention to Steve."

"He took a big risk, following his father into the building," Jace said.

"Maybe he thought doing so would remove suspicion from him." Laura removed the drive from the computer and slipped it into an evidence bag. "It almost worked."

Ramirez and Rogers joined them in the office. "We've been through the whole house," Rogers said. "No medication, though we found a container of castor beans in the back of the pantry."

"We'll get a team out here tomorrow to start looking in the walls and floors," Ramirez said. "Let's go talk to Parker and see what he has to say for himself."

PARKER REMINDED JACE of a life-sized balloon figure that had sprung a leak. Everything about him sagged, from his shoulders to his face. He didn't even look up when Jace and Laura entered the room. They had decided they would question him first, and depending on the progress they made, Ramirez and Rogers would follow up.

A handsome older man with a luxurious white moustache stood to greet the two agents and introduced himself as Gerald Kirkbaum. "I commend you on your dedication to finding the person responsible for these tragic deaths," he said. "But there's been some terrible mistake. Mr. Stroud had nothing to do with those deaths. He had no reason to do such a horrible thing."

Parker didn't look innocent to Jace. In fact, he had never seen anyone who looked guiltier. "We think he did have a reason," Laura said.

She pulled out a chair and sat. Parker still hadn't looked at her. Mr. Kirkbaum remained standing, as did Jace. "You have no evidence—" Kirkbaum began.

"We have evidence," Laura said, speaking to Parker.

"We have a witness who presented us with a bank book, showing the secret account where you've been stashing the money you embezzled from Stroud Pharmaceuticals." She leaned toward him, addressing the top of his bowed head. "This same witness saw you arguing with Gini Elgin when she confronted you about the missing money. And she will testify that she saw you in the garden with the castor bean plants. Castor beans are the source of ricin. But you know that, don't you? We found the castor beans in your pantry."

"Merry is a liar," he said, still not raising his head. "She's upset because I won't marry her, so she told these lies."

"I've seen the financials, and the bank account, and the castor beans," Laura said. "She isn't lying." She leaned toward him, lowering her voice. "How much did you pay Leo Elgin for those bombs? Did you think if you killed your mother and father you'd finally inherit the family business? You could run it the way you saw fit, even sell it if you liked? After all, you'd already killed six people. What were a few more? And hey, your dad was already half-gone, so what did it matter if you killed him?"

"I had nothing to do with that!" Parker's head came up and he straightened, like a puppet come to life.

Jace stepped forward. "Tell us where the other bombs are," he said. "How many did Leo make for you? Six? Or more?"

"No. I had nothing to do with that."

"I've met some heartless people in this job," Jace said. "But a man who would kill his own father, and try to kill his mother—that's lower than low."

"I didn't do it!" His shout echoed in the small room.

"We need to stop this questioning now," Kirkbaum said. "Parker, don't say another word."

But Parker was weeping, tears streaming down his face. He held out his cuffed hands to Laura, pleading. "I only meant to kill Gini. I didn't want to, but she'd found out about the money and threatened to tell my mother. I couldn't let them find out. My dad had already retired and I thought if I kept working on my mother, she'd eventually relent and turn everything over to me. Then no one would have to know."

"You're saying you put the ricin in the Stomach Soother tablets for the purpose of killing Virginia Elgin?" Jace said.

"Yes." The words were barely audible since Parker had buried his head in his hands.

"Parker, you need to shut up now." Kirkbaum leaned over his client. "You're not helping yourself."

"I didn't kill my father," Parker said, raising his head again. "And I didn't try to kill my mother. I never bought any bombs from Leo."

"Tell us more about the ricin," Laura said. "How did you know how to make it?"

"I looked on the internet," he said. "I knew about the castor bean plant because Merry had pointed it out to me. She was really into gardening and knew a lot about plants. I liked that I could make the poison myself, without having to buy anything that might be traced. I had to be careful, but it wasn't really that hard."

"How many bottles did you put the ricin in?" Jace asked.

"A whole tray. Twelve. It was the quickest way, slipping it in as they passed the filler mechanism. I went in one night after everything shut down and ran the machinery myself. I shut off all the security cameras. Then I took the whole lot out before it reached shipping." He frowned. "But I must have missed a few bottles that got slipped into the distribution stream. I put one of the bottles in Gini's desk, to replace the bottle she always kept there. But the next thing I know, all these other people were dying." He covered his face with his hands. "I never meant for that to happen."

Parker was probably hoping they would feel as sorry for him as he felt for himself, but all Jace's compassion was reserved for the six people the man had murdered. "What did you do with the rest of the bottles you pulled off the line?" he asked.

"I buried them."

"Where did you bury them?" Laura asked.

"In my mother's backyard. By the barbecue pit. I didn't know what else to do."

Jace glanced toward the observation window. Ramirez or Rogers would send someone to the Stroud home to collect that dangerous buried treasure pronto.

"When did Merry find out about what you'd done?" Laura asked.

"She saw me in the garden at the plant that day, and she saw me arguing with Gini before that. I guess after she heard how Gini died, she put everything together."

"She was blackmailing you," Laura said.

Parker nodded. "She came to me a couple of days after Gini died."

"She wanted $50,000?" Laura asked.

"That's the thing. She didn't ask for the money at first. She said if we got married right away, she wouldn't be able to testify against me."

No one bothered to point out that this wasn't how spousal privilege worked. "But you didn't marry her," Jace said.

"I couldn't. My parents would have stroked out at the idea. There was no way my mom would have turned over the business to me if I even got engaged to Merry. And I had to get control of the business. So I made a deal to pay her the $50,000 a week and I'd marry her as soon as my mom signed the paperwork to put me in charge."

"How did she react to that?" Laura asked.

"She didn't like it, but I persuaded her it was the only way. She really wanted to be Mrs. Parker Stroud."

"She loved you that much?" Jace tried to keep the doubt from his voice.

"She didn't love me as much as she loved the idea of living in a big house and having everyone in town and most of the state fall over themselves to be her best friend. Or at least, that's how she saw it. I tried to tell her it wouldn't be like that, but she wouldn't listen."

"So Merry knew what you had done, at least since two days after Gini Elgin died," Laura said. "But she told us she didn't figure it out until a few days ago."

"If you know about my bank account, then you saw the payments I made to her," Parker said. "I made the first one on the fourth."

That matched up with the entries in the bank register Merry had given them. "Why did Merry lie to us?" Laura asked. "Did the two of you have an argument?"

"She was getting impatient. She told me I needed to stand up to my mother and insist on taking over the business and marrying her. I tried to tell her that my father had just died—this wasn't the right time, but she wouldn't listen. She said she had waited long enough. But I never thought she'd turn me in."

Laura leaned toward him. "So your agreement with Merry was that when you got control of Stroud Pharmaceuticals, you'd marry her."

"Yes."

"If your parents died, you would inherit the business," Laura said.

"I don't care what kind of monster you think I am, but I wouldn't do that." Parker's voice rose. "What do I have to do to get you to believe me?"

"I believe you," Laura said. "But if Merry thought your parents' deaths would get her what she wanted, do you think she'd try to hurry things along?"

Jace recognized the fear that blossomed in Parker's eyes.

The handcuffed man opened his mouth as if to protest, but no words came out. "She asked me about Leo one day, not long after she figured out what I'd done with the Stomach Soothers," Parker said. "I told her the mad bomber story." He wet his lips. "I didn't think anything of it, but then later, Leo told me Merry had been to see him. He said she'd been really nice and asked about his job, and agreed with him that the Strouds—my mom and dad—were as good as murderers."

"When did he tell you that?" Jace asked.

"We met at the lake one evening, a few days before his mother's funeral. I'd heard what he was saying around town—that my family had killed his mother. I tried to talk some sense to him, but he wouldn't listen."

"What about the money you paid him?" Laura asked.

"It really was for the funeral." He looked pained. "But Merry volunteered to deliver it to him. She said Leo would take it better coming from her, that the two of them were friends now, because they both knew what it was like to get a raw deal from the Strouds."

"That's pretty harsh," Jace said.

"She could say anything she wanted to me now and I couldn't do anything about it."

Laura's chair scraped back and she stood. "That's all the questions we have for now."

She left the room, Jace on her heels. "We need to find Merry," she said as they hurried down the hall.

"You think she planted those bombs," Jace said.

"Yes, and you saw those notes she sent to Donna. She isn't finished yet."

Chapter Nineteen

Merry hefted the second of two large suitcases into the trunk of her car, then slammed the lid. She had spent too much time packing, but it had been hard to decide what to take. She would be gone a long time, and she wasn't sure what she'd need. In the end, she'd consoled herself with the knowledge that she had enough money to buy new things. And what she did have was bound to go farther in South America, right?

Besides, she had a lot more money now. The cops—and eventually Parker—would think she'd just stolen Parker's passbook to turn over to the police, but she'd also taken his passwords, and even the answers to his secret questions that were part of account security. With that information, she'd been able to transfer most of the $10 million balance into her own account. It had been so easy. And with that kind of money, who needed the Strouds? They were nobodies.

She slid into the driver's seat and drove toward town. She had one quick stop before she headed to the airport. In the oppressive afternoon heat, the trailer looked even shabbier than she remembered, the heart-shaped catalpa leaves drooping.

She parked in the shade of that tree and hurried up the walk. The cheap lock popped with one thrust of her credit card between the door and the jamb, and Merry was in and out in less than five minutes. Then again, she'd had a lot of practice delivering her little gifts.

Humming to herself, she pressed down on the gas, the speedometer climbing as she rushed toward the airport.

"She's not here," Laura said as Jace pulled into Merry's driveway. "Her car isn't out front."

"Maybe she has parking in the back," Jace said. He doubted it, but it didn't pay to overlook any possibility.

"I hope you're right." Laura shoved open the door of the truck and raced up the drive, Jace at her heels. She pounded on the front door. "Merry! It's Laura. I need to talk to you. It's an emergency."

No answer. Jace pressed his ear to the door. No sounds of movement inside. He stepped back.

"You need to break the door down."

"Without a warrant?" He feigned shock.

She scowled at him. He stepped back, then aimed a powerful kick at the door, just above the knob. The wood splintered. Another hard kick and it sagged inward. He drew his weapon, and then they went in. "FBI!" he shouted.

The only answer was the low hum of the air conditioning.

"I'll take the bedroom. You search the rest of the house," Laura said.

"I love it when you're bossy," he called after her.

A search of the living room revealed no Merry, but in the dining room, a piece of white paper taped to the table caught his attention.

ALL THAT'S LEFT ARE TWO. GUESS WHO?

Laura appeared in the doorway to the dining room. "She's gone," she said. "There are too many empty hangers in her closet, and there's no makeup or shampoo in the bathroom."

"She left a note." Jace gestured to the table.

Laura glanced at the note, then headed for the door. "I'll call the team while you drive. The local police can put out an APB in case she's driving somewhere."

Jace finished the thought. "Meanwhile, we've got to drive to the airport."

MERRY PULLED INTO the valet lane for airport parking. No more economy lot for her. She handed the attendant her key, flagged down a red cap to take her luggage and gave him the name of her airline. She bypassed the waiting crowd and strolled to the first class desk. "Enjoy your flight, Ms. Winger," the agent said.

Yes! She could definitely get used to service like this.

She glanced around as she made her way to the security checkpoint. No one paid any attention to her. She'd taken a chance, leaving that note, but she figured Laura and her fellow feds would be busy with Parker for the next little while.

The dumb sap. He'd been stupid to think he could get away with poisoning people in the first place, and then he had made things worse by trying to play her. If he had only married her when she asked him to, she would have taken care of everything. Instead, he'd almost gotten himself blown up—twice—and now he was going to jail for the rest of his life.

She reached her gate just as the agent was calling for first class passengers. She handed over her boarding pass and walked down the Jetway to her comfortable seat. Moments later, she was sipping a glass of champagne and contemplating the future. She'd do some shopping tomorrow—buy a new bikini, or several, and clothes more suitable for the tropics. Then she'd visit a real estate agent and look into renting a nice villa. One in a good neighborhood, with security.

She only regretted she couldn't stay in Mayville to hear

about the last two bombs. Leo had balked at making six for her at first, but she had promised to find the person who had killed his mother and make them pay. That, and the promise of mind-blowing sex, had persuaded him. She had never intended to deliver on the sex, but he didn't know that.

Then she had sworn to find him and castrate him if he ever told a soul about her. She had made sure he believed her, too.

Men. They were so easy to manipulate.

The last few passengers filed on and the flight attendants began closing overhead bins and readying for takeoff. Merry leaned back and closed her eyes, some of the tension that had been building these last few weeks easing away. This time tomorrow she'd be sipping a cool drink in the hot sun, planning the rest of a life of luxury.

"I'VE GOT A list of all the flights leaving from Yeager Airport in the next three hours," Laura said as Jace pulled into the valet lane for airport parking. "We're lucky this isn't a bigger airport."

"How many flights?" Jace asked as he handed the attendant his keys.

"Five."

Jace pulled up Merry's picture on his phone and showed it to the attendant. "Has this woman been through here in the last hour or so?" he asked.

The young man studied the photo, then shook his head. "I haven't seen her."

Jace turned as a second man approached. "Have you seen her?" he asked.

The second man's eyes widened. "Yeah, she was just here—maybe half an hour ago."

"What was she driving?" Laura asked.

"A white Chevy sedan."

"Thanks." Jace and Laura sprinted into the terminal.

"You take the desks on the right, I'll take the left," Laura said as they reached the check-in level.

Passengers grumbled as Jace cut to the front of the line at the first desk, but his badge silenced the agent's rebuke. "Merry Winger," he said. "Has she checked in here? She may have been using another name, but she looks like this." He showed the picture.

He struck out at the first two desks, but at the third, the agent verified that Merry Winger had checked in forty minutes before, using a one-way ticket with a final destination of Rio de Janeiro.

Jace texted Laura and headed to security. She met him there and they badged their way to the gate. An air marshal, alerted by TSA, met them. "The plane has already pulled away from the Jetway," the marshal said.

"Then they need to come back," Laura said.

"And don't let her know why the plane is returning," Jace said. "She's already killed at least three people. There's no telling what she'll do if she's cornered."

"Understood," the marshal said. "We'll do what we can to make this seem routine."

MERRY OPENED HER eyes as the speaker overhead crackled to life. "Folks, this is the captain speaking. We've got to return to the gate for a moment. No need for alarm, just a routine precaution. We promise to have you all on your way as quickly as possible."

Merry's stomach fluttered. She flagged down the flight attendant. "Why are we returning to the gate?" she asked. "I have a connection to make in Charlotte."

"You shouldn't have any trouble with your connection," she said. "The pilot is telling us this is only a quick stop."

"But why?" Merry asked, anxiety building. "We were already on the runway. They can't just make us go back."

"It happens." The flight attendant shrugged. "Try not to stress. Would you like another glass of champagne?"

Merry had just accepted the champagne when the flight reached the terminal. But instead of parking at a gate, the plane stopped away from the gates. "What's happening?" Merry asked, trying to see across the aisle and out the window that faced the terminal.

"They're bringing out one of those rolling stairs," a man across the aisle said.

"I bet they're boarding some bigwig who was late for the flight," another man said.

"Maybe it's a celebrity," a woman suggested.

"It's two people," the first man said, craning to see out the window. "Nobody I recognize, though."

Two people. Merry unbuckled her seat belt and scanned the aisle, searching for some avenue of escape. She didn't know for sure that the two people were FBI agents or police, but she wanted to be prepared, just in case.

She stood and the flight attendant hurried to her. "You need to remain in your seat, with your seat belt fastened," the attendant said.

Merry offered an apologetic smile. "I really need to use the ladies' room," she said. "All that champagne."

"I'm sorry, but you'll have to wait a few minutes more." The flight attendant blocked the aisle, refusing to let Merry move past.

Behind her, the exit door swung open. Laura entered first, followed by Jace. "Hello, Merry," Laura said.

Merry shoved the flight attendant aside. Someone screamed as Merry raced past, through the curtain separating first class from economy. "Stop that woman!" Jace shouted.

A man stood in the aisle, but Merry plowed past him, sending him staggering back into the lap of a woman seated beside the aisle.

Someone else grabbed her arm and refused to let go. She jammed her elbow into his jaw, but still he wouldn't release her. She turned to hit him again, then Laura tackled her, taking her to the floor. Strong arms dragged Merry's hands behind her back and cuffed her, and then stronger arms pulled her to her feet.

"Merry Winger, you're under arrest for three counts of murder," Laura said, as a plane full of passengers looked on, several filming the action with their phones.

Merry glared at her. "Only three?" she asked. "I guess you didn't find the other bombs yet."

"Where are the other bombs?" Jace asked.

"As if I'd tell you." She smiled. "It will be so much better if you find that out for yourself."

Chapter Twenty

"We don't know where Merry Winger planted those last two bombs, but her past behavior should give us some clues." Laura addressed the assembled team, consisting of FBI agents, local police and the county's bomb squad and SWAT. She indicated the list of previous bomb locations. "The first three were detonated at Stroud Pharmaceuticals' administrative offices. The fourth went off at Merry's home, deliberately set there by her to divert suspicion."

"So the most likely location for the fifth and sixth bombs is Stroud Pharmaceuticals," one of the SWAT members said.

"Except Stroud is shut down right now," Ramirez said. "There's no one there to be a target of the bomb."

"Yes, I think the key lies in considering the target," Laura said. "The first two bombs at Stroud killed people other than their intended target. We believe Merry set those bombs intending to kill Donna Stroud, who she saw as standing between her and her goal of marrying Parker Stroud. The third bomb, the one that killed Steve Stroud, may have been intended for Donna also."

"One of the two remaining bombs is probably intended to harm Donna," Jace said. "She's unfinished business for Merry."

"Exactly," Laura said. "We've already contacted Mrs.

Stroud and local police have escorted her from her home. We have a team searching there right now."

"What about Parker Stroud?" Rogers studied the white board, arms folded across his muscular chest. "Even though Merry claimed to be in love with him, she threw him under the bus, coming to you with that bank book and her story about seeing him with the castor plant."

Ramirez nodded. "Parker is with his mother at a safe location now, but we should have a team search his house, too."

Laura surveyed the faces of those before her, each tense with the knowledge that lives depended on them making the right guess and finding those bombs. "Any other ideas?"

"We should talk to Leo," Ramirez said. "Maybe Merry told him something about who she intended to target."

Laura mentally kicked herself for not thinking of this earlier. "Great idea," she said. "Let's do it."

Leo was still being held in the local jail, so twenty minutes later Laura, Ramirez, Jace and Rogers crowded into an interview room where Leo Elgin waited. Dressed in a baggy orange jumpsuit, his hair in need of a trim, he looked younger than his twenty-three years.

"We've arrested Parker Stroud for your mother's murder," Jace said. "He's admitted putting the ricin into the bottles of Stomach Soothers."

Leo stared at him. "Parker?" He wet his lips. "Why would he do something like that?"

"Apparently, he was embezzling money from Stroud Pharmaceuticals," Laura said. "Your mother noticed some discrepancies in the accounts and confronted him. He killed her to keep her from going public with the information. We believe the other deaths were to hide what he'd done and divert suspicion away from him."

Pale and clearly shaken, Leo shook his head. "I thought he was my friend. He was always trying to help me."

"Maybe he felt guilty," Rogers said. He sat in the chair across from Leo. "We've also arrested Merry Winger. She told us you sold her the bombs that killed Lydia Green, Angela Dupree and Steven Stroud."

"I sold her the bombs," he said. "She never told me what she was going to do with them."

"Weren't you a little curious?" Rogers asked.

Leo shook his head, emphatic. "I didn't want to know."

"So some woman comes up to you, says she wants you to make her six bombs and you're like, 'Sure. No problem'?" Rogers tilted his head to one side and squinted at Leo. "If this is a side business of yours, building bombs to order, who else have you sold explosives to?"

"Nobody else, I swear."

"So Merry was the first person you made bombs for?" Laura stood behind Rogers and addressed Leo.

"Yes."

"You didn't think it was strange she wanted you to make a bomb—much less six of them?" Laura asked.

"She promised to find the person who killed my mother!" He buried his head in his shackled hands and the room fell silent. Laura scarcely breathed.

At last, Leo raised his head and looked at her, his eyes filled with sadness. "Look, I know it was wrong, but I was so angry. My mother was dead and she died a horrible death. I wanted the people responsible to pay, and Merry convinced me she wanted to help."

"But why a bomb?" Rogers asked. "Why not more poison?"

"She said she had heard I was the mad bomber." He flushed. "I tried to tell her that was just a stupid kid stunt, but she went on and on about it. She…she flattered me. She was really pretty and I was lonely and…" His voice trailed away and he shrugged, his cheeks flushed.

"But how did you know how to build the bombs?" Rogers asked. "Had you done something like this before?"

"No, but I found a lot of information on the internet. And I work with trip alarms all the time, so setting the trigger wasn't all that different."

"What did you think when you heard Lydia Green and Angela Dupree died because of bombs you built?" Ramirez asked.

Leo bowed his head again. "I felt terrible. I panicked and called Merry and tried to get her to return the rest of the bombs. But she wouldn't. She said I didn't need to worry, that everything would work out and the two of us would go away together."

"Where were you going to go?" Laura asked.

"Australia. Or maybe New Zealand." He looked away again. "I guess you think I'm pretty dumb, but she made me believe her."

"There are two more bombs that haven't exploded," Jace slid into the chair next to Leo. "We need to find them before some other innocent person gets hurt. Do you have any idea where Merry put them?"

"No." He angled his body toward Jace. "I promise if I knew I'd tell you. I don't want anyone else to die."

Laura's phone signaled an incoming text. She checked the display.

#5 safely removed from D. Stroud's home. Nothing at P. Stroud's

She glanced up. Jace was checking his phone also. He looked up and held her gaze. *We're getting close*, he seemed to say.

"Leo, did Merry ever mention a name of any particular person she wanted to take out with the bombs?" Laura asked.

"No. We never talked about it. She knew it upset me and she said she would rather talk about me. About us." He had the same dumbfounded look as a kid who had just learned Santa Claus wasn't real. Part of him couldn't believe Merry had lied about wanting to be with him.

"We need to go," Laura said abruptly, and left the room.

Jace hurried after her. "Why the rush?" he asked, catching up to her at the end of the hall. "What set you off?"

"He's still in love with her. She used him to kill three people so far and if she walked in that door right now and said she was ready to run away with him, he'd leave right away, if he could."

"I agree it's twisted, but it's nothing we haven't seen before."

"It just struck me how often love has been used to manipulate people in this case," she said. "Not just Leo, but Parker, too. Merry professed to love him and want to be his wife, but really all she wanted was his money. And even Donna Stroud refused to let Parker have a bigger say in running the company when he could have been a real help to her. Instead, she tried to cover up the severity of her husband's dementia and run things on her own, probably out of love."

"So love—or the wrong kind of love, or the wrong idea of love, can lead people to do bad things," Jace said. "We know that. But we also know the right kind of love can lead to truly wonderful things." He slid one arm around her waist and pulled her close.

She turned to him, fighting against the anguish building inside her. "What are we going to do after this case is over?" she asked.

To his credit, he didn't flinch, or ask her to explain what she meant. "What do you want to do?" he asked.

"We won't be pretending anymore to be husband and wife," she said. "We won't be living together, but we'll still be working together."

"I was getting used to seeing you when I wake up in the morning and at dinner every night," he said. His voice had the low, seductive quality that usually made her weak at the knees, but right now it just made her want to cry. "I was even getting used to all the vegetables you keep feeding me."

She pulled away from him, needing space to think. "Office romances are a bad idea," she said.

"There's nothing against them in the regulations. The Bureau has a history of accommodating married couples."

"Who said anything about marriage?" Panic clawed at her throat. This was Jace she was talking to. Not Jace Lovejoy, her pretend husband, but wild man Jace, who was reckless and cocky and everything she was not.

"I'm not trying to rush you," he said. "I'm just pointing out that if our supervisors don't have a problem with relationships between agents, why should you?"

"I can't talk about this now."

Something flared in his eyes, and she readied herself for a verbal battle. Maybe that was what she had wanted all along, to pick a fight that would lead to them breaking up. At least then she would prove she couldn't depend on a man like him.

"All right," he said, his voice even. "We won't talk now, but we need to talk later."

She didn't have to come up with an answer to that, because Ramirez and Rogers joined them. "We need to go through the list of Stroud employees," Ramirez said. "We think one of them will be the most likely target of the last bomb. You have a list, don't you?"

"It's on my laptop at the trailer," Laura said. "I'll go get it."

"I'll come with you," Jace said.

"No, you stay here." She looked at the other two. If she glanced at him, she might give away all her mixed-up feelings. "You should talk to Merry. See what she has to say. Jace can help with that."

"All right," Ramirez said. "We were just on our way to interview her."

Laura left before Jace could weigh in with his opinion. All she wanted was a little time alone to pull herself together. She needed to bring her focus back to the case, away from the man who had turned her life upside down.

JACE STARED AFTER LAURA. Just when he thought he had torn down the protective wall she had built around herself, she was working hard to build it back up again.

"Come on," Ramirez said. "Let's see if we can get anything out of Merry."

He had expected Merry to be afraid. She had no criminal record and for most people, being handcuffed, fingerprinted and photographed, and locked in a cell was a terrifying experience.

But Merry held her head up and looked him in the eye when he and Ramirez entered the interview room. "Where's Laura?" she asked.

"She had something else to do," Jace said.

"She didn't want to face me, did she?" Merry said.

"Would you prefer that Laura be here for this interview?" Ramirez asked. "I can get her."

"No way." Merry waved her hand in front of her face as if shooing away a fly. "I never liked her. Why would I want her here now?"

Ana sat across from Merry while Jace stood by the door. "Tell us about the bombs," Ramirez said after she had completed the preliminaries for the recording. "Why did you decide to set them?"

"You can't ignore a bomb, or pretend it was an accident. A little mistake. Bombs make a statement."

"What statement do they make?"

"I'm here and you're not going to ignore me."

"Who was ignoring you?" Ramirez asked.

"The Strouds ignored me. They thought I wasn't good enough for their perfect son." She sniffed. "I wonder if Donna thinks he's so perfect now that she knows he's a murderer."

"We found the fifth bomb, in Donna Stroud's car," Ramirez said. "We safely removed it and Donna is fine."

Merry frowned and said nothing.

"Where is the sixth bomb?" Jace asked.

Merry shifted her gaze to him. "You really haven't figured that out?"

"No," he admitted.

She looked amused. "Don't worry, you will."

The look in her eyes froze Jace. Ramirez asked another question and Merry looked away, but the smugness in Merry's gaze was burned on his retinas. She thought she had gotten away with something.

Revenge on someone she didn't like.

He left the room, pulling out his phone as he walked. He texted Laura. Come back. Don't go into the trailer. DON'T.

He punched in her number and listened to the call going through, running now. Then he remembered Laura had the truck. He grabbed a passing officer. "I need your keys."

The cop stared at him. "My keys?"

Laura wasn't answering her phone. Why wasn't she answering her phone? "Your car keys. I need your car keys." He dug out his badge and flipped it open. "It's an emergency."

Something in Jace's expression persuaded the man. He dug a bunch of keys from his pocket. "It's a blue Nissan Rogue, in the employee lot."

Jace found the car and started it, then fastened his seat belt with one hand while he hit Redial for Laura's number. "Pick up the phone!" he ranted as he peeled rubber on the turn from the parking lot.

He drove like a man possessed, barreling down the road with his emergency flashers on, sounding the horn at anyone who got in his way. Laura's phone went to voice mail. He ended the call and hit Redial again.

He was still half a mile from the trailer when she answered. "Sorry, I was on another call. What do you need?"

"Where are you?" he demanded, the car careening wildly as he took a sharp curve at speed.

"I'm just at the trailer. Give me a second."

"Don't go in." His heart pounded as if it would burst from his chest. He could hardly control the car on the rough road. "The bomb. I think the bomb is in the trailer," he said.

"The bomb?"

But he was already racing up the driveway, the car fishtailing as he braked hard and slid to a stop behind the truck.

Laura stood, halfway up the walk, gaping at him. He burst from the car, ran to her and pulled her close.

"Jace, what is going on?" she asked, her voice muffled against his chest.

"I was almost too late." His voice broke, and he could feel the tears hot on his cheeks, but he didn't care. He looked down at her. "I almost lost you," he said.

"I'm right here." She cupped his face in both hands and kissed him. A tender, comforting kiss that he never wanted to end.

The cop whose car he had borrowed arrived first, with Rogers and Ramirez, followed by a bomb squad with a German shepherd that alerted on the front door. "There's a bomb here, all right," a heavily helmeted man called. "Clear the area."

Laura insisted on driving. Shaken as she was, Jace

looked worse. He said nothing as she drove, not to police headquarters, where the others were headed, but to the lake, where they had spied on Leo and Parker. Was that really only ten days ago?

She parked in the lot and turned off the engine. They sat in silence for a long moment, the distant sounds of laughter and muffled conversation drifting to them on a hot breeze through the open windows.

"I guess it's over now," Jace said.

"Everything but the paperwork," Laura said.

"We can go back to Knoxville and our normal lives," he said.

Except her life would never be the same again. She unfastened her seat belt and turned toward him. "What you said before, about us. Being a couple."

"Yes?"

"I want to try. When you came running up to me outside the trailer—no one has ever looked at me that way before—as if I was the most precious thing in the whole world."

"That's because to me, you are."

He pressed the button to release his own seat belt and slid over to her. She tilted her head up for his kiss, but he merely smoothed her hair back from her forehead. "I love you, Laura Smith," he said. "I love how you always play by the rules because you recognize how quickly things can fall apart without them. I love that you're brave but not reckless, and you have the courage to try new things, even when it makes you uncomfortable."

"You make me uncomfortable." She slid her hand around the back of his neck. "In a good way."

"I'll keep working on that." He started to kiss her, but she held him off. "What?" he asked.

"I love you, too. And I've never said that to a man before." She swallowed. "Not even my dad. Do you think that's strange?"

The lines around his eyes tightened. "It's not strange," he said, his voice rough with emotion. "And I'm honored to be the first."

Then he did kiss her, and she fell into the kiss, diving in deep into this crazy lake of emotion that frightened her and thrilled her and made her happier than she had ever thought she could be.

* * * * *

LYING IN BED

JO LEIGH

1

SPECIAL AGENT RYAN VAIL tossed the brochure on the bed. The amazingly comfortable-looking bed, which was a far cry from most of the rat holes he'd been stuck with on various FBI stings and stakeouts. The Color Canyon Resort and Spa was a decadent oasis in the middle of the Las Vegas desert built for people with cash to spend and a yen for excitement and being pampered.

Ryan settled against the headboard, the puffy comforter billowing around him. Straight ahead was a forty-two-inch flat-screen TV. There was a wing chair, a leather love seat, an extravagantly stocked minibar and, if he turned his head to the right, beyond the private patio was a view of a nice little courtyard with a pool and spa pool all in the shadow of the Spring Mountains. It might be February in the rest of the world, but in the Vegas desert it was a balmy seventy-two degrees with copious sunshine on the docket for the rest of the week.

He grinned, pulled out his cell phone and went right to speed dial text.

You're gonna die when you see the bathtub.

He hit Send, adjusted the pillow behind him and checked out his work stuff. Another email update on Delilah Bridges, one of the cotherapists in charge of this barbecue. Four people ran the Intimate At Last retreat weekends, all suspects in a major blackmail scheme. Unfortunately for them, they'd unwittingly targeted a friend of James Leonard, the Deputy Director of the FBI.

Ryan's phone rang, and he knew it was his partner without even looking. "Jeannie Foster. How's my favorite witness for the State?"

"Shut up, you bastard," she said, her voice echoey, as if she were speaking in a vast hall. Or a toilet stall.

Of course, he'd taken a picture of the big-enough-for-a-party whirlpool tub, which he promptly sent her. A moment later, the mother of two cursed him with her usual flair.

"I hate court. I hate lawyers. I hate judges. And don't even get me started on juries. Get me the hell out of here, Ryan."

"It should be over soon, right?"

"Probably around the time of the next ice age. Jesus, they love to hear themselves talk."

"In a few hours you'll forget all about them. This place is something else. If I'm going to be forced to sleep with you, I'm glad it's in this beauty of a bed. Which is actually more comfortable than mine at home."

Jeannie laughed. "It's not the bed, honey, it's all your extracurricular activity. I think you'd have to find a titanium mattress to keep up."

"You're hilarious."

"Nothing is hilarious today," she said. "You get the new updates on Delilah?"

"Yeah."

Her sigh was long and filled with frustration. "Interesting about her father and his criminal record, but dammit, still nothing usable. With all the data we've collected, you'd think we'd have uncovered something more viable."

"Everyone makes mistakes. But," he added, "I'm going to be such a perfect mark, they're gonna wet themselves waiting to get to me. We'll be out of here in a few days."

"I thought you said the accommodations were super deluxe?"

He grinned. This is why he liked his partner, despite the fact that she could be a stick in the mud, what with being married and a mom. She was quick...and needed a vacation as badly as he did after the intensity of the past two months preparing for this sting. "Right. Maybe it'll take the whole week."

"There we go. I have to get back to the torture chamber. I hear they're planning on using the rack next."

"Hey, I'm gonna sign off on this phone, but Ryan Ebsen's cell and laptop haven't finished charging. If there's a God, I should be asleep when you arrive, so don't wake me."

"Coming off another late night, Romeo?"

"None of your business. Go be a witness."

"I'll talk to you in the morning," she said, and then she was gone, and he was faced with the prospect of what to do with the rest of the afternoon.

It would be more fun to play craps or hang out in one of the casino bars, but from the moment he'd checked in, FBI Special Agent Ryan Vail was locked in a vault for the duration of his stay, replaced by the fictitious Ryan Ebsen. Husband of the equally fictitious Jeannie Ebsen. Son of Felicia and Bob from Reseda, California.

Ryan sifted through the file, studying the cover story he already knew inside and out. But when you pretended to be someone else, there was no such thing as too much prep. Ebsen was a regional manager for a business software firm. His lovely bride of nineteen months didn't work because she didn't need to. Not because he brought in enough money to live their extravagant life, but because she had a trust fund. A very hefty trust fund.

But Mrs. Ebsen had been spending a little too much time at the club lately with a very handsome tennis coach, which made Ryan itchy. He doubted they were sleeping together, but there was always a risk that if she started to feel as if the honeymoon was over, she could find solace in the tennis pro's arms. It had been Ryan Ebsen's idea to attend this couple's retreat week, where they would "Learn how to transition to the deeper, more meaningful stage of a committed relationship."

Mr. Ebsen, the scoundrel, really, really wanted to make the marriage work. He'd grown attached to their Brentwood home, the Manhattan pied-à-terre, his Ferrari, the first-class travel. He'd even decided to break things off with Roxanne, the gorgeous receptionist at his office. He was nothing if not serious about this intimacy crap.

He continued to read the email from his team in White Collar Crimes back in L.A. The first report of blackmail had come shortly after a weekend Intimate At Last retreat in Los Angeles, and since it dealt with some historic artwork and blackmail, the L.A. team had taken point on the investigation and now this sting operation. The Vegas office was up to speed, of course. No one wanted a turf war, but there was a time limit on this gig, because in a matter of weeks, the suspects were moving their base of operation to Cancún, Mexico.

So he was on the clock. Since the missus wasn't here, he'd unpack, take a swim, order room service, charge his equipment and himself. Far from the carnal night Jeannie imagined, he'd been up till dawn talking the Long Beach P.D. out of putting his old man in jail. The stubborn idiot had been drunk off his ass again, trying to pick a fight with a half-dozen marines. It was like dealing with a rebellious teenager, only his father was in his fifties.

So sleep tonight, and tomorrow, he and Jeannie would be the very picture of a cookie-cutter couple: powdered sugar on the outside, but filled with lots and lots to lose if a certain trust-fund wife found out about her philandering hubby.

After he'd checked out the room service menu, and thank God there was an expense account because, Jesus, the prices, he opened up his suitcase while he found the sports channel on the TV. His thoughts weren't on the scoreboards, however, but on the reason he needed this operation to succeed beyond all expectations. Deputy Director Leonard was looking to fill a staff position in his Washington, D.C., office. Ryan was a contender in a very narrow pool of candidates. And now that he was in the spotlight, he was going to make damn sure he was a shining star.

ANGIE WOLF SIGHED WHEN SHE heard the voices of the rest of the White Collar Crimes team coming in from their break on the outdoor patio. Damn, it seemed as if they'd left two minutes ago, not nearly enough time for her to breathe let alone hear herself think.

They were a great bunch: competent, dedicated and generally nice people with whom she got along well considering work colleagues were always a crapshoot. But the past two months had been brutal. She'd spent way too many hours in the office and right now she'd give anything to be alone, preferably on a ten-mile run with nothing more to worry about than beating her last record.

Even as she heard them close in on the bullpen, she stayed just as she was, legs stretched out in front of her, ankles crossed, one heel on her desk, leaning back in her chair as far as she could. The fresh air would've been nice, but two of the team members smoked and that she could do without.

"Hey, how come you didn't come out for the lifting of the Red Bulls?"

Angie smiled at Paula, another Special Agent who'd been in charge of the artwork aspect of the operation. The painting in question was a Reubens, stolen during World War II and recovered in the late 1990s. It was worth millions, and had been "gifted" to a New Mexico art gallery, which had then sold it to an anonymous private collector.

The transaction had been legal on the surface, but the granddaughter of the original owner was certain her grandfather had been blackmailed into giving away the family treasure. The Deputy Director of the FBI had been friends with the family since birth.

And now, if Angie's White Collar Crimes team had done their jobs right, the task force was days away from zeroing in on the blackmailers.

Angie realized Paula was still waiting for an answer. Break time was definitely over. "Haven't we spent enough quality time together? Two months of eighty- and ninety-hour weeks? I mean, come on."

Paula flopped into her chair and turned it so she faced Angie. "You can take a break when you're dead. Or tonight, when we go out for drinks. That one, you're not getting out of. We'll use force if necessary."

"You and what army?"

"Me, for one." It was Brad Pollinger, Angie's partner in the field. He was followed into the room by several other members of the group, all of whom cheerfully let her know that they weren't above using every dirty trick in the book to get her to join them.

"Fine. But I'm having exactly one beer." The bullpen was pretty full now, with only Fred MIA, but he was perennially late.

"Don't you have any fun?" Paula eyed Angie's sturdy

low-heeled pumps propped on the desk. Comfort won over fashion every time for Angie. "Ever?"

"I have plenty," she said, although her definition of fun leaned more heavily toward achievement than clubbing. Whether it was cutting a few seconds off her morning run or working on side projects that could get her to the next stage of her ten-year plan, she wasn't much of a party gal.

She'd always been a big believer in setting short-term goals that fed directly into long-term strategies. Even though she'd stopped being a competitive runner, she still kept up the discipline and used the skills she'd picked up as a kid to keep herself on task.

From the beginning of this assignment, she'd realized the potential. With her computer programming skills and familiarity with investigation protocols she could make a significant contribution. And she had.

Angie's new program had led to the revelation about Delilah Bridges's father, that he'd been arrested under an alias for robbery on four separate occasions. It wasn't much as far as real leads went, but it was still a piece of an ever-expanding puzzle. The broader the picture, the more likely the pieces that didn't appear to connect would suddenly come together.

She'd worked damn hard on coding that sucker, a search engine with such a sexy algorithm it had given the guys in Cyber Crimes nerdgasms.

It had also been noteworthy enough to put her in the running for the position with the Deputy Director in Washington D.C. She wanted that job, badly. It would be a huge feather in her cap, the kind of promotion that would set her apart from the crowd. And it would put her squarely in the arena of real power, where she intended to not just stay, but thrive.

"Jeannie's the one having all the fun," came a voice from three desks down. "Can you imagine pretending to be Ryan Vail's wife all week?"

Angie stared at Sally Singer, a normally sedate forensic accountant, checking to see if she was serious.

"Um, yeah, I think Jeannie wins this round," Paula said, laughing, and God, looking a little envious.

Were they crazy? Ryan Vail was a hell of an agent, but he was a player of epic proportions. Everyone knew about his exploits. And while he kept his personal life separate from his work life, he hadn't even tried to keep his reputation from spreading. Legend had it that he'd "entertained" four different Victoria's Secret models, although no one was clear if that had been at the same time or not.

She had to give it to him. His technique was subtle and effective. To her own mortification, his charm had almost worked on her. Admittedly it had been at a party and they'd both had too much to drink, but it still embarrassed her to think about it. Nothing would have come of it, though, because the last thing she wanted was to be another notch on Vail's belt.

"I think you guys are nuts. This week isn't going to be easy for either of them," Brad said as he rolled a quarter over the backs of his fingers in what he called a dexterity exercise, but was in truth his way of coping without cigarettes. "Sharing a bed? Intimacy exercises? I mean, what the hell would intimacy exercises even be?"

"Oh, brother. If you have to ask I feel sorry for your wife," Angie said, and the rest of the crew laughed.

God, she hoped that cut the conversation short because she knew exactly what the exercises would entail. Lots of touching, kissing, maybe even getting naked and she absolutely could not think about Ryan in that context. At least not at work.

"I should have been the one to go undercover with him," Paula said. "Seriously. I would've appreciated the experience so much more than Jeannie."

Brad's laugh was more about disbelief than amusement. "You have a boyfriend."

Paula gave them an innocent smile. "It's not cheating if you're doing it for a case. That's like vacation sex but you still get paid."

"Like hell it's not cheating," he said to more laughter, which said more about their long hours and how punchy they all were than it did about the quality of the humor. "Angie should've been the one to go undercover with Vail. No offense to Jeannie but you two would've looked more like the Ebsens."

Angie snorted, and not with any grace. "Me and Vail? Yeah, right."

Paula shrugged. "You know I hate agreeing with Brad, but I see what he's saying." She tilted her head, glancing at Angie's shoes again. "The right clothes and hair and you two would look as if you'd stepped off the cover of *In Style*."

Angie chuckled. No one else did. Was it conceivable they were teasing her because they knew about her *thing* for Ryan? No, not possible. She barely glanced at him when he was in the office. Absolutely no one knew. Except for Liz, and Liz didn't count. As her closest friend who also happened to be an FBI agent in the San Diego office, she knew almost everything about Angie. But certainly no one at work had an inkling that Angie might have thought about Ryan in a sexual context. A few times. "Shut up. All of you. As if I'd ever volunteer for an assignment with Vail."

"You liar," Paula said, a little louder than was appropriate in the bullpen. "I've seen you check out that ass. Everyone with a pulse has checked out that ass."

"I've got a pulse," Brian said. "Trust me. I have never—"

"I meant people who were into that kind of guy."

"I have," Sally said, raising her hand without a bit of

shame. "And Angie, my dear friend, as cool as you play it, I've seen you blush when he walks by."

"Probably because Vail had done something to blush about." Angie was terrified she'd start blushing right this minute. The subject needed to be changed, although it wouldn't hurt to make a definitive statement. "I mean, come on. To sleep in the same bed as him? To act like his wife? Palmer could've offered to pay off my car loan and no way in hell would I have—"

Assistant Director Gordon Palmer walked into the bullpen, and Angie swung her feet off the desk. Everyone else in the room sat up straight, dropping the banter like hot coals. "We have a problem," he said, as if his demeanor hadn't already tipped them off.

Palmer was a good man, a fair boss and someone who had a knack for assigning the right agents to the right tasks, unlike several A.D.s she could mention. "Agent Foster is being held over in court. Indefinitely. We've been trying to get a postponement, but the judge won't budge."

Angie's chest tightened as if pressed by a vise. All their work, all the hours they'd spent putting this sting together.... This was the final Intimate At Last retreat being held in the United States.

"However," Palmer said, turning toward Angie with purpose. Had he overheard? Was this part of the joke? No, he wasn't the type. "There is one solution."

The pressure in her chest got so heavy she could hardly breathe. "Oh, my God."

"You're up to speed with every aspect of the case," Palmer said, making it very clear he was completely serious. "You helped build the cover stories. I feel certain that you can pull it off."

"Wouldn't Paula be a better choice?" she said, her voice

tight and her hands gripping her chair as if her life depended on it. "She was just saying..."

Paula shook her head, all business. "I don't know the cover, not like you do."

Palmer walked to Angie's desk. "I can't order you to do this," he said, softly now, for her ears only. "And there will be no negative repercussions if you aren't comfortable taking over the assignment. I realize it's a sensitive situation. No one's going to blame you for declining to step in."

The very thought of sleeping in the same bed as Ryan Vail made her skin tingle, made her want to hide under her desk. For all his colorful reputation, he would be a perfect gentleman, she had no doubt, but that didn't mean she could be a perfect lady. Knowing she'd never be with Ryan in real life had no effect whatsoever on what she did with him in her fantasies. The idea of actually sleeping with him... She felt sick with panic.

Taking her own idiotic issues out of the equation, there were several practical reasons to turn down the assignment. She might have helped with the cover stories, but she couldn't step directly into Jeannie's shoes.

However, she couldn't dismiss the short- and long-term benefits of saying yes. She didn't want to let down the team. And if she'd thought writing the search engine code would get her noticed, agreeing to the undercover work would put her front and center in the Deputy Director's radar.

She weighed the pros and cons: pretending to be Ryan's wife all week versus nailing the job in D.C.

She stood. "We don't have much time. Jeannie and I aren't close to the same size so I'll have to get a new wardrobe. We'll need to put my paperwork and computer cover in place faster than is humanly possible."

A.D. Palmer shook her hand. "Thank you, Wolf. Or should I say, Mrs. Ebsen."

2

HE WOKE TO THE BED DIPPING. For a few seconds, Ryan's adrenaline spiked until he remembered where he was. He groaned at the bright red numbers on the clock. "One a.m.? What the…?"

The rest of the question got lost in the dark, but it didn't matter, because Jeannie didn't answer. He didn't blame her, she must be exhausted. At least she hadn't turned on the lights. And he had asked her not to wake him. "You okay?"

She tugged sharply on the covers, pulling more of them to her side of the bed. But she didn't confirm or deny.

Ryan craned his neck until he could just make out her head on the pillow, her back to him, hunched and tight. Must have gotten stuck at the airport or something. If she didn't want to talk about it, fine.

He curled onto his side hoping to find the dream she'd interrupted. It had been nice. Smelled nice. He sighed as he closed his eyes, thinking vaguely that he'd been right that sharing a bed with her was no big deal. Especially when he considered what else was going to take place in the next few days.

It was amazingly quiet; they weren't in the hotel proper, but a separate group of bungalows that had their own locked gate, their own pools, even an exclusive bar. That's why the retreat cost an arm and a leg. So they could be near the secluded Namaste courtyard where the private couples retreat would take place. Too bad he had to work. This was the best vacation spot he'd been to in years.

He sighed as he let himself slip deeper and deeper into sleep.... The scent came back, a little like the beach and jasmine, low-key and sexy like—

His eyes flew open. His heart thudded as his pulse raced and it had to be the dream. The dream had gotten him confused. That's all. No need to panic. That was Jeannie next to him. For God's sake, who else would it be?

So why wasn't he turning around? Even in the dark, it would only take one look to know for sure and then he would cool his jets and go back to sleep. Undercover jitters. It happened. Not to him, but he'd heard tales. Nothing to see. No chance in hell the boss would do something insane like pull a switch at this stage of the game.

Moving slowly, not wanting to disturb her, Ryan twisted until he could see his bed partner. He hadn't used the blackout curtains because he never did—might have to see in the middle of the night. Like now. Just to check. Just to be certain.

He swallowed as his gaze went to the back of Jeannie's head. *Shit.* It was a trick of the moonlight. Jeannie's blond hair looked darker, that's all. And longer. He bent closer, grabbing his side of the mattress so he wouldn't tumble on top of her, then took a major sniff.

"What the—" Ryan sat up so fast the whole bed shook. His hand flailed in his search for the light switch, but even after he'd found it he didn't blink.

It wasn't Jeannie. The woman next to him. Wasn't. Jeannie. Jeannie smelled like baby powder and bananas. The woman next to him smelled exactly like...

She groaned and as she turned over, he whispered, "No, no, no, no."

Special Agent Angie Wolf glared back at him with red-rimmed eyes. She wasn't supposed to be here. In the bed. With him.

"Jeannie is being held over in court," she said, her voice as gruff as the hour. "They weren't able to get a postponement. If you'd answered your phone or picked up your messages, you would know that. Palmer asked me to take her place. I would prefer not to be here, but we really don't have a choice if we want to salvage the operation. Now, turn off the light and go back to sleep. Please."

It took him a minute to digest what she'd said. Eventually he nodded. "Okay."

She punched the pillow, looked once more in his general direction and said, "Oh, and if you wake me before eight, I'll kill you with my bare hands," then pulled the covers over her head while Ryan thought of five different reasons he should get up and go straight back to L.A.

That would end any chance he might have had for the D.C. job, but hey, he was a good agent. He could still rise to the top, even if he had to climb stairs instead of ride the elevator. Which would leave one of the other candidates to slip right into that sweet, sweet position working for the Deputy Director. For example, the woman sharing the goddamn bed.

What he couldn't do was pretend to be married to Angie Wolf. This operation was possible because Jeannie and him, they had seen each other in their underwear before. It had been funny. No embarrassment whatsoever. Hell, he was pals with her husband. He played with her kids. They were cool, him and Jeannie, no matter what cockamamie new-age tantric yoga tofu-covered bullshit they might have to sit through.

Angie Wolf was a whole different kettle of fish. She was hot, for one thing. Hot as in smokin' hot. Tall, lean, small up top, but on her it worked, and legs... Man, those runner's legs. Her dark hair was straight and thick and flowed halfway down her back, and he'd found himself too often staring into her cocoa-colored eyes.

Worse than that, he'd almost broken one of his cardinal rules because of her: he did not cross the line with anyone connected to the job. But at last year's Halloween party they'd come uncomfortably close. He'd been joking, sort of, but then there was this heat between them, and he'd realized that the fire had been smoldering for a long time, probably since they'd met. But A.D. Palmer had interrupted what had been dangerously close to a kiss and she'd stepped back. He'd laughed as if it was no big deal, as if his heart hadn't been beating a wicked drum solo in his chest or that he'd been half-hard just from the scent of her perfume. They'd kept their distance since. Sixteen months later they still had to be careful because the pull hadn't diminished one iota. At least not for him. She was kind of hard to gauge.

God, just a few hours ago, he'd been laughing about the Intimate At Last brochure. Body work. Couples massages. *Delightful homeplay assignments.* Shit. How was this supposed to work now?

Once the light was off, he stared into the shadows of the room. He wasn't about to fall asleep anytime tonight. Angie Wolf was going to be his wife. For a week. Holy hell.

THE FIRST THING ANGIE thought when she woke up was how surprised she was that she'd slept at all. She'd assumed sharing a bed with Vail would have kept her wide-awake for the entire night, but the exhaustion of the day had won out. At least the bed was big enough that they wouldn't have to touch. The thought of feeling his bed-warmed body brush against hers was enough to cause a surge of panic that woke her more efficiently than a cold shower.

"I'm ordering coffee," he said, shifting behind her. "You want?"

She exhaled as she remembered her role. Not the one as his wife, but as his partner. "Yeah, thanks."

The sound of the bedding rustling as he reached for the phone caused her muscles to tense and her jaw to tighten. So much for her resolve. She'd made a choice yesterday. She could have refused the assignment. As with everything worth having, and there was no doubt that the job in D.C. was, compromise and sacrifice came with the package.

No matter what her personal feelings were toward Ryan, her only task this week was to play his loving, entitled, slightly insecure wife so that Ryan became the perfect target for blackmail. The end. Nothing else mattered. Not sharing a bed, not the intimacy exercises they would participate in, not the inevitable touching. As long as they were both completely clear that no "optional" nudity was going to occur under any circumstances, they'd be fine.

Behind her, Ryan hung up the telephone, then the comforter shifted as he stood. Angie stayed frozen on her side just long enough for things to get really awkward. A quiet huff broke the silence and a moment later, the bathroom door closed.

She rolled onto her back and the way she relaxed told her just how tense she'd been. She hadn't moved all night. Good thing because she'd been so close to the edge she could have very easily fallen right on the floor.

A shower would help things immensely. Personal issues aside, yesterday had been a killer. She'd barely made it on the last flight to Vegas. Getting into character had been insanity. While she'd had to suffer a mani/pedi, two of the L.A. team had hit Rodeo Drive armed with her measurements and crossed fingers to pick up a complete designer wardrobe.

Underwear. Bras. Shoes. Earrings. She hadn't had someone buy her panties since she'd been twelve.

Her own style was business casual, built around the fact that she carried a Glock in a shoulder holster. She'd be more comfortable dressing up as a vampire than pulling off Prada or bebe.

The bathroom door opened, and there was Vail. Shirtless. Wearing UCLA Bruins sweats that hung low on his sharp-edged hips. Of course, he was sculpted like a professional athlete, a swimmer, damn him. Even worse, he had a Hollywood–handsome face to go with it. Dark hair, piercing green eyes, goddamn chiseled jaw. She let out a groan but immediately stretched, trying to make it seem natural, and not a reaction to the six-pack and the shoulders-to-hips ratio.

He tried to fight a grin, not very convincingly, then took a few more steps toward the big dresser. "The bathroom's all yours. I showered last night."

Angie threw the covers back and swung her legs over, determined to get her act together. What she needed was to talk to Liz, who couldn't have picked a worse time than yesterday to be incommunicado.

"You gonna sleep in your clothes every night?" Ryan asked. "I suppose it wouldn't blow the gig, but I imagine it won't be very comfortable."

"Yeah, no, it was late," she said, keeping her head down as she went to get her suitcase. Why wasn't the room bigger? Like the size of Montana? "At least the room's nice."

"So is the minibar."

She didn't look up at him. "I don't think the budget's going to cover twenty-dollar beers." The snick of the pull handle on her suitcase seemed alarmingly loud, but then everything since she'd agreed to this…situation had felt excessive.

To give Ryan credit, he was being extremely civil. She'd been worried he'd be in her face about the change in plans.

She'd also imagined him very, very pissed. But then, they were officially on the job, and working for the government made acceptance of the absurd a necessity.

Ryan was a good agent. He was dedicated. More than that, he was smart. He wasn't as concerned with rules and regs as the brass would like, but that wasn't a big deal, not to her. He got the job done. He could be pleasant. Nice, even. He'd never been anything but professional, even after they'd had that brief...misunderstanding at the Halloween party. Hell, he'd moved on without missing a beat.

It was as a man that he failed spectacularly.

No, that wasn't fair. He had different values than her own, that's all. It wasn't up to her to judge someone's sexual practices. If he wanted to sleep with the entire female population of Los Angeles, it was his own business.

She made sure she didn't look too anxious as she made her way to the bathroom, but slamming the door might have given him a clue. When the back of her head bumped the door she realized that she'd done nothing but behave like a child since she'd opened her eyes. Not moving, not looking at him, avoiding his touch. The man didn't actually have cooties, and she would eventually have to meet his gaze. Touch him. Act like a professional. Act like his loving wife.

The first thing she did was turn on the shower. The second thing was to pull her iPad out of her suitcase and turn it on to Skype.

Liz answered the call in seconds. "I got your message. What the hell have you gotten yourself into?" she asked, and Angie could see her redheaded friend perched at her breakfast counter, still wearing her Nike running gear. In front of her was a glass of orange juice and a bowl, probably oatmeal.

"I'm already in Vegas," Angie said, keeping her voice low. She didn't want Ryan to hear, God no. "With Ryan Vail."

"Holy crap, Angie. Did you not have a choice?"

"Yes and no. I mean, how could I tell Palmer I didn't want to step in? The whole case would've gone down the drain."

"What are you going to do?"

"The job."

"But..."

"I know!" Angie said. "God, why weren't you around yesterday? I have to sleep in the same bed with him."

"Oh, sweetie, that is the least of your worries. Do you know what tantric massages are like?"

Angie closed her eyes. "Stop it. That's not helpful."

"Well, I'm not sure what I can do from here." Liz lifted the iPad and brought it up until her face almost filled the screen. "You can do this. I know you can do this, because you are fierce and you are a woman to be reckoned with. Besides, Ryan isn't about to cross any lines with you. In fact, I'd bet a million he's going to go overboard to make sure nothing hinky could even be implied."

"I wish I could fit in a run," Angie said. "I'm exhausted, but I'm wired."

"Find time later. What do you have to do right now?"

Taking a deep breath, Angie let her friend's steady voice calm her down. "Shower. Dress like Angie Ebsen. Coordinate our stories so we don't contradict each other. Go to the first session. Introductions, filling in forms. Then lunch, and after that, there's some kind of bonding ritual. God, Liz, a *bonding ritual*."

"Don't think about anything past lunch. Introductions are a piece of cake. You know the backstory, you're expected to be nervous. You'll be fantastic." Liz smiled broadly, and damn if that didn't help, as well.

"Now go get clean, then put on your disguise. Break it down like your training schedule. I'll be in the field, but you can call me during the day. I shouldn't be late, though, so we can Skype tonight, okay?"

"Sounds good. Thanks."

"No problemo. Later."

The screen went dark, Angie clicked off the tablet and stepped into the shower in no time. She'd already solved her first problem. No way she could have lasted the week with people calling her Jeannie. Thankfully Brian had thought of a way out of that little mess. Angie would be her middle name, the one she preferred. The computer guys had woven it into all the paperwork and background references.

The story of the Ebsens would remain intact. Unfortunately the team had used a lot of Jeannie's personal history for Mrs. Ebsen's childhood, and because Jeannie and Ryan had known each other so long, no time had been wasted filling in all those details.

Now those blanks would, by necessity, have to be replaced with Angie's past. And Ryan needed to give her the Cliff's Notes version of his history, as well.

With the shower running, she stripped, grabbed her toiletries and used her time to visualize herself as Angie Ebsen. She imagined the way she'd carry herself as someone wealthy, who had high-level expectations about service and general conversation. She could see herself playing the part, she really could, up until the point where she had to act as though she was in love with Ryan.

God, this was going to be tricky. Even in her own head, all she could picture was the humiliation of that single horrifying moment if, no, not if...*when* Ryan figured out that she still wanted him. How he'd been the man in her fantasies for more nights than she cared to admit.

She stared down at the unbelievably expensive engagement and wedding rings on the third finger of her left hand. She was so screwed.

RYAN REALIZED HE'D BEEN staring at the bathroom door for a while and that he might want to move before Angie finished with her shower. He shook his head as he turned back to the dresser to get ready for their first day of marriage.

He supposed they'd have to talk about it now. *It* being the distance they'd been maintaining for over a year. The polite nods without eye contact, the apologies that followed accidental touches. Walking on eggshells like that at work had been bad enough, even though their jobs required minimal interaction. But behaving that way here would ruin the mission.

What they needed was to be all over each other. Just shy of obsessively on his part, a little less so on hers. Jeannie and he had been A-OK with that plan. They'd practiced until they'd been able to stop cracking up with each vaguely sexual touch. But with Angie he faced the opposite problem.

Every touch was sexual with nothing vague about it. Hell, the slightest brush of Angie's skin had caused a chain reaction that left him unsettled and heading toward hard. Thank God he wasn't a teenager anymore, or he'd have had to walk around the office with a textbook handy to cover himself. As it was, he always managed to make a quick exit or distract himself long enough to settle down, but that wouldn't be a viable option when they were in public here.

He pulled out a pair of khakis and a striped polo shirt, selected, along with the rest of his wardrobe, by a personal shopper who specialized in outfitting guys who made fifty times Ryan's yearly salary. Even his boxer briefs and socks were ridiculously expensive, and he paid attention to his clothes.

The sound of the shower registered and, of course, his brain went straight to a very detailed picture of Angie naked with water running down her chest, a drop hesitating on the edge of her rigid nipple, streaking down her stomach only to get caught in the trimmed thatch of dark hair that signaled the approach to his happy place. Never mind that he hadn't actually seen her naked. He had a good eye and could connect the dots.

And right there was the crux of the problem. The big, elephant-size problem.

In order to make the sting operation a success, they would have to break every boundary they'd very carefully set in place, consciously or not, at the risk of his libido overtaking his good sense.

Angie was not the kind of woman who would make exceptions for special circumstances. Even if they hadn't been colleagues, she wasn't his type of woman at all.

Physically? No question. She was a wet dream even when she wasn't in the shower. But he suspected she wanted someone she could count on. Someone who would be there for the long haul. A man who would be an excellent husband and father. A stand-up kind of guy to share her life with.

He wanted a woman who didn't particularly care who he was, as long as there was a bed and he could keep up his end of the bargain.

So not only were he and Angie required to mix business with pleasure for an entire week, they already knew that getting too close was playing with fire. Hell, all they'd done was consider, for like five minutes, hooking up, and they'd both backed off so fast they'd left skid marks.

This arrangement did not bode well. For either of them.

As soon as he was finished dressing, he speed-dialed Jeannie.

"I was going to call you."

Ryan sat on the edge of the bed, leaning his elbows on his knees. "How is this gonna work?"

"She can do it," Jeannie said, in her *I'm being serious* voice. "We spoke last night and she's completely committed to getting the job done. Just spend as much time as you can this morning going over your personal histories. Between the two of you, you'll make it happen. I doubt there's going to be anything heavy on the first day."

"We can still postpone this. A family emergency or something. Before they meet her."

Jeannie's silence had him wishing he'd kept that last thought to himself. She didn't know about the thing between him and Angie. Didn't need to. No one did.

"What's wrong with you?" Jeannie said finally. "Delaying could blow the whole sting. We've all worked too hard to get this far. Sometimes we've just got to roll with the punches. I figured you better than anyone could deal with that."

"I know, I know. You're right."

Again she hesitated. "Is there something you want to tell me?"

"Nope. Nothing. I'm good."

"Okay. You two look great together. You're the perfect bait. Hey, get the evidence we need to proceed and you can come on home. Easy as pie."

"Jeannie?"

"What?"

"You can shove that pie where the sun don't shine."

"Why, Ryan Vail, I never."

"Yes, you have."

Her laugh made him even sorrier she wasn't here. But their conversation told him he'd better get his act together fast. "The trial going okay?"

"Same crap, different day. I'm really sorry, kiddo. I would have been there if I could."

"I know."

"Call me tonight, let me know what I'm missing."

"If I can, I will." He disconnected, shoved his phone in his pocket, hoping like hell there would be nothing to tell. Ever. That he and Angie would pull this sting off with no hiccups, and then he'd be on his way to D.C. to a new job before he had to give her another thought.

A minute later he still hadn't moved and room service was at the door.

THE COFFEE WAS ALL SET OUT on the patio when Angie left the bathroom. Two laptops were open, one on the table which Ryan was staring at, the other on the dresser. That laptop had to be Ryan Ebsen's because the screen saver consisted of revolving pictures of Ferraris.

She debated unpacking, but she needed the caffeine too desperately to wait.

Outside, it was surprisingly warm for February in the high desert, and the view of the mountains was beautiful. Ryan had a large cheese Danish on his plate, but in front of her seat at the round glass table was a yogurt-and-fruit parfait with a bran muffin on the side. She stared at the breakfast, then looked up to meet Ryan's gaze, but only for a second. "What's this?"

"Sustenance." He poured her a cup of coffee, then put the carafe down.

"Thank you." Interesting that it was the exact breakfast she would have ordered for herself.

"You're welcome. Look," he said, meeting her gaze. "I believe what's required here is to barrel through all notions of propriety and just get down to how the hell we're going to pull this off."

Angie knew she was blushing, she could feel the heat rise on her cheeks. "Can I at least have a cup of coffee first?"

"Yeah," he said, easing up, at least somewhat. His posture was still stiff and he could only hold her gaze for a few seconds at a time.

She proceeded to put the cream in her coffee, to take a few moments as she sipped to catch the view and try to relax.

Ryan looked different in his Ebsen clothes. She'd never imagined him in khakis and a too-tailored-to-be-off-the-rack polo shirt. The suede bucks were the perfect touch to put him on the Street Style map on *GQ*. He'd always dressed sharply, but this change made him look rugged and elegant at the same time, and she'd better stop thinking about him in or out of clothes and get down to work.

After another big sip of almost hot enough coffee, she gave him a nod.

"Okay," he said. "Starting with registration, we're going to be the Ebsens to everyone at the hotel, so from this moment forward, we're in character. We won't be able to pull it off 24/7, but the more we practice, the easier it will get. Your part shouldn't be too tough. I'm playing a ruthless bastard, so you won't have to act much, at least not to start."

She flinched at his words until she saw the way his mouth quirked up. Joking, just joking. Everyone in the unit, including Ryan, kidded around, often with really black humor, and as of yesterday afternoon, it had never made her blink. Now, though... Pulling out a smile, she said, "I don't think you're a bastard. I think you're going to be very good at this."

After a questioning look he cleared his throat as he reached down beside his chair and brought up a thick file folder.

"All right, then," she said. "You want to go first?"

"Go first?"

"I need you to tell me as much as you can about the parts of your real life you used to fill in your cover background. We let you and Jeannie handle that aspect because she knows things about you that the rest of us on the team don't."

"Right." He paused, obviously thinking over what he wanted to make public and frowning as if he wanted to be anywhere but sitting across from her. "I, uh. Huh. Maybe we should... How about you tell me what you know about me and I'll confirm, deny, fill in."

Bad idea. Really, really bad. It would be just like her to say some idiotic thing she'd made up in her head about him. Or ask a question that had nothing to do with the sting. "That seems more complicated than it has to be. And frankly, confusing."

He looked out at the distant mountains. "I'm not trying to be evasive, but what Jeannie knows, she's learned over the last three years."

"I understand. She's your partner. Kind of like a wife in a way."

"A wife?" He laughed. "We're not that close."

"You know what I mean," she said, saw the fleeting panic in his face and considered that maybe he didn't. "Have you ever lived with a woman?"

"No." He seemed affronted. "No," he repeated, this time drawing out the word and meeting her eyes. "You?"

She started to shake her head but stopped herself. "Nope, never have lived with a woman. I was trying to get you to think in terms of what you'd expect a wife should know about you."

He rubbed his eyes, and murmured, "Maybe you should go first."

Dammit. Angie was going to have to take the lead on this and she'd been counting on following his example. "Okay," she said finally, reminding herself to be cool and act her age. "We have one shot at these people, so when I'm finished, you can ask me any questions you like. And then we'll discuss exactly how far we're willing to go to see this through to the end."

3

"I KNOW YOU BUILT Jeannie's tennis playing into the cover story, but I'm just okay at tennis so we'll have to be careful there. Running is my thing," Angie said, and Ryan nodded because he already knew that. "In fact, I run every morning and I plan to stick to my schedule while we're here." She paused. "Do you want to write some of this down?"

He shrugged. "I will when I need to. But I already knew you were a runner."

"Really?" she asked with a slight tilt of her head.

"Yeah, you know, that 10k you did in August?"

The head tilt was now accompanied by narrowed eyes. "I don't recall talking about that at work."

Ryan stared at her. Damn. There was a risk of getting too close to the line if he spoke to her about her runner's body. Hell, it was obvious that she was dedicated to the sport. He flashed back to the picture he'd envisioned of her in the shower and he grabbed a pen, then ducked inside the room for a moment to grab a blank piece of paper and cool himself down. By the time he returned to the table, he was fine. "I must've heard someone mention it, but yeah, I'll write it down."

She seemed to buy that answer and turned to gaze thoughtfully through the sliding-glass door. "I'm not exactly sure what kind of subjects are going to come up during the intimacy exercises, so I'm gonna cover a broad spectrum. Um, I don't like roses. Of any color. If a man were to—" Her gaze shot back to him. "You'd send me a simple fresh-cut mixed bouquet if you were to do that sort of thing. Nothing fancy and prearranged."

He took notes. Flowers. Shit, he wouldn't have thought of that, though he'd seen Jeannie buy carnations on the corner after work. He liked that Angie didn't care for fancy arrangements, although he couldn't imagine why it made any difference.

"Good Lord, how much can you write about flowers?"

He looked up. "Which one is your favorite?"

"Tulips, lilies, no, lilies remind me of funerals. Anything but roses and lilies."

"Got it."

"I don't drink much, because of the running. But I don't mind sour apple martinis or white Russians. I can't see Mrs. Ebsen throwing back a Miller."

Ryan smiled. "I don't think I'd marry anyone who didn't like beer."

"I didn't think you'd marry anyone for any reason."

"That's true," he admitted, returning his eyes to the paper. "Back to Mr. and Mrs. Ebsen. I know you like sports in general so let's get that squared away."

She nodded. "I cross train in mixed martial arts, a beach volleyball league and ballet, but I watch basketball. I'm not into football at all, or hockey, sorry. Baseball bores me to tears, so let's just stick with basketball. You do like basketball, right?"

"Not as much as hockey, but yeah, I'm a Lakers man." He'd bet his official Gretzky jersey that she already knew that. He'd won the office pool several times. Just like she'd known he was into hockey. He remembered a disagreement they'd had about Larry Bird that had taken place before the Halloween incident.

"Good," she said. "We met at a sports event, then. A championship game."

He pulled out his own phone and started punching keys. "The 2010 Finals, there was a fund-raiser in one of the owner's suites. How does that sound?"

She nodded and scribbled on the margin of her report. "Perfect."

"Why don't we make that our safety topic, then. I don't think anyone would question it. We're pretty athletic looking. Meanwhile, what are you going to do about your name?"

"Tell them I go by my middle name, Angie."

"That'll work." He looked up from his phone.

Angie rose and stretched over to reach the coffee carafe. After topping off his cup, she tended to her own. It was interesting seeing her dressed as Angie Ebsen. Her blouse was red with big sleeves but snug around the waist. Nice, but not nearly as great as the slim, black pants. Completely unlike anything she wore to the office.

He'd never thought much about how she neutralized her looks by the clothes she wore. As far as he could recall, she completely avoided anything that hugged her figure, which was a damn shame.

"My favorite extravagant restaurant in L.A. is Mellise, which is somewhere the Ebsens would go," she said, sitting again, and allowing him to relax. "Do you know it?"

"Yep, it wasn't far from where I grew up. What about Matsuhisa?"

"Never been, but I have been to Nobu. If anyone asks, we'll use Matsuhisa or Mellise, okay?" She sipped her own coffee, then took a bite of bran muffin. If her surprised smile was anything to go by, she liked it a lot.

"What else do people want to know when they first meet?" he asked, anxious about the time they had left before they had to report to the workshop. "No kids, so there's that."

Angie swallowed, then dabbed her lips with her napkin, drawing his gaze. "The cover story takes care of a lot. Where we live, no pets. My parents being filthy rich, me attending school abroad, which Angie Ebsen doesn't like to talk about. Simple."

He went back to his notes, afraid she'd caught him staring. "I can't think of anything else."

"No questions?"

He shook his head.

"Okay, now you fill me in."

Ryan looked up, the urge to get out of this strong, but he couldn't think of one reason she'd believe. He'd have to tell her what he could, and let her ask her questions. It wasn't as if his life was anything horrible, or even that much of a secret. He simply preferred to keep work and personal life separate. It was easier and cleaner to let his coworkers believe what they wanted. Some of which was actually true.

ANGIE COULD BE WRONG, but she got the feeling Ryan's hesitation was more about figuring out what not to say than how to fill her in on his life. He had to know she'd heard the stories. It wasn't as if anyone said anything terrible about him. On the contrary. Men seemed to be jealous, but not enough to make him a target, and the women she knew...well, they were mostly like Paula or Sally if they weren't happily married, like Jeannie.

Finally, after finishing off his Danish and the last of his coffee, he said, "I grew up in Santa Monica with my father. Don't know much about my mother. She left when I was a kid. No siblings. I don't have any other hobbies except sports, and yes, even though it's less convenient, I work out at Gold's."

"Oh, I'm sorry."

"It's not that big a deal. In a pinch I'll go to the FBI gym."

"I meant...about your—"

"That was no big deal, either. Anyway, I graduated from UCLA. We already talked restaurants, I run, but it's not my thing, and I play tennis occasionally. I prefer a pickup game, but what the hell."

"So if someone in the group asks us to double at tennis? Remember I'm only so-so."

"Then let's give that a pass. We'll need to be *on* every time we're in public. At least if we go to the casino, there's lots of distractions. The important bit is to get me into a situation where I can confess my sins. That'd probably be with Delilah or Ira. They're licensed and have to honor client confidentiality, but if the opportunity arises with the other two staff members, I'll jump on it. No telling who's involved in their scheme."

Angie nodded, trying to digest all the data Ryan had rushed through. No mother? Wow, that had to have been rough. But it might explain why he played the field as if his life depended on it.

"What about movies?" he asked.

"I'm in favor of them."

He rolled his eyes, which was a good thing, in her opinion. Things had grown a little tense. "Fine. Spoilsport. I liked *Date Night. Sin City. To Kill a Mockingbird. African Queen. Harold and Maude.*"

Ryan inhaled. "I saw one of those movies."

"Let me guess. *Sin City.*"

His eyes narrowed. "That was a trick, wasn't it? You didn't like *Sin City* at all."

"I have no idea what you're talking about."

"Yeah, right," he scoffed, but it was friendly. Nice. Getting closer to the comfortable ballpark.

"So what are your favorites?"

"I know you're expecting all the Bruce Lee and Chuck Norris movies that have ever been made, but that wouldn't be true."

"You don't like Bruce Lee and Chuck Norris?"

"Not *every* one of their movies, no."

"Seriously, guy flicks exclusively?" she asked.

"I've gotten misty over a film or two. I'm not that much of a stereotype."

"Misty, huh? Like when Shaun had to kill his mom in *Shaun of the Dead* or when Rose let DiCaprio go in *Titanic*?"

Ryan's eyes widened. "You liked *Shaun of the Dead*?"

Angie couldn't help laughing.

"What?" Ryan looked hurt. Actually hurt. "It's a classic."

She smiled very slowly. "I agree. But for the purposes of this exercise, you go with *Shaun,* I'll go with *Titanic*. It explains so much in so few words."

"You're mocking me. You shouldn't make fun of someone's taste in films."

"You're right." She pursed her lips, trying to keep the straight face she'd struggled to find. "So we won't even start with novels."

"Can I ask one thing, though?"

Angie nodded.

"Is it a genetic thing with women, *To Kill a Mockingbird*?"

"It's more a Gregory Peck thing, I think. Also, how incredible Atticus is with Scout." She thought for a moment. "But maybe it's genetic."

Ryan seemed satisfied with that, and for the next while they ran through a quick list of favorite foods, best vacations, mountains versus beaches and family pets.

At least the questions and answers had helped ease some

of her concerns. "You know, I agree that there's not going to be a lot of intrusive questions, not on the first day, but we want to set the tone accurately. The single most important thing about both of us is my family fortune. So let's get really clear about why the Ebsens are here. I don't know you've been cheating on me, but do I suspect? Jeannie said she hadn't decided yet, that she was going to take her cues once she spoke to the staff, but I'd like to hear your opinion."

Ryan looked pensive for a moment, and she hadn't noticed before but when he was thinking, he looked straight down, not to the right or left. Unusual. "I think it works better if you're a little suspicious, which will mean keeping me close. I also think that, for today at least, we act like happy lovers but not ridiculously so. We're nervous. Not sure what to expect. So we stick together, hold hands. Whisper a lot. Don't stand out from the crowd. We can always switch gears as we get more comfortable."

He took a look at his watch, then excused himself, closing himself behind the bathroom door. She knew he had his phone with him, and at his unexpected exit she wondered if he was ducking out to privately call Jeannie. Or maybe another woman. None of her business, she reminded herself, not in this room. Why couldn't she have been partnered with Brian? He would have been a nightmare, too, but in a totally different way. At least with Brian, there was no fear of being caught ogling like a lovesick teen.

While Angie polished off her yogurt she thought about what Ryan had said so she wouldn't end up blowing their cover in the first five minutes. With the notable exception of the attraction situation, she was actually getting a little revved about this sting and what they were about to do. It had been a while since she'd been assigned to the field, and though she loved her computers more than Paula loved her cats, there was an adrenaline rush with casework that went unmatched, even by winning a major race.

An undercover assignment called on skills that were rarely used in any other type of investigation. Which was terrifying, and also exciting, although it would have been even more thrilling if they could have made the actual bust, but that wasn't up for debate. Besides, the blackmail text likely wouldn't come until after the week was over.

As long as she kept the goal firmly in mind, she should be fine. Jeannie had offered her services as her coach, and Angie had promised she wouldn't hesitate to call if she felt out of her depth.

"We don't have much time left," Ryan said, coming back outside, and powering down his laptop. "You okay with everything so far?"

"Fine. Anything else you need me to know?"

He held up a hand as he put the computer into a hard case and locked it. After that was in the closet, along with the rest of the luggage, he went to the dummy laptop on the dresser. He pulled out his wallet and extracted a small rectangle of clear plastic, which he was able to attach to the monitor seconds before it closed. If anyone opened it, the card would slip out, but not be observed. Clever.

He turned back to her and she was caught off guard once more at how broad his shoulders looked in that polo shirt. She shook the thought away, angry that she'd even think such a thing.

"Tonight," Ryan said, all business, "we'll have a much better idea how to proceed. For now, we stick to small talk and distractions. If anyone asks something we're not sure about, we plead 'sore subject' and move on."

"Good." Angie put her hands on the armrests ready to go, but Ryan slipped into his chair and leaned forward, capturing her attention fully.

"As for how far I'm willing to go, I want to make it perfectly clear that I will do my utmost to avoid any delicate situations. If we get stuck, I'll keep in character, but I'll do my best not to make you uncomfortable."

She inhaled slowly. His declaration wasn't a surprise, but it was welcome, nonetheless. Even though she'd tried not to imagine situations in which they could be forced into that kind of intimacy, way too many had come to mind. The massages, of course, and what if they were the only two who didn't jump onto the clothing-optional bandwagon? Would that make them look suspicious? Would that scream undercover cops?

Regardless, none of that should matter. Awkward stuff always happened on undercover operations. It was part of the job. Still, it was going to be damn weird. After that Halloween incident, she'd told herself that there was no way in hell she and Ryan were ever going to see each other naked. This week, it would be a miracle if they could avoid it.

PURPLE WALLS AND PURPLE carpet made it very clear why they called the main workshop space the Lavender Room. The giant bean bags on the floor arranged in a big circle were pretty much what Ryan expected, or should he say dreaded.

"What's that frown for?" Angie asked.

"I thought bean bags went out in the early eighties. But instead, they just continued to grow. Those are huge." Ryan gave her the smile that terrible joke deserved, and it felt great when she grinned back. Picturing the two of them curled up together on the bulging bag of polystyrene pellets just became a little more comfortable. For about a minute.

Jesus. A whole week of foreplay and no main event.

What the hell was it going to take to get him to stop thinking about her as anything more than a fellow agent? His gaze moved from her smile to the red blouse to her thigh-hugging trousers. The outfit made everything worse. At work, in her nonfitted suits she wore sensible shoes with small heels. Something she could run in. Today, the heels on her sandals had to be five inches. She was tall without them, but standing next to him like this, their eyes were almost level, and he was six-one. There was no way he could fool his brain into seeing her as anything but stunning. Beyond tempting. Sexy.

"Six couples," she said.

He nodded, then turned away, checking out the rest of the room. Two exits, a bank of closed windows. The carpet was industrial, the tables in the back standard and there were two whiteboards, a blackboard and too many posters of greeting card couples on the walls.

The long tables with chairs had clipboards in front of each of twelve seats, along with the ubiquitous seminar water carafes and glasses.

"There's Delilah," Angie said, bringing Ryan's attention back to her. She nodded toward a tall, attractive woman walking up to the whiteboard. Delilah had blond hair that reached past her shoulders. A nicely proportioned body and a broad smile completed the very-professional package.

"Older than her brochure picture."

"Not by much," Angie said, and they were both speaking softly, moving slightly away from a couple who hovered nearby. "She's pretty."

"Damn relaxed."

"She would be. This is old hat for her."

Delilah wore dark slacks and a sensible button-down white shirt. She would have looked at home in any business setting, and that surprised him. "I pictured flowing robes and too many flowers."

"I guess they left that up to Ira," Angie said, scoping out the tall, slender male therapist who'd just walked in.

"An aloha shirt?" Ryan watched Ira Bridges approach Delilah and put his hand on the small of her back. His salt-and-pepper hair brushed against his shoulders. Garish flowers covered the pale, roomy shirt. Ryan wouldn't be surprised to find he wore a ankh necklace or an infinity bracelet. "Tell me he's not wearing flip-flops."

Angie leaned just enough to the left so she could tell. "He is."

Ryan sighed. "They're going to play that pan flute music, aren't they? I hate the pan flute."

Angie poked him in the side with her elbow, dislodging his train of thought. It didn't hurt at all. In fact, it was more of a gentle nudge but it had been enough to remind him that her skin was slightly tan and looked like silk.

He held his breath, afraid to move. She'd never have done that back in L.A. under any circumstances. Angie would have cleared her throat, turned toward him, said something, but she wouldn't have touched him like that. Angie Ebsen not only would, but should, and the touching would soon be a hell of a lot more intimate than an elbow to the ribs.

Another couple entered the room, which was what Angie had been alerting him to in the first place. He had no doubt he would learn more about these ten strangers than he wanted to. So he smiled as he cataloged his first impressions of the group. All of them were nervous and most of them held on to each other in some way because their partner was familiar and safe.

He reached with his left hand and found Angie's right. She jerked at the initial touch, but he didn't look at her. He kept his own slightly nervous smile on his face, and sure enough, she caught on and slipped her hand into his.

And he'd thought the elbow was memorable. God only knew what it was going to be like when they had to hug or kiss or he had to rub warm oil into her lush, lean body....

He cursed Jeannie and the entire legal system for putting

him in this ridiculous position, and then he cut that nonsense straight out because Ryan Ebsen would be sizing up the men in the room and checking out the wives. Special Agent Vail would be looking for the other two staff members, and sizing up Delilah and Ira.

Neither of them would have an elevated heart rate because he was holding Angie's hand.

"Come in, come in." Ira Bridges welcomed the newcomers as he headed for the door. Delilah had written: *Intimate relationships satisfy our universal need to belong and the need to be cared for* in a clean, easy to read cursive on the whiteboard.

"There are nametags on the end of the tables," Ira continued, his voice friendly, his smile wide and earnest. "Find a seat and please fill out the three-page questionnaire so we can get that out of the way. When you're finished, come into the center of the room and find a spot...on the floor." Ira beamed at the surprised murmur. "That's right. Surprise is a wonderful part of intimacy, and it's also a large part of this week, so keep on your toes."

Ryan leaned close to her ear and whispered, "I'm going to grab us seats."

She jerked sharply, caught off guard, her eyes wide and her lips parted. He wanted to apologize but as soon as she settled, he wanted to surprise her again.

"I'll get the nametags," she said, then hurried away, glancing back at him once.

He walked more sedately to his chosen seat then stared at the papers in front of him without seeing a word. The last time he remembered touching Angie on purpose had been a brush of fingers across the back of her hand. He'd wanted her then, but it had been at the party, and she'd been dressed as Scully, and though he'd never tell a soul living or dead, one of the main reasons he'd gone into the Bureau was because of Dana Scully and the *X-Files*.

Not the best thing to think about when there was so much on the line. The sting, the convictions, the promotion. After pouring himself a glass of ice water and downing half the drink in one go, Ryan started filling out the paperwork on the clipboard.

The first page looked like something he'd find at a doctor's office. Some overarching medical issues, which were easily dismissed, some personal info about family and work and hobbies and that kind of crap. Since they were using their own basic backgrounds, he was able to fill in the blanks in short order. He kept checking the still-open door, glad to have his mind occupied.

"Here." Angie dropped his nametag, already filled out, in front of him. When she sat, she shifted the chair closer to his.

He didn't acknowledge the tag, just slapped the sticky side to his shirt. Then he flipped to the second page of the questionnaire. "Shit," he said, under his breath.

"What?"

"Page two."

Angie checked out the material before she looked at him. "What's the problem?"

"You need to go first. Just make sure I can see your answers."

Her brow furrowed for a moment as she studied him, but she relaxed quickly with a nod. He went back and fiddled with page one while she attacked the intimacy portion of the opening challenge.

The first question alone had stopped him in his tracks.

I think of my partner lovingly many times a day.

He doubted he'd ever thought lovingly of anyone. Not that he didn't have good thoughts about people, especially about women, but lovingly? "What does that first question even mean?" he asked, keeping his voice low.

"We're in love," she said. "You'd think of me lovingly a lot."

Right. They were in love. If anything, he should go overboard on this questionnaire. Still, he'd take his cues from Angie, follow her lead. Make it appear that it was love with a background note of desperation, that brought them to this retreat, desperation with a mask of love that made them want to put in the effort. No sweat as a concept, but he hadn't really thought through the language issue.

Statement two was no better:

We feel warmth and connection at least twenty minutes a day.

Who the hell knew how many times they felt connected? He felt *connected* to the L.A. Kings hockey franchise, at least when they were winning, but that lasted the length of the game.

He leaned closer to Angie with a sigh. "This is gonna suck. Even if they don't play new-age CDs."

She snorted. Daintily. Whispered, "It'll be fine. Go with your instincts. Pretend they're asking about you and your personal trainer. Trust me, all the answers will make perfect sense."

He probably should have been insulted by that, but it actually made him laugh. He decided that when he was in doubt, he'd go with the opposite of his instincts, and he should be okay.

He glanced again at her paper, then stayed for a while, reading. Most of her responses were unsurprising given her backstory. The one about initiating sex equally made him blink. She'd given that a "Happens often." Good to know.

Confident that he now had the game down, he tackled his sheet, filling in the numbers for Ryan Ebsen, a man dedicated to keeping his wife and her checkbook. By the time he reached the end of the third page, he figured this thing with Angie was going to work out just fine.

Then she stood up, leaned over the table to grab another pen, and he got a load of her picture-perfect backside.

Nope. No. This thing with Angie was gonna kill him. Dead.

4

"THE FOOD WAS REALLY GOOD," Angie said, sipping her coffee from the back of the Blue Room. The group lunch hadn't been nearly the ordeal she'd stressed over, but there had certainly been moments.

The whole lot of them had walked the short distance from the Lavender Room, passing another group, all of them holding fruity umbrella drinks. Angie had been tempted to switch her allegiance, or at the very least call room service for a cocktail of her own. Especially after she got a load of the weird as hell layout of their new location.

The lunch tables had been set up in odd configurations: some were long family style, some round that could seat eight, a couple of them could accommodate four and only one table for two. There were more seats available than participants and each seat had a complete table setting.

Delilah had asked them all to sit. Anywhere they chose. With no more than a glance between them, she and Ryan went for the round table for eight where, for the most part, they'd eaten and listened to other people talk. The person to her right had been Luke, husband to Erica. Luke had spent the bulk of the meal's two courses telling her how he was only at this workshop because of Erica and how the whole point of intimacy was sex, and since they had sex pretty much every night, what was the point? He also mentioned the cost three or seven times.

Fortunately it hadn't been difficult for her to play her role. Primarily because Ryan had kept checking in with her. Not with words. With a look, a smile, a roll of his eyes. Each one a string between them, connecting, strengthening, woven together like a safety net. That tie relaxed her enough that she was able to answer the few questions asked without overthinking or stumbling.

The one time she'd tripped up was when she turned to find him staring across the table at Tonya Bridges, the yoga and tantric massage instructor. He'd looked riveted, interested. But then he'd turned back to the man to his left. Chris looked to be in his fifties. The two went on to discuss basketball until it was time for dessert and they'd all been "invited" to find different seats. Ryan had taken her by the sleeve and pulled her straight to the back of the room, to the table set for two where they hid like the bad kids during assembly as they watched the most confusing game of musical chairs ever.

"I think Ira's wearing patchouli oil," Ryan said as he fiddled with his linen napkin. He'd gotten coffee, nothing else, while she'd fixed herself a small plate of fruit. "Think he's actually old enough to be a hippie?"

Ryan wasn't looking at her, but that was okay because she was too busy scoping out the room to look at him. Their little table was situated close to the desserts. There were only three choices: a crème brûlée, a New York–style cheesecake, which was calling Angie's name, and a bowl of fresh fruit. She ate another piece of cantaloupe and decided the cheesecake had to be a billion times better. "Delilah hasn't had any work done I don't think," Angie said, pushing her grapes around. "Which makes me like her more, and also makes me question her involvement."

"What? Why?"

"They've been living in L.A. and Vegas for years. Plastic surgery is practically required by law for any woman over the age of forty."

He looked at her, clearly disbelieving. "That might be true for celebrities, but—"

"Ellen Fincher."

Ryan tossed the napkin all the way past the table, which Angie doubted he meant to do. "Get out."

Ellen was Palmer's administrative assistant. Angie knew for a fact she was forty-seven, because Angie had been at the birthday party. Ellen's present to herself had been eye lifts and some lipo. "Oh, I'm right."

"I'll take your word for it, but why does that make Delilah a more trustworthy person?"

"If she had a ton of illicit money, she'd probably have a nip or a tuck. She's pretty, but she's starting to droop. On the other hand, she could be saving every last penny for her dream retirement in Cancún."

"Or maybe she's just not that vain. You know—" Ryan stopped talking as Zach, the banker from Orange County, came by. Rachel, his wife, followed shortly thereafter, and all four of them chatted about how fantastic the food was until the couple wandered off.

Angie would have been fine with that if Zach hadn't been eating his damn cheesecake right in front of her. But after four bites she'd broken like a dime-store toy. "You want anything?"

Ryan shook his head staring once more at Tonya, who was sitting at one of the long tables, talking with two other couples.

Angie refilled her coffee, then said, "Screw it," even though no one was near enough to hear her, and picked up the biggest piece of cheesecake on the table. As she took her first bite, standing there like a heathen, she did a quick scan of the room. No one had left, even though they were perfectly free to do so. Marcus had cornered Olivia and Kyle. Delilah had both Paul and Natalie and Chris and Hannah.

Ryan watched Angie come back to the table. She sat down, both pleased and troubled that they were alone once more and murmured, "We're the only ones without a staff member."

"Yeah, I was thinking that we should probably move."

"Not near Marcus," she said after she'd swallowed another bite of the incredible cheesecake.

"We'll have to talk to him at some point."

"Not now. I spent five hours with him when you excused yourself after the main course."

He blinked at her. "I was not in the bathroom for five hours."

"My point exactly." She'd rarely run across anyone as beige as Marcus. Not simply his skin tone, his dishwater hair and his clothes, but his voice and his whole demeanor were so dull it was almost mesmerizing. He could put whole cities to sleep. "Now that I think about it, it's the perfect disguise."

"What's that?" Ryan's lips were already quirked up a hair, which made her throat tighten for a second.

"Being so boring people will do anything to avoid you."

Ryan's smile broadened. "How come I didn't know you were funny?"

That wasn't what she expected him to say. "I have no idea. And I don't think I am. Not funny funny. I'm intermittently amusing."

"You're under-the-radar funny. I imagine it would be very entertaining to sit next to you during bad movies."

"Now that I know your taste in films, that's never going to happen."

"Excuse me? *Shaun of the Dead.*"

"You said bad movies."

He laughed outright, and she hoped that Delilah and Ira were watching because this moment would convince anyone she and Ryan liked each other very, very much.

"ALL RIGHT, EVERYONE, are we ready?" Delilah glanced around at each couple, smiling serenely, until her gaze stopped on Ryan. "Is there a problem, Ryan?"

"Nope," he said, eyeing the bean bag chair. "None."

Problem was putting it mildly. This was exactly the nightmare he'd dreaded. Only worse. They hadn't been back in the Lavender Room for five minutes when the woman had described their very first bona fide intimacy exercise. Of course, it involved a bean bag chair. One chair. To be shared by him and Angie. At the same time. Hell. For a second he'd seriously thought about faking an allergic reaction to something he'd eaten at lunch. But Angie would know. Not to mention they were on the job.

"Come on, Ryan, move it," she whispered, her impatient voice edging toward panic.

He looked around, saw that all the other couples were in place, the husbands somewhere between lying and sitting, their wives cuddled on top of them. Slowly he lowered himself into the torture pit. Once he arranged himself as best he could he stared up at Angie, waiting for her to join him.

She hesitated, briefly met his eyes, then concentrated on her feet.

Ha. *Yeah, real easy, right?* He killed all hints of a satisfied smirk as he offered her his hand.

Ignoring it, she plopped down, none too gracefully, then swung a leg over him. He sucked in a breath, pretty sure she hadn't meant to hit him there.

"Um, sorry, if I—"

"Don't worry about it." His voice came out wrong, more like a fourteen-year-old going through the change.

He refused to say another word. Just laid there and let Angie do her thing. She'd figure out exactly how they were supposed to be situated. At least her knee had eliminated the possibility of his cock getting involved, so that was something.

"Is this supposed to be comfortable?" he asked, his lips very close to Angie's ear as she lay with her head on his shoulder.

"I have no idea." She adjusted again.

Every time she moved, Ryan tensed another notch. Delilah had asked for one partner to be "enveloped" by the other in order to listen to their heartbeat. First off, he didn't think Delilah knew what enveloped meant, but that wasn't the issue. Having Angie curl up in his arms? Touching him from shoulder to calf? Mother of—

"You're squeezing," Angie said.

"Huh?"

"My elbow. Tightly."

Ryan jerked his hand away, but it turned out to be a load-bearing hand and Angie slid down his chest until they reached a brand-new level of discomfort. Especially when her knee ended up on his inner thigh. Perilously near the first event.

"Oh, boy," she said.

He swallowed a moan.

Then she made things a hundred times worse by trying to scoot back up using that damned knee. Against his thigh. He bit his lip and most definitely did not whimper.

"Sorry, sorry."

He moved, too, attempting to keep his privates out of jeopardy while they struggled to get into position.

"That's wonderful," Delilah said from the front of the room. "Now that you're all settled, I want you to listen to the sounds of the rain forest and become aware of your breathing."

"Settled?" Ryan whispered. He hadn't known a whisper could be high-pitched. He didn't dare look around the whole room, but the couples in his line of sight looked as cozy as lovebirds. The bastards. "We're doing this wrong."

"What would you suggest?" Angie whispered back, her frustration making him feel a little better. "We don't fit on this thing."

"Everyone else fits. You have to relax."

"Me? You're as tense as a bowstring."

"If you'd just arrange yourself over me like—"

"I'm not a lap blanket."

Her knee moved again and he was running out of thigh. "Stop. Please." He wasn't above begging. "They're all waiting for us." He'd managed most of that sentence with his teeth clenched.

Angie lifted her head. "They're not all *settled*. Erica looks completely pissed at Luke, and Olivia's sitting on the carpet."

"Ira's doing something with the iPod player. Where's Delilah?" Ryan didn't particularly care, but maybe if he distracted Angie she'd stop moving.

"Must be at the front of the room. Come on. We can do this," Angie said. "We've just got to coordinate."

"That's what I've been trying to say." He took in a deep breath and let it go slowly. "I'm going to just lie here. I won't move an inch. All you have to do is get comfy. In fact, I won't even watch, that way I won't anticipate or react. Deal?"

She rested her head on his chest again. The warmth and weight of it made Ryan close his eyes before he'd planned on it.

"Deal," she said.

"Angie? One favor?"

"What?"

"Watch the knee."

His eyes weren't merely closed they were clenched. Which

did nothing to stop him from hearing her sharp, soft, "Oh. Sorry."

Ryan couldn't imagine how they must look to the therapists. To the blackmailers. Maybe it would help if he pretended it wasn't Angie crawling all over him, but Jeannie.

That was good, good, excellent, he could picture her hair and the stupid second earring on her right ear, but then Angie's scent caught him by surprise and Jeannie vanished like his humor.

Instead of throwing in the towel he pictured the woman he'd met at Bordello back in L.A. Terry, Mary, Carrie?

And there it was. Nothing magical, no, because his balls still ached, but he improved. Relaxed, at least to the point he wasn't going to snap his spinal cord. He pictured the short-haired brunette on her large four-poster bed. God, she'd been flexible. He'd been tempted to call her again, but hadn't.

When she'd wrapped her legs over his shoulders, head arching back on the pillow, he'd had to... How had the image in his head turned into Angie? When? Hell, even with the ache in his groin his cock was getting interested.

"That's the ticket," Delilah said softly from really close by.

Ryan's eyes opened to find her crouching next to their bean bag.

"I thought you two were going to need some special assistance but you worked it out. Don't worry that it took a few moments to find your comfort zone. Being in a group like this requires some new skills. Trust me, it gets easier."

Angie's head, which was now in its proper position on his chest, lifted. "I think we're good, but thanks for checking on us."

Delilah patted the side of the bag. "That's what we're here for." She rose, walked away until Ryan couldn't see her at all.

Angie had draped herself over him with her left hand on

his ribs, her front pressed to his side and her leg now safely thrown across his own.

As he put his hand gently on her shoulder her muscles seized beneath his palm, which caused him to go from uncomfortable to suicidal in seconds. With both of them stiff as statues, he grew hyperaware of every part that touched every other part.

"This position, curled around each other in total harmony, is home base," Delilah said, speaking to everyone now, her voice as calm as a summer breeze. "It's where you go when you need to feel safe. You can use this position in your own rooms or in here, any time you feel at all uncomfortable or restless. In fact, your homework for tonight is to recreate this position when you go to bed. Let your partner reassure you with their body, their breathing."

"Are you kidding me?" Angie said, her whisper quavering with panic.

"Well, shit," Ryan said, closing his eyes again, this time trying to pretend he was anywhere else on earth.

ANGIE SHOULD HAVE TOLD Ryan she'd meet him back at their room, rather than waiting for him outside the workshop space. Leaving without him would only add fuel to the fire. She doubted the afternoon session could have been more of a spectacular failure.

If Ryan was never approached by the blackmailer, she would be perfectly justified in blaming herself. She'd been more nervous lying in his arms than when she'd had sex for the first time. Okay, bad analogy. As if she wasn't having enough trouble keeping her thoughts on the assignment.

Some Special Agent she was. Rookies with one day on the job would have handled themselves better than she had.

Yet, she managed a smile as the other couples left the room. All of them were touching. Every single couple. Chris and Hannah held hands. Kyle and Olivia were so busy gazing into each other's eyes they almost walked into a pole. Paul had his arm around Natalie and before they reached the gate, he'd pulled her into a kiss that made Angie ache.

She and Ryan were nothing like them. They were awkward and self-conscious, and if anyone paid attention for more than five minutes they'd see there was no love between them. Worse, there was no familiarity and that's what was going to blow this whole sting out of the water.

She wanted to go for a run. At the very least, she wanted to talk to Liz. She'd understand, and she'd help Angie find some perspective.

Ryan, who'd been talking to Zach, finally made his way out the door wearing a smile that looked genuine. She thought of dessert in the Blue Room, of how nice that had been, and how the minute they'd had to fake real intimacy, they'd completely fallen apart. The irony was not lost on her that what they needed to get through a five-day-long intimacy workshop was a five-day-long intimacy workshop.

"Zach and Rachel asked us to join them for drinks in the casino tonight," he said when he rejoined her. "I said I'd let them know."

"We can sure talk about it."

Ryan kept walking into her personal space, and when his arm went over her shoulder, she did her damnedest not to react. But she could feel her jaw tense, her arms stiffen. With a conscious effort she relaxed and slid her arm around Ryan's waist. "Did they say what time? I'm ready for a drink right now."

The two of them walked down the winding pathway, between buildings and manicured lawns, everything oddly green for February, for a desert. "No specific time, and no pressure. It was an open invitation," Ryan said, his smile gone now that they were out of anyone's sight. "But I won't feel comfortable seeing anyone until we work a few things out."

She slowed her step. "I'm sorry," she said, at the exact time he said the same two words. Stopping completely, she looked at him. "Why are you sorry?"

He glanced around as if searching for the person Angie was talking to, or maybe just to avoid meeting her gaze. "I was incredibly out of character. No way you missed that."

"I was the one— I froze, I was awkward. Everything we'd talked about went out the window."

Ryan shook his head and got them moving again. "Okay, so we both sucked. What are we going to do about it?"

"Talk some more. Tell jokes. I don't know… Maybe talk about what we were like growing up?"

His brow furrowed. "That's… Let's think some more."

A waiter pushing a room service cart came at them, and Ryan tugged her onto the grass so the man could pass. He put both hands on her shoulders while they waited, and all the reasons she'd been horrible during the intimacy exercise rose to the surface in great neon letters, along with the very obvious solution.

The path clear once more, Angie covered Ryan's hands with her own, keeping him behind her. "We need to kiss," she said, knowing exactly what she was getting herself into. She'd have to put on the most durable armor in her mental wardrobe to pull this off. To kiss him until it felt right. Until it was as natural as breathing.

She tensed, waiting for his response. But he didn't say anything. Maybe he hadn't heard her. Probably a good thing, because the more she thought about it the more her belly clenched, and that wasn't helping at all.

To get to a comfort level would take a considerable amount of kissing. And touching. Could she really handle that? Of course she could… She had to, or risk disgracing herself, him, the entire team and the Bureau. The one thing she had on this job, no matter what, had been her self-confidence. If she blew this because of some ridiculous crush on an impossible man, she would lose far more than a job in D.C.

His hands squeezed her shoulders, sending an unwelcome shiver through her body. "You're right."

"About what?"

"Kissing."

The panic returned, stealing her breath and freezing her body. Thank God he was still behind her and she didn't have to look him in the eye.

He hesitated, then turned her around to face him. His gaze locked on hers, his hands settling on her waist. "We have to get rid of this awkwardness between us or we need to pack up and go home."

"I agree. Totally. Of course." She forced a smile, casually placed a palm on his chest, as if kissing him was no big deal, and hoped he didn't see her pulse leaping from the side of her neck. His heart rate wasn't exactly coasting on idle, so that helped.

"Jeannie and I did it."

"Did what?"

Ryan smiled, probably because her voice had climbed three octaves. "Practiced kissing."

"Really?"

"Yep, until we could do it without laughing."

"How long did it take?"

"Um, far longer than either of us liked."

"Ah." She cleared her throat. "We'd better get to the room, then."

"Yeah," he said, but he didn't move.

Someone else, a young woman clutching a book, passed them, but that's not why Angie hadn't lowered her hand.

"Just to be clear," he said, "we're talking about kissing, right? Just kissing?"

She felt a blush flower on her cheeks. "Yes. There's no reason for us to change any of the ground rules. Kissing. Touching. Until we're okay with it—" Her breath caught. "You and Jeannie, you didn't practice doing—"

"No. Jesus." Ryan loosened his grip. "No. No."

"Right. Of course not." Angie stepped back on the path, and took hold of his arm as they continued the trip to the room, reminding herself twice to ease her grasp. With every step she repeated her goal to shake this absurd *thing* for Ryan and shoved away all other thought.

When he had his card key out, breathing became an issue as her heart pounded faster and faster. This was it. The moment of truth.

As soon as the door closed behind Ryan, she turned, ready as she was going to get.

But Ryan wasn't even looking at her. He pulled out a slick gadget that looked a lot like a cell phone but was in fact a nifty little electronic sensor.

Angie couldn't decide if she was grateful that Ryan could still think about protocol or if she should be insulted. Given how close she was to an arrhythmia, she decided she would be grateful and use this moment as a reminder that this kissing business was exactly that: business.

Ryan walked the complete perimeter of the room using the scanner that was the most sophisticated frequency detector in the world, disappeared into the bathroom for a moment, then went to the dresser to make sure no one had tinkered with the Ebsen laptop. Finally he joined her by the door, and up close, she could see he wasn't quite as composed as she'd imagined. "I'm getting a scotch," he said, as if she'd needed more proof than the panic in his eyes.

Her whole body sagged in relief, but before she let herself

ask for a drink of her own, the stakes flashed through her mind like a sign from on high. She grabbed Ryan's shoulder, pushed herself against his body and pulled him straight down into the kiss of her life.

5

THE VELVET SHOCK OF HER mouth on his sent Ryan stumbling back against the wall. She'd caught him off guard, nearly knocked the air out of his lungs. But he caught on quickly, abandoning every thought but to read her cues and give her what she needed.

He touched the tops of her arms, and while she didn't exactly jerk completely away, her body stiffened with tension. However this ended, it had to begin with feeling comfortable and safe.

Keeping his hands gentle and his mouth closed, he consciously relaxed. It wasn't a piece of cake. The idea that he was kissing Angie was messing with him something fierce. All the carefully constructed barriers that had helped him keep his distance had been crumbling since last night, and together with the "safety" position and now this, he felt defenseless. But he couldn't simply let go and have at her. She wasn't a one-night stand. He knew Angie's last name, and a whole lot more, and he wasn't about to call the shots.

She pulled back from him, not away. Just enough to breathe for a minute. To whisper, "I don't know if I can do this."

"Course you can. We can. Use your imagination. Who's your favorite actor?"

"What?"

They were so close together that with every word came a soft gust of her breath. He recognized the scent of wintergreen breath mints. "Who's the hottest guy you can think of?"

The way she blushed was startling. She must really like whatever actor she was thinking of, but that wasn't the point. He didn't want her embarrassed. "All right. Forget that. Did you ever have an unrequited crush?"

Now she turned her head, and the tension of a minute ago had been nothing. What kind of a past did Angie have? "An ex-boyfriend?"

"Yes," she said, so excitedly he jumped. "I have an ex-boyfriend. From my first year of college."

Because she was looking at him again, Ryan forced down his grin. He risked squeezing her arms a little more tightly, and yeah, okay, now they were getting somewhere. She wasn't exactly in a Zenlike state of calm, but she was a hell of a lot better. "Close your eyes," he said, keeping his voice low and calm. "Picture…?"

"Steve."

"Steve," he repeated. "How you felt when he kissed you, and how good it was." He pulled her closer, waited until the little furrow on her forehead disappeared. Then he kissed her.

This time, her lips weren't pressed together so tightly air couldn't have escaped if it tried. Her hands, which had gripped his shirt so firmly she'd nearly ripped the seam, had softened, and the energy that had been coursing through her body had shifted from electrical fence to a strong buzz.

Then her tongue swept across his lower lip, just a tease, a taste of what came next, and oh, hell, in his quest to make things easier for her, he'd forgotten that he was the one actually kissing Angie.

He probably should have stopped things right there. All she'd have to do was keep imagining he was this safe and comfy ex from college. Instead, he moved his hands to her back, tilted his head until their mouths were a perfect fit and kissed her like he'd wanted to for a very long time.

ONE SECOND, IT WAS STEVE on her lips and it was all so simple. The next, she wanted to climb Ryan like a tree and never let go.

Her moan would have been embarrassing if she'd had any brain cells left, but what he was doing with his tongue and how his large hands were stroking her back as if he couldn't get enough had fried all her synapses, leaving her helpless to do anything but kiss him back.

Those hands of his had reached the curve just above her behind. He paused and it felt important to tell him to continue, which she did by thrusting her hips forward.

Message received, and good grief he grabbed each cheek, pulled her close and oh, he was clearly aroused. The more they rocked against each other the thicker and hotter his erection became.

Considering she was Kegel squeezing to beat the band and panting into his mouth as if she'd just finished a marathon, she couldn't exactly complain.

God, he could kiss. He should quit the FBI immediately and become a professional— She lurched back, so roughly they had to take a few steps to catch their balance. He'd let go of her, and she…she remembered who he was and who she was and, "Oh, my."

Ryan, still obviously hard and flustered, cleared his throat. His lips glistened. "Well, that wasn't too bad," he said.

A burst of laughter escaped before she could stop it.

"It wasn't," he said defensively. "For a first time, given the circumstances, we did okay. We learned some things."

Things? Like, say, that *he* was the hottest guy she could think of? That Ryan was her unrequited crush? As if more proof was needed, she'd practically dry-humped the guy into coming. She made a sound. A sort of croak. Definitely not a word. But she couldn't look at him. She turned around and stared at the wall.

He very sweetly didn't comment on it. "Listen," he said, "we're two healthy adults with fully functioning hormones. It would have been more surprising if we hadn't responded so, uh, enthusiastically."

"Is that what happened to you and Jeannie?"

"What?"

Angie spun back. "When you two kissed?"

"We didn't..." He shook his head. "No. It wasn't like that."

Well, that was good, because it would have been creepy if they had. "You know what? I'm really feeling tight from sitting so much all day. I think I'll go for a run."

"A run? I thought we were going to keep kissing until we felt comfortable."

"Yeah, that was the plan, but you're right. For a first time, we did great, and the next time we'll do better, and we're probably not going to have to kiss in front of anyone, anyway. So I might as well do a few miles...."

"What about drinks at the casino?"

"You should go. Tell them I was tired. Which is true. I am tired. Unless you think it's important for the case—"

"No," he said, before the last word had time to settle.

The urge to look down was so strong she thought something in her brain might actually break. At the thought, she glanced. Quickly. His erection was still there. She could only imagine the kind of self-discipline it took to speak to her so calmly.

"The only reason we'd go is to make our cover stronger," he said, "but I'm thinking we'll skip it tonight."

Angie made a break for it. She pulled open her drawer, nearly yanking it out of the dresser. But she got her running gear, including socks, after only three tries. "Great. I'll just—"

She hurried to the bathroom and closed the door behind her. All she could think about was getting out of this hotel room, pounding the pavement until she could figure this damn thing out. There had been a single moment when things had gone to hell. Before she came back to their room, back to the bed they shared, she vowed to find the line between kissing him as part of the job and kissing him as the fulfillment of her fantasies, and stick to the proper side.

Ryan had tried to watch television, but he couldn't disconnect from kissing Angie. He'd thought taking care of himself in the shower would give him enough relief that he could think again, but he couldn't get any kind of distance.

She'd been gone half an hour. He supposed he could eat, but he should wait for her to come back because they were supposed to be in love and recommitting themselves to their marriage. They were supposed to be a lot of things—professionals, for one. Rational adults, another.

He clicked off the TV and almost threw the remote against the wall, but instead he grabbed his gym gear. After he'd changed, he left a note on the bed, then he and his towel headed for the fitness center. Like Angie, he thought better when he was doing something physical, and the hotel had a lot of decent equipment. He'd pass on the free weights, but the machines would give him a good sweat.

The path meandered, as did all paths in this resort, except for the one to the casino. It reminded him of how they set up grocery stores, forcing people to walk by the expensive ticket items in order to buy the milk. The casinos paid for everything in this town, and it never ceased to amaze him that those damn slot machines were in every gas station and supermarket.

As he rounded the curve of the fitness center building, he heard familiar voices. Tonya and Ira along with another couple, maybe Luke and Erica? Ryan was in no mood to join in what sounded like a jovial chat, so he stayed where he was, moving a little closer to the building where it was darker.

Eavesdropping was something of a relief. It was work related and he didn't have to be alone with his thoughts. There was Tonya pimping her early morning yoga workouts, and Luke inferring that it was somehow girly. Jesus, the man was a Neanderthal. Ryan gave Luke's marriage a year, tops.

Goodbyes came shortly after, and the three of them, everyone but Ira, walked right past Ryan, who decided to stay where he was until he could see what the therapist was up to. He'd probably left for his room, but Ryan gave it a minute, just in case.

"A fickle lady," Ira said, but his voice got soft at the end as he spoke into a cell phone. Doppler effect; he was walking. No, pacing, because there was more and his voice grew louder. "...dime to win. On the second, I want number four to win, six to place. Third, gimme two to win. Fifth, three to win."

Ryan moved closer to the edge of the building, keeping himself against the wall. He'd been to enough races to understand that Ira was placing bets on the horses, and that the dime he'd mentioned was a thousand dollars. So his bets for that particular track were in the five to six thousand dollar range.

"Yeah. Not tonight. Tomorrow, early. Seven-thirty. Okay."

Ira's voice had grown closer, and the last thing Ryan wanted was to be caught skulking. He hurried back to the path and moved forward with his head down, almost running into the man.

"Excuse me," Ira said, holding his hands out in front of him.

They would have touched if Ryan had taken one more step. Instead, Ryan did the pardon-me shuffle as he smiled. "Sorry about that."

"On your way to the fitness center?" Ira asked.

Ryan nodded. "Angie's catching a run, so I'm gonna grab a quick workout before dinner."

"Good for you. I should do more of that myself. But not now. Late for a private session."

Ryan nodded as the older man walked away, his steps quick, his hands fisted in his pockets. Why in hell would a man staying at a casino with a major sports book place bets with a bookie? Only one thing Ryan could think of, and that was secrecy. Ira wasn't playing for peanuts, but there was nothing in the intel already gathered that indicated he had a gambling problem.

That opened up a whole new arena to investigate. How was he financing his hobby? Did anyone else on the Intimate At Last team know he was a gambler? Was the blackmail his source of funds?

Ryan pulled his own cell phone out of his left pocket, double checking that it was his personal iPhone. Ryan Ebsen's cell was an older-model Nokia that was simpler to clone. He speed dialed Jeannie. It was afterhours, or almost, but that meant she'd be out of court. Probably at home having a great dinner with the family, not worrying about kissing people and inappropriate erections.

"What's up?"

"New information."

"Okay, wait a sec."

Ryan heard her yell for her husband although her voice

was muffled. There was a discussion that lasted so long he'd made it inside the gym and had staked out a private corner where he could see all entrances and exits. There were only three people in the place, and he didn't know any of them.

"I'm back," she said, finally.

"I forgot what I was going to tell you."

"Shut up. You try having a family and being a secret agent at the same time, then come bitch at me."

"Secret agent?"

"According to my children, yes."

"According to me, too, double-oh-seven and three-quarters. Listen, I overheard Ira Bridges making a bet to a bookie. I know Santa Anita's running, but the track doesn't matter. The fact that he was betting several thousand dollars was interesting, however."

"Really? Oh, that's good. That's very…motivational."

"My thoughts exactly. He was on the down-low making the call, no one else in sight. But that doesn't necessarily mean he's kept it secret. Suspicious, though. I think he's going to meet someone at seven-thirty tomorrow morning. It could be a phone call, but I doubt it. I'm gonna go running with Angie at seven, circle around his bungalow. See if we can't get eyes on the guy or a license plate."

"Don't get caught."

"Yeah, I needed that reminder, me being a rookie and all."

"What the hell's wrong with you?" She snorted. "Your job is to play the loving couple. Our best shot at nailing these bastards is you getting targeted. I'll get the info to Parker and the rest and see what they come up with."

"Good." He rubbed his temple. Naturally she was right. "Thanks."

"So how's it going with Angie?"

"What do you mean?"

Jeannie puffed some air at the receiver. "I mean, how's it going with Angie?"

Ryan opened his mouth, then closed it, editing his thoughts. "Fine," he said. "Fine."

The huff of air was replaced by a derisive laugh. He knew that laugh all too well. "What?"

"Took you a hell of a long time to get to fine, kiddo. What's going on?"

"Nothing. You know. All that touchy-feely crap. Ira wears an aloha shirt, okay? There are bean bag chairs."

"That's swell, but how's it going with Angie?"

"She's not you," he said, hating that it sounded a lot like the way her kids whined about going to bed. "I was ready for you."

The silence that came back at him wasn't the friendly kind. It made Ryan nervous, and he found himself pacing, but still sweeping his surroundings for anyone who could be listening in. He shouldn't have to explain his discomfort, not to Jeannie. She'd spent a lot of time ragging on him about how they were going to be his longest relationship, how with women, he was made of Teflon, sliding in then sliding out, no fuss, no muss. Jeannie understood that he wasn't built for romantic relationships. She didn't make him want things he shouldn't.

"It's the touchy-feely stuff, right?" she asked. "We figured there was going to be a lot of physical contact."

"We weren't wrong."

"Okay, so today you realized that this wasn't theoretical, that you're undercover as a married man. The way I see it, you have about three hours left to freak out about it, and then you'd better get your act together, Ryan. Seriously."

"I'm not freaking out."

"Yeah, you are. I can't say I blame you. If the situation were reversed, and they'd stuck me with any other guy on the team, I'd have been a mess. Privately. Because I would know that my feelings are the last thing on earth that matter for the rest of the week."

"Well, you're a damn saint, Jeannie."

"Fine, be pissed at me. Just remember that you're the one who wants Washington so badly. You're the one who's determined to play Ryan Ebsen down to his short hairs. You two are going to touch each other. A lot. You'll have to kiss a time or two. And you're sleeping next to her. If junior won't behave, you have exactly one option. You keep it in your pants. That's it. There's not a plan B or a deal you can work out. Everyone's counting on you. Because you're the man in the spotlight. If anything, you need to make it easier on Angie. She's taking one for the team, and don't get smart with me, because you know what I mean. It was brave of her to step into this part with zero prep."

He scraped his teeth over his lip, then put the phone down while he slugged the padded back of a weight machine. Then he put the cell to his ear again. "Well, hell, when you say it like *that*..."

"All righty, then. Where are you, in the fitness center?"

"Yeah." He heard the relief in her voice, and it made him more determined than ever to get his thoughts in line. "You know it's not about Angie, right? This would be a problem with anyone who isn't you."

Her pause told him he should've left well enough alone. "Yeah, I know. Look, my tribe is going to revolt if I don't give them sustenance. You, work out. Hard. Think whatever you need to, then get clear. Get focused. Eye on the prize, kiddo. Eye on the prize."

After a brief goodbye, he shoved his phone in the correct pocket, then went to the elliptical, set it for maximum resistance and started pumping. The key was control and focus.

He was better at that than anyone he knew. Completely capable of putting away any feelings he had for Angie Wolf while still giving the performance of his career. Dammit.

6

Angie sat on the edge of the whirlpool bathtub, the steam from her shower redolent with the cucumber scent of her body wash. Liz Copper was front and center on Angie's iPad. In the background was the interior of Liz's SUV and the ambient sounds were a random car horn or an airplane. Liz could have been halfway home by now instead of listening to Angie whine as she sat in the Bureau parking lot.

"Hey," Liz said, "I'm sorry, but I don't understand the problem."

"It's Ryan," Angie said, her jaw clenching with the need to be quiet. Ryan wasn't in their room, but that didn't mean he couldn't come back any second. "I completely forgot myself and what I needed to accomplish. *I* kissed him. *I'm* not supposed to do that. I'm supposed to be in character, not wanting to jump the guy I work with five days a week. For God's sake, Liz, you know how risky this part is, and we're on day one."

"Again," Liz said, so calmly Angie wanted to punch her. "I don't see the issue."

"Stop it. You're not dense."

"You are, apparently. Look, Angie, this is one week out of your life where your future depends on you acting as if you love the man you're supposed to be married to. The more the lines blur between you and your character, the more effective you're going to be at playing the part."

Angie's head reared back. "That's insane. And inappropriate. And...and wrong."

"Why?"

"Because when this week is over, I have to go back to L.A."

"Not for long. Look," Liz said, leaning closer, making her head look very big. "You're attracted to him. A lot. I was there at that Halloween party, remember? I saw the way you two looked at each other. So use it. Make it work in your favor."

"That's not right."

"Have I ever advocated using someone like that in real life? No. But in this case... Think of it as pulling a Ryan. Trust me, he'll be thrilled. At least until he finds out you're going to D.C. instead of him, but hey, all's fair when seeking promotions that will pull you up several rungs on your career ladder."

Angie sighed, her instincts battling for dominance. "Let me get this straight. Are you saying that I should seduce him? While on the job?"

Liz blinked a little. "I'm not saying you should. I'm suggesting that in this case, it wouldn't be a bad thing to go with the flow. He wants you, you want him, that's a fact. The only reason you two haven't already gotten together is because of the job. Well, now the job is to convince two marriage counselors that you're hot for each other. Think of it as method acting."

"There's something fundamentally flawed about what you're saying, I know there is."

"Kiss him again tonight. If it feels wrong to go farther,

stop. But if it goes to the next step, don't beat yourself up for it. That's all I'm saying."

If it had been anyone else, Angie would have already laughed off the idea and moved on. But Liz really did know her better than anyone else. She was protective of Angie. Had been since their first year in college. "Okay. I'll let you know what happens. But I have to get out of this bathroom. For all I know he's right outside the door."

"Good luck," Liz said, then she was gone, and Angie put away her tablet. Her gaze moved to her reflection as she went to the door. She'd dressed in Angie Ebsen's clothes, a sheer white camp shirt over a silk tank, with winter-white jeans, the russet belt the only color in the outfit. It would have looked better if she'd been more tan, but she didn't actually live the life of an heiress.

She did have to play one, though, so it didn't matter whether Ryan was on the other side of the door or not. Now, if she could only erase her entire conversation with Liz.... Instead, she set her shoulders and walked out, ready to face him, face whatever the night would hold, but thank goodness she was alone. Her gaze went to his note. No indication of what time he'd written it, but even if he had spelled it out she couldn't begin to guess when he'd return.

Her stomach rumbled. No wonder, it was coming up on eight. She figured they'd go to one of the hotel restaurants, be seen together, maybe find the others in the bar, after all. She'd put on makeup.

Unsure what to do now, she thought of cracking open the minibar. She still didn't think the Bureau would pick up the tab, but she did get a per diem.

At least the run had done her good. Of course, Liz's "Go for it" pep talk had undone most of Angie's calm. Thinking of seducing Ryan made her hyperventilate, but she could sit with the notion of seeing where things led. Being open to entertaining the idea that there could possibly be more than kissing between her and Ryan. Maybe.

She stared at the door, then at the fridge, then back at the door. It seemed ridiculous to wait for an unquantifiable time, and though she didn't like interrupting anyone's workout—tough. She got her cell, dialed Ryan's.

He answered as the door to their room opened, his voice echoed in twin spaces. "I suppose you're wondering where I am," he said, smiling at her.

Eye-rolling was becoming something of a reflex. "You didn't say."

He still had his phone to his ear as she put hers back in her purse. When she looked up again it was to find him eyeing her, but not cynically at all. His gaze hovered over her chest for a few seconds then moved slowly down until he reached her shoes, yet another ridiculously high pair of strappy nonsense. With her heart thudding and praying he wouldn't notice that she was utterly panicked, she found a smile that almost felt normal.

"They're impossible to run in," she said. "I'd break my ankle in five steps. I don't know why they insist on putting TV cops in these high-fashion things. It's absurd."

He let his phone hand drift down as looked up. "To be fair, they only do that to the female TV cops."

"Ha, ha."

"You do look damn nice in them," he said. His workout was all over him, and it was a good look. The sweat on his shirt reminded her of her own before she'd showered. The flush of his neck and face was pretty close to indecent. "Did the fitness center live up to the brochure?"

"Oh, yeah. You'd like it."

"I'll stop in sometime."

"Whoever picked out your wardrobe did a hell of a job,"

he said. "You could be about to step onto a yacht. Did you want to go meet the gang for drinks?"

"Dinner first would be nice. I'm starving."

He nodded and headed for the closet. "Give me five minutes. Oh, and I overheard Ira making some impressive wagers with a bookie."

"Really? Why a bookie?"

"My question exactly."

As he gathered his clothes, he filled her in, and by the time he'd reached the bathroom, they'd gone over a quick half-dozen possible explanations. "I'll call Parker," she said, grateful beyond measure that the conversation had turned to the case and that she could breathe again.

"I spoke to Jeannie, already. She'll take care of it."

"You told Jeannie?" Angie wasn't sure why that surprised her, but it did. There was no reason for him to hold on to the information until he talked to her, and yet there was a niggling pressure in Angie's chest that felt too much like jealousy.

Ryan nodded, completely casually, as he should. "I'll be right out. Why don't you look over the menus, decide where you'd like to eat."

The only thing good about this brand-new overwhelming awkwardness that had taken up every available cell in Angie's brain was that she no longer felt weird about the kissing.

God, this assignment was going to kill her. The only way to survive would be to take it one second at a time, be present, stop projecting. They had a new lead, and who knew what else they'd find out next?

She just had to make sure she was in bed early enough to get some decent sleep. Then actually get to sleep. In the morning she planned on running. Then she was going to attend the morning yoga session, try to bond with Tonya. At the very least, the two of them shared a body consciousness that if played right, could lead to conversations outside the purview of the intimacy retreat.

Big stuff, all of it. She really did need to sleep. And to disregard all thoughts of Liz's idiotic suggestion.

"I THINK WE SHOULDN'T even try to find Ira with his bookie," Angie said.

Ryan stared at the big red 1:43 a.m. on the nightstand clock. It was hard to miss, lying on his side, facing away from Angie. "No?"

"We've been here one day," she said. "Give it time."

It wasn't exactly easy to hear her, as she was lying on her side, facing away from him. And the way her words were slightly muffled, he assumed she had her mouth smooshed on her pillow. The same mouth he'd kissed a few hours ago. He had to stop obsessing about that. Twice he'd gotten hung up on studying her lips and lost track of the conversation. "I keep thinking we need to do more."

"Tonight was good," Angie said, as if she was trying to convince him. "With Marcus in the restaurant, and then Tonya at the bar."

"Yeah. But not for long enough, and honestly I couldn't tell if they were being friendly or milking us for info. Well, most of us. Did you notice how Tonya physically stepped back when Zach started talking about the exercises? Tonya can't stand him, which I get, but the important part is that it was amazingly easy to tell she couldn't stand him. She's not a very accomplished actor. Not that an extortionist has to be a good liar, but it would help."

"Huh, no. I didn't see any of that. I was occupied for most of that discussion."

Yeah, he'd noticed. "I think Kyle and Olivia want a threesome with you."

The sheets rustled and the mattress wobbled on her side. "What? Why would you say that?"

Angie's voice was a lot clearer and nearer. Ryan had a quick debate with himself as to the wisdom of turning to look at her. So far, watching the clock had worked pretty well, but the clock wasn't going anywhere, and he wanted to see her reaction to his observation. He turned. "How did you not notice?"

"We weren't talking about anything. Restaurants in L.A. There was no mention of beds or sex or anything like that."

He could make out her features thanks to the augmented moonlight. She'd taken off her makeup leaving her skin soft and not quite as pale as was recommended by the AMA. He probably wouldn't have known that fact if he hadn't seen her come out of the bathroom, but now, half in shadow, he wanted nothing more than to brush his lips over those smooth cheeks. "They were eating you alive," he said.

"I'll admit they got up into my bubble, but I would have noticed if it was anything more than that."

"Would you?"

"What, you think I have no life experience? I'm not a kid."

"Okay, okay," he said, realizing too late that mixing this discussion with the ability to see her had been a stupid move. "I take it back. I was completely mistaken."

She turned with a flounce and a punch to her pillow. He thought about what an idiot he was for bringing up the topic in the first place.

Then she turned again. "Why did you think so?"

The clock changed from 1:45 to 1:46. "It was the personal space thing. That's all."

"No, come on. That's not why."

"It is."

She huffed.

He only imagined he could feel the warmth of her breath

on the back of his neck. "I don't know. I guess I thought they were both checking you out."

A sigh this time, then some kind of movement he didn't want to know about. "They were doing that to you, too."

He turned. "Kyle was?"

Angie's mouth quirked up and so did her eyebrows. "Oh, really?"

Ryan mimicked her eye-roll. He knew she was messing with him because she'd already admitted to being oblivious, but he'd let her have her fun. "I'm wondering how I didn't catch that. They were obvious as hell when they were looking at you."

"Well, you were in no position to judge because you were bending over to pick up Tonya's napkin."

He grinned. Yeah, he'd picked up the napkin, but Angie was still full of bull. "Okay, that's good information to have. Maybe we can use it."

Again, she huffed at him, but this time it was somehow suggestive.

"Get your mind out of the gutter, woman. For the case. If the two of them are interested in some extracurricular activity, maybe I can exhibit some interest in return."

She gave up the whole back-to-back business and her shuffling made him turn around. She ended up sitting cross-legged with her sleep T pulled over her knees. It was plain blue, nothing special and Ryan figured it wasn't part of the disguise, but something she wore regularly.

"How," she asked, "would you go about doing that?"

Ryan sat up, too. They were supposed to have come home on the early side so they could get some sleep before taking their six-thirty run. "Subtly. In the presence of at least one of our suspects."

"That could potentially mean that you'd come on to Kyle

four different times. I don't care how subtle you are, that's going to make waves."

"We're supposed to make waves."

Angie shook her head. "Not the kind you're talking about." She sat straighter. "We're supposed to be working on our marriage. Not looking for orgies."

"Some would argue the added spice would keep the relationship more interesting."

"Yeah, like who?" Her head moved, just a little, and he really, really wished he could see the details of her face. "You?"

He almost lost it then, but pretended to yawn. "I won't get myself into anything I can't get out of. I promise."

"That's good," she said, lying down again under the white duvet. "Because it would blow our cover all to hell if I had to come sweeping in to save your ass."

"I see what you did there," Ryan said, grinning at her even though she couldn't see it. "Save my ass. You're a riot."

"So you've said."

"Being a riot is not the same thing as being funny."

Another punch to the pillow, observed this time, and her hair flowing over the ghostly white of the case made his smile fade and his stomach clench. It was too easy to talk with her, to lose track of how she affected him until it was too late. His cock wasn't hard, but it wasn't ignoring the circumstances, either.

"You set the alarm for six o'clock, right?" Angie asked, her voice lowered and missing the teasing he found he liked very much.

"Yeah."

"Okay. Good night."

"You, too." He took his time settling back into his safety position, thinking about the giant gap between his idea of safety and Delilah's. But Ryan also knew that a bed didn't exist that was large enough to make this deal with Angie one of the most difficult challenges he'd faced. Despite his determination, his promises to himself to stop thinking of her as anything but a coworker, there was no way.

He'd seen Kyle and Olivia scoping Angie out and he'd wanted to pull her away so fast he'd have left smoking tracks. He wasn't bothered by jealousy much. When he was younger, yeah, but in the past ten years he never put himself in a situation where there would be any competition. The women he picked had already picked him.

This, now, this was something else. And he was starting to realize how unprepared he was. The defenses he'd built up only worked in the scenarios he manipulated. This bed? This assignment? A thousand and ten miles from his comfort zone.

ANGIE CROSSED PERFECTLY manicured nails as she waited to see if Liz was there to get her call. If not, Angie would try her cell phone, but she had to be fast because Ryan was waiting for her. While she'd spoken to Liz earlier that morning, she needed another dose of best friend.

Just before Angie was about to hang up, Liz's face came into view. "What happened?"

"Nothing."

Ryan's voice, muffled, stopped Angie cold. "Are you speaking to me?"

She hadn't remembered to turn on the water. "Nope," she said, loudly. "Talking to myself." Then she turned the sink's spigot on full blast, hoping it was enough.

"Show me that dress," Liz said.

"Shh. Whisper."

"He can't hear *me,* you idiot. Now, show me the dress."

Angie did, but only because Liz wasn't going to let it go. When she whistled, Angie winced, sure Ryan had heard that. She pulled the tablet up so she was face-to-face with her friend. "Your theory about sleeping with him is ridiculous," she said, whispering, but with as much venom as she could muster.

"Okay." Liz said it with complete nonchalance.

"I'm not kidding. It's stupid. I'll have to see him in the office."

"Fine."

"Liz!"

"What? I'm not arguing with you."

"Delilah and Ira gave a class on pleasure props today."

"Pardon?"

Angie sat back down on the side of the tub. "You heard me. We had to play with everything from riding crops to gray silk ties. No one was naked or anything but the only thing worse than having Ryan Vail suck flavored lube off my finger was when I had to practice, uh, binding him while he gave me hints and smiles."

Liz took in a deep breath and let it out slowly.

Angie could see she was struggling not to laugh. "It wasn't funny."

"I can see how it wouldn't be. I'm sorry you had to go through that."

"Thank you," Angie said, the sympathy easing her discomfort hangover.

"Why are you calling me?"

She noticed that her friend was in her sports bra with her hair up. She was in her bathroom, too, and the sound of the tub filling was kind of loud. "Tonight I have to be all over him at the casino."

"Ah. Well, I guess you just do what feels right, Angie. Go with your instincts."

"He screws up my instincts."

Liz's condescending smile made Angie want to slap her. "Go take your bath."

"In all seriousness, hon, you can do this. You're the most

focused person I've ever met. When in doubt, remember the promotion. Do what's necessary to get it."

Angie nodded, knowing her friend's words were wise but unsure that she could follow the advice. "I'll try. But don't be shocked if I call you in the middle of the night."

"I have to work tomorrow," Liz said, her voice whiny and high.

"Tough. It's your fault for being a good friend. I'll talk to you later." Angie clicked off, not feeling one iota better. After she shoved the tablet in her case, she checked herself in the mirror, feeling equally hot and embarrassed. She'd never worn a dress like this, ever, and even though the material squeezed her like a giant Ace bandage, she felt more naked than she did wearing a bikini. It not only emphasized the curves she had, but created new ones. A person would think she had boobs in this Hermes concoction. Then there was the question of the length. Or the lack thereof. Her fingertips skimmed the bottom hem, for God's sake.

The shoes didn't help. The ludicrously tall heel was the same purple as the dress, but that was the only attempt at matching. The strap around her ankle was orange, the platform black patent and the peep-toe a dayglo pink. The instructions were to carry a white clutch with this mess of Crayola colors. She had no idea why.

One final look at her face, painted with far too much makeup, and she turned the knob, ready for a night at the casino.

From the back, Ryan looked great. He'd put on a jacket that fit him very well, emphasizing his broad shoulders and trim waist. When he turned around, the picture was even more alluring. She had a thing for athletic bodies, the clean lines of a ripped stomach and the masculinity of a perfectly muscled chest. The shirt he wore was white, elegantly simple and just a tad too snug. The slacks were black like the jacket. No tie. Classic shoes. Altogether stunning.

"Holy…"

Angie looked up and was taken aback to see the expression on Ryan's face. His eyes got wide and full of pupil, a slight flush tinted his cheeks, and then there was his dropped jaw. "What?" She looked down, wondering if something unfortunate had popped out.

"Wow," he said. "You continue to be very surprising."

"It's too much, isn't it?" she asked. "I have a couple of other choices in there. I look like a hooker, don't I? Oh, God. I do."

"No," he said, stepping toward her but stopping more than an arm's length away. "You look fantastic. You look like you should be on the cover of Vogue or on a red carpet, making all the actresses hate your guts."

Angie couldn't help the grin that tugged at her lips. "Really?"

"Yeah. It's perfect. Everyone in the casino is going to notice you. Actually both of us. Because they'll all be wondering what the hell you're doing with a guy like me."

"Oh, come on, Ryan. You're just fishing. You know you're gorgeous in that. It looks like it was tailor-made for you."

"It was. It cost a fortune. The best part is that because it's bespoke, I don't have to return it."

"Oh." She looked at the dress she'd suddenly come to like more than anything else she'd ever worn. "I suppose I'd better not spill any wine on this thing. I have no idea what designer dresses go for, but I can't imagine they're cheap."

"On the other hand, if you stain it carefully, it might not be returnable."

"That would be defrauding the American people."

"Only technically. I see it as doing the people a favor.

Any citizen who sees you in the dress is going to be very impressed with the FBI."

"I'm not going to wear my badge with it."

"You should. You should be on the cover of *FBI Monthly*."

Okay, that deserved the eye-roll. "There is no *FBI Monthly*."

He smiled. "They'd start one, if they knew you could be on the cover."

The blush that had started when he'd said, "Wow" had taken root, and while she liked the compliments, she could only deal with so many. "You know what? Give me a minute, would you? I, uh, need to brush my teeth."

Ryan's surprised look was cut off by her shutting the bathroom door.

Angie steadied herself on the sink as she tried to find the breath Ryan had stolen. She wasn't used to such extravagant attention for her looks. Yes, she understood she was attractive, but attractive hadn't counted for much in her life. Everything was about strength, athletic ability and intellectual achievement. That had been enough to contend with, and hearing Ryan talk about her that way, look at her with those eyes. It was great, and also not easy to deal with. But she needed to. Confidence was a key part of Angie Ebsen's character, and tonight, Angie would be on display.

She swiped a bit of toothpaste on her tongue, just in case, then stood up straight. Flicking her hair back, she pretended she was the woman she was playing, who wielded her sexuality the way Angie wielded her weapon.

When she stepped out of the bathroom, Ryan was standing by the bed. He gave her a long, considering look from the top down.

"Let's hit it," she said as she picked up her small bag and made a beeline for the door. "But not too fast because walking in these shoes is the most dangerous part of this assignment."

"I could argue that one," he murmured, but it was low, as if he hadn't meant for her to hear. He made it to the door first and held it open for her.

The night was chilly enough that if she'd been herself Angie would have worn a jacket. At least it wasn't a long walk to the casino, and she'd suffered through worse. She waited for Ryan to join her, picking up the pace as they moved along the well-lit pathway. Slowly, so she could get her feet under her.

She'd thought he might touch her once, but that only happened when they had to step aside for someone passing. Three times, his arm had moved behind her, but there'd been no contact. It was too close to the not-quite massage they'd suffered through all afternoon. "You know how earlier I said I could feel the energy of your body?"

Ryan slowed down even more. "Yeah?"

"I lied because that's what Delilahexpected me to say. I didn't feel anything."

"Oh. I felt yours."

They were almost at the entrance. She stopped.

"You all right?"

Angie thought about asking him if he was telling her the truth, but why would he lie? "I will be," she said. "I'm always nervous before the start of a race."

He leaned in and rested his hand carefully on her bare lower arm. "You're going to knock this out of the park. Just go with your instincts."

That was two votes for instincts, and for once, she didn't overthink it. She simply leaned forward the few inches between them and kissed him on the lips. It was meant to be a quickie, but his arm snaked around her back and he pulled her close as he licked the crease between her lips until they parted for him.

A girlish laugh and a low wolf whistle registered seconds before the glass doors to the casino slid open. It took her a second to realize Ryan had pulled back.

7

A WALL OF NOISE HIT RYAN from the casino, rock music from somewhere near the entrance, bells and dings and chimes from hundreds of slot machines, laughter, cheers from the craps tables. No wonder the doors were so heavy, not just to keep the desert heat out, but to mark the distinction between the casino and the courtyard.

Still, as he walked with Angie, the taste of her on his tongue, none of the glitz and sparkle could hope to compete with this incredibly surprising version of the woman he'd thought he'd known.

A cocktail waitress passed, forcing him to step closer to Angie and he struggled for a second against his need for more contact. He gave in, though. His hand at the small of her back, because while they were in the casino there was no question about who he was. Ryan Ebsen would feel proprietary about his wife, especially considering the hungry looks that were coming from every direction. Even the pit bosses stared as he and Angie passed the table games. The players, including those who had no chance in hell, stopped in midmotion, their hunger blatant. But then that was what a casino was all about.

"Of course, all the restaurants are at the back of the building," Ryan said, moving his mouth closer to her ear. "At least we can keep an eye out for any of the gang."

"I'm not ready to see anyone yet," Angie said, "but God, please tell me that band doesn't play all night."

"You're probably out of luck with that. Did you decide which restaurant?"

"Let's see if we can get in to Hachi first. It's still early, so I don't think we'll have too much of a wait."

Ryan nodded, then noticed that the open staring had eased up considerably. He smiled as he realized it was because they were passing the banks of video poker machines. These folks never looked up. Angie could have been stark naked and not be noticed.

Okay, perhaps he shouldn't think about Angie being naked. Especially when there was no hiding a thing in that dress of hers. Every curve was on display, perfectly wrapped like the most stunning present ever.

"Why are you slowing down when I'm so hungry?" Angie asked, tugging at his sleeve.

Somehow they'd separated. Unacceptable. But instead of the sexuality of his hand on her back, he went to the opposite end of signaling ownership and took her hand in his.

The move startled her, but she got back on track in a few seconds. "Have you seen any of the foursome?"

"Nope," he said, although to be honest he'd been distracted.

"I haven't even found any of the couples," she said as they moved closer to the perimeter, past the steakhouse and the Italian bistro. "I guess this is why the sessions start so late in the day."

"Lots of playtime. Smart to have an intimacy workshop at a casino where there's maximum stimulation of the senses and the endorphins are already swimming."

"Right now, all I care about is sushi. If we can, let's get a table by the window. Get seen."

"I'll do my best," he said as he led her into the foyer of the elegant and ultramodern Japanese restaurant. There was a small line, but the place wasn't packed. He pulled a fifty out of his wallet, reluctantly left Angie standing by the large art thing that looked strangely woodsy, then went to the tuxedo-clad maître d'.

Not five minutes later, they had their window seat, facing each other. It was going to be a long night, so he passed on having a drink and as expected; so did Angie. The food selection was huge, and if they'd had time, he would have gone for the chef's menu, but they needed to be out there, at center stage.

Instead of choosing between the spicy tuna and the sea urchin, he kept stealing glances at Angie. More than eating at the group lunches or room service, this felt like a date. He figured Ebsen would feel the same way, given his goals. As soon as they filled out their sushi orders, he reached across the table for Angie's hand. "You, my love, have been causing quite a stir."

She stared at where he touched her. "How's that?"

"That dress is probably illegal in most states. You're a stunner."

"Trust me, it's the dress more than me. It's actually uncomfortable as hell."

"Really? Too tight?"

"Too much. Too clingy. I'm not used to being so on display."

"You'd never know it. You walk like you own the place."

She looked down, differently this time, a shy move, something to hide the blush that stole up her cheeks. "Thank you," she said, but her voice was lower. Softer.

The waitress came then, and he let Angie go, but man, he didn't want to. And that scared the hell out of him.

IN HER WHOLE LIFE, ANGIE had never felt ornamental. She'd been a loner, a second fiddle, a third wheel, but never arm candy. Looks weren't the currency of worth in her family. Only achievement. Even though she wore Angie Ebsen like a costume, Angie Wolf was still inside and she wasn't sure how to feel about his compliments and the way he looked at her. Flattered, yes, but uneasy, as well.

Sipping a sour apple martini, standing slightly behind Ryan as he threw the dice at the craps table, Angie distracted herself by taking another long look past the immediate crowd to the casino floor beyond, seeking out anyone having anything to do with Intimate At Last.

A loud cheer interrupted her search, making her tense with the knowledge of what came next. Ryan, continuing his wicked winning streak, turned halfway toward her, far enough to wrap his hand around her waist and pull her into a kiss.

He tasted like whiskey and excitement as he thrust into her mouth. While it was perfectly in character, each kiss set her heart pumping as she struggled to remember that none of this was real.

When he finally pulled away, it was only long enough to reach for the dice. Thankfully he didn't ask for her to blow on them, because she couldn't have pulled that off. Besides, Angie Ebsen would never have done something so lowbrow. It was bad enough that she continued to wince each time he returned his attention to the game.

A bump to her elbow made her spill a few drops of her martini, and a quick, deep-voiced apology followed.

She smiled, a reflex more than anything. "No problem."

The man, who had to have fought his way into his slot at

the table, didn't turn immediately to the game. Instead, he tilted his head, looking concerned.

He wasn't as tall as Ryan, not quite as good-looking, although again, Ryan was unfairly handsome. The man whose shoulder brushed against hers wore a natty retro shirt and had a television smile. "Is that a sour apple martini? I'll get you another."

"Don't worry about it," she said, aware of what was going on. Just because she wasn't used to casinos and skintight dresses didn't mean she hadn't had to deal with her fair share of pickup lines.

"I insist," he said, leaning closer.

The arm around her waist surprised her, but only because it hadn't been preceded by a cheer. Ryan wasn't even looking at her. Everything about him had gone into caveman mode. He stood ramrod straight, his nostrils flared, his pupils darkened his eyes and he pulled her so close he practically bent her sideways.

"Is there something we can do for you?" he said, and hell, if she thought the stranger's voice had been deep, Ryan's was just damn dangerous.

"Nope, nope." The man stepped back, not accepting the challenge. "Sorry to have disturbed you."

Ryan didn't move. Not an inch. From her quick glance, Angie realized he was holding up the game. The interloper ceded his territory to the alpha dog and crept off. It was like something from a nature documentary.

"You okay?" he asked.

His voice was still low, but it had softened as he moved in so close she felt his breath on the shell of her ear. She wondered if he'd had one drink too many, because this didn't feel like part of the game plan.

"I'm fine," she said, frowning. "But you're supposed to be neglecting me."

"Sir," the croupier interrupted. "Would you like to pass on the dice?"

Ryan dropped his hold on Angie and turned a brilliant smile on the waiting crowd. "Do you guys want me to pass the dice?"

Like a flash mob, the entire group yelled out some version of "No way," quite a few of them with far more cuss words. Angie could only see him from an angle, but even she recognized the power he exuded, and if she hadn't believed all the stories about his legendary conquests before, she did now.

She polished off her drink and looked around for a cocktail waitress. Ryan evidently threw the ideal numbers, and his fawning audience grew even more exuberant.

She didn't find the waitress but she did discover Marcus sitting at the circular bar in the center of the room. He was alone, his back toward the bar, watching the craps table. Actually, he seemed to be watching Ryan through the space created by the dealers.

Curious that he hadn't looked her way. Also curious that for the first time, Marcus seemed tense. He was leaning forward, his weak chin jutting out, the martini glass in his hand gripped tightly enough for her to notice. Perhaps he was sizing up Ryan as a likely target. If so, tonight's performance should help nudge him in the right direction. The blackmailer had waited until after the retreat was over to send the initial text message, but the move to Cancún could be enough to change the M.O.

Ah, something else snagged his attention. He pulled a cell phone out of his pocket, put his glass down on the bar behind him and started texting.

It occurred to her that there had been at least two cheers since she'd turned her attention to getting another drink. Which meant that Ryan was ignoring her. Good. All part of the sting. Now it was her turn to react. With a pronounced pout, she left the table and headed for the bar.

As she made her way she looked past the stares and outright leers to get a broader picture than she'd been able to while standing behind Ryan. To her left were the big glass doors to the courtyard, and to her right, the hotel lobby, which was separate from the spa lobby. They were equally flashy, but this one didn't inspire calm and relaxation. Soft mood music would never be heard in this cacophony, for one thing. Here, the front desk looked as if it was made of black oil and the uniforms of those who worked it were that much tighter on very fit bodies.

She checked back to find Marcus still texting, looking serious but less intense, but she slowed her step in a delayed reaction to something she'd seen by the front desk.

Looking again, she found what had caught her eye. Tonya Bridges, behind the desk, speaking to one of the assistant managers. Angie recognized the dark suit and the lapel pin that signified the man in charge.

Without another thought, Angie shifted her trajectory. Not in a straight line to Tonya where she stood, but where Angie estimated Tonya would be in a few minutes. Angie walked very slowly, which did nothing to discourage a couple of young men who needed to be cut off from the booze.

Ignoring their attempts to speak with any kind of coherency, Angie observed Tonya quickly scan several pages before the man pulled her into a conversation. Tonya gave off every indication that she didn't want to speak to Mr. Assistant Manager. Visibly worked up, he grabbed her just above the wrist.

Angie was no longer walking slowly. All her danger alerts had gone red at that touch. Tonya smiled, but even at this distance, which was closing by the second, Angie could see how strained it was.

Held up by a large party of tightly packed revelers, Angie didn't lose her cool. She waited the minute it took for the group to pass. There was Tonya and the man who'd touched her, and they were separate now, his hands by his side, his posture tight.

Angie was just within hearing range when the manager said, "Let me know if you need any more faxes. Anytime. At all."

Tonya looked back at him for a moment, then pressed on, right into Angie's path.

"Hi there," Tonya said, quickly folding her paperwork and sticking them in her purse. Her voice was as breezy and casual as she'd been this morning at yoga. "I saw you at the craps tables. Ryan looked like he was having a heck of a lucky streak."

"Yeah," Angie said, glancing back to the table. She wasn't able to see Ryan from this angle, but she did catch a glimpse of Marcus, still sitting at the superlong, elegant open bar that went all the way around the pit where the band continued to knock out terrible covers of Journey and Kansas. She brought her gaze back to Tonya. "He's on fire."

Tonya gave her a questioning head tilt. Angie had already thought about what her reactions should be in this situation. She'd specifically had Tonya in mind, given what they suspected about her father's gambling activities. Quick as a wink, Angie slapped on a loving smile, complete with an indulgent eye-roll that wouldn't have fooled a high school girl let alone a woman raised by two therapists.

"I gather you don't play," Tonya said. She looked great in black skinny jeans and a blue silk short-sleeved blouse. She'd gone heavier on the makeup without overdoing things, and Angie had a strong feeling she was on the hunt, but not for the fax man.

"Oh, no," Angie said, exaggerating her expression. "If I'm

going to give away my money, I want it to go to something that needs it. This casino is doing fine without me."

Tonya chuckled, but there was no humor involved. "No, the house always wins. Were you headed somewhere specific?"

Angie looked back again, this time catching a quick glimpse of Ryan and a young woman who seemed to be standing very, very close. "No," she said. "Well, I was trying to find a cocktail waitress."

"Are you all right?"

Angie turned back, lowered her eyes, avoiding the other woman's. "Peachy," she said. Then she shook her head. "I'm sorry. I didn't mean…"

"No, it's okay. Why don't we head toward the big bar. If you want to, that is."

"You're not booked?"

Tonya smiled, but the grin didn't hold. She was looking behind Angie's shoulder.

When Angie followed her gaze, she saw Ira walking past the table games, and she wondered if he was heading to the sports book. A few seconds later, Delilah followed him. There was no smile on her face, either.

"I can't believe it," Angie said, making sure she was looking at the craps table.

"Can't believe what?" Tonya asked, her voice very strained.

Angie sighed. "Nothing. Just, Ryan's having himself a time."

Tonya started walking more toward Ryan than the bar. It was interesting that being with Tonya, who was very attractive, had a sort of dampening effect on the men around them.

They didn't speak until they were midway between the still-texting Marcus and Ryan, who'd picked up not one, but two admirers. They were both young, college age, probably.

Over twenty-one, at least, but not by much. They weren't touching him, but they were clearly in his orbit. Rooting him on with a lot of hair-touching and giggling.

He couldn't have been rolling the dice this whole time, and when she moved slightly to her left, Angie saw that he'd lost a considerable number of chips. The ones he reached for were black.

"Wow, those are hundreds," Tonya said, then pressed her lips together.

"It's not the money," Angie said, stepping a few inches closer to her would-be friend. "He knows he can't go too crazy or my business manager will take away his cards. Still, I hate gambling. I've always hated it."

"Oh?"

"Ryan isn't a compulsive gambler." Angie made sure she sounded defensive.

Tonya didn't say anything, but questions were there in her eyes.

Angie bit her lip, then sighed. "It broke up my family. Among other things."

"I see," Tonya said. "Believe me."

Okay, so Tonya knew about her father's gambling problem. It was clear from her reaction, from the way she looked at Ryan. "Anyway, it's no big deal. Most of the time, he's wonderful. And we don't come to Vegas often."

"No, I'm sure you don't."

Angie smiled bravely. "What about that drink, hmm? I'm getting desperate."

Tonya returned the grin, and they headed once more toward the bar, but she stopped two steps in. So sharply, Angie had to turn around to find out what had happened. Of course, she knew it was the sight of Marcus that had stopped Tonya. It was evident there was no love lost between those two. And who was that standing next to him?

Angie put herself next to Tonya, then faced Marcus and his flashy companion. Now Angie understood the shocked expression on Tonya's face. Marcus was trying to find the woman's tonsils with his tongue. The woman was several inches taller than him, had long, curly red hair that had to be out of a bottle. And her dress made Angie's look like a tent. Especially across the bust. When the two of them came up for air, Angie was surprised again to find out the woman was legit gorgeous. A ten, at least. Marcus was a two on his best day.

"Is that Marcus's girlfriend?"

Tonya barked out a laugh.

"Oh, God." Angie turned her head, feigning acute embarrassment. "I didn't mean..."

"It's fine. Marcus has...special needs."

Looking back at Ryan, Angie guessed that he'd seen the Marcus-and-call-girl show, as well. But that didn't matter in the least because one of Ryan's young admirers had gone from looking to touching. "Damn him," she snapped. "I don't even know why we bothered."

Silence followed, and Angie didn't have to look to know that Tonya had seen Ryan's new best friend. Angie made sure she looked hurt, but not surprised. This was not new behavior she was witnessing.

Then, Ryan touched the blonde. His fingertips brushed her cheek as he swept back a loose strand of hair. Something inside Angie twisted. It was crazy because the jealousy she'd felt when Ryan had spoken to Jeannie was nothing compared to the body slam she felt now. Which she was supposed to be faking and not experiencing all the way down to her stupid polished toes. The sudden itch to pull the blonde out of his reach scared the hell out of her.

She abruptly turned away and met Tonya's sympathetic eyes. Angie swallowed hard and tried unsuccessfully to force a smile. This was good, she told herself, she was supposed to look as if the rug had just been pulled out from under her. After all, the man she loved had just broken her heart in two.

"Look," Tonya said. "Why don't we get out of here? I'm sorry I said anything at all about Marcus. He's a good guy, and he doesn't mean any harm."

Angie nodded, heading for the doors. "It's all right. Everyone's got something to hide. I hope I haven't given you the wrong impression about Ryan. He can be very sweet. He loves me. He does."

"I've seen you two together," Tonya said, keeping up with Angie's quick steps. "It's obvious he's mad about you. Casinos are just bad news, that's all."

Behind her, Ryan's voice carried over the noise of the slots, of the music, calling her name. She didn't want to stop. Not just because of the role she was playing. Seeing him with that girl rubbing up against him had been painful enough, but when *he'd* touched *her*...

She needed to leave, now. Get away from Tonya, from the job, from everything until she could clear her head. Somehow she needed to make sense of the churning in her stomach, the tightness in her chest.

But before she could make her final move, a hand gripped her arm, and a fresh cascade of unwanted emotions poured through her. When she turned to look at Ryan's stricken face, she didn't have to act at all.

8

RYAN'S HEART LURCHED in his chest as his focus narrowed to Angie and only her. The look of betrayal she'd given him hit low and hard, as if he'd done something unforgivable.

He hurried back to the craps table, and as he stuffed chips into his pockets he called out Angie's name. He didn't have to fake his desperation.

How had that one look made it stunningly clear that she wanted no part of him? Not even sure he'd picked up all the hundred-dollar chips, he darted through the crowd to the exit and chased after Angie and she was fast, even on those heels.

It was Tonya who brought some reality back to the situation, and he was damn grateful for it. He'd caught her reflection in the glass display case, and just like that he was back in the game. Shit, the past couple of minutes…

Tonya followed him with no attempt to hide what she was doing. Worried for Angie's safety? Gathering more data for possible blackmail?

He sped up for a few paces. "Angie, wait."

She didn't look back.

Fine, he could deal with that, at least until they got to their room. If he didn't have a heart attack first. His reactions were messed up. He needed to calm down, let her keep ahead of him. Make sure he gave himself time to turn off the weird and unexpected panic that made it difficult to breathe.

They'd passed the gate to their private courtyard. A few folks were using the spa pool, people from their group. None of the suspects. Ryan didn't pause but the clicking of Tonya's heels stopped. He walked more quickly now that they were a few feet away from their bungalow. Angie opened the door before he had a chance to get out his card key and he had to hustle before it closed behind her.

Once inside with the bolt locked, he let out a long breath. He almost asked her what the hell she'd been doing, but he didn't dare say a word before he checked the room for surveillance. He put his finger up to his lips. Angie's startled nod told him that she wasn't thinking clearly, either. The bug sweeper had been locked away along with his real cell phone. He took out both, put the phone in his pocket and began the scan.

Angie hadn't moved. "I'm going to get ready for bed," she said. "Do you need anything in the bathroom?"

"Yeah, give me a second," he said as he hurried to make sure the room was clean. No red lights went off as he scanned, which wasn't surprising. A moment later, he left the bathroom to Angie.

With her night things held close to her chest, she barely looked at him as she slipped past him and closed the door.

He continued the sweep, wanting to be done. He'd have preferred to use the time alone to regroup. The fact that he'd confused reality and work bothered him a hell of a lot. He'd fought hard to keep work and personal business separate but more than that, he had no need or desire for this kind of… emotion. He didn't get entangled. Not ever. Now he felt up to his ass in alligators, unable to find solid ground. It sucked.

At least there were no red lights on the sweeper as he moved it carefully through their room. This particular device could detect not only all kinds of radio frequencies but pinhole lenses of tiny cameras. Finally he was assured that no one had planted a bug, but that still left one more item to check. He went to the laptop he'd left on the dresser.

The plastic tab was no longer in place. Someone had screwed around with the laptop.

Everything extraneous left his thoughts as he replayed each word they'd said since they entered the room. Habit and discipline had insured that neither of them had misspoken. There was no camera in the dummy computer for just this reason. However, there was a microphone.

He was at the bathroom door in three strides. Of course it was locked, why wouldn't she lock it? But he had to get in there, now, because whoever had been in the room might be listening to everything, and she needed to be on her toes until their team in L.A. had a chance to check out the hard drive.

He knocked. Loudly. "Hey, sweetie. What did you lock the door for? Was I really such a bad boy?"

He leaned against the door, but got nothing. Not even the sound of the water running. When it opened, he nearly knocked her over, but he did manage to grab on to her shoulders. Her naked shoulders. A towel covered her breasts, but the naked part was far more important.

"Are you drunk?" She was stiff in his hands but allowed him to walk her backward until he could close the door.

Releasing her was more difficult than it should be, which pissed him off. This was business, dammit. "Someone's been in the room," he said, leaning in, noticing that the only clothing she had on was a red thong. He considered running out and getting her a blanket to cover herself with, but a tilt of her head stopped that thought in its tracks.

"Well?" she asked, clearly having had to wait too long for him to explain.

"Wait," he said, letting her go in order to turn on the water in the shower. He thought about dunking his head under the spray, but that would be admitting far too much. When he straightened, she was close enough to him that he could see the small gold flecks of her dark brown eyes. Still, he leaned in. "No cameras. No radio frequencies in any part of the room. It's the laptop. We need to get it scanned," he said. "Right now."

Angie's eyebrows rose and her towel lowered, but only a little.

Calling Jeannie forced him to move back. As he hit her speed dial, he made the mistake of glancing at the mirror. Christ. Angie's bare back made his cock stir. Which was nothing compared to the view of her nearly naked behind. The thong made it sexier than if she hadn't had a thing on.

"What's wrong?" Jeannie's voice was rough with sleep and annoyance.

Turning his gaze to the bathtub, he explained about the laptop.

"Any other signs of intrusion?" Jeannie asked, not pissed anymore.

"Nope, that's it."

"I'll see that it gets done. Leave your phone on. I'll have someone text with the outcome. Just keep being a happy couple until we get this sorted."

"Right," he said. "Tell them to hurry." When he hung up, he found Angie leaning against the sink, her towel still in place and her expression pensive. He should have gone back to staring at the tub, but he couldn't, despite the fact that they'd had their first real confirmation that the blackmailer was scoping them out.

"There's no camera on that computer," Angie said.

"What?"

"Whatever they loaded on to the computer isn't video."

He blinked, nodded, brought his thoughts to heel. "That's

the upside." He looked at the cell phone again, urging it to ring, despite the fact that no one could have possibly searched the hard drive yet. Like a man under a spell, he couldn't help but stare once more at Angie, at the way her dark hair swept over her shoulder, the curve of her hips. "I wonder if it was just us," he said. "Or if whoever it is will be trying to surveil everyone. That might be the approach across the board."

"Not everyone would have brought a laptop."

"True. But I imagine they have options. Anything quick. In and out, because it's a risk, breaking in like that. Maybe someone on the hotel staff working for them? Someone with a master key?" He glanced at his phone again. Focused on it as if his thoughts could make it ring. "Did you get anything useful when you left the craps table? I should have asked. Was there something else to tell Jeannie?"

Angie's inhale drew his gaze, and he just gave it up. As long as they were in the bathroom and she was undressed, he was physically incapable of not looking. Unbelievable. Thirty-two years old and this was his life.

"Tonya knows Ira's a problem gambler," she said, talking faster than normal as if she would forget if she didn't spit it out. "And Marcus likes high-priced hookers."

"I saw him with that redhead. She had to cost him a pretty penny."

"From what Tonya said, it's a regular thing with him. I also saw her leaving the front desk office. The assistant manager had faxed some pages for her. I only got a glimpse of them, not enough to see what they were, but it made me wonder. Intimate At Last has an office here, on site. There's no way on earth they don't have a fax machine. So what was she faxing so late on a Wednesday night that couldn't have waited till morning? Why not use the hotel's business office for guests if it was something she didn't want her partners to know?"

"Well, hell. The only one we haven't caught doing something hinky is Delilah."

"She's probably the mastermind. At least she's clever enough not to get caught."

"I don't know." Ryan shook his head, trying to piece together the night, what he'd want to put in his report. "Marcus was watching me like he knew something. Or maybe he was waiting to hear something back. For example, that our computer had been breached. You'd left the craps table already—"

Angie nodded, clearly clicking with the notion that Marcus had been up to no good. She pushed off from the sink. "If we can get a trace on whatever he did to the computer—" She gestured with her arm. The one holding the towel.

Her breasts were perfect. Small, pert, with hardened nipples that made his mouth water.

Her gasp made him turn away, guilt slamming him in the gut. He knew she'd covered herself again, but he wasn't sure at all what to say.

She cleared her throat. "Um, there's no camera on the laptop," she said.

Keeping his eyes low, he nodded. "We've already established that."

When she didn't respond, he dared a glance. Angie, with very wide eyes and pink cheeks, motioned to the door with her chin.

"Oh," he said. "Sorry. Sorry. I—" Now the sound of the water seemed exceedingly loud and he noticed she'd been in the middle of taking off her makeup because there were cotton balls on the counter and a bottle of something blue open. "There's no reason for me to wait in here."

"Not that I can think of," she said, looking at everything but him. When he moved, she moved, skittering around trying to keep herself as covered as she could. Only, there was a flash of her from the side, a reflection in the mirror as he took the few steps to the door.

The swell of her breast made his pace stutter and his hand slip on the knob. The nipple was hidden, but it was too late. He'd seen it, the exact shade of pink and how her areola was like a perfect halo. The modest glimpse of side breast shouldn't have knocked him for a loop, but it was the most erotic thing he'd seen tonight.

He was out the door in a flash, upset, embarrassed and more confused than ever. "Well, that happened," he said softly, not sure whether he should laugh or offer to sleep in the bathtub. In the meantime, he put on his pajamas, keeping himself away from the computer even though he couldn't imagine there was anyone watching.

Changing wasn't easy, though, because his body was clearly trying to make a point. His brain filling him with urges and memories that made it hard to breathe. His cock, on the other hand, was being a son of a bitch, already more than half-hard. Like a man obsessed, he imagined kissing her now, when he knew so much more. Wondered what it would feel like to meander up those mile-long legs of hers, first with his hands, then with his mouth.

In perfect and swift retribution, Angie walked out of the bathroom just as he pressed his palm against his now very hard and insistent erection. A second later, the cell phone rang, but the damage had already been done.

ANGIE DID HER BEST NOT TO STARE. Not that he didn't deserve to be stared at, but she was above that sort of thing. What was important now was the report from the team. She needed the distraction more than she could say, especially since she'd realized in the middle of washing her face that she could have put on her sleep shirt the moment Ryan had entered the bathroom.

"That's a relief," Ryan said into the phone. He'd turned his back on her, the chicken. Too late. She just wished there was a way to delete the image that was now burned into her brain forever. It wasn't as if those pajamas were especially thick or tight fitting. Or that his hand hadn't been *right there*.

Although he had looked amusingly like a kid caught with his hand not just in the cookie jar, but with a fistful of Oreos. Quite a fistful, in fact.

"No, okay. We'll work on it tomorrow. Maybe an email from Roxanne wouldn't be out of the question?"

Oh, so, keylogging. She imagined it would be hypervisor based, software running underneath the operating system, becoming a virtual machine that would reproduce itself on the blackmailers end. At least, that's what she'd look for first. She would have asked Ryan to put the call on speaker, but his back was still turned.

At least it wasn't just her. Angie wished it wasn't so late, as she'd love to talk to Liz about, well, everything, but that would have to wait. What Angie needed this minute was to put herself to bed. Because falling asleep was the only possible way out of the mess in her head. Unfortunately, despite being tired enough to face-plant in the middle of a run, she was also chock full of adrenaline and raging hormonal influences.

Even so, she put her clothes away and parked her bathroom case, then slid beneath the sheets. Ryan was either listening to a very long explanation of computer tech or was waiting until his hard-on deflated.

Finally he made a quick dash to the bathroom. She wanted to be snarky about that, but in truth, he was being considerate. He didn't want to make her any more uncomfortable than she'd been. God, when she'd lowered the towel…

She closed her eyes as she positioned herself on her side,

facing away from Ryan's sleep spot. Nothing needed to change. Outwardly, at least.

So much had happened since they'd gone to dinner she could barely get things straight. The way she'd reacted to Ryan in the casino was a major issue. Made more immediate than ever now that he'd seen her, and she'd seen what she did to him.

It wasn't a terribly big surprise. This thing between them had been burning like a slow fuse, and hell, maybe Liz was right and they should just bow to the inevitable. But the idea of sleeping with her partner while in the middle of a case felt fundamentally wrong.

Nothing about this case wasn't fundamentally screwed up, even without adding sex.

The bathroom door opened, and in quick order, she felt the bed dip and the covers move.

"No trace of a microphone," he said, calm as could be. "Whoever it was is key—"

"Keylogging, yeah, I figured. I assume we're going to use that to our advantage." She started to roll onto her back, but stopped short.

"The team is working on that. Getting together some scripts. A push by Roxanne to keep the affair going. Something like that."

"Good," she said, closing her eyes. A sudden and vivid picture hit her. Of Ryan in his pajama pants, pressing down on his cock. Followed immediately by the way he'd stared at her when the towel had slipped. She bit the side of her cheek to keep steady. The last thing in the world she wanted was for him to hear something weird in her voice. "Who'd you talk to?"

"Arnold. He said that a trace will take time, especially because whoever uploaded the program knew his stuff."

She nodded. "So not a game changer. We keep doing what we've been doing."

"Yep," he said.

Silence fell, and while it should have been a comfort, it was the opposite. Her nipples had hardened. Just like that. Hard like erasers and she found herself pressing her palm on her breasts, which just reminded her again of his hand and his pajamas....

Angie was reasonably sure she was going clinically insane. What the ever-loving *hell* was she doing to herself? Only a complete masochist would continue to somehow forget that Ryan was not her boyfriend, her lover, her husband, her dream man, her *anything* except her partner. Regardless of erections. Regardless of dubious advice from friends.

There just didn't seem to be anywhere for her to hide. No switch that would let her turn off the thoughts. Even during her run this morning, her last bastion of sanity had been filled with thoughts of Ryan and sex. Sex and Ryan.

Perfect. Wonderful. She should be getting the FBI Special Agent of the Year award any minute now.

"What was that sigh about?" Ryan asked.

"Frustration," she admitted, and winced at what he undoubtedly thought she meant. Great, the incredibly uncomfortable silence came back to make everything worse.

"I have to admit, it's harder than I thought it would be," Ryan said, his words soft and half-mumbled.

"What is?" Angie did roll over this time. Onto her back, so all she had to do was turn her head to see him. At least, see him in shadow. Because he couldn't mean what she thought he meant.

"Pretending."

She froze as his response derailed her. She understood the word but not what he meant. Pretending to be married? Pretending they hadn't been hot for each other for ages?

He turned until he was lying on his side facing her. Then, as if he hadn't already stolen her breath, he reached over and took her hand in his.

She wished she could see his eyes more clearly, even though she was pretty sure about his intention. The next bit would be up to her. If she slipped away from his grasp, they could hold on to their very rocky status quo. If she reciprocated…

Before she could talk herself out of it, she pulled away.

9

"I MEAN, TONIGHT," HE SAID, as if he'd never touched her. "It was weird flirting with those girls. Acting like a jackass at the table. Not my style, that's not me."

"You were very convincing. I'm sure what Tonya and Marcus saw helped the case. You looked like a man trying to puff himself up, to make himself feel more powerful. That's exactly what you were supposed to do."

"True," he said. "I think we both did really well tonight."

Except for the part where she'd completely lost touch with reality. But he didn't have to know that. "Agreed."

"So, six?"

"Yeah. Thanks."

He leaned over and did something to the clock, then ended up with his back to her once more.

She stared at him, the shape of his head, the edge of his T-shirt, his shoulder rising and falling with his breath. It was tempting to take another stab at understanding him. For all the seeing each other in compromising positions, all the touching and kissing they'd practiced, this talk right now was by far the most intimate thing that had happened since she'd arrived.

What she didn't know was if that was a good thing or a

bad thing. Keeping her distance felt like a matter of survival, but opening up to Ryan might end up being the linchpin to this whole operation. Perhaps if they became real people to each other, the mystique left over from the night that almost was would go away.

Knowing the real man would certainly change the fantasy Ryan she'd been carrying for so long. It was ridiculous to think her reaction this evening had been about Ryan himself. She didn't know him well enough to feel anything more than physical attraction, and that had never been enough for her. Her fantasies weren't built on anything but lust and fiction. Until this week, it had felt like being in lust with a character in a TV show.

STARING AT THE CLOCK wasn't in any way helping Ryan relax. At the very least it should have bored him to sleep. But the night ahead of him was destined to be uncomfortable in every possible way.

She wasn't sleeping, either. He could tell from her breathing, her small movements. What he needed was a brain wipe, but what he might be able to get was something less provocative to replace the miasma of erotica starring his bedmate that continued to plague him. "Tomorrow I'm going to sign up with Marcus for a private session. Give him an opportunity to ferret out some damning information."

"Oh, God," she said.

"I know. I haven't wanted to avoid something this badly since my old man gave me *the talk*."

"Oh, that," she said. "How old were you?"

"Twelve." He stared at the window, so aware that she was a matter of inches away from him it was hard to think. "I'll give him credit. He was creative about it."

Angie shifted. "What do you mean?"

Without looking he could tell she was on her back again.

"Books weren't his thing. Neither was a straightforward conversation. What he did tell me wasn't exactly orthodox."

"No 'When a mommy and daddy love each other very much…?'"

He laughed, the sound surprisingly bitter even to his own ears. The heat in his face made him yank on the comforter. "Why are we talking about this?"

"You brought it up."

"I really, really don't want to think about getting a massage from Marcus."

"Understood. Carry on, then. He was creative…?"

Ryan's sigh was more telling than he wanted to admit. But at this point, talking about his father, which was his least favorite topic in the world, was preferable to letting his mind have free rein. "It wasn't the mechanics that he'd gotten wrong," he admitted. "It was the entire subject of women."

"Oh?" Of course Angie sounded surprised. He never discussed his private life. Not even with Jeannie.

"He's sure as hell not anyone's idea of a model father." Ryan tried to make it sound as if he were joking but the attempt fell flat. "He lives his life as if he's in a pulp novel from the fifties."

"For example…?"

"Chauvinistic crap about a woman's place, blah blah blah. You know that old saw, 'A man wants a maid in the living room, a cook in the kitchen and a whore in the bedroom'? That was…is…his credo."

When she didn't say anything for a weirdly long time, he couldn't hold out any longer. He used rearranging his pillow as an excuse to not only settle on his back, but to look at her.

Even in shadow, he had no difficulty filling in the details. No cover would be thick enough, ever again, and wasn't that completely screwed up. He bit back a groan that would have made everything worse.

ANGIE WAS GLAD, NOW, that she was staring at the ceiling. Things had just gotten very personal. She could sense his embarrassment as if his thoughts had weight. If she didn't do something soon, this would be the last time he'd open up to her, of that she felt certain. The risk seemed worth it. She faced him, moving that much closer to the middle of the bed, but being the chicken she was, she stared at her hand instead of meeting his eyes.

"My mother gave me the talk. She had a book of some kind that explained everything in excruciating clinical detail. With pictures. It was horrifying."

"I can only imagine."

"A week later, I got to go over the entire subject again, with my father. Evidently he'd found my mom's book and thought he could do better."

The bedclothes rustled. His warm breath swept gently over her hand, and when she looked up in surprise they were only inches apart. One-quarter turn more and they'd touch.

"How long did it take you to recover?"

It took her a second to remember what he was talking about. "There is no recovery. Only shudders when the thought swims to the surface."

He did laugh then. "How old were you?"

"Still in middle school. Hadn't been kissed yet. Never really thought about boys. I was too caught up in training."

"Track and field."

"Yeah. That was our religion. Competition in general. My family is really into overachieving. In every aspect of life. Needless to say, they weren't thrilled to discover I wanted to work for the Bureau. They had me penciled in as an attorney. After all, they already had two doctors in the family. I would have rounded out their résumés." She shrugged, tempted to move her hand closer, just to feel more of his breath.

"They must be really proud of you now."

She checked to see if he was being sincere. Ryan's free hand moved scant inches across the mattress until he touched her. It was different. Surprisingly sweet. "Not yet," she said.

"What? I can't imagine any parent not being proud of you. Look what you've accomplished and you're not even thirty. You were what, in the top five at the academy? You're the highest-ranking woman in hand-to-hand in the whole damn country. Which is chicken feed next to what you can do on a computer. You've made a major contribution to forensics, Angie. That's like winning all the gold medals and a bag of chips on the side."

She laughed. Thank goodness he'd given her a reason, because even though she didn't want to, her eyes had filled with tears. How was this moment even happening? Ryan was the least sentimental person she knew. Whom she thought she knew.

After she pushed her hair back, she rested her hand on Ryan's. Gave him a little squeeze to say thanks. When she went to pull away, he stopped her. Stopped her breathing, too.

He sighed and his breath warmed her neck. "This is not a good idea," he said.

Right. At least they were on the same page. "No, it's not."

"We're not..."

"God, no."

"But," he said. "We do need practice. Kissing, I mean."

"We do," she said, but the conversation was slipping away from her, the timbre of his voice and his closeness taking over.

He inhaled a long breath between his teeth. "I don't know about you, but I'm not going to sleep anytime soon."

"Maybe it'll be relaxing. Practicing, I mean." Who was she kidding? They were on a precipice with a lot hanging in the balance. Did she want to pull herself back up to the ledge, or let herself fall? With her heart pounding and her fingers crossed, she said, "Tomorrow we're going to the hot springs. We'll have to touch a lot."

"The hot springs," he echoed, his voice a gruff whisper. "Right. It'll be…hot."

The hand that wasn't holding him up took all of Angie's attention. It had moved from his side to just above her right cheek. Almost touching her. Slightly tickling as he pushed some wisps of hair back.

"Hot," she whispered, even though she didn't really know why.

It wasn't just his hand that was moving now, but his whole upper body. Achingly slowly. Giving her plenty of time to say no.

"It's just…" His voice had become even rougher, softer, making Angie strain to hear.

She had to lift her head off the pillow. To hear.

"Say yes," he whispered, inches away from her, so close to her parted lips they might have touched. "You need to say it. Say something."

Her wince wasn't planned. Neither was the hand to his chest. "Wait a minute."

She felt him stop breathing again, still completely. A lot of rapid heartbeats went by before he moved back. Not just back but away.

As she lost contact, she thought about grabbing his T-shirt, pulling him down, but she couldn't.

"I'm sorry," he said. He cleared his throat, and repeated the words twice. By the time he grew quiet, he was as far away from her as he could get on the bed. "I have no excuse. That was completely unprof—"

"Stop." She tugged at his arm, forcing him to move until she could see his profile in the moonlight. "Please, stop. I'm not…" Holding up her index finger, she closed her eyes so she could concentrate. When she opened them again, she felt calmer, although still unbelievably shaken. "I'm not saying no like that."

"What?"

"Not like, no, this is wrong or bad. More like no, this is something we'd better think about. I was kind of swept away there, and I need to be here. This isn't a minor decision."

He didn't say anything for a long time. They both were breathing as if they'd just come back after a quick jog, and she had to squeeze her legs together to ease the pressure, but finally, he said, "We really are all wrong for each other."

"Yes, we are." She felt the urge to pull the covers up to her chest, but she didn't. "That doesn't necessarily mean—"

"It's this undercover bullshit—" he said, breaking in. "I had no business—"

"I was jealous," she said, louder.

"What?"

"Of that girl at the craps table."

Silence. Then, "Huh."

"I know. Ridiculous. And you're right. This role-playing stuff and the kissing. I didn't expect… I didn't know what to expect. This is so far outside my range of experience…."

"No one on earth has experience doing what we're doing."

"I know. I do. But it's really complicated. Between us."

Ryan's hand moved halfway across the bed, as it had before. She wished he would stop doing that because she couldn't help the reaction it caused. The way it made her ache.

"For what it's worth, I think you're really brave," he said.

"What? Why?"

"You just dove into the deep end of the pool. Jumped in without a life vest, without any prep at all. For this sting? That took one hell of a lot of courage."

"The whole operation was on the line."

"Doesn't negate my point."

She smoothed down the comforter. "I'm not that altruistic. I'm going after the job in D.C. You did hear what I said about me and my family, right?"

"Yeah, I get it."

"But thank you."

She had no reason to believe he was smiling when he said, "You're welcome." Still, she was pretty sure he was. If she flipped on the light right now, she'd see it. See his strong jaw and his humor in the face of their impossible situation. Made so much worse by the months she'd spent making him into her fantasy man. Here, in the flesh, she'd seen his toes. The way he pulled on his bottom lip. How he looked when he was out of his depth and when he still had sleep in his eyes.

Her hand went out to meet his and this time their fingertips brushed. It felt startling and intimate and sweet. And if she had half a brain, she'd roll back onto her other side, roll all the way back to L.A. before it was too late. Because the only thing that had changed since that long-ago party was that she wanted the real Ryan now.

THE TOUCH OF HER FINGERS on his got his poor confused cock revving up again. Granted, it had never softened completely, not even after her "no" had penetrated past the layers of brain-fogging lust. Thank God it was dark and there were covers. Thank God they were talking and it wasn't horrible and weird and that she didn't want to leave this very minute.

It wasn't as if he'd planned on seducing her. He knew what that was like, exactly what that was like, and tonight he had not been hunting. He'd been…cast in a spell.

Yeah, that totally sounded macho. Cast in a spell. What were these stupid exercises doing to him? New-age music was dissolving his brain.

Her nails came into play, and he hissed at the sensation. For Christ's sake, a fingertip was not supposed to be a huge erogenous zone. Everything was out of proportion, and damn, he wanted to be next to her, her body pressed to his.

"Were you drunk?" Angie asked.

"When? Tonight?"

"No. Halloween."

"Oh. No. Not particularly. At least not until after."

"After the party?"

"After I realized what I'd done. How I'd come on to you. Not my finest moment."

"Hey, we didn't cross any lines."

"I crossed one of my own."

She sighed, and he closed his eyes, wishing he had that sound on tape so he could hear it over and over again. He'd like to fall asleep to that sound.

"I was very tempted."

His eyes shot open. "What's that?"

"Halloween. I wanted to."

"Seriously?"

"Yeah. But I'm glad we were interrupted. Because we work together and all."

"Which is why—"

"Exactly," she said. And then she moved closer to him, pulling the bedding with her.

He could reach much more than her fingertips now. He could feel the shift in the air, in his rapid pulse as he skimmed over her amazingly soft skin. "In a way, we are technically on vacation."

She laughed. "Technically we're not, but I do see your point. It feels as if we're on vacation. As if the rules don't apply here."

He nodded. "Exactly. I mean, we're sleeping together. Every night. Kissing each other. Our homework is to hold you in my arms and we were supposed to wash each other's hair." Then he swallowed, and willed his erection to simmer the hell down, because getting too hopeful here could end badly. For both of them. The important thing was to let her call the shots.

But hoping was acceptable. Unavoidable.

Her position had changed, her head was no longer resting on her palm. It was on her pillow, and he was about ten seconds away from turning on the light because he had no idea what she was thinking.

When her fingers trailed up his hand to his inner arm, then all the way to the crook of his elbow, he began to get a clue.

"It's late," she said.

"Yep." His voice didn't sound half as squeaky as he'd feared.

"I'll never get back to sleep now."

He could hear the quaver in her voice. She teased him with touches so light they were barely there, making his entire nervous system ache with the need to be inside her. Jesus.

As a measure of self-defense, he turned over so he was on his stomach. That he was inches away from Angie was, well, perfect.

"I'm extremely attracted to you," he said. "Just to be clear. But I'll stop this right now if you need me to. I won't touch you, or make jokes, or even insinuate anything that could make you uncomfortable. I mean it."

"You're saying what happens next is up to me."

"I am." His free hand itched to turn on the light, to know if she was smiling, or frowning, or—

"Yes," she said. "Yes."

He'd known from that first day that Angie was going to kill him, and he was damn sure this would be the moment.

10

ANGIE HELD HER BREATH, waiting. She'd said the word, but she couldn't follow through. She wanted to, God, she did, but her body was in some kind of shock or something, because—

Ryan pressed up against her, holding her gently as one hand slipped behind her neck and the other ran down her arm. His lips brushed hers. With a so-soft "Thank God" she might have missed it, he deepened the kiss.

Despite all the verbal foreplay, the tease and the tension, she was unprepared for the shock of his body. She wanted his clothes off. Hers, too. Now, right now because she needed the contact everywhere. She wanted to be wrapped up in Ryan, to do everything all at once.

Their lips and tongues were ravening, insatiable, so eager each time they parted she had to gasp in as much air as she could, only to immediately return to drowning in sensation.

He made soft noises as he kissed her, as he reached down to the bottom of her sleep shirt and snuck his hand underneath. The sounds were low, and growly and she doubted he even realized he was making them, but each time, her hips arched of their own accord.

It took her a few minutes to realize she was being equally loud and demanding, growing more impatient even as she grabbed on to his rock-hard ass as if she never planned to let it go.

The heat and hardness of his cock bled through his poor pajamas as he rocked into her. He'd better have condoms right next to him or else there would be big trouble.

He broke from their kiss, murmuring something that sounded like "Up, up, up," until her dazzled brain understood he wanted to take off her clothes.

Of course, she obliged, but as soon as her nightshirt went flying across the room, her hands were yanking on his pajamas, tugging as if wanting him naked was enough to make him so.

"Wait," he said. "Wait, I need to..." And he went too far away from her, whole inches, it wasn't fair, and then he whipped his T-shirt off. "Close your eyes."

"I want to see."

"I know," he said. "That's why you have to close your eyes."

"What the hell are you talking about?"

He growled, literally, then said, "Just close them for one second."

She did, but she wasn't happy about it until the light right above the headboard came on. "Oh."

"Exactly."

She should have waited another thirty seconds to open her eyes again, but there was entirely too much to see. His chest, of course, but seeing that wasn't the good part. Touching, playing with his sparse, dark hair and his little peaked nips, now that would be something to remember.

It occurred to her that it might be rude that she'd been staring at his chest the whole time the light had been on, but when she glanced at his face, she realized he hadn't noticed.

She did like the way his lips had parted and how his own eyes looked utterly dazed.

"You're incredible."

Her hands went to her barely-B-cup breasts, but quelled the urge to cover herself. For God's sake, he'd already seen them. His pupils were huge, he was practically drooling. So she captured her nipples, which were pretty long, between her middle and ring fingers.

Ryan groaned as if she was hurting him.

When she looked down to see the outline of his erection pressing against the soft cotton of his pj's, she arched her back. It might have been her imagination, but the wet spot over the crown of his cock seemed to get larger.

"You're killing me," he said. "I knew you would. But I never guessed. If I could move, I would have those panties off you right now. I would bury myself between your thighs for the rest of my life."

"That's sweet," she said, "but how about you take off the rest of your clothes first."

"What?"

She nodded, looking straight at his bottoms.

He exhaled as he followed her gaze. "Okay, but you have to put your hands somewhere else. Please."

Her chuckle stopped dead as Ryan got up on his knees and pushed his pajamas down. Oh, the cloth hadn't lied. He was impressive. And eager. She didn't even blink as he bared himself completely. She'd seen so much of his body but she couldn't have imagined how the sight of him like this would affect her.

Every part of her reacted with want. Between her legs, her breasts, her breathing, the very feel of her skin, the flush that spread like honey all through her body. "Condom," she said, the word breaking on the last syllable.

He had started toward her, inching across the bed on his knees, but he stopped, turned just enough for her to ogle the single most stunning bare male ass she'd ever seen, and she'd seen Michelangelo's *David*. Ryan yanked open his bedside drawer and struggled with his wallet.

His cursing got creative for a minute, and then he pulled out two packets and threw the wallet on the floor.

"That's ambitious of you."

"I was a Boy Scout. Now, please, dear God, if you have any mercy in your heart, please let me take off those panties."

She smiled as she made herself ready. Her hands, as they adjusted her pillow, actually trembled. Somehow she managed to kick the sheet and comforter down far enough. When she looked up she found Ryan gripping his thick erection, on his knees right next to her.

"You're stunning," he said, his voice husky and thick.

"What I am is impatient," she said, lifting her hips a few inches.

"Stop, stop, don't help. Not yet. Let me… Just let me."

To see him so undone, and before they'd even started made her heart pound and her flush deepen. She'd never felt more desired or more beautiful. It sent a rush through her that felt better than winning any race.

He positioned himself between her knees, gently parting them until she was spread enough for his liking. Then he ran his hands up her thighs, stopping when he reached the edge of her underwear. He slipped underneath the white cotton and his eyes closed for a moment as he brushed his fingers outward for a few inches, then back to the center, where he explored, with only his fingertips, across that exquisitely sensitive skin between thigh and labia.

Her squirming made him open his eyes, but he didn't speed up and he didn't move closer to where she wanted him, the bastard.

If he didn't pick up the pace, she was going to start flicking her nipples, which she might do, anyway, because God, they were so tight, and she was so ready. "Ryan," she said, surprised that the word came out so breathy.

He grinned wickedly, and bent down, still not removing her panties. With widely parted lips, he covered her exactly where she ached the most, and warmed her with his hot breath.

She knocked his chin with her arched hips, but he didn't seem to mind. "You need to remember something," she said, seconds away from ripping off the last of her clothes. "I'm top of the class in hand-to-hand."

He laughed as he pulled the crotch of her underwear to the left, baring her, at least partly. The growl returned, and then there was his tongue sneaking between her lips and finding her swollen clit with uncanny precision.

She cried out, pushing up into that hardened tongue, impossibly aroused. It wasn't like her. Ryan had barely touched her, and yet she could already feel the beginning of her climax building deep inside. She'd grabbed on to the sheet so tightly she was afraid it might rip, but dammit, something had to give. Now.

RYAN COULDN'T BELIEVE HOW amazing she tasted, how hard her clit was between his lips as he sucked the nub until Angie was a quivering mess beneath him. Her legs were holding him down, heels digging into his back, but he didn't care. He doubted she even realized she'd done that. Doubted she could think anymore.

He went back to flicking, fast and hard, then when her thigh muscles tensed he pushed two fingers inside her.

She came like a bottle rocket. He hoped the bungalow had thick walls because she was loud. And gripping his fingers so tightly he could scarcely imagine what it would feel like to bury his cock inside her.

He pulled back, letting her legs fall to the bed and taking

her panties down at the same time. For a moment, he simply looked at her. The full body blush, the way her dark hair was wild on the pillow, her breasts with those gorgeous nipples rising and falling with her gasps. She was magnificent naked. Long lines, sleek and defined, and damn how she made his cock pulse as he looked at her beautiful sex. Lips thickened and damp, pink and perfect, and all he wanted to do was give her pleasure. Bring her to the brink over and over again, until she begged him to stop. And when they were both dripping with exhaustion and wrung-out from pleasure, he'd hold her in his arms just to feel her breathing.

With shaky hands, he opened the condom, and carefully sheathed himself. For once, he was grateful for the barrier. He needed the dampening effect because he was one clench away from coming.

He lifted those amazing legs again, kissing her inner thighs as he brought them to his shoulders. She had another aftershock with his lips on her skin, and that was intense all by itself. He'd done that. Given her that.

He had to stretch to get hold of the free pillow, but he was able to tuck it neatly under her, planning to get a much better view of that behind when they weren't so occupied.

She'd opened her eyes, finally. Dark as night, slightly damp eyelashes that worried him for a moment, but her smile let him know she wasn't crying. "Oh, my God," she said. "That was…"

"Only the beginning."

She rolled her eyes, but not the way she'd ever done it before. "You're going to kill me."

"I know the feeling."

Letting her hips down, he positioned himself, his whole being urging him to thrust now, now, now. "Angie. Look at me."

She did. She met his gaze, and damn if there weren't sparks.

"Keep your eyes open," he said, his voice barely recognizable. He rubbed himself between her lips, groaning at the slickness, then found where he belonged. "As long as you can," he whispered, needing to watch her right back. To see her come apart.

He pushed forward into the wet heat of her, and every part of him was there, right there where they were joined. Every part but his eyes as he watched her head go back, her mouth open in a silent cry, the perfection of her neck as she arched. For him.

When he was fully in her, he had to stop. No choice. His gasp reminded him to breathe again, his shudder was like that kick the moment before sleep.

He wanted to stay there for as long as she'd have him, but his cock needed friction.

Moving inside her became a symphony, every push building to an inevitable crescendo. Ryan wanted to see her eyes, watch her body, stare at his cock each time part of himself disappeared. As he thrust faster, his world narrowed and there, the pool of heat that signaled the start of it, his balls tightening, his muscles tensing tighter and tighter.

She spasmed around him, her climax squeezing his cock and it was as if all his atoms came apart, a supernova that made him see spots behind his eyelids and sent his heart racing so fast he thought he might just die.

Some time must have passed, though, because he could feel his burning lungs and his aching thighs, and when he looked down, there she was, the light making her skin look golden.

All he wanted to do was fall where he was and do nothing for a week, but instead, he pulled out of her, reluctant to leave then forced himself to climb out of bed to take care of business.

When he came back, she slowly moved her head so she could look at him. "You're here."

"I am."

"I'm glad."

He grinned. "Me, too." Then he pulled up the bedding, grabbed the pillow she'd pushed to the side and settled next to her.

She rolled into his arms as if she'd always known the way.

11

"Angie." Her shoulder was being tugged, and that needed to stop right now. "Angie, we're late. We slept through the alarm." She turned over so quickly she kicked Ryan. "Sorry. What time is it?"

"A quarter to ten."

"Oh, no."

Ryan, looking dazed and disheveled said, "Go shower. And leave me some hot water."

She scrambled to pull her act together, not sparing even a moment to be embarrassed about doing it naked.

Once she was under the spray, she started to relax as she soaped herself, acutely aware that Ryan had touched every inch she covered. Memories of a few hours ago filled her mind's eye like a really sexy slideshow. He'd caught her off guard so many times it left her breathless. She'd imagined him slick and dangerous, smug with his expertise as he showed her his wicked bag of tricks.

Instead, he'd been almost selfless. Oh, he'd gotten off all right, but his ego had left the building. His focus had been on her. So attuned he anticipated every desire. The memory made her shiver as the hot water cascaded down her back.

She jumped at a loud knock, then Ryan's panicked voice. "Angie, sorry but we've really got to move it."

"I'll be right out." She got busy, his tension sparking her own. They'd never been late before, she'd missed her run, yoga, coffee, dammit, her talk with Liz. And here she'd been off in the clouds daydreaming as if what had happened was one of her fantasies.

She stilled as her happy buzz abruptly went down the drain. As it hit her, exactly what she'd done. God, oh, God. She'd slept with him. She'd said yes. He'd offered to back off, but she'd just pulled him closer, and had the best sex of her life. With Ryan Vail.

Hell, she hadn't just said yes, she'd thrown away her ethics and reason, and now the memory of him inside her was so vivid she wanted to cry. How could she still want him when it was all so wrong?

Maybe that's what Liz had been getting at. Having sex with Ryan hadn't magically changed the fact that they were never going to be a couple. Not even friends with benefits. She knew she wouldn't pick things up when they went back to the office, and he certainly wouldn't want to. Maybe that's why the sex had been so unbelievably hot. Because he was taboo. She worked with him. He was completely the wrong man for her. Of course, it would probably be awkward as hell, but they both deserved that.

Well, they'd done it. Fine. Experiment over. Now she could concentrate solely on the job.

So why did her hand shake as she turned off the water, just because he was right outside the door? A part of her was glad they were late. There'd be no time for stolen glances, mumbled regrets. They had to jump into work. Which they were screwing up by being late.

As soon as she pulled her towel off the rack she realized she hadn't brought in her clothes. But she didn't want to leave the bathroom naked. It didn't matter that he'd already seen her. They were back on the clock. There was a clear line of demarcation, last night to this morning. She wrapped herself tightly in a towel.

He was waiting at the door as she opened it, clothes in his hand, his impatient gaze taking in everything. "I'll be quick."

"Should I wait? Go ahead without you?"

"Whatever." Their gazes met for an instant before he closed the door.

His single word answer made her feel both relieved and terrible. She didn't like the dip in her tummy that told her she'd been dismissed, but his cool nonchalance was exactly what they needed to find their footing again. They'd have to get into their roles damn quickly, but they each needed to get grounded in reality before that happened.

As she threw her clothes on, she reminded herself yet again that they only had one job to do. Make the suspects believe Ryan was ripe to be blackmailed. It had already begun with the break-in, but for it to stick, they needed to keep in character, keep to their routines. Be goddamn professional FBI agents.

She wouldn't put the sting at risk again.

Behind her, Ryan's shower turned off, and she pulled a brush through her hair. She didn't even have time to put on makeup, which was one of the central keys to Angie Ebsen.

Great. Just great.

The rush to get to the Lavender Room had precluded much talk, for which Ryan was profoundly grateful. Turned out they missed the brief meeting, anyway. Today was their trip to the hot springs, which they'd completely forgotten, because what they'd done in that bed was enough for him to forget his own damn name. They weren't going just to soak, but to do some sweaty, physical exercises on the bank surrounding the springs, to be followed by comfort and support in the hot water.

They did get their things-to-take list and a colorful tote bag marked with the Intimate At Last logo. He didn't miss the irony, and he'd be damned if he'd carry that sucker to the bus waiting for them out front.

Sex with Angie hadn't been surprising. Normally his only concern was that he and his partner both got off, and that the woman didn't resent his quick departure after the fireworks were over. But with Angie, his orgasm had been more about her pleasure then his own.

He chalked it up to the cumulative effect of pretending to be in love with her combined with the inherent physicality of the masquerade. He'd have to be a damn sight more careful about separating his role from his life. Angie was the first woman in a hell of a long time that he had to see the day after.

With a few minutes to spare, he and Angie had settled in a comfortable bench seat on the minibus. Their thighs touched and she muttered a "sorry" and angled the other way. It made him wince. Would she have done that two days ago? Or was he reading too much into her every move?

In the fifteen minutes they'd had to change again and pack their tote, they'd managed to say perhaps a dozen awkward words. Angie had behaved like a textbook agent and had barely looked at him, and he'd gone along with it because it was hands down better than talking. But even after they'd pulled up the bedding, the room still smelled like sex, making it difficult to pretend that they hadn't taken a giant step over the line. She had the right idea, though. Play the part, forget about the rest.

He leaned his head against the window while they waited for late arrivals Luke and Erica and concentrated on his agenda for the day. He needed to get Ira and Delilah to see him as vulnerable and desperate. He'd screwed up with his wife the night before, in front of the whole casino. So today would be about kissing Angie's butt.

Not a wise thing to think about when she was sitting so close. The clean scent of her was already driving him wild, and they had a full day of togetherness to get through.

If only he could stop the quick flashes of memory, of the way she'd tasted, how it had felt to enter her for the first time. He shifted on the seat and looked around regaining his bearings. What he saw surprised him.

He leaned slightly toward Angie. "What's everyone so pissed at us for? We're not even the last ones on the bus."

She didn't make a big deal about checking out the group. "They're not pissed, they're curious."

"About…?" He coughed, trying not to choke. "You don't mean—"

"No." Her eyes narrowed, she gave him a long, drawn-out look. Feeling like an ass, he pretended his mind hadn't gone straight to the gutter.

"I'm pretty sure everyone has heard about me storming out last night after catching you with your coed," she said, finally, resettling another inch away.

"I didn't notice anyone but Tonya and Marcus," he muttered, painfully aware that he'd been overly focused on Angie in that dress.

"All it would have taken is one person. Now they're all waiting to watch you grovel."

"Yeah," he said. "I'll bet. Maybe I won't give them the satisfaction."

"Oh, you'll grovel," she whispered, then followed through by leaning back, frowning at him and turning so she was sitting sideways.

Across the aisle Hannah didn't even try to hide her interest. She gave him a quick evil eye, then smiled with theatrical flair at Angie, the picture of a sympathetic friend.

Okay, this was good. All wasn't lost. Playing the part of the guilty husband was no stretch. In fact, it was a little too real. From the moment he'd opened his eyes this morning he'd felt guilty and that was another thing he hadn't expected. Guilt about women hadn't been part of his repertoire for years.

Right there, that was the central problem. He shouldn't have ever thought of Angie as anything but a colleague. The moment he'd seen her as a woman, everything had begun to unravel. This morning, he'd seen shame in her eyes, at least when she could make herself look at him. By the time they'd arrived at the Lavender Room, she'd gotten her act together, but he knew what he'd seen. It upset him more than he cared to think about.

Last night had been an eleven for him, more memorable than any encounter he'd had in years. That scared the crap out of him, with good reason, but dammit, he also didn't want regret to overshadow everything else.

He couldn't imagine she felt anything but regret. After all, he was the player of players, his reputation built on solid evidence augmented by rumors that he never bothered to squelch. In the real world, she'd made it clear she wasn't the least bit interested in the likes of him. Maybe that's what appealed to him.

Whoa, he backed out of that thought at the speed of light.

Too much was happening at this retreat. All of it coming fast and furious. He'd said too much, relaxed his guard, let his feelings take control.

That stopped right now. This minute. Everything was at stake here, and he didn't just mean the case.

During the rest of the drive to Hoover Dam, Angie spoke and laughed with most of the women on the bus, all chummy and rolling their eyes about *men*. Ryan stared at the high desert landscape, going over his plan to ask for help once he got

Ira on his own. It didn't matter that he'd rehearsed before. He didn't dare think about anything else.

Ryan would admit to the affair, to the prenup, to his desperation to keep Angie happy. But the kicker would be an earnest confession that despite his behavior, he loved his wife and that it would kill him to lose her.

He doubted he'd have a bit of trouble acting the part.

Angie hadn't gone in the hot springs yet. She was purposefully keeping back now that they'd finished their first round of tandem exercises.

The first time they'd touched—she'd fallen back into his arms and let him catch her, which was supposed to build trust. It probably would have worked if the feel of him hadn't felt like a body blow. But they'd played on. Touching with their sweaty bodies, holding each other. Staring into each other's eyes.

At least their difficulty would read like they were a couple in trouble.

The idea of taking some time alone in the hot springs was tantalizing, but this break wasn't for feeling better. It was for confiding in Delilah.

So she stared at the rock formations and the way the native plants poke out of every crag and furrow, knowing Delilah would come check on her. The last time Angie had been in Vegas it had been summer, over a hundred and ten outside. Today it was mid-seventies and the sky was ridiculously blue. She stared up at the bouncing waterfall, leaping from rock to rock on its way down the canyon. When she turned, she could almost see the entrance to Sauna Cave through the tamarisk bushes.

It was difficult not to seek out Ryan. He was on the opposite side of the big shelf of rock, huddled next to Ira. The two of them had started talking the minute the break had begun, and even though Angie knew Ryan was telling the story they'd crafted, she had to wonder if he was as distracted as she was.

He was too good an agent to let his personal issues interfere with the assignment, and she'd thought she was right on par with him. And she had been. Until she'd let down her guard, allowing her hormones to subvert her intelligence.

Seems she could only hold on to her rationalizations for so long before she reverted to a doubting mess. Mostly she felt disappointed in herself. She'd thought she was stronger. That she could handle herself in any given situation, even something as tricky as pretending to be in love.

She'd been wrong. Regardless, she had to put all her personal turmoil aside and keep her head in the game. If only she'd been able to talk to Liz.

Yes, her friend had encouraged her to go for it, but once Angie explained the very real consequences, Liz would be there to help. Liz was an agent herself, and she understood that the success of this sting was the only thing that mattered. Wasting time trying to read into what Ryan was thinking... He was completely in character, none of his issues bleeding through, and she needed to step up and do the same.

"You mind some company?"

Angie spun around at Delilah's voice. The woman exuded compassion and comfort, and for a second, Angie wished she could tell her the true story and get her counsel. Instead, she nodded, and instantly her eyes filled with tears. "Ryan's a good husband," she said. "He really is, you know."

"I believe you." Delilah took Angie's hand in her own. "Tonya told me that you seemed upset about his behavior at the casino last night."

Wiping her eyes with her free hand, Angie nodded. "It wasn't the gambling I minded."

"No?"

Delilah was so close to her that Angie had to be careful of every move. She avoided the older woman's gaze and her wince lasted but a second. "He doesn't mean anything by his flirting. He can't help it. Women come on to him all the time. But that's because he's very sweet and so good-looking. I was the one who started things with him when we first met, so I can't blame them for trying."

"If you know it's harmless, what bothered you?"

Angie sniffed. "I guess I'm just the jealous type." She laughed, but it was rueful and matched her small shrug. "I didn't know until I met Ryan that I could be jealous. I haven't had a lot of good experiences with men. Mostly because of the trust fund."

"Oh?" Delilah walked them over to an outcropping large enough for both of them to take a makeshift seat. "Your family is wealthy?"

"Very," Angie said. "We're not old money, third generation with me. But I'm an only child and my father was the one who inherited, so there wasn't a lot of practice dealing with men. I mean men who weren't with me for the money."

"Ah. Trust issues."

"Trust fund issues. After my third boyfriend turned out to be a lying bastard, yeah, you could say I came to some conclusions. But Ryan, *he* wanted the prenup. He gets nothing if we get divorced. It would be ridiculous for someone who was only after my money to do that."

"But deep down, you still think he's another fortune hunter?"

"Yeah, maybe," Angie said, after a moment, then shook her head. "I don't know. I'm probably not being fair because of my own baggage. That's why I jumped all over coming to this retreat when he suggested it. I want to believe in him and love him properly, but I'm not sure I can."

Delilah squeezed Angie's hand. "After this is over, I

can't recommend strongly enough that you consider marriage counseling. Ryan's crazy about you. I can see it as clear as day."

Angie couldn't help but smile. That conclusion proved that Delilah hadn't bothered to look past the superficial. But then, this whole sting had been predicated on the fact that the therapists would see only what the Bureau wanted them to see.

It would have ruined everything if Delilah had gotten close enough to realize that while Ryan liked sex, and he liked Angie, there was no possibility he was crazy about her.

"You flinched."

"What?" Angie straightened to attention. "I did?"

"When I mentioned that Ryan is crazy about you." Delilah genuinely looked sad. "For a minute, let's consider I can see something in each of you the other can't right now. Ryan cares, of that I am certain. But I think he has trust issues of his own. It could be very powerful for you to work on it together and that's why I want you to seriously explore counseling. But also?" Delilah waited until Angie met her gaze. "Give yourself a break. You've had some stinkers. They leave a mark."

Angie nodded, but in her head she was hearing Delilah sound certain that Ryan cared. Her ridiculous heart pounded as if the words had been true, and that was the trouble with what they'd done last night. This surging emotion was terrific for Angie Ebsen. But it nearly crippled Angie Wolf, because she would be the one returning to L.A., working in the same office as Ryan.

And there he was, heading toward the hot springs with Ira. It was eighty-five degrees in the water, and everyone splashing around looked relaxed and happy. Three couples had decided to let it all hang out, but Angie didn't care. She wanted to be done with this part of the afternoon. Return to the resort, slip into her familiar running clothes and run as far as her legs would carry her.

"Thanks," she said, as she stood. "I'm glad we spoke."

"Anytime." Delilah squeezed her shoulder. "Please think about what I said." Then the woman went to join Ira, passing Ryan with a smile.

He came straight up to Angie, took her hands in his. "You okay?"

She nodded, afraid she was close to tears. It would be okay, though, the fake Angie would—

He pulled her into his arms and kissed her. Not a peck, not a tease, but a full-on blistering kiss that stole her breath. Of course, Ira and Delilah were watching. Everyone was. But Angie's talk with Delilah had left its mark, and she wasn't sure how her character should respond to this very public declaration. She started to pull away, but the hand at the small of her back and the groan that only she could hear stilled her thoughts.

They'd gone from zero to sixty in five seconds. She felt dizzy with flashes of their night. God, she remembered his body as if she'd studied it for years, the hard planes and the soft skin. Her hand went to his thigh, the indent that had flexed when he walked naked from the bed to the bathroom.

She had to squeeze her own thighs together at the primal reaction he stirred in her. Her breasts were pressed against his chest, but with each breath she could feel how her nipples had beaded, and how they ached for more than the material of her bathing suit top.

The sound of catcalls from the hot springs hit her like a slap in the face and she jerked back, dislodging his hold as if they'd been fighting.

Ryan's lips were still wet and parted, his eyes filled with a level of hurt she couldn't understand at all. Why hurt? It couldn't be, because Delilah was wrong. Ryan was a consummate actor, that's all. That's all any of it was. Even if her heart didn't want that to be true.

She was in trouble. Her reaction to him was so not part of the charade it wasn't funny. No more. No more sex with him. Not again; not ever. It was imperative that she get herself together. Everything was at risk. Her career, this sting, her dignity.

Her job was to play this role. If not for that, she'd have never touched him, never kissed him and, by God, she'd never have been in the same bed as Ryan Vail.

Frantic to get away, she opened her mouth to tell him she was going to get in the water. Nothing came out so she just started walking, leaving Ryan behind, sure he was watching her and wondering what the hell had just happened.

IT WAS AFTER SIX WHEN THEY finally made it back to the room. Ryan had gone with the flow, acting the chastened and groveling husband, but Angie's performance had been all over the place. One second she'd been hot, the next freezing, and while he considered himself an intuitive guy, he'd been lost.

Of course, they hadn't been able to talk about it until now.

"Listen," she said as she put down her tote bag once Ryan had completed his search for bugs. "You go ahead and use the shower first. I'm going for a run before dinner."

"Right now?"

She was standing by the round table at the far end of the room, her arms crossed over her chest. Her nod and smile were equally awkward.

"Want to tell me what's going on?" he asked.

"Nothing."

"Noth—" He stopped, took a breath as he tossed his sunglasses on the dresser. "Did you have a plan for the evening? Aside from running?"

"I don't know," she said, turning to her tote and pulling

out first the towel, then her sunscreen. "Debrief. Sleep. I'm wiped out."

He almost asked her why she was going running then, but it seemed unwise. "Okay," he said. "Enjoy yourself. I'll be cleared out of the shower by the time you get back."

She abandoned her unpacking to grab her shoes, but instead of putting them on, she just waited until he was at the bathroom door.

"Would you like me to order some room service for dinner?"

"No," she said, looking anywhere but at him. "That's okay. But go ahead if you want that. I'm probably going to pick up a salad from the café."

Again, he stopped himself from asking the obvious question. But what was the point? Dammit. He didn't want her running off before they talked this thing through; he just wasn't sure how to stop her. Or even if he should. It was increasingly evident last night had been a spectacular error, but they still had a case to work here.

She'd put on one shoe, and was about to slip into the other. "Angie."

She froze. Just stopped moving at all.

"We should talk."

Her answer came after what felt like far too long. "We will. But I need to think."

"Okay. Whenever you're ready."

She kicked into gear again and in a moment she was at the door, a small backpack he'd never seen before strapped on. It was too little to carry all her clothes in case she wanted to book a separate room. She didn't look back.

He used his long, hot shower as his own time to think. The fact that she'd run was actually a good thing. She'd set the future terms of the game very clearly. In her own way, she'd said everything that needed to be said.

Rather than put her through any more discomfort, he decided to clear out for the evening. After he dressed, he wrote her a note, letting her know he was going to see if he could find Marcus, set up the massage thing. He'd catch up with her later, and they'd talk in the morning.

The words he used were straightforward, all business. Surely she'd read between the lines and realize he wouldn't bring up last night again.

He had no illusions that he wouldn't think about it. But he'd keep his thoughts, and anything that wasn't the job, to himself.

12

NOT ONLY HAD SHE RUN at least six miles, but Angie hadn't changed into her sports bra and running gear. Big mistake. Especially with the backpack. Small wonder, since mistakes were becoming something of a specialty. It was ironic that it was the bra that had done the most damage. She was so small it didn't seem possible, but the way her stride worked and the position of the material under her right arm hadn't gotten along since the half-mile mark.

She really needed to shower, to eat, to sleep. But first, she needed her friend. And perspective. She found herself a nice little corner in a building not only far away from the room, but primarily used by staff. There was a patch of green about the size of the backseat of her car, and she was still breathing heavily after her post-run stretch.

She dialed Liz, hoping very hard that she was home, because Angie didn't want to face Ryan with only her own thoughts in her head.

Liz connected, and Angie felt so grateful she nearly cried. God, she was tired.

So was Liz if her flushed face and heaving breath were any indication. "What's up?"

"You want to go shower before I hit you with my news?"

Liz walked her to her kitchen. Although the view was weird as hell, bumpy and dizzying, but Angie heard the way her sneakers squeaked on her kitchen tile, the soft *whump* of her fridge opening because the door tended to stick, and knew Liz was pulling out OJ before she saw the bottle. Liz always pulled out a bottle of OJ first, with a water chaser. She gulped a few times, then brought the tablet's camera up. "Talk to me, I missed you yesterday."

"I followed your advice. Kind of."

"What adv— Oh, do not say this unless you're telling me the absolute truth. You slept with him." Liz sat down hard enough to make the chair groan, then straightened the iPad again.

"Yes. But not because I was 'going for it.'"

"What the hell does that mean? And where are you? That's a horrible sound."

Angie looked down the path and watched as a huge cart full of sheets rolled noisily past. "I'm hiding. Near the laundry, evidently."

"Good choice. Anyway, back to the earth-shattering news. Why did you sleep with him?"

Angie closed her burning eyes. "I may have gotten three hours of sleep last night, but I'm probably off by two and a half hours. It's complicated."

"Start from the beginning."

"I have no patience for beginnings. Bottom line is that I got confused. I let down my guard. He saw me half-naked, okay? What was I supposed to do? We'd been bugged, and he came in the bathroom. And then he got hard, and he was wired, and there was all this adrenaline."

"Okay. Getting some of this. Thinking this wasn't a slam against the wall, rip your clothes off and do it on the floor kind of encounter, even with the adrenaline."

"You'd be correct. It was, however, a confess things about

your life and family and other intimate stuff, then be totally decent about it, and smell so damn good kind of encounter."

Liz's eyebrows had gotten comically high on her forehead. "That's the most perfect thing I've ever heard. I couldn't have written it better. Me? I go for against the wall, but you love all that confession crap. And men being decent. So what's your damage?"

"I. Work. With. Him."

Liz waved her hand so dismissively it was a good thing they were hundreds of miles away from each other. "You are so busy trying to meet every unrealistic expectation of that insane family of yours, you are missing the best parts of things. Last night was the marrow of life, Angie. The thing you'll remember when you're seventy. You won't give a rat's ass about this assignment by then, you know that, right?"

Maybe calling Liz wasn't the smartest move. "That's all well and good and dramatic and poetic and all that other shit, but the truth is I'm not seventy and I have a lot at stake here. I can't be this off balance. It's day three. We've still got two more to go, and I can't imagine getting in bed with him tonight."

"Why not?"

Angie wiped her face with her hand, and looked at her friend, who was calmly drinking her orange juice. "Please be here for me. Be on my side. I need you."

Liz lowered the bottle. "Sweetie, I am here for you. I have been and will continue to be here for you. However, I will also consider the fact that the broader picture is not what you're looking for at the moment. So here's what you do. Talk to him. Tell him you're confused, and you desperately need to sleep. That you don't regret what happened, but it probably won't happen again. How does that sound?"

Angie nodded. She could do that. She could say those things. They made sense. They sounded as if an adult had come up with them. And it didn't leave any room for arguments. "Thank you. Perfect. But do me a favor?"

"What?"

"Email me those exact words because I'm too tired to remember them."

"Will do. And I'll be here all night, so if you need me, call. Cell phone or Skype, whatever will work best. If not, please be in touch tomorrow, okay? I'll worry."

"I promise." She disconnected, put the iPad in the backpack and made it back to the empty room ten minutes later. Starving and wobbly, she called for a room-service dinner, then made it into the shower and stayed there for a long time.

When she was dressed again, just jeans and a T-shirt, she found Ryan standing by a room service cart signing for her dinner. He'd gone for the same look, in a pair of jeans that she hadn't seen before. They must have been his own, not part of the wardrobe, because the wear was obviously from his body, not some artificial distress. His snug T-shirt was tucked into those close-fitting Levi's, and before she could attempt to stop it, her body reacted with a hunger that had nothing to do with the scent of pasta.

Her forehead dropped with a thunk to the wood of the open door. It hurt.

"You okay?"

She stood up straight. Ryan was alone, standing by the ottoman where her meal had been laid out. "I should have called you. Asked if you wanted me to order something."

"I ate. With Marcus."

"Ouch."

"Not the most fun I've ever had. You should eat, though, if this is the first thing you've had since lunch."

Her stomach reinforced his point, and after stashing her things, she sat in the big wing chair and practically stuffed half the pasta into her mouth in ten seconds.

Forcing herself to slow down, she dared another glance at Ryan. The jeans and T-shirt look was just as effective from the front, although there had been a special something about his butt and how the denim curved. It didn't help that he was leaning against the round table across the room, staring at her, arms and ankles crossed, and dammit, she had to stop thinking about him as a man.

"Why don't you fill me in on Marcus?" she said, then turned her attention to her salad.

"I gave him a very similar story to the one I told Ira. Didn't want it to be verbatim, because I assume they talk to each other. This time I went for more of a physical angle. Asked him if he'd teach me how I could use nontraditional methods of showing you how much I loved you."

Swallowing her bite carefully, she gave him a quick glance. "Nontraditional?"

"Yeah, massage. Oils. Candles. All that crap. He was far too eager to show me."

Angie caught the tail end of his full body shudder. "Eww."

"Hey, sometimes we have to take one for the team."

She popped a cherry tomato in her mouth, reining her thoughts back, and then back further.

"The point is, he knows about the affair, the trust fund, that I'm desperate. The only one who might still need more convincing is Tonya. Thoughts?"

"I've been trying to figure out a way to find out about her stealth faxing, but honestly, I can't. I'm guessing she's up to speed with our situation by now."

"Yeah?" he said, and his arms came down so he could grab the edges of the table.

Angie switched her gaze back to her salad. This was becoming a serious issue. They were having a work discussion. There was no thinking about his body during work discussions, period. "I'll try to have a friendly talk with her in the morning, poke around, see if she was included in the conversations from the hot springs."

"Maybe talk to her about that tantric massage thing?"

Thankfully Angie hadn't been eating because she'd have spit the food straight out. She knew just enough about tantric methods to know it was done naked, with no parts left un-massaged. "And I would do that why?"

"Maybe because you want to keep me interested." He kind of shrugged one shoulder, the move casual, but the rest of him tense. "Maybe Angie Ebsen doesn't want to kick her husband to the curb just yet."

This was bad. Horrible. She couldn't read him. Even staring straight into his eyes. She had no idea which Angie and Ryan he was talking about. A flash of an image hit her, Ryan on the bed, *in her*, and she darted her gaze away, knocking her napkin to the floor. She picked it up slowly, willing the heat to dissipate from her face. So, so bad.

EVEN THOUGH LEANING against the table edge was becoming more uncomfortable by the second, Ryan didn't dare move. With his ankles crossed and bending slightly forward, his half-hard dick was hidden, and that's the way it would stay until he settled the hell down.

All she'd done was eat her dinner. Drink some water.

He'd reacted as if she'd done a pole dance wearing nothing but red high heels, but try explaining that to his cock.

They'd been discussing the case as if they were in the bullpen back in L.A., and what had he done? Brought up tantric massage. Yesterday he could've gotten away with it. She would've automatically assumed it was about the case. But after this morning?

Eventually they were going to have to sleep. Share that bed again.

That was it. Bottom line. No room for error, so they'd better get over this thing and get back on point.

She was staring at him when he looked up, her brow furrowed and her napkin dangling from her fingers. "About last—"

"Oh, hell," he said, cutting her off and pushing away from the table. "I'm two hours late checking in with Jeannie." He pulled his cell from his pocket and made a beeline for the door. "I'll be back."

He hadn't looked at her as he'd made his escape, and that, he figured, was the most chicken-shit thing he'd done in his life. Including hiding in the school library for an entire year to ditch a gang of bullies.

He didn't want to talk about last night. The note couldn't have been plainer. Of course, Angie didn't have to know that given a choice, he'd probably make that same mistake all over again.

He was pathetic. He stared at his cell as he walked down the pathway, trying to think of ways he could avoid calling Jeannie. Man, he was just racking up the points, wasn't he?

Why did he still want Angie so much? He'd been there and done that. The mystery had been solved. And yet all day, he'd wanted nothing more than to be near her. To touch her, to smell and taste her. He'd had a miserable time at the hot springs, even when he'd been allowed to touch her. To kiss her. Shit.

Jeannie was going to kill him, but she was his only hope of getting himself straightened out. When he was far enough away from the bungalow and in a good position to see if anyone was around, he pressed Jeannie's number.

She answered after the first ring. "About time. You know I have kids to put to bed."

"Yeah, well, I told you to get goldfish, but did you listen?"

"Ha. You're a scream. Tell me what's going on."

The first part was easy. He went through the night at the casino skipping the in-room entertainment, then told her about not only the field trip but his meeting with Marcus. Then, it got tricky.

"What aren't you telling me?" she asked.

"Why would you ask that? I've told you everything about the case."

"That's why," she said. "I'm not just a pretty face, you idiot, I know you. What did you do?"

"Me? Why do you always assume I've done something wrong?"

She didn't say anything. She didn't have to.

Ryan sighed. Deep down he'd probably known she'd ask, and maybe getting it out there would ease his guilt, although he doubted she'd offer absolution. "Okay, but I didn't force her. We mutually decided that—"

"You slept with her. Dammit, Ryan. You had one thing you weren't supposed to do. One thing."

"I had a lot of things I wasn't supposed to do."

"Not helping your cause."

"Fine. It was an error. We both realize that."

Jeannie went radio silent. She wasn't supposed to do that. A real friend would reassure him that this, too, would pass. "You've talked?" she asked finally.

"Not precisely."

"Meaning, no, you've been avoiding the conversation like the plague."

"I'm getting a new partner when I get back. You suck."

"Stop it," Jeannie said. Her voice had lost all humor. "This is not a minor deal, Ryan. I expected better of her, for God's sake, but it's not like you, either. Did you ignore everything we talked about?"

"There were circumstances," he said, hearing how weak that argument was, but not having anything better.

"Yeah. Your dick got hard. That's not a circumstance, honey. That's a breach of conduct. Even if it'll never be reported, it is not how two agents on assignment behave, even when the situation is as tricky as the one you're in. I have to admit, I'm disappointed."

He sighed, and if he'd been near anything, even a brick wall, he'd have smashed his hand through it. "Yeah. Me, too."

"You need to discuss this with Angie. No making jokes about it, either. Tell her you're sorry."

"But—"

"Be the bigger man, Ryan. Dammit. You are the bigger man. You've never done anything like this before. I know it's been tough. I get that. But you can't afford the luxury of letting your personal feelings get in the mix."

He didn't have an answer to that, either. Just a profound sense of his own shame. "Yeah, I screwed up. No excuses."

The silence grew, but his pacing stopped. He needed to listen to what Jeannie had to say, as hard as it was to hear. She was his friend. The first honest-to-God friend he'd ever had. She was the only person in his life who dared to tell him the absolute truth.

"I think," she said, and he had to press the phone close to his ear because her voice was so low, "that when you get back from this assignment, you and Angie need to have a different kind of conversation."

"What do you mean?"

She sighed. "I think you like her. Maybe more than that."

He squeezed his eyes shut. "What?"

"You know what I'm saying. She's not like the women you normally date. And, kiddo, unless there was something serious happening in your head about Angie, there's no way you would have put so much in jeopardy to get laid."

His heart was hammering in his chest, and he wanted to

run for the hills, but kept the phone up, and opened his eyes. "I still… Shit, Jeannie, it's like I…"

"Feel something?"

He took in a deep breath, then gave it up. "Yeah."

"Put it on the back shelf until you get home. Your first duty is to the job. You got that?"

"Oh, yeah. Big time."

"Fine. Talk to her, and let her know you want to discuss it after. Don't leave that part out."

"Are you kidding?" He was starting to sweat now. If he could gauge Angie's reaction it would be different, but he had no idea what she was thinking, outside of that one look of shame that still haunted him. "How do I know she'll even want to do that?"

"Ryan, she didn't put her career on the line on a whim, either."

"All right, but…"

"Go talk to her before you two have to crawl between the sheets. Let her know she's not going to have to worry about you doing anything else unprofessional. Then for God's sake, don't do anything else unprofessional."

"Okay." He ran a hand through his hair and thought about going to the gym to duke it out with a punching bag, but he put that aside. He owed Angie the courtesy of an apology. "Thanks. I'll give you a call tomorrow night."

"Anytime. And Ryan?"

"Yeah?"

"You made a mistake. It happens. You move on."

"Right. Go put the kids to bed."

She gave him one last goodbye and hung up.

He disconnected, put the phone back in his pocket. This next part wasn't going to be fun, but it would also be a relief. He wasn't going to let his life be run by lust. That was his old man's game, not his.

But what Jeannie had said about him and Angie needing to talk once they returned to L.A.? She was wrong. Angie was great, but they weren't the right mix. Not even for one night, let alone more.

Angie had the TV on HBO, to a movie she'd been wanting to see for ages. Pity she couldn't concentrate for more than a minute at a time.

Ryan had been gone for an eternity. She'd put her dinner plates outside the door, changed into her sleep shirt, washed up, brushed her teeth and crawled into bed, once again all the way at the very edge. If she thought she wouldn't look like a complete nutcase, she'd have taken every cushion and pillow and put them straight down between them like a bundling board. She'd still know he was there, but it would be so much easier if she didn't have to see him.

No matter how much he wanted to avoid her, she'd realized while he'd been gone that she needed to talk to him. It wouldn't be pretty, but one thing she'd learned over the past few days was that nothing got fixed without communication. Their impossible situation had crossed over the line last night, but that didn't mean they couldn't regroup.

Competition running had taught her that dwelling on mistakes was a waste of valuable time. Learn from them, then let go. To rehash was the gateway drug to losing, and she and Ryan were so close to the end of this assignment that to blow it now would ruin everything.

Her promotion was on the line, and if she'd been back in L.A. that would have been the only thing in her life that mattered. All her efforts would have been tailored to the furtherance of that goal. Here, just an hour's flight away, the D.C. job was an afterthought, a footnote.

She didn't want things to be weird with Ryan when they finished out the week, but that ship had probably sailed. It wasn't that big of a loss. She'd barely known him. An almost indiscretion at a party, a foolish mistake during a stressful time? The problem was the illusion that they were more to each other than was true. Forced togetherness and a couple of personal revelations did not make a relationship. It didn't even make a friendship.

Her logic was impeccable, and that should have been that. The crushing sadness that made her gut ache begged to differ.

She noticed that the action on the screen had become a steamy love scene, and as quick as her clicking finger could move, she turned to the nature channel. Shark Week seemed safe enough.

Finally, after squinting through a terrible circle-of-life moment where something cute got eaten, Ryan came back inside. He seemed subdued, but that was in comparison to his manic desperation to escape. "How's Jeannie?"

"Good," he said. "She'll pass on the info to the team in the morning."

"Great. Brad told me that Gordon and Director Leonard are pleased with our reports so far. He heard it directly from Ellen, which is as good as hearing it from the horse's mouth."

"No kidding. That's great. That's...great."

Angie closed her eyes. Her next move needed to be made with a clear head and it seemed looking at Ryan, especially wearing those jeans, clouded her judgment. "Are you going to run out again if I bring up last night?"

"No."

Surprised at his vehemence, Angie's eyes snapped open. "What does that mean?"

"It means no. I'm not going to run out again."

"Okay," she said, hitting the mute button. Maybe she should have just turned down the volume. It was really quiet. "Because it wasn't completely my fault."

The look he gave her was this close to a slap. "I never—"

"I know. I know, but dammit, this is awkward."

"And I'm sorry about that," he said, but softly. Humbly.

"We both got carried away," she said, matching his tone. Wishing she hadn't gotten in bed yet. It would have been easier to walk around.

"I'm not sorry," he said. "I don't want you to get that impression. Not about..." He waved his hand in a general way at the bed. "Just the timing. The situation."

Angie held herself still. "Tell you the truth? It wouldn't have happened if we weren't here."

He took two steps away from the table, then stopped. "So you regret the whole thing?"

"No. Not, no. I'm not sure what I feel, exactly. Confused, I guess. But not shocked."

Tilting his head slightly to the right, he closed one eye as if that would help him understand better. "Explain?"

"I find you very attractive," she said. "But even disregarding the work situation, I doubt I'd have acted on that. I'm not good with casual sex."

"And I'm not looking for anything but."

Her smile had to look as cockeyed as she was feeling. "In the interest of full disclosure, however, I will admit that it's... difficult not to think of you like that now."

"Well, we are supposed to be acting like lovers."

"But I'm not supposed to be feeling like a lover."

He inhaled, then stopped. Just held his breath and stared at her. Long enough for heat to climb up her face.

"I meant—"

"I know what you meant," he said. "At least I think so. Because I've been feeling that myself."

That was a hell of a thing to hear. Coming from anyone other than Ryan Vail, it would have been a game changer.

"But we both know our feelings aren't real," he said. "They'll be gone the minute we're out of this predicament."

"Right," she said, nodding a little too enthusiastically as she tried to ignore the fist in her chest. "Exactly. We just have to get through the next two days, then boom, all our problems will be solved."

"As long as we don't touch each other."

The moment the words came out of his mouth, she realized that was going to be impossible. Not sure what she was supposed to say to that, she just sat there and tried not to react.

"I mean, we don't touch each other unless there's someone there who's supposed to see it."

She nodded. "That works. That's good. That's the rule, then. No touching unless someone else sees it."

Ryan opened his mouth as if to say something, then closed it again. "For what it's worth, I also happen to like you. And that part's not going to disappear when this assignment is over."

Angie winced and pressed her mouth together tight. Of all the things, he had to go and say that. Just when she was making peace with the cold, hard fact that Ryan wasn't the least bit interested in anything but a casual screw. But she'd asked for honesty. "Well, dammit," she said. "I like you, too."

13

AFTER ONE OF THE MOST miserable nights of her life she had barely survived the excruciating morning with the group. She'd known massage lessons were on the program, but she hadn't realized it would be a lab situation where they learned on each other. Now, with only a few bites of lunch in her tummy, she was overdosing on caffeine. That likely wouldn't end well…unless it made her sick and she had to bow out of this afternoon's session. Not a bad idea.

"You want more coffee?" Ryan asked as the last of their plates had being cleared.

"Sure do." She smiled. "Thanks."

Giving her a suspicious look, Ryan left her, Tonya, Zach and Rachel at the table, after making sure no one else wanted anything.

Angie watched him go, glad that he wasn't wearing his own worn jeans because every minute of this morning had been torture, and she didn't need any more visual aids, thank you. He still looked fantastic. Especially with his shirt off. On a massage table. Smelling like a wicked mix of cinnamon and spices from the organic oil she'd used to rub him down.

Ryan put her fresh cup on the table. Her gaze went to his

thighs, enjoying how even the high-end jeans molded against him, and she let out a sigh.

The laughter from her tablemates sent her into a tailspin, hoping she hadn't sounded like a dopey schoolgirl.

"I can sell you guys a bottle of that massage oil at cost," Tonya said, pretty much confirming Angie was being a twit.

Ryan happily took her up on her offer, but then he'd been deeply in character all day. Angie concentrated on her caffeine input, ignoring everyone. Especially him. She should ask for hazard pay, is what she should do. Because come on. He still smelled like warm chai and sex.

Tomorrow was the final day, thank goodness. The team hadn't been able to trace who'd installed the program on their computer, but they'd managed to send a few emails from the fictitious Roxanne that would lead the blackmailer to believe Ryan was a perfect mark.

She remembered so clearly when she'd first heard about the art scam from Deputy Director Leonard. It had felt like such an intellectual exercise—setting up the sting, writing the database program. How in hell had she gotten here? Learning how to turn on her pretend lover with oil and touch hadn't been covered in any of her FBI training.

At least there were only two more sessions for sure, and Delilah had hinted that there would be something special as a farewell. Although Angie was seriously contemplating cutting things short. The idea stirred a whole pot of conflicting emotions. This morning's exercise had blurred the lines nearly to oblivion. In spite of all her logic and reasoning, her goals, her plans, the reality of everything, she'd found herself aching with desire for the stupid man. When she'd massaged his shoulders, a shower of sensual memories swamped her, making it hard to breathe, to think, to find her footing.

The professional that was still inside her knew the faster she could get out of here, the better off she'd be.

All things considered, she and Ryan had done everything they could do to establish their vulnerability. The keylogging incident was a bonus none of them could have predicted, totally in their favor. If she could come up with an exit that reinforced what they'd accomplished, she wouldn't hesitate. The longer they stayed, the more likely they were to slip up.

"What's the plan for after lunch?" Ryan asked, surprising Angie until she saw Ira standing by him.

"We're switching things up a little."

"No more massages?"

"No. Something else."

The troubled way Ira was looking at Ryan had Angie thinking that even if she didn't feel sick, she was getting to be a good actress. Ryan seemed uneasy, too. Then, Ira smiled and stepped over to Zach and Rachel. He kept the grin, though, no worried gaze in sight.

"Wow," Ryan whispered as he turned to Angie. "I can't wait for the next session to start."

"The worst has got to be over, right?" she said, referring to his earlier session with Marcus.

Ryan shuddered, and she held back her laugh because what he'd gone through was not amusing at all. The pale man with the hooker fetish had actually put his hands on Ryan's body. Above the waist, of course. Still. Eww.

"We have time to go back to the room," he said. "You gonna stay and guzzle more coffee or join me?"

She basked in his slow easy smile, annoyed that her heart actually fluttered. It had ceased to matter that she wished she felt nothing more than respect and camaraderie. Life as she knew it before making love with Ryan was already crumbling around her. Why delay it? "Let's go. I want to change shirts, and I have a proposition for you."

Ryan wasn't liking this one bit. Especially the part where he had to go first. So far the only thing he'd liked about today was Angie's suggestion that they leave early. Even that sucked as far as propositions went, and the plan only shaved off a day. But trying to keep his hands off her made every minute matter.

They were in the Lavender Room and if he never saw the color purple again, it would be fine with him. The much-hated bean bags had been shuffled off to one corner and the massage tables from the morning session had disappeared. Now there were twelve chairs in pairs that faced each other in a broad circle. He was sitting so close to Angie that his knee was nearly touching hers. Not by choice, because being this near her was dangerous. But at least their proximity meant that unless they spoke loudly, whatever they said to each other wouldn't be overheard. It was, according to Ira and Delilah, a matter of trust.

"The first timer will be set for thirty minutes, the second for thirty-four minutes." Delilah spun slowly around as she explained the exercise. "You will remain seated for the entire time. Once the first chime goes off, everyone stops speaking. Be sure to make and keep eye contact until the second chime. For the first thirty minutes, you may speak to each other, but you must remember not to be judgmental or sarcastic or dismissive. Everyone clear?"

Ryan was barely listening. He was too busy thinking about the private instruction he and the other men had received a few moments ago. Ira had explained that the point of this psychological torture experiment was to reveal something intimate, something they'd never told anyone before, and then let the conversation take its own course. And to pay particular attention to the last four minutes of eye contact.

Ryan had about forty-five seconds to decide if he should make something up that might be true for Ebsen, or to tell

Angie about a part of his life. That would have been a no-brainer, but he knew that Ira would be paying particular attention to him during this exercise from hell.

"And so," Delilah announced. "We begin."

Silence all around him wasn't making his decision easier. His thoughts darted from topic to topic in an attempt to find some piece of business he could build into a convincing fiction. Something with heart, something that would sound true, and painful and like a secret held close to the vest, but everything seemed stupid or was from some movie he saw on TV, or had too many guns involved.

He knew Angie had no idea what to expect, except that he was supposed to speak now. From the way her eyes darted to the right, then widened at him, he knew someone was coming to help them get started.

"When I was fourteen, my father brought home a prostitute," he said. "For me."

Angie got very still. Her breathing stalled for a moment, then started again, but she hadn't blinked.

He was having some trouble on that account, himself. Of all the things in his life, why the hell had that slipped out? Could he change tracks now? Take it back?

Ira's goddamn patchouli smell hit him before the man himself crouched beside him. "You can say anything you wish to say. Remember, there are no mistakes. The only requirement is willingness."

Ryan was willing to smash the moron's face in, but he just nodded, getting the message that if Ebsen wanted to save his marriage, he'd better cut open a major vein.

"She was young," Ryan said, lowering his voice while leaning toward Angie. But he didn't say another word until Ira in his ugly aloha shirt walked away.

While he could have switched the topic, one look at Angie stopped him. He'd already said too much, and he didn't want her thinking he'd been traumatized for life. It was better to tell her the truth then leave room for her to make stuff up. "She was over eighteen, I know that, because he told me. She also looked a whole lot like my mother. Same dark hair cut blunt at the top of her neck. Green eyes like her. Same kind of body. Short, curvy. Her top was cut so low I could see her bra. It was red.

"I've never been so embarrassed about anything in my whole life as when she walked into that room. She had two glasses with her. Scotch shots. I'd had beer before, and I'd tried some booze with my friends, but this was drinking my old man's scotch with a hooker. Of course, I was horny, I was fourteen and smothered in puberty, but I was dying, too. Because my father was in the other room. He knew exactly what we were supposed to do. That she'd be naked. She'd see me naked."

He paused, not wanting to give Angie an opening but not wanting to talk, either.

"Was she nice to you?"

Of all the questions she could have asked, that's what she led with? "Huh. Yeah. She was okay. She didn't point and laugh. At that age, I wasn't exactly *Playgirl* material."

"You were a child. He'd go to jail for that now, if not then."

"Yeah. Probably. If I'd told anyone."

"You never told anyone? Not even a friend?" she asked.

He inhaled sharply, wondering why the hell he was telling *Angie?* What was he doing? His heart had been beating fast since they'd walked into the room, now he was pretty certain he was headed for a stroke. He shook his head.

"You didn't want to brag about it?"

"I wanted to forget it ever happened." He leaned back, wishing the chairs were farther apart.

"Did you?"

He shrugged his shoulders. "It was...memorable. Even the horrible parts."

"There were good parts, too?"

Leave it to Angie to keep looking for that silver lining. "One or two."

Interestingly Angie was the one mirroring his body language, even though that had been part of his instructions. She'd leaned back when he had. Her right hand was fisted to match his left. Their knees were touching now. Barely, though, mostly his pants and hers brushing against each other. He scooted forward on his chair far enough that he could feel her.

"Wow, your father sounds like a real sweetheart and a dream dad."

That made him laugh. Good for her. He had no idea how much time had passed, and he wanted the damn chime to happen so he could stop. Even though the eye contact thing was going to be a bitch. The two of them kept dancing around each other. Looking away, looking back, over and over.

"I had some difficult things happen to me when I was young," she said. "I told you about the whole sports connection, but what I didn't say was that my parents forced me into situations that were far too complicated for a child my age. But what your father did was child abuse. My God, you were so young."

The bark of a laugh that was meant to disabuse her of her dramatic notions came out way more pathetic than it should have. "Look, I wasn't scarred for life, if that's what you're thinking. It was a crappy thing to pull on your own kid, which is why, by the way, I have no plans to have children of my own, but it wasn't a deal breaker. I went on to kick ass in school. In college. Anything I ever wanted I went after hard, and here I am, so there's no use wringing my hands over my childhood issues. We all have crap happen to us, and some of us turn that into motivation. I'll never be like him. Never."

The way she looked at him told him exactly how much she believed him on that last score. His back straightened. "I'm not denying that my attitude toward women hasn't been damaged. But we play the hand we're dealt."

"I didn't say—"

"You didn't have to. It's fine. I'm not unhappy or wishing I could be something that I'm not."

"No, of course you're not." The sympathy in her eyes irritated him. "I admire you."

"Because I had a bad childhood?"

"I admired you before today."

"Even after we...?"

Her lips parted and curved up slightly. She must have licked them while he'd been talking because they glistened. If he could have, he'd have leaned over and kissed her.

"Where was your mother in all this?" she asked very gently.

He shrugged. "No idea."

"You okay with that?"

"Yeah. I think she was lucky to get out."

"She left you behind."

"She did."

Her hand went to his knee and he felt it all the way up his body. As if her touch were made of sparks. It was just her *hand*.

He covered it with his own. The flare transformed into a warm diffusion of comfort that settled right next to the steady and unceasing arousal that had taken root near his spine.

It was Angie who leaned toward him this time. He mirrored the move, guessing she might want to whisper something, just to make sure no one else could hear.

He was wrong. She moved straight on in for a kiss that caught him completely off guard. It wasn't much, compared to what they'd done before. Just lips, soft and sweet. But damn.

He barely heard the chime go off.

After the chime, Angie pulled back. Not far, though. Before she could meet Ryan's gaze, she had to clear her head. She closed her eyes, took a deep, cleansing breath and let it out slowly. When she looked again, it was straight into his unwavering gaze.

It was a revelation.

The urge to turn away was profound, not from looking, but from being seen. Of course, she'd held eye contact before. Never so intentionally and never with someone who'd just poured his secrets into her lap.

Her lips parted and she had to struggle to fill her lungs, as if the room itself were losing oxygen. Her eyes flicked down and took in his strong jaw, the gap between his lips, the first hint of stubble on his chin, but then she returned to the connection, to the pull.

The next urge was to talk, to make a joke, to hide behind words, but that wasn't allowed, and how long had it been? A minute? It had to have been at least a minute.

God, his eyes were so dark. His pupils had taken up all the room, and she knew it was an illusion that she could see herself reflected. If the old proverb had been right and she was peering into his soul, the view was less poetic than she'd been led to believe. The only thing she could read was want. Then again, perhaps that's why she thought she could see herself.

His hand moved, a slow drift to gripping her lightly around her wrist. Then his thumb went to her pulse point, and he rubbed, back and forth. Delicately. She wanted to watch, of course, but she held steady. The edges of his eyes crinkled, and she knew exactly which smile he'd put on. Could picture its every detail.

What was he seeing in her? How sad she felt for his childhood? How brave she knew he was? He made so much more sense now. It was as if he'd handed her his Rosetta Stone, and she had a whole new view of the path he'd taken. At least, some of the path.

It was tempting to think the revelation explained all of him. Just because there was such an obvious correlation didn't mean there weren't a hundred different stories that would change the picture dramatically.

She couldn't help wondering, though, if he would ever find a way out of the fortress he'd built around himself. Now, though, she wanted to kiss him again. They were going home tomorrow morning. While she'd been in the shower during their break, Ryan had received the go-ahead from Gordon, and the team was busy setting up their departure, complete with a verifiable paper trail.

So this really would be the last time she could kiss him. She had no business being upset at the fact, but there it was. She moved in closer, with no doubt at all that he was on board.

Just as her lips brushed his, the chime rang. Ryan's hand disappeared, he jerked back as if she'd been about to slap him and before she could get her bearings, he was out of his seat and across the room.

A moment later, he was gone. The session wasn't over. Other couples were kissing, were touching. All of them deeply involved with their mates. Angie looked at Delilah, who gave her a sympathetic smile.

Ira approached, then crouched down beside her. "It happens sometimes."

"What's that?"

"Fear. That he revealed too much. That he was too truthful. People, particularly men, aren't used to that level of intimacy."

"It was extreme."

"Believe it or not, this is a good sign. Even though the session isn't over, I think you ought to go after him."

Angie nodded, still in shock, not just from Ryan's vanishing act but the thirty-four minutes that had preceded it. She collected her purse from the back of the room and slipped outside, not wanting to disturb the rest of the group. If she hadn't been so worried about Ryan, she would have breathed a tremendous sigh of relief. Instead, she hurried toward the bungalow, to their room, wondering if she should, in fact, walk in or knock, or just give Ryan some time alone.

When she walked in, Ryan had his suitcase on the bed, and a bundle of folded clothes in his arms. If she was reading him right, and she was pretty sure she was, he was leaving. Now.

14

"Ryan?"

He didn't turn around. In fact, he sped things up, shoving his belongings into the case as if they'd wronged him in some way. "There's no reason to wait until tomorrow," he said. "We're done. We might as well get back to L.A., start the paperwork."

"I'm all for leaving," she said, "but don't you think this might look a little suspicious?"

He glanced at her, then walked to the dresser. "What difference does it make? Today, tomorrow."

"Because of the session we just had."

"What does that mean?"

His words were brusque, and yeah, okay, she understood. He'd opened himself up to her in there, not something he was used to. However, they had to think this through and not let his self-consciousness mess up the finale.

"It means that we should take a minute." She walked over to her side of the bed, sat by her pillow. He'd have to look at her if he was going to continue to pack.

"It was your idea to get out of here."

"And we put the plan in motion. Gordon agreed to our leaving in the morning."

"That's just a technicality."

She closed her eyes as she gathered her equilibrium. Not even ten minutes ago, the two of them had been gazing into each other's eyes, and she'd felt a connection to Ryan that had gone so deep she'd seen that her feelings for him were more complex than just a crush. To find him like this made her all the more aware of what a mess she'd gotten herself into.

Although Ryan tried to look as if everything was normal, panic was just below the surface. Given what she knew about him now, that made a world of sense. "Can we at least take a breather?"

His chin dropped to his chest and he sighed deeply. "I can't believe how I blew it in there."

"What?"

"I have absolutely no idea if Ira or Delilah was listening." He slammed the dresser door shut and walked to the window, tension rippling through his every motion. "I couldn't get it together fast enough, and I should have been better prepared. I don't even remember half of what I told you, and for all I know I completely contradicted everything I'd told Ira at the hot springs. God dammit, I bet I said some things to Marcus this morning that put Ebsen's mother in the picture. If they put two and two together—"

Angie joined him at the window and put her hand on his shoulder.

He jerked as if she'd shocked him.

"You didn't blow anything," she said. "Ira and Delilah weren't near us."

"How do you know? We were too busy staring at each other—"

"I know. You know it, too. Both of us have been trained to always be somewhat aware of our surroundings."

He shook his head, his jaw tensing, and that little vein on his forehead had made an appearance.

"You were amazing," she said, squeezing his shoulder. He must have felt it even through his tension. "What those two saw were two people deeply engrossed in each other. We couldn't have done a more convincing job if we'd rehearsed for months. They would never doubt that we were exactly who we said we were, that you are deeply frightened of losing everything that matters to you. And that I would be devastated if I discovered you'd been with someone else."

"That's the voodoo talking," he said. "I don't know what it was about that exercise, but come on. That was like hypnosis or something."

She couldn't disagree, truth be told. It had felt as if they'd been mesmerized. "It doesn't matter. What happened in that room was the icing on the cake." She dropped her hand, but she didn't step away. "You were great."

His eyes slammed shut so tightly it was painful to watch, and the urge to hold him filled her.

He spun around and before she could even understand what was happening, she was in his arms and his lips were on hers, the kiss so desperate it made her gasp. He took advantage and used his tongue while his hands ran down her back pulling her tight against his body. She hung on to his sides as if her life depended on it. As if his did, too.

"It's over," he said, his lips brushing hers. "We aren't breaking the rules." He kissed her again, grasping the back of her head with his broad hand and tilting her just enough that their mouths locked together like pieces of a puzzle.

It was impossible to think when he kissed her like that, when her body wanted so badly to let him in.

When he reached underneath her blouse to caress her skin, she jerked her head back, the sensation dizzying. Ryan didn't give her a second to adjust. His mouth moved down her neck, licking, nipping, his low moan a rumble that was felt more than heard.

"Wait, Ryan, wait. We can't."

"No, shhh, no. We can. It's over, and we're done and I can't stop thinking about you, haven't stopped since I was inside you." He lifted her blouse, the silk slipping up her back and her bra, until it was over her head.

She could stop things right now. If she didn't let go of her grip on him, he wouldn't be able to finish undressing her. Not without a struggle, and there was no way in hell he would do that to her, no matter how frantic he seemed.

When he straightened, when he finally met her gaze, his desperation was written on his face and in the tension that strained his muscles. He'd been through so much. Not just what had happened all those years ago, but today. He'd laid himself bare in front of her, the most private confession she'd ever heard.

She wanted him so much her body ached, even as she understood what a risk it was. If she gave in… No, if she chose to be with him one more time. This was her heart she was playing with. He'd be fine, he'd go home and everything would go back to normal. She couldn't say the same.

It was just turning dark outside, the room filled with shadows and quiet, except for their heated breathing. All she had to do was say no.

Instead, she released his polo shirt, and his shoulders sagged with relief. When he lifted her blouse off, he moved carefully and he never turned his gaze away.

She was the one to reach behind and unhook her bra, letting it fall to the floor.

"Oh, Christ," he whispered right before baring his own chest and pulling her close once more.

She sighed as her nipples pressed against him, as his arms tightened around her. She leaned into him, abandoning any pretense, thrilled insensibly by the small noises Ryan made as they drowned each other in kisses. He maneuvered them until her legs hit the side of the bed.

He broke away and cursed. "What idiot put a suitcase there?" Looking as if it hurt, he released her and dispatched the wretched thing, his clothes leaving a trail from the end of the bed to the wall.

When he turned back to her, he stopped, lips parted on an inhale as he studied her, starting with her naked breasts but returning to her face. "I don't want to make a mistake here," he said. He flexed most of the muscles she could see from his arms to his jaw. Her own wince surprised her, but only until he whispered, "I'll just get..." as he picked up her blouse from where she'd let it drop.

She took it back and tossed it on the seat of the leather chair. Then she put her arms around his neck and brought her mouth close to his ear. "Take me to bed, Ryan Vail."

His lips were on hers so fast it was like magic, and he was fiddling with the buttons on her slacks, not having much success. Covering his hands, she said, "Let's make this simple. Strip."

The laugh wasn't a big one and his attention stayed on her as he toed off his loafers and slipped out of his jeans.

God, he looked good in those black boxer briefs. She loved how obviously he wanted her. But then she was being pretty obvious herself with her body blush and hard nips.

She made a little show of taking off her panties. They were the palest pink, a match to the bra that was somewhere else. He finished removing his socks, and when he stood up tall and oh, so erect, she wanted to do *everything*.

THE ROOM WASN'T CHILLY, but his skin was so hot that a shiver shot down his spine. Or maybe that was from looking at Angie, so beautiful it made him throb. What had been a mad rush to have her, to lose himself inside her, had become something else. Part of him wanted to throw her down on the bed, take her hard using every trick in his large arsenal.

Instead, he pulled her close again, taking a minute to savor that stunning body rubbing against him. She felt better than anything. If he could package the sensation, he'd be the richest son of a bitch in the world.

"Oh…" She turned the breathy word into a hum while she ran her hand slowly over his chest.

"Did anyone ever tell you you've got amazingly soft skin?" he asked.

"I think you might have mentioned it. A couple of times."

He sighed before he caught her bottom lip between his teeth and gave it a little tug. After he let it go, he lapped at that tempting flesh and found himself drowning in the taste of her.

Finally she pulled back. "We gonna do this standing up?"

"We could try," he said. "But I think we'd have to be closer to the wall. Leverage."

Her laughter was as addictive as every other single thing about her. "Let's not get carried away. I'd hate for you to break something important just before we go home."

"That's a deal." He took her hand and helped her lie back, no clever moves, no showing off at all. He simply paid attention, holding back the covers even though he'd have preferred doing it on the comforter. But Angie had goose bumps and she seemed to like having the covers available.

When he settled himself beside her, they rolled together so easily it shocked him. He wasn't sure what was happening here. He should be putting as much distance between them as possible, racing for home and his real life. If not that, then applying his go-to recipe for fixing what ailed him by burying himself in someone new, a mystery to be solved in the span of an evening.

He'd broken every rule with Angie. He'd let her in where

no one was allowed. Thank God this was it. That they were going back to where things made sense. But for now, for the few hours they had left together, he wanted to stop thinking so damn much. Let it be.

"This is…"

"What?" he asked.

She shrugged, then kissed his shoulder. "Nothing." She looked up at him. The room was filled with the gold of the sinking sun, making her look tanned and sexier, if that was even possible.

After a kiss that made his cock harder than it had any right to be this early in the game, he started a systematic, highly detailed deconstruction of one Angie Wolf. By the time he reached his destination, he wanted her to be a quivering mess, begging for release. Which he would give her, all in good time.

If he made it that far, himself.

It was her long, graceful neck that lured him in to start. Using his lips, tongue and a hint of teeth, he got the party in gear. She tasted like honey and smelled like the beach. By the time he was nibbling his way across the divide between neck and shoulder, she'd bucked her hips twice as she squeezed his flesh wherever she could grab. It was her soft whimpers that made his cock jerk, though, that and knowing he was safe for the rest of the night.

ANGIE MOANED AS RYAN'S fingers entered her, a prelude, but delicious on its own. He was all over her and she'd never dreamed she'd ever actually feel ravished, but she did, as if he was taking her apart and putting her back together piece by piece.

The desperate noises she couldn't hold back were the same for pleasure as want, and how did that even work?

His finger pumped, which had her lifting her hips even as

he pinned down her back. His lips were on her right nipple, sucking and flicking to beat the band, and then his thumb came into play right *there,* steady as he pushed and licked and made her thighs tremble.

In one shocking moment, he abandoned her completely but before she could do more than cry out, he'd flung the comforter back. "I need to see," he said, then he went straight back to killing her with wicked bliss.

Her hand was in his hair, mostly running through it, but when he did something noteworthy, which was about every other second, she tugged. The first time it happened, she'd felt terrible about it, but the second time the way his body jerked and his low moan told her he not only didn't mind, but that he liked it.

Ryan switched his attention to her other breast and the sweet torment made her moan. Gorgeous, too much, and not nearly enough. His thumb, though, had most of her attention. It was the slow circle with the perfect pressure that was doing her in.

She tugged again, actually lifting his head back until their eyes met. "My thighs are two seconds away from meltdown, and I'm going to come and you won't be in me."

His slow grin was as full of mischief as his dark eyes. "I won't be in you yet."

"I can't hold on. You'll be sorry, because I'll be worn out."

"You're a long distance runner, sweetheart. I know what you can do."

Her legs gave out. Dislodging his hand just as she was starting the wind up. "I warned you."

"I think," he said, easing his head and hair away from her relaxed fingers, "that I'm going to make you come three ways tonight."

"Huh?" she said, eloquent as ever.

"First," he whispered, after a quick kiss goodbye to her right nipple, "with my mouth."

She watched him slide over, all strong limbs and flexing muscles, until he was between her legs.

"Then, with my fingers." He paused for a hello kiss to the very top of her sex before he maneuvered her legs over his shoulders.

"After that—" he met her gaze again, more predator than mischief maker "—with my cock."

She let her head drop to the pillow. There was no response to what he'd said. None. She thought about laughing, but she didn't want to waste the energy. If his objective was to wring her out like a wet cloth, well, he was going about it the right way.

"Fine," she said, her hands flopping up near her head. "Do to me what you will."

His chuckle was the kind that sent all kinds of shivers directly to the good parts. "I intend to."

IT WAS SOME UNGODLY HOUR, and she was tapioca and overly sensitized at the same time. She couldn't move and could barely catch her breath. He was beside her, gasping away. Where his hip touched hers felt as if they were melting.

He'd done it. All three. In that order. Like a magic trick because she wasn't one of those multiorgasmic women the magazines were so impressed with. *Three times.* Holy crap. Shouldn't there be an award or something? At the very least one of those parchment paper certificates, signed by the Commissioner of Amazing Sex.

Her head was only half on the pillow, there were at least two spots she didn't want to sleep on and, if she'd had the wherewithal, she'd turn on the air conditioner.

It occurred to her that while this part of the sting had certainly ended with a bang, tomorrow would begin a very different operation. They were heading back to normal. To being on the same team. Sleeping in different places. Acting like FBI agents.

Which would all look much simpler once they were dressed. Especially in her own clothes. With her sturdy, two-inch heels and her slightly baggy work suits. She'd get back to running her regular routes, dive into the post-assignment paperwork which was an achingly familiar slice of boring that felt like home.

Ryan and her? She turned her head far enough to see his eyes were closed and his body seemed completely relaxed. He deserved a rest. Not just from the sex, but for stepping so far outside his comfort zone. All week, actually.

No, the two of them wouldn't pick up where they left off. Not possible, not after what they'd been through. If it had just been sex, that would have been one thing, but they'd been intimate. She'd been closer to Ryan than she'd been with any other man in her life.

You didn't just walk away from that with a tip of the hat.

She couldn't imagine what it might be like, because of their jobs, because of so many things, not the least of which was working in the same office on the same team.

But then, one of them would probably be shipping out to Washington, D.C. If the blackmail text came through. If there wasn't someone more qualified, or more on the Deputy Director's radar. If it wasn't her, she was going to put in for a transfer to cyber crimes, so that would help.

She'd miss him. More than she could have imagined. It might have been a lot of role-playing and spy stuff, but he'd been incredibly open with her. She knew him now, seeing with such clarity that it wasn't the length of time that mattered, but what was shared that made people…close. He must know her, as well. Somewhere in this long, strange week, he'd changed from being an occasional fantasy to a man she cared for. Deeply.

RYAN OPENED HIS EYES AND stared straight up into the dark. He wanted to wake her again, bury himself in her body, in her pleasure and his own.

What he didn't want was the twisting sick feeling that was eating him alive. The memory of what he'd said to her burned inside him like a flare before the flash.

What the hell had he done?

15

A SHAFT OF SUNLIGHT brought Angie from dream to foggy awareness. Memories of the night came first. She wallowed in how it had felt to have Ryan's arms wrapped around her, the way he'd kissed her insensible, how her muscles had tightened in those last few seconds before release. Stretching her legs now brought an unexpected ache to her calves and thighs. She was in damn good shape but she was tempted to skip her run and soak in that sadly unused whirlpool tub.

Ryan wasn't next to her, which was a shame, but she knew he was in the bathroom. Must have heard something during the foggy part. Ah, there was a gurgling message from her stomach, angry at her for not eating dinner last night. God, she was starving.

The hell with yogurt and bran, she wanted something decadent. Eggs Benedict or French toast. *Hash browns.*

Where was he? Opening her eyes, finally, she got her watch from the bedside table, shocked that it was 8:20. So late she'd probably have to choose between the soak and the meal, and a run was out of the question.

The bathroom door opened. Ryan was already dressed in jeans, although not the worn ones, and a slate-gray short-sleeved shirt. His hair wasn't even wet, so he must have showered a while ago. He was staring at his cell phone until she cleared her throat. She grinned, looking forward to his good morning, wondering what he had in store for her.

"Hey," he said, giving her a glance and a smile that felt like an absent pat on the head.

She must have interrupted something important for him to act so dismissively. It shouldn't have disappointed her. Certainly not this much. They weren't on vacation, and if he'd gotten a message from Gordon or Jeannie, his behavior was entirely appropriate.

"You hungry?" she asked, watching him scroll through messages on his smartphone.

"Sure," he said, not even giving her a glance this time. "Go ahead and call room service. I'm trying to book the soonest flight out."

"What's the rush? Let's have something wonderful for breakfast." She grabbed her sleep shirt from the floor and slipped it over her head.

Ryan looked her way, but didn't meet her eyes. "I just want coffee."

"Did something happen?"

He lowered the phone and went to the patio window to stare outside.

With every step her insides tightened. What the hell was going on?

"I just want to get back to L.A.," he said, his voice as expressionless as the glimpse she'd had of his face. "Get started on the next part of the case."

"Okay," she said, not meaning it at all. She wanted him to look at her, to have the man she'd slept with look back at her. Things had happened between them that couldn't just vanish into nothing.

The only thing she could think of was that he was having a delayed reaction to the intimacy exercise yesterday. She'd known at the time that it was way out of his comfort zone, so, yeah, it was understandable that he was freaking out a bit, but to treat her like a one-night stand? No, that was just…no.

If that was the case, and she honestly couldn't come up with anything else, then he was probably embarrassed, which made her ache inside. Did he think she was going to tell anyone about what he'd said? That she would mock him for revealing so much of himself?

She walked over to him, even though he'd gone back to hiding behind his cell phone while keeping his back to her. She rubbed his arm, gently, the way she'd touched him yesterday. He'd found comfort in her then, and she hoped he'd feel it now.

Instead, he tensed.

"Hey," she said softly. "If this is about the thirty-four minutes, don't worry about it, okay? I consider what you told me privileged information. I'll never say a word about any of it. I'm just really honored that you trusted me enough to open up." She laughed a little, feeling her face heat. "For what it's worth, I thought you were amazingly brave."

Ryan took a step away from her, glancing at her once more, but only for a moment, and she couldn't tell if he was angry or embarrassed or what. "Look, nothing I said yesterday was about me. It was the job. That was all made up bullshit designed to make it look like I'd do anything to keep you. My personal life is just that. Personal. Sorry if you got confused." He paused, keeping his eyes averted. "About any of it."

Angie stood very still, trying to calm the surge of emotions so she could think. No way he'd made all that up yesterday. No way. The best actor on the planet couldn't have pulled that off.

And what the hell did he mean by any of it? Was he dismissing that they'd had amazing sex, that they'd made a real connection? Good God, she knew they wouldn't be strolling into the office holding hands.

But for heaven's sake, he couldn't even look at her. That body language in a suspect would signal guilt from a mile away. He was deflecting, that's all. He'd crossed every boundary he had for himself, and now he was trying to reclaim control the best way he knew how.

It was sad, and it was a lie, but it made her feel like an utter fool. She'd done it again. Let herself believe that he was someone other than the notorious Ryan Vail. God, she was an idiot.

But she couldn't deny that the overwhelming sensation right now was hurt. Deep, stabbed-in-the-back hurt. He had a right to his feelings, including shame and anger and whatever, but she felt slapped in the face, which she didn't deserve.

"If you haven't already, you should let the team know about the change of plans. Call Delilah and tell her whatever the hell you want, just don't blow everything we've managed to accomplish so far." She headed toward the bathroom. "You know what? I'll call Delilah. You just get us out of here."

Ryan looked her in the eyes for the first time that morning, and instead of making things better, the cool *nothing* she saw there made everything a hundred times worse.

DESPITE THE EXPENSE, ONCE they'd landed in Los Angeles, Ryan took a taxi to his apartment in the arts district downtown. Not that he used the place for anything to do with art. He kept meaning to tackle the bare wall situation but he'd never found sufficient motivation. Frankly, all he gave a damn about was his bed and the shower. He'd shelled out a hell of a lot on both of them, and considered it money well spent.

His place was on the fifth floor, and as always the elevator smelled like pine-scented chemicals. He'd lived with much worse. One of the reasons he'd moved into this high-tech, overpriced high-rise was the twenty-four-hour security. Also the weekly maid service. But mostly the security.

Unlocking the door relaxed his shoulders and he felt as if he could breathe for the first time since this morning. He left his suitcase by the couch, dropped his armful of mail on the counter, then headed back to his bedroom.

It was seven-thirty. He'd hoped to be back from Vegas earlier, but there'd been one mess up after another. The whole damn day had been a nightmare. He fell across his bed, the big old navy-blue comforter and the unbelievably great mattress made things somewhat better. If he thought he could sleep through the night he would have just let go, but it was too early and he was too wound up.

Being alone for a while would do him a lot of good. Christ, what an assignment. He'd better get that D.C. job, that's all. Then he wouldn't have to see Angie in the bullpen, in the elevators, in his head. He winced at how he'd been such a royal bastard to her. But it had been the right decision, even though it had killed him to see how hurt she was. He couldn't afford to regret it. But he couldn't help it. Every time he'd looked at her. Or thought about her. Or remembered how it had felt to be inside her.

His actions this morning had been in both their best interest. They were in the real world now and he had to work with Angie until he got the new job, so what was he supposed to do? Pretend he had feelings for her? That would have been much crueler. At least now, they both knew what was what, and they could return to the slightly uncomfortable but workable situation they'd had before Intimate At Last.

Ryan rolled over, spreading himself across the California King. *This* was precisely why he never went after a woman who was in any way connected to work. He'd broken his own rule and now he was paying the price. So he liked her.

So what? He'd liked a lot of women and somehow he'd managed to separate work and pleasure.

Jeannie was going to crucify him. If she found out he'd screwed up a second time. Who was he kidding? She'd find out. Somehow. He wouldn't tell her and he knew without any question that Angie wouldn't, either, but Jeannie had a kind of radar with him that by rights should creep him the hell out.

If that didn't make him want to leave the country on the first plane out, he didn't know what would. But since he couldn't get out of town, at least he could stop obsessing and get back to living his own life. Shower first, then go.

Zero Sum sounded right. It was the kind of club where it didn't matter what night of the week it was or who was behind the bar. He'd find himself a friendly woman who wanted nothing more from him than a few drinks and a couple of decent orgasms.

By ten-fifteen, he had his scotch rocks in hand, and three women in sight that were contenders. There was a petite brunette with a sexy overbite. Unfortunately she was with a friend, so that could be a problem. But he set his sights, made his plan and went for it.

ANGIE SHIFTED ON HER COUCH. It should have felt fabulous to be home. It didn't. There was nothing edible in the fridge, but she couldn't bring herself to look through her take-out menus. Her iPad sat next to her, turned off.

Three hours she'd been home. Showered, done laundry. Put on a nightgown, not a sleep shirt. She'd meant to call Liz, but she didn't think she could handle anything her friend had to say. Sympathy might just kill her.

The thing was, she'd done it to herself. Ryan had been nothing but Ryan. She'd known it, and she'd known the outcome, and she'd still opened herself to him. Opened her feelings. Opened her heart. Stupid. So stupid.

The only thing she'd done right all day was that she hadn't cried. She wouldn't. Not over him.

RYAN PAID HIS BAR TAB, NOT really surprised he hadn't scored. He'd stepped back into the real world too abruptly, that's all. Give him a day or two, a trip to the gym, and he'd be back to himself. He had to be back to himself because this was nuts.

The whole time he'd been talking to the short brunette, he'd been thinking about Angie. He wanted her. There was a physical ache inside him that one touch from her could cure. Or maybe that was hunger. He'd stop and get something on the way home, because his fridge was empty. Even his mustard had gone bad.

Despite it being out of the way, he stopped by a Korean place that was open late and ordered some bulgogi and cha dal with a side of kimchee then ended up eating it in his Mustang.

It wasn't hunger.

"SO WHAT WAS IT LIKE?" Paula asked, scooting her chair over to Angie's desk, bringing a skinny hazelnut venti latte as her bribe. "Sleeping with Ryan?"

"Awkward," Angie said, as rehearsed. She'd stood in front of her mirror for far too long making certain her expressions gave away nothing. "Very, very awkward. The whole time was. And I owe whoever picked out my clothes a giant slap upside the head."

"Come on. Don't be like that. I know you guys had to kiss and stuff."

Angie hadn't even put her purse in her bottom drawer yet, and already she wanted the day to be over. The month to be over. She'd had a horrible night's sleep, and coming back to the office had been almost as hard as telling her parents she wasn't going to go to law school. Wearing her own clothes had been difficult, which pissed her off. Not thinking about Ryan had been impossible.

"He's a good kisser, isn't he?"

"Paula, I swear to God, you have got to let up on this. We weren't away filming a reality show. It wasn't at all like that. It was weird, and I'm grateful it's over."

"Okay, jeez, I'm sorry. I mean you guys were sharing a room. I looked up tantric massage. What was I supposed to think?" Paula had the decency to blush, for about two seconds, then she said, "Tonya Bridges isn't going with the gang to Cancún."

"What?" For the first time since the casino night, Angie felt herself come down to earth. "She never said a word."

"Well, according to public records in the state of Nevada, she's applied for a massage license in Clark County. The paperwork was registered the day before yesterday."

"Hmm. That explains the furtive faxes. I wonder why she wants it so hush-hush? What kind of business is she planning to establish?"

"We're working on it. Now apologize with something juicy, would you? We can't talk about it when Jeannie gets here because she thinks we're perverts."

"We are perverts." Sally who was practically running to join them, stole Brad's chair to horn in on the prime desktop territory next to Paula. Why did all the women in this team have to come to work so early?

"She claims nothing happened," Paula said in her second snottiest voice. "That it was awkward."

"Because it was true, you troublemaker. I said it was awkward but we got through it. We planted all the right information, now we just have to wait for the right response. And fill out reams of paperwork." Angie finally stowed her purse in the drawer. "So if you would act like the professional, well-trained agents that you are, tell me what else has happened since I left."

"Joanna Tighe from ERT is getting married to Ken Westerly, you know, the guy from SWAT."

"Good for them, but I was asking about the actual work we do. In our office."

"Boy," Sally said, "did you have to sign up to get that stick up your ass or was it included in the workshop?"

Angie closed her eyes. It was a losing battle, and she had to either give them something or come up with a legit excuse quickly. Terrified of giving anything away, she went with an excuse.

"I'm sorry. I'm exhausted. I had a bad night after a rough week. I promise we'll all talk another time, okay? We'll do lunch soon, I promise."

Sally and Paula, both looking as if she'd betrayed some unwritten but important female coworker code, moped back to their own desks and Angie took comfort from her still-hot coffee.

Too bad nothing seemed to warm her up. Not the late night shower that had turned her pink from the heat, not huddling under her thick duvet. It was as if she'd been hollowed out, left empty and confused.

The thing was, she'd been *so wrong*. Missed the mark by a light-year. It had felt special. Magical. Real. Where had she gotten lost? Yes, she got it that the thirty-four-minute exercise had sealed her fate, but that wouldn't have been enough on its own.

Probably, it had begun with the very first kiss. Or maybe it had started at the Halloween party, and she hadn't realized the depth of the problem. She never should have agreed to the assignment.

Something had told her it would be dangerous. God, if she'd only known.

She took another sip while she turned on her computer. It was still twenty minutes from the opening bell, but her team consisted of overachievers and rabid gossips, so it wasn't at all surprising that the only two still missing were Jeannie and Ryan.

The thought that he'd truly be here, in person, in a matter of minutes, stole her breath. Tendrils of panic were snaking around her chest, and she used every trick her coaches had ever taught her about calming down.

She had to get her act together, that's all there was to it. This was the office. She was, despite her behavior in the past few days, a professional. This would not break her.

As she logged in her user name and password, she remembered how it had been right after that stupid party. The truth of him had been so much clearer back then.

Then she'd started letting him into her fantasies, and that had been the beginning of the end. It probably wouldn't have done lasting damage if Jeannie hadn't been held up in court. Angie could have gotten along with him up until the day she got the job with the Deputy Director.

Now, she didn't even deserve that job. Not after the fiasco that had been the Las Vegas sting. She just prayed that Ryan would be the chosen one, because at least he'd be across the country. Out of her sight, and eventually, out of her head. She'd gotten in bed with a viper and been shocked that she'd been bitten. Who's fault was that?

Knowing all that, it should have been a simple thing to shake it off. Like a side stitch or shin splints. It shouldn't make her want to curl up into a ball and hide from the world. She shouldn't feel worse than when she'd broken up with Steve.

Her sigh was too loud, her posture slumped, and if anyone looked at her right now they'd see she was on the verge of tears. All the effort she'd put into practicing to appear cool and calm had gone down the drain even before work had officially begun.

If she had any self-preservation instincts, she'd pack up and go home before it was too late.

Turning to pick up her cup, she froze. It was already too late. Ryan had arrived, and he couldn't have looked more carefree and happy.

16

RYAN KEPT HIS SMILE IN PLACE, made sure his movements weren't tense and that he didn't shy away from meeting anyone's eyes. Especially Angie's, although that lasted about five seconds.

On the inside, he wasn't handling things, as well.

He masked the ache in his chest by making the rounds, going from desk to desk in the bullpen, being his typical smartass self. Slyly inappropriate innuendoes were traded with the men, completely different more politically correct innuendoes with the women. Angie was last, and by that time he'd found his rhythm. He probably should have gone into acting instead of the Bureau. The money was better and the women hotter.

Well, no one was hotter than Angie.

It was all he could do not to let his gaze sweep over her. To linger on her neck as her remembered scent blossomed in his mind, nearly as real as when he'd had his nose buried in the soft spot right behind her ear. Other recollections hit him in a jumble. How her fingers felt on his arms, the way she squeezed his hips with those strong legs, pulling him closer even though they'd been as close as two people could be. God, the way she'd tasted.

"...at four."

Ryan blinked, a splash of panic bringing him to the present. He thought briefly about nodding, then somehow unraveling what Angie had just said, but gave that up as a losing battle. "I'm sorry. I was miles away. Could you repeat that?"

"Which part?"

He could feel heat rise to his cheeks and he wondered again what earthly good had ever come from the act of embarrassed blushing. "All of it."

"Late night?" she asked. She didn't look angry or particularly invested in his answer. Kind of indifferent. Which was good. So why did it sting?

He nodded, and this time the truth wasn't at all hard to admit. He'd tossed and turned doing everything he could to think of anything but her and failing miserably. How she'd managed to completely upend his well-ordered life. He might've gotten three hours.

"We have to write up the week," she said, sorting through papers on her desk, probably so she didn't have to look at him. "Separately, then go over our conclusions together. Palmer wants the team in his office at four."

"So much for getting out of here early."

"Well, life is tough all over."

Her clipped response was only slightly more obvious than the underlying weariness she was trying to hide. Before last week, he wouldn't have noticed. Wouldn't have cared.

Clearly, she hadn't had a peaceful night, either, although it had taken him some time to see her as she was, rather than how he pictured her. The glow had dimmed, her skin looked pale.

"Was there something else?"

He shook his head. "Let me know when you're ready for the wrap-up."

She nodded then turned to her computer. In profile the

tension in her shoulders was obvious, as was her desire to have him leave.

He obliged. It was only when he'd booted up his own computer that he let himself think about the past few minutes. She'd barely looked at him. Granted, they hadn't spoken for long, but her gaze had darted all over the place, most often landing on the bridge of his nose or his right ear. He hadn't realized how accustomed he'd become to reading her through her eyes. Sometimes they were so expressive it was as if she'd given him the key to her thoughts.

Complete avoidance said even more.

At least before when they'd danced around each other it had involved a little teasing, some heat, but always, there'd been respect.

He'd certainly managed to screw that up. She'd probably never really look at him again, and she certainly wouldn't want to laugh with him, or ask his opinion about work. About anything.

It shouldn't matter so much. It did, though, because he honestly liked her. Admired her. She didn't use her looks to get ahead, to manipulate anyone, as a crutch. He knew that because he did all of those things. The statistics were there, and he'd decided early to go with them, exploit every advantage he had.

Playing the handsome card wasn't evil or even unethical, but it was the easy way out. Also, it was something his father had done. Still did. His old man had been a model when he was younger. He still reminded people of Clooney, at least until he had a few. Then he got ugly. The kind of ugly that had nothing to do with mirrors. But by then, it was usually too late for whatever hapless woman had been deceived by his packaging.

The horrible thing was, Ryan was sure his own behavior wasn't going to change anytime soon. And yet, in retrospect, he should have handled yesterday morning with more tact. But that was the only part he regretted. As for the rest? He'd done Angie a favor.

THANKFULLY ANGIE WAS sitting across from Gordon Palmer with Ryan to her right. Jeannie sat next to him, and the rest of the team fanned out around the large conference table. The pretence of normalcy was easier in a group.

The private wrap-up had been accomplished in record time, but at least they'd had the comfort of FBI-speak to hide behind, paperwork and notes to focus on. Not that she'd gotten through it scot-free. Despite her efforts, the worst kinds of memories kept breaking through. All the different ways he'd looked at her. The way he smiled as if she were someone extraordinary. Most often, what she'd seen during those thirty-four minutes.

The pitchers of water were a big clue that the meeting was going to be a long one. Angie sat up straight, prepared to focus solely on the business at hand. She hadn't gone through that sting only to lose it when they were so close to the finish line. Now that everyone was settled, Gordon leaned forward to begin.

"We've received two interesting pieces of information this morning from the Vegas bureau. They've got hard evidence now that Ira's bookie has been dipping his pen into illegal ink. The only thing that matters in our case is that they were able to seize the operation's books. Ira lost well over fifty thousand dollars in the past few months. There's sure to be more as the Vegas team digs deeper. It's possible the amount of money he's lost this month alone is responsible for the second piece of data. The suspects have moved their flights up. They'll be out of the country at the end of this week."

Angie looked at Ryan, just as he looked at her. He seemed as surprised as she was.

"Was there a ticket for Tonya?" Ryan asked, jerking his gaze back to Palmer.

"Yes."

"So she still hasn't broken the news," Angie said. "Do we have any more intel on that business of hers? Is it a real thing, or a ruse or what?"

"Vegas has tails on all four of them." Gordon looked pointedly at Angie and Ryan. "We're all waiting on the text, which has to be coming soon. They're not going to want to leave without their nest egg. I'd expect to hear from them no later than the weekend."

Ryan leaned back in his chair. "Since Ebsen doesn't have access to multimillion-dollar art, we know they're going to ask for cash. So how do they expect to get the money out of the country?"

"If the blackmailer is Ira working alone, he may need to clear up his debts." Jeannie's gaze went to Ryan, then turned to Angie.

Brian leaned in. "If it's Tonya's game, she could be keeping the cash to help open up her business here, but that could also mean we won't necessarily hear so quickly."

Ryan nodded. "Marcus has some tricks up his sleeve. I'm not sure what, but he has some power issues. That milquetoast persona he's got going doesn't quite cover the rage. It wouldn't shock me to find out he's behind everything."

"Marcus?" Jeannie asked. "He's probably too busy with his call girls."

"Expensive call girls." Angie glanced quickly at Jeannie, but switched over to focus on Brian instead. Jeannie had looked…off. But Angie couldn't think about that right now. "This woman must have charged a couple of grand. We have no idea how often Marcus indulges. It could be nightly, for all we know."

"Yeah, but according to Tonya the family knows about

his hooker hobby. Which could mean they're all involved with the blackmail."

Angie shook her head. "Maybe everything comes down to Delilah, and she's just so good at blackmail and manipulation that she didn't leave us any breadcrumbs. She looks squeaky clean and that could mean she's smarter than all of them put together. Which could explain why Tonya changed her ticket. A last-minute escape attempt."

That set up a few minutes of chatter around the table. Not Angie, though. She was still caught up in trying to figure out what was going on with Jeannie. Had Ryan told her what had happened? Did Jeannie blame her for having sex while on the case?

Angie thought about her conversation with Liz. They'd talked for over two hours the night before. Liz had been furious at Ryan on Angie's behalf, which was nice, even though none of it was Ryan's fault. Liz had tried to convince Angie to talk to Ryan, to clear the air, but there was nothing to clear. He'd made his stand, and she'd known from the start that this was the most likely outcome. What was she supposed to say, "No fair, you were supposed to have changed for me?"

The thought swamped her with shame, but thankfully, Gordon brought the meeting to order again.

"Everyone got copies of the reports from Angie and Ryan? I want to go over the conclusions, see if we've missed anything. Then I want each of you to get the two of them caught up. Paula, why don't you start us off reading page one."

Perversely Angie found herself turning to Ryan instead of Paula. He was looking down at the papers in front of him, and he seemed unnaturally still. Also, his chair was upright. Ryan liked to swagger even when he sat, well, leaned back. His hands weren't moving at all. Normally he was a fiddler. No nearby pen was safe from his fingers, rubber bands were particular favorites and he'd bent more paperclips per meeting than anyone she'd ever seen. But there he was, head bowed, motionless, as if his vitality had flown the coop and left his body behind.

Watching him made her uneasy, and if she'd been sitting next to him she might have touched the back of his hand or rubbed his shoulder with her own. Despite everything. It was too much like looking at an imposter, and she didn't care for it. The squeeze of tension in her chest swelled as she tried again to understand how things had fallen apart so drastically in such a short period of time.

She should have looked away. She meant nothing to him, and in return, she should do herself a favor and feel nothing for him.

His eyes closed. Slowly, as if he had to think about what he was going to do. Then his head swiveled toward her until he was staring right at her. The expression on his face was neutral. Almost. Because his gaze made her stop breathing, made her lean back in her chair. Made everyone else in the room seem to disappear.

She couldn't guess what he was thinking. Only that it wasn't about their report, or even about the case. All she knew for sure was that he'd lied to her. Whatever was going on between them, the thirty-four minutes and their night together hadn't all been an act.

MIDWAY THROUGH SALLY's overview of the Intimate At Last financials, Ryan's phone rang. The sound brought everything to a standstill even though it wasn't particularly loud. Everyone present knew that particular ring tone was Ebsen's.

He pulled it out of his pocket. It was too soon for a blackmail text. But then nothing about this case had gone as expected. The blocked number told him it was the text they'd been waiting for. He knew from the interviews with the victims that they wouldn't be able to trace the call, that it would be routed and rerouted in a convoluted trail that ended somewhere in Romania. He clicked View Now.

Dear Mr. Ebsen: If you wish to continue your very pleasant life with your beautiful wife, with your expensive car and your many elegant vacations, you will be at Du Par's on Ventura Boulevard tomorrow night at 12:00 a.m. You will be alone, you will not be wearing a wire, and you will have with you $500,000.00 in cash, in hundreds, in unmarked bills with no dye pack and no tracers and no bugs and no hint that anyone, including the police, has been alerted. You will sit at the counter with a suitcase beside you. You will order coffee and you will not look around. If you do, your wife will receive every photo and every text and every email that is on your cell phone and computer. The suitcase will be taken. You will remain at the diner until 1:30 a.m. You may then return to your delightful life.

He nodded, so that the room understood this was the text. This was the ball in play. But there were still photo attachments to be looked at.

He began the slideshow. There was Ebsen's ex-mistress. Next was a photo of breasts. Nice ones that hadn't actually belonged to the woman who was pictured as his lover. She was a Special Agent out of the San Diego office, matter of fact.

Then came a series of pictures of emails and texts. From Ebsen to Roxanne, from her to Ebsen, deleted emails and deleted texts. He looked up, met Gordon's eye. "Well, we were right about them cloning the SIM card and the laptop."

"Let's hear it," Palmer said.

Ryan clicked back on the original message and as he read, half the people in the room took every word down.

"That's awfully smug," Jeannie said.

Angie nodded. "Sure. They've already gotten away with

it. We have no idea how many times. This transaction is a done deal. It could be from any one of them or all of them."

"All right," Palmer said, looking his version of pleased. "We know the timeline. We'll have the money ready. This is going precisely to plan."

"Whoever's running the pickup can't get back to Vegas by plane that late." Ryan looked over at Angie, a reflex, but one he'd have to curb if he didn't want to get jolted out of his thoughts. "I doubt there are any trains. So, they'll be driving. Unless the blackmailers are also in L.A."

"We're following the money," Angie said, but Ryan kept his gaze on Palmer. "They don't have the tech to discover our bugs, so we can wait it out until it changes hands."

"Are we absolutely sure the Vegas team has to take the bust?" Ryan had been okay with the deal up until about two minutes ago. "We did do all the heavy lifting."

Palmer's pleased smile disappeared. "It will show up in your files as a joint operation. Don't sweat it. We all know what everyone did for this sting." He looked right at Ryan as he spoke, then at Angie.

Ryan hoped to God that Palmer didn't know everything that happened, but he nodded at his boss, anyway. At least the hand-off would be up to him. He couldn't wait to see who was going to show up to take the cash.

"What's going on?"

Angie wasn't using Skype, so she couldn't see Liz's face, but she could picture her friend perfectly. Worried, mostly because of how wrecked Angie had been last night. Probably because Angie couldn't keep up any kind of facade with Liz even over the phone. "I'm sorry. It's been insane. I'm on a stakeout. Well, actually, I'm a block and a half away from the surveillance van in my car at the moment. I just wanted to touch base."

"I wish you'd reconsider talking to Ryan."

"I'm thinking about it. He's been gone all day, acting out a day in the life of Ryan Ebsen. Being at work without him felt weird."

"In what way?"

"Damn it, I missed him. I can't stop thinking about him. I don't believe it was all an act. We connected, I'm sure of it. The thing is, I'm positive that he knows all that, too. He just doesn't like that he'd gotten involved. Especially with someone at work. So this feeling, this boulder in my chest, it's all my problem, not Ryan's. It hurts like fire, Liz. It just gets worse and worse."

"Oh, boy." Liz's voice was softer, careful. "Angie, honey. I think you went and fell in love with the guy."

Angie closed her eyes and willed herself not to let the sudden hot tears fall. "I didn't."

"Right." Liz sighed. "The good news is, it won't actually kill you. The bad news is, you'll kind of wish it would."

It took a minute of the heel of her palms pressed against her closed eyes, but Angie won the fight. No tear dropped. Only the penny. But if this was love, she wanted nothing to do with it.

"I've got to get back to the van. Ryan should be coming soon."

"Good luck," Liz said. "You know I think you should still talk to him. Outside of work."

"Goodbye, Liz. Thank you." Angie put her cell in her jacket pocket, locked up the car and walked back to the surveillance van, which had been parked down the street from DuPar's diner. It smelled like a men's locker room. Which wasn't the bad part. There were four other people in the van with her that all had very defined tasks. She was a guest, and therefore, she wasn't allowed to complain that she couldn't see, couldn't hear and technically shouldn't even speak.

So she tucked herself into the corner and waited till Ryan Ebsen's red Ferrari came into view. Their team was in place, with backups and hidden cameras using new stealth tech, and the wired money and cars that would physically follow the cash to see where it ended up.

She refused to think of anything but the stakeout and the money transfer. Every time something personal popped up, she squashed it like a cockroach. This moment would justify everything that had happened to her since they'd been assigned this case. It would make up for being in the most awkward and ultimately painful situation of her life. She'd be damned if she was going to miss a second of it on some insane emotional idiocy.

"He's on the Boulevard," Max said. He was their electronics guy, the one who'd come up with the nontraceable cash tag. "Everyone stand by."

Angie took him at his word and stood, as cramped as it was. All she wanted was for this night to be over. For the case to be turned over to the Vegas office. And for Ryan to be safe. Even though he wasn't the kind of man for her. Despite the fact that it was likely that she'd become more attached than was wise to the part he'd played instead of the man himself.

The truth was, he didn't love her. *He didn't love her.*

There was nothing to be gained by talking it out with him. She still stood by the decision she'd made this morning to put in for a transfer to Cyber Crimes. Just in case the D.C. job fell through, of course. She'd covered her bases, given herself a backup exit strategy. No matter what happened, she wasn't going to spend any more time working in the same office as Ryan. Not if she could help it.

"He's here." Max's voice was calm and low, but the words constricted Angie's chest, and she maneuvered herself so she could see one of the monitors.

That car was captivating, but it couldn't hold a candle to

Ryan himself. God, he looked nervous. Of course. He was a consummate actor deep in his character.

He carried the suitcase with him into the brightly lit diner. The cameras they'd put in place an hour after the text showed every seat in the house. Particularly at the counter. But no one turned to look at him.

He ended up taking a stool to the far right, where there were the fewest customers. He put the case next to his feet, as ordered. An agonizing twelve minutes later, a tall blonde walked through the front door.

"I'll be damned," Angie muttered.

Everyone in the van looked at her.

"It's Marcus," she said, her gaze glued to the woman. "I mean, he's in on it. She's got to be one of his call girls. Clever."

The blonde didn't even bother to sit down. She just picked up the suitcase and walked straight through to the back entrance, where the exterior camera showed her getting behind the wheel of a white Chrysler. A moment later, she took off into the night.

By the time Ryan left the building at exactly one-thirty, the Ferrari was gone.

17

IT TOOK FOREVER TO GET HOME. He'd had to go to the house they'd set up as belonging to the Ebsen's first, then sneak off super-spy style in Jeannie's minivan. By the time she dropped Ryan back at his apartment, he was more exhausted than he could ever remember. It felt as if he hadn't slept in years, not days, and now that the adrenaline had worked through his system, he was running on fumes.

That didn't seem to matter to his beleaguered brain. As he stripped for bed, letting his clothes drop at his feet, he replayed every word Jeannie had said to him on the longest drive of his life. He'd confessed his sins, and she'd put him through hell for it. Truth was, he didn't mind. It wasn't half of what he deserved. The only thing he took exception to was Jeannie's advice to talk it out with Angie.

What Jeannie didn't know was that he'd already thought of that. The number of imagined conversations he'd attempted must have been in the dozens, each one falling flat or worse, making him want to wring his own neck.

They all began with, "I'm sorry. I messed up."

The bed beckoned, but there was still one thing he had to do. Booting up his laptop took forever and made him very aware that it was damn cold wearing just his boxers on his metal desk chair, but doing anything about it was out of the question. One click opened a new document and he started typing. Once he got going he realized the short message he'd envisioned wouldn't be sufficient so he kept on until he'd said everything he'd needed to. Literally dizzy with fatigue, he copied the text and found the two, no three, contacts for his email. Then he pasted his note, saved everything, shut off the machine and somehow made it back to the bed. And sleep.

DEPUTY DIRECTOR LEONARD had arrived at ten that morning, although Angie hadn't seen him. She supposed he was being personally filled in on the success of their mission by A.D. Palmer. Rumor had it Leonard was going to stay on for a while, probably to conduct interviews.

Angie wasn't fussed. The only thing worrying her was that it was almost noon and Ryan hadn't made it in to the office. She wasn't pining away for him. The opposite was true, in fact. She needed to prepare herself to see him. To get her thoughts in order as she ruthlessly shoved her feelings to a dark, small box in the back of her mind.

Not knowing when to expect him was messing with her timing. The last thing she needed today was that kind of distraction.

The Vegas team had taken over once the white Chrysler had crossed into Nevada. The go-between had gone to a very expensive high-rise condo just off the Strip, which was immediately put under surveillance. She hadn't left again.

Despite Angie's realization that the woman had to be one of Marcus's call girls, all the staff of Intimate At Last were being watched. Each of them had been seen at least once during the morning, but no one had left their homes.

Her office phone rang, and it was the Deputy Director's assistant, asking her to come to the third floor temporary office. She popped a mint as she went to the elevator, amazed at how calm she felt. At least about this.

On three, the elevator doors opened. Ryan stood directly in front of her. It took her so by surprise that Ryan had to block the doors from closing.

"You've been here all morning?" she asked.

"An hour." They traded places, but he kept the elevator stalled.

She had questions, but the director was waiting, so... "It went great last night."

"I heard you were in the van."

She nodded, then motioned with her chin toward the director's temporary office down the hall. "I have to..."

"Yeah," he said, looking as if he wanted to say more. Instead, he moved back in the car, letting the doors close.

The walk to Leonard's office wasn't nearly long enough. But she managed to settle, to get back some of her calm before she tapped on the door.

She took the offered cup of tea just to have something to hold on to. Of course, she'd met Leonard before, but she doubted he remembered her.

"Congratulations on a job very well done," he said, gesturing for her to sit in the guest chair.

"Thank you, sir."

"Not just for your software program, but for stepping into a very delicate situation."

She nodded, smiled, took a sip of tea that really needed some sugar. "Thank you," she repeated. God, how she hated interviews.

"I received an interesting email this morning," he said, rising from his chair to walk around his desk. He leaned back against the dark wood, and Angie remembered Ryan standing just that way in their hotel room.

"Oh?" she said, in another stunning moment of grace and intelligence.

"Special Agent Vail had a lot to say about you."

That took her so by surprise that she had to put the tea down on the console table. Luckily she didn't have to respond verbally, because she wouldn't have known how to begin.

"He was quite impressed with how you handled yourself in such a potentially awkward situation. The Bureau doesn't make it a habit of asking our agents to go as far as you had to. I can't imagine that it was easy."

"It wasn't. But I assure you, Agent Vail made all the difference. He was deeply committed to making sure the sting was successful. The lion's share of the responsibility rested on his shoulders."

Leonard's smile was brief, but knowing. "He warned me you would say that." After a strangely intense stare, the director leaned forward a couple of inches. "I'll be frank with you, Agent Wolf. I asked Vail to meet me earlier to offer him the position in my office."

"Good choice, sir," she said, hoping he understood that those weren't idle words.

"He turned me down. Said you'd be the right person for the job. That with your computer skills and your adaptability and skill as an agent, you'd be an unbeatable asset."

Angie's mouth opened, but nothing, not even a breath escaped as she tried to make sense of what she'd just heard. He'd turned down the job? That was crazy. Absolutely nuts. She knew he wanted it. That he'd be great at it. Hell, even the Deputy Director knew he was the right man for the position. "I'm flattered," she said, finally, "and confused, to be honest with you."

"That's probably because I haven't asked." He smiled again, this time it was more open. "Which I'm doing right now. I think both you and Agent Vail would make excellent additions to my staff, but I only have the budget for one of you. The job is yours if you want it."

She should have been jumping on the offer without a second thought. Last week, she would have. Her family would have been so proud. A lot had changed since then. "Thank you, sir. I appreciate the vote of confidence. But I'm afraid I'm not going to be able to accept."

To say he looked surprised was an understatement. "Excuse me?"

"I submitted a withdrawal of my application this morning. I've decided to apply for a transfer to Cyber Crimes, here in Los Angeles. I believe it's where I can do the most good, and frankly, working in programming suits me."

Now it was the director's turn to appear a little shell-shocked. He was a distinguished-looking man in his elegant navy suit, and she'd never seen him ruffled. Until now.

She almost apologized again, but decided against it. "Agent Vail had no idea about my decision, sir. For what it's worth, I think your first choice was the right one. He's the most impressive agent I've ever worked with."

"Thank you for your candor, Agent Wolf." He studied her for a long, uncomfortable moment, then continued with a short speech about what the move to D.C. would do for her career. The professional pep talk was eerily close to too many she'd heard from her parents.

It was her reaction that was different. She didn't feel as if she were sitting on the hot seat destined to disappoint someone. No, she'd weighed the pros and cons and took responsibility for the choice she'd made. From this point forward, the only person she could disappoint was herself, but only if she didn't try her best.

She sipped, nodded when it was appropriate, but it was obvious when the director recognized that she'd already made up her mind. With a faint smile of defeat, he straightened.

She stood, held out her hand.

He shook it with a certain gravity, which she understood. "I'm regretting my budget restrictions even more after speaking to you both. But I agree you will make a considerable contribution to the Bureau working in Cyber Crimes."

She smiled as he let her go and took a huge breath once she was back out in the hall. It was only with great determination that she started walking again, because *Ryan had turned down the job. For her.*

Okay, so maybe Liz had a point about the whole talking thing.

AFTER A TERRIBLE NIGHT, Ryan had gotten to work a few minutes late. He hadn't seen Angie at all after her interview with Leonard yesterday. He'd even stuck around for a while after hours, but she'd been locked up in meetings with the tech heads from Cyber Crimes. He'd spent his night at home, staring at his cell phone, debating between calling her, showing up at her place or trying one more time to make something happen at one of his night spots.

In the end, he'd fallen asleep on the couch, and woken late with a stiff neck and the lingering memory of a dream. About her. About them.

The 9:00 a.m. call from the Supervisory Special Agent in Las Vegas came directly to Ryan, and his two-finger whistle brought everything to a halt in the bullpen. He put the phone on speaker. "You've got our attention," he said.

"At 7:22 a.m. we arrested Marcus Aldrich for extortion under Penal Codes 518-527 inclusive. We've obtained full warrants for all material including computers, cell phones and any and all electronic devices belonging to or rented by the Intimate At Last staff. Delilah Bridges, Ira Bridges and Tonya Bridges are officially persons of interest in the case and won't be leaving the country anytime soon. Well done, Los Angeles."

The team burst into applause with more than a few members whooping it up. Ryan found Angie's gaze and held it. Whatever else had happened, this was their victory. They'd come through for the team and for the Bureau. He hadn't always believed they would, so this was a good thing. A damn good thing.

She smiled. Picked up her phone. He watched her type a text from about fifteen feet away. It wasn't a surprise that his cell rang.

I would like to speak to you. Tonight. At your apartment. After work.

Despite his desire to speak to her, it took him a minute to respond. He wasn't sure he wanted to hear what she had to say. Most likely that she'd accepted the D.C. job. He figured she'd heard about his letter to the Deputy Director, but that didn't excuse his behavior last week. No matter what, there was no happy ever after ahead, not for the two of them. It was surprising enough that he found he wanted one, even though he wasn't sure he had what it took to make Angie happy.

He'd like to try, though.

Next life, he'd know better. This life, he texted her a quick You bet. She'd have her say, and then he'd figure out what was next for him. He'd stick around in White Collar and milk this victory for all it was worth, then take a look at what was available. He was free to go anywhere, maybe take on Major Crimes or tackle Terrorism. The only place he wouldn't look was Washington, D.C. He couldn't bear the idea of working in the same office with her again.

He put his cell away as Gordon Palmer walked into the room, causing yet another swell of celebration.

"Great job, everyone," he said. "We'll continue to support the Las Vegas team as we head toward convictions and restitution. You all deserve a raise. You're not going to get them, but you deserve them."

He got a laugh, even though it wasn't all that amusing.

"Now get back to work. We've let too many of cases slide these last few months. It's time to play catch-up."

The transition back to work mode was smooth, but unsettling. Ryan wanted the assignment to be over. To get back to normal. But normal had left the building.

Somehow, he was able to read an entire brief without thinking of what would happen after work at his place. But he kept sneaking glances at Angie. Surprisingly, she kept sneaking glances back.

ANGIE STOOD OUTSIDE RYAN'S door, unable to bring her hand up to knock. He knew she was standing there. She'd told him she was coming, and he'd buzzed her in, but that didn't matter. She was scared to death and there was still time to make an escape. He wouldn't press her about it. They were already riding a tidal wave of awkward. But if she knocked and he let her inside, and she did what she'd come to do, there was every chance that wave might drown her.

But not doing the thing that needed to be done? She would regret it forever. It was all about choices. Especially the hard ones. So she knocked, and he must have been standing right there, probably looking at her through the peephole, and wondering if she'd lost her mind.

The answer was clearly yes.

She hadn't been in his apartment before, although she'd been to the building. Once, a long time ago. He'd met her in the lobby and she'd driven the two of them to a weapons seminar. She'd expected the white walls, but she hadn't been prepared for the emptiness. It was as if no one lived there.

More like a home used by undercover agents than anyone with a real life.

It made her sad and scared for him, although she wasn't sure why about that last part.

"You want something? I've got coffee. Uh. Coffee. Oh, water. Tap water."

"I'm good, thanks."

They hadn't moved from next to the door. He'd closed it, done up the dead bolt. Some things became a habit when you worked in law enforcement.

The silence stretched between them, and Angie knew that because she'd called this meeting, she'd need to be the one to speak first. If only she'd thought of that before right this second.

"Want to sit?"

His couch was masculine and leather, dark brown, big. There was a coffee table that was some other kind of wood, and while she was no decorator, she could tell the two didn't go together. But she didn't want to sit there. In the kitchen, a small table had four utilitarian chairs. Those would do.

She took off her jacket and put it, along with her purse, on the coffee table. Then she arranged two of the chairs in the plentiful empty space, facing each other. A few feet apart.

Of course, he recognized the setup as the one they'd used in the thirty-four-minute exercise. The look of dread on his face wasn't surprising. She'd blindsided him on purpose. "You can say no," she said. "But I'd appreciate it if you didn't."

He stood still for a really long time. He was in his work clothes, sans jacket. He'd rolled up the sleeves of his white Oxford shirt and removed his tie. He bore a striking resemblance to Ryan Ebsen. Both of them were as masculine as that huge couch, but thankfully much better-looking.

"If this is to yell at me, couldn't we just do that standing up?"

"I'm not here to yell at you," she said. That he thought so surprised her.

"Why not?"

"Because you didn't do anything wrong. Well, maybe you could have been nicer, but no. I won't be yelling."

He moved, stepping closer so abruptly it startled her. "I was a jackass. Of all the people in the world, you did not deserve me being such an unmitigated prick."

"True."

He snorted, as if she had to be nuts. "That's it?"

She nodded. "You were just being yourself. I knew what we were doing there was an act. You could have softened the blow, but I suppose I needed the wake-up call."

He met her gaze. She didn't shy away, just let him look. Her visit was more about her than him in the long run, but it was also about them. About clearing the air; and while he'd started that ball rolling, she wanted to steer it in the right direction.

Stepping over to the chair, she didn't sit, just waited, prepared for him to bow out. God knew, Ryan was nothing if not averse to emotions of any kind. But maybe, perhaps, hopefully, their days at the workshop had opened a tiny crack in the giant fortress he'd built to protect himself.

With a rueful shake of his head, he sat down in the awful chair. That's when her heart started pounding double time. She figured she could get through this as long as she didn't stop to think. No crying, either. Under any circumstances.

She sat across from him. Judged the distance, then scooted in an inch. Then she set her watch alarm for thirty minutes.

"When I was ten, I had won a race at a district-wide meet. It was nothing, really, but it was held at a high school that had a proper track and there were ribbons and too much screaming from parents. I won my race, and my team also won the relay. So I came home with two ribbons, which my parents put up on a really large poster board in the family room.

"Anyway, they had some company over, I don't remember who. It was late, but I needed to use the bathroom, and had to walk down the hallway to get there. I passed the family room on the way, and I heard my father talking. I slowed down when he said my name.

"He said that I was built like a thoroughbred. That he'd always known that I was going to be a champion, and today was just the beginning. He'd bet everything he owned that I'd end up in the Olympics, and that I'd be a gold medalist. He planned on building a special display case for those medals.

"Then my mother started. About how I was a natural, how coaches were lining up, wanting to take me under their wings. They were being very picky, and if it meant moving to another state, they'd move. Because I was going to finally bring home the gold."

Ryan had leaned forward. But he hadn't looked away from her, not at all. "Sounds like a lot of pressure."

"I was utterly terrified," she said. "I shook so hard I had an accident in the hallway. Luckily it was a hardwood floor, so I was able to clean it up, but I ended up throwing my pajama pants out my bedroom window, then tossing them in a trash bin the next day. I was humiliated, but more than that, I knew without any doubt whatsoever that I was not going to be an Olympic champion. Not only was I not that fast, but I didn't care about it. I mean, competing was okay, but I didn't want to get up hours before school to train, dedicate my life to the sport.

"I wanted to go on sleepovers and playdates and I had it bad for horses, but I knew in that moment that I would forevermore have to do everything I could to make them proud of me, but in every way, not just on the track. I've lived my whole life trying to be that perfect person. Let me tell you. It's exhausting."

He sighed, finally looked down, but only for a moment. "I'm sorry you had to go through that."

"I don't think they meant any harm. They wanted what they saw as an ideal life for me. They had no way of knowing that conversation was going to set the direction of my life. That it would become the foundation of who I believed I was. How I was destined to fail."

"But you studied computer tech in college."

"My scholarship was in track and my major was pre-law. It nearly killed them when they realized I truly didn't have the talent for either. It's never been the same between us. Never."

"Do parents ever get it right?"

"Some more than others," she said.

He nodded, and she knew he was thinking about his father. About the way his mother had discarded him.

"But at some point," she said, "I realized I had to let go of what they wanted from me, and become the person I wanted to be." Angie cleared her throat, because this was coming up on the hard part. The part where she put her heart in her palm and let the chips fall.

"I'm not sorry I went to Vegas," she said, and he had to lean in a little closer because her voice wasn't coming out very loud. "But especially, I want you to know that I'm not even a little sorry about what happened to us personally. I've been attracted to you for a long time, and while I understand you aren't interested, I'm okay with that. What I don't want is for us to be weird with each other. Besides realizing how amazing sex could be, I found out so many other more important things. You were careful with me. You were creative and clever, and you always had my back…every minute and—"

"Stop," he said, and Angie gasped because she hadn't noticed that his eyes had changed, that he wasn't commiserating with her any more, he was in pain.

"What? I'm sorry. I—"

"Don't apologize, for God's sake, don't. And don't you dare say that I was careful with you. I was reckless. I thought you were just another…"

He stood. He walked all the way into the kitchen, opened up a cupboard and pulled out a bottle of Johnnie Walker. He poured himself a shot, and then brought down a different kind of glass and poured another shot for her. But he downed his standing by the counter, then just stood there, staring at the white cupboard.

Finally he walked back to her. Offered her the drink. She shook her head.

He sat again. Swallowed hard, put the drink on the floor, reached over and took her hands in his. When he met her gaze, she wouldn't have looked away for all the money on earth. "I'm so sorry, Angie," he said. "I was a complete bastard to you. I took advantage of the situation. I was unprofessional, and it was unforgivable. I just wanted you so damn badly.

"And then, that last night in our room, I got scared. Truly terrified, like you standing in that hallway. You aren't like any woman I've ever been with. I didn't want to let you go, and that was…unprecedented. You're the most amazing person I've ever met, and you've kind of messed everything up. I've tried to slide back into my life, but I can't. You're everything I didn't know I was missing."

"What?" The rug had not only been pulled out from under her, but she'd lost the ability to put two words together.

"If I were any other man, I'd never let you go again. I'd move heaven and earth to make you happy."

That helped her find her voice. "If you were any other man, I wouldn't want you."

The way he smiled broke her heart. "You don't know. You couldn't know."

"You don't, either," she said. "God, if you weren't going to Washington... And hey, that letter—"

"If I wasn't going to... What?"

"Oh. Leonard hasn't contacted you yet?"

"I'm seeing him tomorrow afternoon, but I wasn't told the agenda."

"He's going to restate his offer. I'd already decided I wanted to stay in L.A. and transfer to Cyber Crimes."

"But working with the Deputy Director is a huge opportunity. It'll open doors, put you in the center of the action."

"I know. But it's not what I want. Although, hearing you'd turned him down, that you'd written a letter on my behalf..."

"That letter was only the truth."

"Thanks. But now you can take the job with no regrets."

He stood up again, paced his sterile living room. When he ended up at the window, he turned to her again. "It's three thousand miles away."

"Yeah."

"You wouldn't be there."

The way he was looking at her and the tone of his voice kicked up her heart rate to the power of ten. She wasn't even sure why. "I know."

"I'd rather stay here. Near you. Which is a problem. Because I am not the kind of man who sticks around."

She stood up, weak knees and all. "Ryan."

"I hated that you were going to leave. I can't stop thinking about you. But, Jesus, I'm such an incredibly bad risk, I have no right to even be telling you this."

She met him at the window, aching for him, for them. This was the crossroads. Decisions made now would echo for a lifetime. "I would hate it if you didn't take the job, then found out you'd made a mistake."

"I'd hate it worse if I missed the one chance I had to be with you. There'll be other promotions."

The alarm went off, making both of them jump. She silenced it quickly. "I don't think I want to do the four minutes of silence."

"No?"

She shook her head. "I think we could find something better to do."

He pulled her into a kiss that stole her breath but not her reason. This unlikely man was the one for her. She'd want to kiss him for the rest of time.

He pulled back, but didn't let her go. "You're risking a lot here."

"I know. Remember that whole 'I learned to choose who I wanted to be' part?"

"And that includes me?"

"We've already been married, so dating should be a piece of cake, don't you think?"

His grin was slow in coming, but when it hit, it lit her up inside. "I never dreamed I would say this in my lifetime. Angie Wolf, I'm in love with you. And I will do everything in my power to make you proud and happy you're choosing me. But only if you understand, I have no experience when it comes to love or relationships."

"You're off to a great start," she said. "Besides, I already know you're a quick learner."

"I am one lucky son of a bitch," he said, seconds before he pulled her into the kiss of a lifetime.

* * * * *

PRIDE AND PREGNANCY

SARAH M. ANDERSON

To Dorliss Jones and Lynn Orr, who were wonderful next-door neighbours to my grandmother and have read every book. You've been asking for Yellow Bird for years – so here he is!

One

"Judge Jennings?"

Caroline looked up, but instead of seeing her clerk, Andrea, she saw a huge bouquet of flowers.

"Good Lord," Caroline said, standing to take in the magnitude of the bouquet. Andrea was completely invisible behind the mass of roses and lilies and carnations and Caroline couldn't even tell what else. It was, hands-down, the biggest bunch of flowers she'd ever seen. Andrea needed two hands to carry it. "Where did those come from?"

Because Caroline couldn't imagine anyone sending her flowers. She'd only been at her position as a judge in the Eighth Circuit Court in Pierre, South Dakota, for two months. She had made friends with her staff—Leland, the gruff bailiff; Andrea, her perky clerk; Cheryl, the court reporter who rarely smiled. Caroline had met her neighbors—nice folks who kept to themselves. But at no time had she come into contact with anyone who would send her *this*.

In fact, now that she thought about it, she couldn't imagine anyone sending her flowers, period. She hadn't left behind a boyfriend in Minneapolis who missed her. She hadn't had a serious relationship in…okay, she wasn't going to go into that right now.

For a frivolous moment, she wished the flowers were from a lover. But a lover would be a distraction from the job and she was still establishing herself here.

"It took two men to deliver," Andrea said, her voice muffled by the sheer number of blooms. "Can I set it down?"

"Oh! Of course," Caroline said, clearing off a spot on her desk. The vase was massive—the size of a dinner plate in circumference. Caroline hadn't gotten a lot of flowers over the course of her life. So she could say with reasonable confidence that the arrangement Andrea was carefully lowering onto her desk was more flowers than she had ever seen in one place—excepting her parents' funerals, of course.

She knew her mouth had flopped open, but she seemed powerless to get it closed. "Tell me there was a card."

Andrea disappeared back into the antechamber before returning with a card. "It's addressed to you," the clerk said, clearly not believing Caroline would receive these flowers, either.

Caroline was too stunned to be insulted. "Are you sure? There has to have been a mistake." What other explanation could there be?

She took the card from Andrea and opened the envelope. The flowers had been ordered from an internet company and the message was typed. "Judge Jennings—I look forward to working with you. An admirer," was all it said.

Caroline stared at the message, a sinking feeling of dread creeping over her. An unsolicited gift from a secret admirer was creepy enough. But that's not what this was, and she knew it.

Caroline took her job as a judge seriously. She did not make mistakes. Or, at the very least, she rarely made mistakes. Perfectionism might be a character flaw, but it also had made her a fine lawyer and now made her a good judge.

Once she'd found her footing as a prosecutor, she'd had an impeccable record. When she'd been promoted to judge, she prided herself on being fair in her dealings on the bench, and she was pleased that others seemed to agree with her. The promotion that had brought her to Pierre was a vote of confidence she did not take lightly.

Whoever would spend this much money to send her flowers without even putting his or her name on the card wasn't simply an admirer. Sure, there was always the possibility that someone unhinged had developed an obsession. Every time she read about a judge being stalked back to his or her house—or when a judge and her family in Chicago had been murdered—Caroline resolved to do better with her personal safety. She double-checked the locks on doors and windows, carried pepper spray, and had taken a few self-defense classes. She made smart choices and worked to eliminate stupid mistakes.

But Caroline didn't think this bouquet was from a stalker. When she'd accepted this position, a lawyer from the Justice Department named James Carlson had contacted her. She knew who he was—the special prosecutor who had been chasing down judicial corruption throughout the Great Plains. He'd put three judges in prison and forcibly retired several others from the bench after his investigations.

Carlson hadn't given her all of the details, but he had warned her that she might be approached to take bribes to throw cases—and he'd warned her what would happen if she accepted those bribes.

"I take these matters of judicial corruption seriously," he had told her in an email. "My wife was directly harmed by a corrupt judge when she was younger, and I will not tolerate anyone who shifts the balance on the scales of justice for personal gain."

Those words came back to her now as Caroline continued to stare at the flowers and then at the unsigned note. Those flowers were trying to tip the scale, all right.

Damn it. Of course she knew that people in South Dakota would not be less corrupt than they were in Minnesota. People were people the world over. But despite Carlson's warning, she'd held out hope that he was wrong. He had stressed in his email that he didn't know who was buying off judges. The men he'd prosecuted had refused to turn on their benefactors—which, he had concluded, meant they either didn't know who was paying the bills or they were afraid.

Part of Caroline didn't want to deal with this. Unknown individuals compromising the integrity of the judicial system—that was nothing but a headache at best. She wanted to keep believing in an independent court and the impartiality of the law. Short of that, she didn't want to get involved in a messy, protracted investigation. There was too much room for error, too much of a chance that her mistakes might come back to haunt her.

But another part of her was excited. What this was, she thought as she stepped around her desk to look at the flowers from a different angle, was a case without a resolution. There were perpetrators, there were victims—there was a motive. A crime needed to be solved and justice needed to be served. Wasn't that why she was here?

"How long do we have before the next session starts?"

she asked, returning to her chair and calling up her email. She had no proof that this overabundance of flowers had anything to do with Carlson's corruption case—but she had a hunch, and sometimes a hunch was all a woman needed.

"Twenty minutes. Twenty-five before the litigants get restless," Andrea answered. Caroline glanced up at the older woman. Andrea was staring at the bouquet with an intense longing that Caroline understood.

"There's no way I can keep all of these," she said, searching for Carlson's name and pulling up his last email. "Feel free to take some of them home, decorate the office—strew rose petals from here to your car?"

She and Andrea laughed together. "I think I will," the clerk said, marching out of the office in what Caroline could only assume was a quest to find appropriate containers.

Caroline reviewed the emails she and James Carlson had exchanged before she opened a reply and began to type. Because one thing was clear—if this were some nefarious organization reaching out to her, she was going to need backup.

Lots of backup.

Sometimes, Tom Yellow Bird thought, the universe had a sense of humor.

What other explanation could there be when, the very morning he was scheduled to testify in the court of the Honorable Caroline Jennings, he had received an email from his friend James Carlson, informing him that the new judge, one Honorable Caroline Jennings, had received a suspicious bouquet of flowers and was concerned it might be connected to their ongoing investigation into judicial corruption in and around Pierre, South Dakota?

It would be funny if the situation weren't so serious, he

thought as he took a seat near the back of the courtroom. This trial was for bank robbery, and Tom, operating in his capacity as an FBI agent, had tracked down the perpetrator and arrested him. The robber had had the bank bags in his trunk and marked bills in his wallet. A cut-and-dried case.

"All rise," the bailiff intoned as the door at the back of the courtroom opened. "The court of the Eighth Judicial Circuit, criminal division, is now in session, the Honorable Caroline Jennings presiding."

Tom had heard it all before, hundreds of times. He rose, keeping his attention focused on the figure clad in black that emerged. Another day, another judge. Hopefully she wasn't easily bought.

"Be seated," Judge Jennings said. The courtroom was full so it wasn't until other people took their seats as she mounted the bench that Tom got his first good look at her.

Whoa.

He blinked and then blinked again. He had expected a woman—the name Caroline was a giveaway—but he hadn't expected *her*. He couldn't stop staring.

She took her seat and made eye contact across the room with him, and time stopped. Everything stopped. His breath, his pulse—everything came to a screeching halt as he stared at the Honorable Caroline Jennings.

He'd never seen her before—he knew that for certain because he'd remember her. He'd remember this *pull*. Even at this distance, he thought he saw her cheeks color, a delicate blush. Did she feel it, too?

Then she arched an eyebrow in what was a clear challenge. Crap. He was still standing, gawking like an idiot, while the rest of the court waited. Leland cracked a huge smile, and the court reporter looked annoyed. The rest of the courtroom was starting to crane their necks so they could see the delay.

So he took his seat and tried to get his brain to work again. Caroline Jennings was the judge on this case and she was his assignment from Carlson—nothing more. Any attraction he might feel for her was irrelevant. He had testimony to give and a corruption case to solve, and the job always came first.

Carlson's email had come late this morning, so Tom hadn't had time to do his research. That was the only reason Judge Jennings had caught him off guard.

Because Judge Jennings was at least twenty years younger than he had anticipated. Everyone else who had sat on that bench had tended to be white, male and well north of fifty years old.

Maybe that was why she seemed so young, although she was no teenager. She was probably in her thirties, Tom guessed. She had light brown hair that was pulled back into a low ponytail—but it wasn't severely scraped away from her face. Instead, her hair looked like it had a natural wave and she let it frame her features, softening the lines of her sharp cheekbones. She wore a simple pair of stud earrings—diamonds or reasonable fakes, he noticed when she turned her head and they caught the light. Her makeup was understated and professional, and she wore a lace collar on top of her black robe.

She was, he realized, *beautiful*. Which was an interesting observation on his part.

He had no problems noting the physical beauty of men or women. For Tom, the last ten years had been one long observation of the human condition. Looking at an attractive person was like studying fine art. Even if a woman's physical attributes didn't move him, he could still appreciate her beauty.

But his visceral reaction to a woman in shapeless judge's robes was not some cerebral observation of conventional beauty. It was a punch to the gut. When was the last time he'd felt that unmistakable spark?

Well, he knew the answer to that. But he wouldn't let thoughts of Stephanie break free of the box in which he kept them locked up tight. He wouldn't think about it now. Maybe not ever.

He sat back and did what he did best—he watched and waited. Judge Caroline Jennings ran an efficient courtroom. When Lasky, the defense lawyer, started to grandstand, she cut him off. She wasn't confrontational, but she wasn't cowed by anyone.

As he waited for his name to be called, Tom mentally ran back through the email Carlson had sent him. Caroline Jennings was an outsider, appointed to fill the seat on the bench left vacant after Tom had arrested the last judge.

She was from Minneapolis—which was a hell of a long way from South Dakota. In theory, she had no connection with local politics—or lobbyists. That didn't mean she was clean. Whoever was pulling the strings in the state would be interested in making friends with the new judge.

Once, Tom would've been encouraged by the fact that she had already contacted Carlson about an unusual flower delivery. Surely, the reasoning went, if she was already willing to identify such gifts as suspicious, she was an honest person.

Tom wasn't that naive anymore. He didn't know who was buying off judges, although he had a few guesses. He couldn't prove his suspicions one way or the other. But he did know that whatever group—or groups—was rigging the courts in his home state, they played deep. He wouldn't put it past anyone in this scenario to offer up a beautiful, fresh-faced young judge as a mole—or a distraction.

"The prosecution calls FBI Special Agent Thomas Yellow Bird to the stand."

Tom snapped to attention, standing and straightening his tie. He should've been paying more attention to the trial at hand than musing about the new judge. The prosecutor had warned him that this particular defense lawyer liked to put members of law enforcement on the spot.

As he moved to the front of the room, he could feel Judge Jennings's gaze upon him. He didn't allow himself to look back. He kept his meanest gaze trained on the accused, enjoying the way the moron shrank back behind his lawyer. It didn't matter how intriguing—yes, that was the right word. It didn't matter how *intriguing* Judge Caroline Jennings was—Tom had to see justice served on the man who'd pulled a gun on a bank teller and made off with seven thousand dollars and change.

All the same, Tom wanted to look at her. Would she still have that challenge on her face? Or would he see suspicion? He was used to that. He'd been called inscrutable on more than one occasion—and that was by people who knew him. Tom had a hell of a poker face, which was an asset in his line of work. People couldn't figure him out, and they chose to interpret their confusion as distrust.

Or would he see something else in her eyes—the same pull he'd felt when she'd walked into this courtroom? Would she still have that delicate blush?

Smith, the prosecutor, caught Tom's eye and gave him a look. Right. Tom had a job to do before he dug into the mystery that was Caroline Jennings.

Leland swore Tom in, and he took his seat on the witness stand. Roses, he thought, not allowing himself to look in her direction. She smelled like roses, lush and in full bloom.

Smith, in a forgettable brown suit that matched his equally

forgettable name, asked Tom all the usual questions—how he had been brought in on the case, where the leads had taken the investigation, how he had determined that the accused was guilty of the crime, how the arrest had gone down, what the accused had said during questioning.

It was cut-and-dried, really. He had to keep from yawning.

Satisfied, Smith said, "Your witness," and returned to his seat.

The defense lawyer didn't do anything for a moment. He continued to sit at his table, reviewing his notes. This was a tactic Tom had seen countless times, and he wasn't about to let the man unnerve him. He waited. Patiently.

"Counsel, your witness," Judge Jennings said, an edge in her voice. Tom almost smiled at that. She was not as patient as she'd seemed.

Then the defense lawyer stood. He took his time organizing his space, taking a drink—every piddling little thing a lawyer could do to stall.

"Today, Counselor," Judge Jennings snapped.

She got a lawyer's smile for that one before Lasky said, "Of course, Your Honor. Agent Yellow Bird, where were you on the evening of April twenty-seventh, the day you were supposedly tracing the bills stolen from the American State Bank of Pierre?"

The way he said it—drawing out the *Yellow Bird* part and hitting the *supposedly* with extra punch—did nothing to improve Tom's opinion of the man. If this guy was trying to make Tom's Lakota heritage an issue, he was in for a rude awakening.

Still, Tom was under oath and he responded, "I was off duty," in a level voice. This wasn't his first time on the stand. He knew how this gotcha game was played, and he wasn't going to give this jerk anything to build off.

"Doing what?" That smile again.

Tom let the question linger in the air just long enough. Smith roused out of his stunned stupor and shouted, "Objection, Your Honor! What Agent Yellow Bird does in his free time is of no importance to this court."

The defense attorney turned his attention to the judge, that oily smile at full power. "Your Honor, I intend to show that what Agent Yellow Bird does on his own time directly compromises his ability to do his job."

What a load of bull. That perp was guilty of robbing a bank, and his defense team was throwing everything and the kitchen sink at the prosecutor's witnesses in an effort to throw the trial. Tom knew it, the prosecutor knew it and the defense attorney definitely knew it.

But none of that mattered. All that mattered was the opinion of Judge Caroline Jennings. She cleared her throat, which made Tom look at her. Then she leaned forward, elbows on her desk. "How so, Counselor?"

"Your Honor?"

"You're obviously building toward something. My time is valuable—as is yours, I assume. Someone's paying the bills, right?"

It took everything Tom had not to burst out laughing at that—but he kept all facial muscles on complete lockdown.

The defense lawyer tried to smile, but Tom could tell the man was losing his grip. Clearly, he'd expected Judge Jennings to be an easy mark. "If I could ask the question, I'd be able to demonstrate—"

"Because it sounds like you're fishing," Judge Jennings interrupted. "What illegal activity are you going to accuse Agent Yellow Bird of?" She turned her attention to Tom and there it was again—that *pull*. "Any crimes you'd like to admit to, just to save us all the time?"

Tom notched an eyebrow at her, unable to keep his lips

from twitching. "Your Honor, the only crime I'm guilty of is occasionally driving too fast."

Something changed in her eyes—deepened. He hoped like hell it was appreciation. All he knew was that he appreciated that look. "Yes," she murmured, her soft voice pouring oil on the fire that was racing through his body. "South Dakota seems made for speeding."

Oh, hell, yeah—he'd like to gun his engine and let it run right about now.

She turned her attention back to the attorney. "Are you going to make the argument that violating speed limits compromises an FBI agent's ability to investigate a crime?"

"Prostitutes!" the flustered lawyer yelled, waving a manila envelope around in the air. "He patronizes *prostitutes*!"

An absolute hush fell over the courtroom—which was saying something, as it hadn't been loud to begin with.

Shit. How had this slimeball found out about *that*?

"Your Honor!" Smith shot out of his chair, moving with more animation than Tom would have given him credit for. "That has nothing to do with a bank robbery!"

This was ridiculous, but Tom knew how this game was played. If he displayed irritation or looked nervous, it'd make him look shifty—which was exactly what the defense wanted. So he did—and said—nothing. Not a damn thing.

But his jaw flexed. He was not ashamed of his after-hours activities, but if Judge Jennings let this line of questioning go on, it could compromise some of his girls—and those girls had been compromised enough.

"That's a serious accusation," Judge Jennings said in a voice that was so cold it dropped the temperature in the courtroom a whole ten degrees. "I assume you have proof?"

"Proof?" the lawyer repeated and waved the manila envelope in the air. "Of course I have proof. I wouldn't waste the court's valuable time if I couldn't back it up."

"Let me see."

The defense lawyer paused—which proved to be his undoing.

Judge Jennings narrowed her gaze and said, "Counselor Lasky, if you have evidence that Agent Yellow Bird patronizes prostitutes—*and* that somehow compromises his ability to trace stolen bills—I'd suggest you produce it within the next five seconds or I will hold you in contempt of this court. Care to start a tab at five hundred dollars?"

Not that Tom would admit this in a court of law, but Caroline Jennings had just taken that spark of attraction and fanned it into a full-fledged flame of desire, because the woman was amazing. Simply *amazing*.

Lasky only hesitated for a second before he strode forward and handed the manila envelope over to Judge Jennings. She pulled out what looked to be some grainy photos. Tom guessed they'd been pulled from a security camera, but at this angle he couldn't see who was in the pictures or where they might have been taken.

He knew what they weren't pictures of—him in flagrante delicto with hookers. Having dinner with hookers, maybe. He did that all the time. But last he checked, buying a girl dinner wasn't illegal.

Even so, that the defense lawyer had the pictures was not good. Tom had a responsibility to those girls and his tribe. But more than that, he had an obligation to the FBI to make sure that what he did when he was off the clock didn't compromise the pursuit of justice. And if Judge Jennings let this line of questioning go on, Tom's time at the truck stops would be fair game for every single defense attorney in the state. Hell, even if this criminal wasn't found guilty, another defense lawyer would try the same line of attack, hoping to be more successful.

"Your Honor," Smith finally piped up into the silence, "this entire line of questioning is irrelevant to the case at hand. For all the court knows, he was meeting with informants!"

Not helping, Tom thought darkly, although again, he didn't react. If people suspected those girls were turning informant, they'd be in even more danger.

Judge Jennings ignored Smith. "Mr. Lasky, as far as I can tell, this is proof that Agent Yellow Bird eats meals with other people."

"Who are known prostitutes!" Lasky crowed, aiming for conviction but nailing desperation instead.

Smith started to object again, but Judge Jennings raised a hand to cut him off. "That's it? That's all you've got? He ate—" She turned to face Tom and held out a photo. "Is this dinner or lunch?"

Tom recognized the Crossroads Truck Stop immediately—that was Jeannie. "Dinner."

"He ate dinner with a woman? Did she launder the stolen money? Drive the getaway car? Was she the inside woman?"

"Well—no," Lasky sputtered. "She doesn't have anything to do with this case!" The second the words left his mouth, he realized what he'd said, and his entire face crumpled in defeat.

"You've got that right." Amazingly, Judge Jennings sounded more disappointed than anything else, as if she'd expected Lasky to put up a better fight. "Anything else you have to add?"

Lasky slumped and shook his head.

"Your Honor," Smith said, relief all over his face, "move to strike the defense's comments from the record."

"Granted." She fixed a steely gaze on Lasky.

Tom realized he'd never seen such a woman as Judge Jennings—especially not one for whom he'd felt that spark. He wanted nothing more than to chase that fire, keep fanning those flames. Stephanie would have wanted him to move on—he knew that. But no one else had ever caught his attention like this, and he wasn't going to settle for anything less than everything. So he'd stayed faithful to his late wife and focused on his job.

Except for now. Except for Caroline Jennings.

There was one problem with this unreasonable attraction.

She was his next assignment. Damn it.

"Agent Yellow Bird, you may step down," she said to him.

Tom made damn sure to keep his movements calm and even. He didn't gloat and he didn't strut. Looking like he'd gotten away with something would undermine his position of authority, so he stood straight and tall and, without sparing a glance for the defense attorney or his client, Tom walked out of the courtroom.

There. His work on the bank robbery case was done. Which meant one thing and one thing only.

Caroline Jennings was now his sole focus.

He was looking forward to this.

Two

As Caroline headed out into the oppressive South Dakota heat at the end of the day, she knew she should be thinking about who had sent the flowers. Or about James Carlson's brief reply to her email saying he had contacted an associate, who would be in touch. She should be thinking about the day's cases. Or tomorrow's cases.

At the very least, she should be thinking about what she was going to eat for dinner. She had been relying heavily on carryout for the last couple of months, because she hadn't finished unpacking yet. She should be formulating her plan of attack to get the remaining boxes emptied so she could have a fully functional kitchen again by this weekend at the latest and make better food choices.

She wasn't thinking about any of those things. Instead, all she could think about was a certain FBI agent with incredible eyes.

Thomas Yellow Bird. She shivered just thinking of the

way his gaze had connected with hers across the courtroom. Even at that distance, she'd felt the heat behind his gaze. Oh, he was intense. The way he'd kept his cool under fire when that defense attorney had gone after him? The way he'd glared at the accused? Hell, the way he'd let the corner of his mouth twitch into a smile that had threatened to melt her faster than ice cream on a summer day when he'd said he was guilty of speeding?

So dangerous. Because if he could have this sort of effect on her with just a look, what would he be capable of with his hands—or without an audience?

She hadn't had the time or inclination to investigate the dating scene in the greater Pierre area. She assumed the pool of eligible men would be considerably smaller than it was in Minneapolis—not that she'd dated a lot back home. It'd been low on her priority list, both there and here. Messy relationships were just that—messy. Dating—and sex—left too much room for mistakes, the kind she'd dodged once already.

No, thank you. She did not need to slip up and get tied to a man she wasn't even sure she wanted to marry. Her career was far more important than that.

Besides, she spent most of her time with lawyers and alleged criminals. Her bailiff was married. It wasn't like an attractive, intelligent man she could date without a conflict of professional interest just showed up in her courtroom every day.

Except for today. Maybe.

Because there was that small matter of whether or not he patronized prostitutes. That was a deal breaker.

Lost in thought, she rounded the corner of the courthouse and pulled up short. Because an attractive, intelligent man—FBI Special Agent Thomas Yellow Bird—was leaning on a sleek muscle car parked two slots down from her Volvo. Her nipples tightened immediately, and only one thing could soothe them.

Him.

She shook that thought right out of her head. Good Lord, a man shouldn't look this sinful—and in those sunglasses? He was every bad-boy fantasy come to life. But she'd watched him on the stand and seen flashes of humor underneath his intense looks and stoic expressions—and that? *That* was what made him truly sexy.

Was secretly lusting after an FBI agent in a great suit a conflict of interest? God, she hoped not. Because that suit was amazing on him.

"Agent Yellow Bird," she said when he straightened. "This is a surprise."

One corner of his mouth kicked up as he pulled his sunglasses off. "Not a bad one, I hope."

It wasn't like they'd had a personal conversation in court today. There'd been several feet of plywood between them. She'd been wearing her robes. Everything had been mediated through Lasky and Smith. Cheryl had recorded every word.

Here? None of those barriers existed.

"That depends," she answered honestly. Because if he were going to ask her out, it could be a very good thing. But if this was about something else…then maybe not so much.

His gaze drifted over her, a leisurely appraisal that did nothing for Caroline's peace of mind right now. She'd thought she'd been imagining that appraisal in the courtroom when she'd met his gaze across the crowded courtroom and everything about her—her clothes, her skin—had suddenly felt too tight and too loose at the same time.

No, no—not lusting after him. Lust was a weakness

and weakness was a risk. The heat flooding her body had more to do with the July sun than this man.

As his gaze made its way back up to her face, a look of appreciation plain to see, she knew she wasn't imagining *this*. When he spoke, it was almost a relief. "I wanted to thank you for having my back today."

She waved away this statement, glad to have something to focus on other than his piercing eyes. "Just doing my job. Last time I checked, eating dinner wasn't a conflict of interest." Unlike this conversation. Maybe. "I have no desire in being perceived as weak on the bench. I run a tight ship."

"So I noticed."

This would be a wonderful time for him to assure her that he didn't patronize prostitutes—in fact, it'd be great if he didn't eat dinner with them at all. She tried to keep in mind what Smith had said in his objections—perhaps Agent Yellow Bird had been meeting with informants or some other reasonable explanation that could be tied directly to his job.

Strangely, she wasn't feeling reasonable about Agent Yellow Bird right now. She steeled her resolve. She couldn't be swayed by a gorgeous man in a great suit any more than she could be influenced by cut flowers. Not even loyalty could corrupt her. Not anymore.

Everything about him—his gaze, his manner—was intense. And, at least right now, they were on the same side. She'd hate to be a criminal in his sights.

"Well," she said, feeling awkward about this whole encounter.

"Well," he agreed. He shoved off his car—an aggressive-looking black thing with a silver stripe on the hood that screamed *power*—and extended his hand. His suit jacket shifted, and she caught a glimpse of his gun. "We haven't been formally introduced. I'm Tom Yellow Bird."

"Tom." She hesitated before slipping her palm into his. This didn't count as a conflict of interest, right? Of course not. This was merely a...professional courtesy. Yes, that was it. "Caroline Jennings."

That got her a real smile—one that took him from intensely handsome to devastatingly so. Her knees weakened—weakened, for God's sake! It only got worse when he said, "Caroline," in a voice that was closer to reverence than respectability as his fingers closed around hers.

A rush of what felt like electricity passed from where her skin met his, so powerful that Caroline jolted. Images flashed through her mind of him pulling her in closer, his mouth covering hers, his hands covering...

"Sorry," she said, pulling her hand back. She knew she was blushing fiercely, but she was going to blame that on the heat. "I generate a lot of static electricity." Which was true. In the winter, when the air was dry and she was walking on carpeting.

It was at least ninety-four out today, with humidity she could swim in. She was so hot that sweat was beginning to trickle down her back.

He notched an eyebrow at her, and she got the feeling he was laughing. But definitely on the inside, because his mouth didn't move from that cocky half grin.

Her breasts ached, and she didn't think she could blame that on the sun. She was flushed and desperately needed to get the hell out of her skirt suit to cool down. What she wouldn't give for a swim in a cool pool right now.

Alone. Definitely alone. Not with Agent Tom Yellow Bird. Nope.

"About the flowers," Tom said, looking almost regretful about bringing up the subject as he leaned back against his spotless car.

Caroline recoiled. "What?" It wasn't as if the fact that she'd received the bouquet wasn't common knowledge—it was. Everyone in the courthouse knew, thanks to Andrea passing out roses to anyone who'd take some. Leland had taken a huge bunch home for his wife. Even Cheryl had taken a few, favoring Caroline with a rare smile. Caroline had left the remaining few blooms in her office. She didn't want them in her house.

Had Agent Yellow Bird sent them? Was this whole conversation—the intense looks, the cocky grins—because he was trying to butter her up?

Crap, what if Lasky had been right? What if Agent Tom Yellow Bird was crooked and prostitutes were just the tip of the iceberg?

Suddenly her blood was running cold. She moved to step past him. "The flowers were lovely. But I'm not interested."

Damn, she was tough.

"Whoa," Tom said, holding his hands up in the universal sign of surrender. "I didn't send them."

"I'm sure," Caroline murmured, stepping around him and heading for her car as if he suddenly smelled.

"Caroline," he said again, and damn if it didn't come out with a note of tenderness. Which was ridiculous. He had no reason to feel tender toward her at all. She was his assignment, whether she liked it or not. It'd be easier if she cooperated, of course, but he'd get to the bottom of things one way or the other.

He was nothing if not patient.

She began to walk faster. "I appreciate the gesture, but

I'm not interested. I hold myself to a higher standard of ethics and integrity."

What the hell? Clearly, she thought he'd sent the flowers. The idea was so comical he almost laughed. "Wait." He fell in step beside her. "Carlson sent me."

"Did he?" She didn't stop.

He dug his phone out of his pocket. If she wouldn't believe him, maybe she'd believe Carlson. "Here." Just as she made it to her car, he shoved his phone in front of her face. She had to stop to keep from slamming her nose into the screen. "See?"

She shot him an irritated look—which made him smile. She was tough—but he was tougher.

Begrudgingly, she read Carlson's email out loud. "'Tom—the new judge, Caroline Jennings, contacted me. An anonymous person sent her flowers and apparently that's out of the ordinary for her. See what you can find out. If we're lucky, this will open the case back up. Maggie sends her love. Carlson.'"

She frowned as she read it. This was as close as Tom had been to her and again, he was surrounded by the perfume of roses. He wanted to lean in close and press his lips against the base of her neck to see if she tasted as sweet as she smelled—but if he'd gauged Caroline Jennings right, she probably had Mace on her keys. Given the way she was holding her body, he'd bet she'd taken some self-defense classes at some point.

Good for her. He liked a woman who wasn't afraid to defend herself.

The moment that thought popped up, Tom slammed the door on it. He didn't like Judge Jennings, no matter how sweet she smelled or how strongly he felt that pull. This was about the case. The job was all he had.

She angled her body toward his, and a primal part of

his brain crowed in satisfaction when she didn't step back. If anything, it felt like she was challenging his space with her body. "And I'm supposed to believe that's on the level, huh?"

God, he'd like to be challenged. She was simply magnificent—even better out of her robes. "I don't play games, Caroline," he said. No matter how much he might want to. "Not about something like this."

She studied him for a moment. "That implies you play games in other situations, though."

His lips twisted to one side and he crossed his arms, because if he didn't, he might start smiling and that was bad for his image as a no-holds-barred lawman. "That all depends on the game, doesn't it?"

"I put more stock in the players."

So much for his image, because he burst out laughing at that. Caroline took a step back, her hands clenched at her sides and her back ramrod straight—which was completely at odds with the unexpectedly intense look of… longing? She looked less like a woman about to punch him and more like…

Like she was holding herself back. Like she wanted to laugh with him. Maybe do even more with him.

If he slid an arm around her waist and pulled her into his chest, would she break his nose or would she go all soft and womanly against him? How long had it been since he'd had a woman in his arms?

It absolutely did not matter—nor did it matter that he knew exactly how long it'd been. What mattered was cracking this case.

"I don't sleep with them."

"What?" She physically recoiled, pushing herself closer to the door.

"The prostitutes," he explained. "I don't sleep with

them. That's what you're worried about, isn't it? What I do in my free time?"

"It's none of my business what you do when you're off duty," she said in a stiff voice, shrinking even farther away from him. "It's a free country."

That made him grin again. "This country is bought and paid for, and you and I both know it," he said, surprised at the bitterness that sneaked in there. "I buy them dinner," he went on, wondering if someone like Caroline Jennings would ever really be able to understand. "They're mostly young, mostly girls—mostly being forced to work against their will. I treat them like people, not criminals—show them there's another way. When they're ready, I help them get away and get clean. And until they are, I make sure they're eating, give them enough money they don't have to work that night."

"That's…" She blinked. *"Really?"*

"Really. I don't sleep with them." For some ridiculous reason, he almost let the truth slip free—he didn't sleep with anyone. It was none of her business—but he wanted to make sure she knew he operated with all the ethical integrity she valued. "Carlson can back me up on that."

"Who's Maggie?"

Interesting. There was no good reason for her to be concerned about Maggie sending Tom her love, unless…

Unless Caroline was trying to figure out if he was attached. "Carlson's wife. We grew up on the same reservation together." He left out the part where he'd gone off to Washington, DC, and joined the FBI, leaving Maggie vulnerable to exploitation and abuse.

There was a reason he didn't sleep with prostitutes. But that wasn't his story to tell—it was Maggie's. He stuck to the facts.

The breeze gusted, surrounding him with her scent. He

couldn't help leaning forward and inhaling. "Roses," he murmured, his voice unexpectedly tender again. He really needed to stop with the tenderness.

She flushed again, and although he shouldn't, he hoped it wasn't from the heat. "I beg your pardon?"

"You smell of roses." Somehow, he managed to put another step between them. "Is that your normal perfume, or was that from the delivery?" There. That was a perfectly reasonable question to ask, from a law-enforcement perspective.

"From the flowers. The bouquet was huge. At least a hundred stems."

"All roses?"

She thought about that. "Mixed. Lilies and carnations—a little bit of everything, really. But mostly roses."

In other words, it hadn't been cheap. He tried to visualize how big a vase with a hundred stems would be. "But you're not taking any home with you?"

She shook her head. "I didn't want them. My clerk got rid of most of them. Leland took home a huge bunch for his wife."

"Leland's a good guy," Tom replied, as if this were normal small talk when it was anything but.

"How do I know I can trust you?" she blurted out.

"My record speaks for itself." He pulled a business card out of his pocket and held it out to her. "You don't know what you're up against here. This kind of corruption is insidious and nearly impossible to track, Caroline. But if there's anything else out of the ordinary—and I mean *anything*—don't hesitate to call me. Or Carlson," he added, almost as an afterthought. He didn't want her to call Carlson, though. He wanted her to call him. For any reason. "No detail is too small. Names, car makes—anything you remember can be helpful."

After a long moment—so long, in fact, that he began to wonder if she was going to take the card at all—she asked, "So we're to work together?"

He heard the question she didn't ask. "On this case, yes."

But if it weren't for this case…

She took the card from him and slid it into her shirt pocket. He did his best not to stare at the motion. *Damn.*

She gave him that look again, the one that made him think she was holding herself back. "Fine."

He straightened and gave her a little salute. "After this case…" He turned and headed to his car. "Have a good evening, Caroline," he called over his shoulder.

She gasped and he almost, *almost* spun back on his heel and captured that little noise with a kiss.

But he didn't. Instead, he climbed into the driver's seat of his Camaro, gunned the engine and peeled out of the parking lot as fast as he could.

He needed to put a lot of distance between him and Caroline Jennings. Because, no matter how much he might be attracted to her, he wasn't about to compromise this case for her.

And that was final.

Three

For a while, nothing happened. There were no more mysterious flower deliveries—or, for that matter, any kind of deliveries. The remaining half dozen roses on Caroline's desk withered and died. Andrea threw them away. People in the courthouse seemed friendlier—apparently, handing out scads of flowers made Caroline quite popular. Other than that, though, things continued on as they had before.

Before Agent Tom Yellow Bird had shown up in her courtroom.

She got up, went for a jog before the heat got oppressive, went to the courthouse and then came home. No mysterious gifts, no handsome men—mysterious or otherwise. No surprises. Everything went exactly as it was supposed to. Which was good. Great, even.

If she didn't have Tom's card in her pocket—and that electric memory of shaking his hand—she would have been tempted to convince herself she had imagined the whole thing. A fantasy she'd invented to alleviate boredom instead of a flesh-and-blood man. Fantasies were always safer, anyway.

But...there were times when she could almost feel his presence. She'd come out of the courthouse and pull up short, looking for his black muscle car with the silver stripe on the hood, but he was never there. And the fact that disappointed her was irritating.

She had not developed a crush on the man. No crushes. That was that.

Just because he was an officer of the law with a gun concealed under his jacket, with eyes that might be his biggest weapon—that was no reason to lust after the man. She didn't need to see him again. It was better that way—at least, she finally had to admit to herself, it was better that way while his corruption investigation was still ongoing. The more distance between them, the less she would become infatuated.

Tom Yellow Bird was a mistake she wasn't going to make.

It was a good theory, anyway. But he showed up in her dreams, a shadowy lover who drove her wild with his hands, his mouth, his body. She woke up tense and frustrated, and no electronic assistance could relieve the pressure. Her vibrator barely took the edge off, but it was enough.

Besides, she had other things to focus on. She finally finished unpacking her kitchen, although she still ate too much takeout. It was hard to work up the energy to cook when the temperature outside kept pushing a hundred.

Still, she tried. She came home one Friday after work three weeks after the floral delivery, juggling a couple of bags of groceries. Eggs were on sale and there was a recipe for summery quiche on Pinterest that she wanted to try. She had air-conditioning and a weekend to kick back. She was going to cook—or else. At the very least, she was going to eat ice cream.

She knew the moment she unlocked the front door that something was wrong. She couldn't have said what it was because, when she looked around the living room, nothing seemed out of place. But there was an overwhelming sense that someone had been in her home that she didn't dare ignore.

Heart pounding, she backed out of the house, pulling the door shut behind her. She carried the groceries right back out to the trunk of her car and then, hands shaking, she pulled her cell phone and Tom's card out of her pocket and dialed.

He answered on the second ring. "Yes?"

"Is this Agent Yellow Bird?" He sounded gruffer on the phone—so gruff, in fact, that she couldn't be sure it was the same man who had laughed with her in the parking lot.

"Caroline? Are you all right?"

Suddenly, she felt silly. She was sitting outside in the car. It wasn't like the door had been jimmied open. It hadn't even looked like anything had been moved—at least, not in the living room. "It's probably nothing."

"I'll be the judge of that. What's going on?"

She exhaled in relief. She was not a damsel in distress and she did not need a white knight to come riding to her rescue. But there was something comforting about the thought that a federal agent was ready and willing to take over if things weren't on the up and up. "I just got home and it feels like there was someone in my house." She winced. It didn't sound any less silly when she said it out loud.

There was a moment of silence on the other end of the phone, and she got a sinking feeling that he was going to tell her not to be such a ninny. "Where are you?"

"In my car. In the driveway," she added. Cars could be anywhere.

"If you're comfortable, stay there. I'm about fifteen minutes away. If you aren't, I want you to leave and drive someplace safe. Understand?"

"Okay." His words should have been reassuring. He was on his way over and she had a plan. But, perversely, the fact that he was taking this feeling so seriously scared her even more.

What if someone really had been in her house? It hadn't looked like a robbery. What had they been after?

"Call me back if you need to. I'm on my way." Before she could even respond, he hung up.

Wait, she thought, staring at the screen of her phone—how did he know where she lived?

She turned on her car—all the better to make a quick getaway—and cranked the AC. She knew she shouldn't have bought ice cream at the store, but too late now.

She waited and watched her house. Nothing happened. No one slunk out. Not so much as a curtain twitched. It looked perfectly normal, and by the time Tom came roaring down the street, she had convinced herself she was being ridiculous. She got out of the car again and went to meet him.

"I'm sorry to bother you," she began. "I'm sure it's nothing."

Then she pulled up short. Gone was the slick custom-made suit. Instead, a pair of well-worn jeans hung low off his hips and a soft white T-shirt clung to his chest. He had his shoulder holster on, which only highlighted his pecs all the more. Her mouth went dry as his long legs powerfully closed the distance between them.

If she had been daydreaming about Agent Yellow Bird

in a suit, the man in a pair of blue jeans was going to haunt her dreams in the very best way possible.

He walked right up to her and put his hands on her shoulders. "Are you all right?" he asked, his voice low.

That spark of electricity moved over her skin again, and she shivered. "Fine," she said, but her voice wavered. "I'm not sure I can say the same for the ice cream, but life will go on."

He almost smiled. She could tell, because his eyes crinkled ever so slightly. "Why do you think someone was in your house?" As he spoke, his hands drifted down her shoulders until he was holding her upper arms. A good two feet of space still separated them, but it was almost an embrace.

At least, that's how it felt to her. But what did she know? She couldn't even tell if someone had been in her house or not.

"It was just a feeling. The door wasn't busted, and nothing seemed out of place in the living room." She tried to laugh it off, but she didn't even manage to convince herself.

He squeezed her arms before dropping his hands. She felt oddly lost without his touch. "Is the door still unlocked?" She nodded. "Stay behind me." He pulled his gun and moved forward. Caroline stayed close. "Quietly," he added as he opened the door.

Silently, they entered the house. Her skin crawled and she unconsciously hooked her hand into the waistband of his jeans. Tom checked each room, but there was no one there. Caroline looked at everything, but nothing seemed out of place. By the time they peeked into the unused guest room, with the remaining boxes from the move still haphazardly stacked, she felt more than silly. She felt stupid.

When Tom holstered his gun and turned to face her, she knew her cheeks were flaming red. "I'm sorry, I—"

They were standing very close together in the hall, and Tom reached out and touched a finger to her lips. Then he stepped in closer and whispered in her ear, "Outside."

For a second, neither of them moved. She could feel the heat of his body, and she had an almost overwhelming urge to kiss the finger resting against her lips. Which was ridiculous.

What was it about this man that turned her into a blubbering schoolgirl with a crush? Maybe she was just trying to bury her embarrassment at having called him out here for nothing beneath a more manageable emotion—lust. Not that lust was a bad thing. Except for the fact that she still had no idea what he did in his spare time or whether or not it broke any laws. And there was the unavoidable fact that acting on any lust would be a conflict of interest.

They were actively on an investigation, for crying out loud. It was one of the reasons she couldn't read romantic suspense novels—it drove her nuts when people in the middle of a dangerous situation dropped everything to get naked.

She was not that kind of girl, damn it. So instead of leaning into his touch or wrapping her arms around his waist and pulling him in tight, she did the right thing. She nodded and pulled away.

It was harder than she'd thought it would be.

When they were outside, she tried apologizing again. "I'm so sorry that I called you out here for nothing." She didn't enjoy making a fool of herself, but when it happened, she tried to own up to the mistake as quickly as possible.

He leaned against her car, studying her. She had met a lot of hard-nosed investigators and steely-eyed lawyers in her time, but nothing quite compared to Tom Yellow Bird. "Are you sure it was nothing? Tell me again how you felt there was something wrong."

She shrugged helplessly. "It was just a feeling. Everything looked fine, and you saw yourself that there was no one in the house." She decided that worse than feeling stupid was the fact that she had made herself look weak.

For some ridiculous reason, this situation reminded her of her brother. Trent Jennings had been a master of creating a crisis where none existed—and he was even better at making it seem like it was her fault. Because she'd been the mistake, the squalling brat who'd taken his parents away from him. Or so he was fond of reminding her.

That wasn't what she was doing here, was it? Creating a crisis in order to focus the attention on herself? No, she didn't think so. The house had *felt* wrong. Then something occurred to her. "Why are we outside again? It's hot out here."

"The place is probably bugged."

He said it so casually that it took a few moments before his words actually sank in. *"What?"*

"I've seen this before."

"I don't understand," she said, wondering if he was ever going to answer a straight question. "You've seen *what* before?"

For a moment, he looked miserable—the face of a man who was about to deliver bad news. "You have a feeling that someone was in your house—although nothing appears to have been moved or taken, correct?"

She nodded. "So my sixth sense is having a bad day. How does that mean there are bugs in my house?"

One corner of his mouth crept up. "They're trying to find something they can use against you. Maybe you have some sort of peccadillo or kink, maybe something from your past." He smiled, but it wasn't reassuring. "Something worse than speeding tickets?"

The blood drained from her face. She didn't have any

kinks, definitely nothing that would be incriminating. She didn't want people to watch when she used her vibrator—the thought was horrifying. But…

It would be embarrassing if people found out about her lapse of judgment in college. Although, since her parents were dead, she wouldn't have to face their disappointment, and the odds of Trent finding out about it were slim, since they didn't talk anymore.

But more than that…what if people connected her back to Vincent Verango? That wouldn't just be embarrassing. That had the potential of being career ending. Would she never be able to escape the legacy of the Verango case?

No, this was fine. Panicking would be a mistake right now. She needed to keep her calm. "I stay within five miles of the speed limit," she said, trying to arrange her face into something that wasn't incriminating.

Tom shrugged. At least he was interpreting her reaction as shock and not guilt. "They want something on you so that when they approach you again and you say you're not interested, they'll have a threat with teeth. If you don't want them to inform the Justice Department about this embarrassing or illegal thing, you'll do what they say. Simple."

"Simple?" She gaped at him, wondering when the world had stopped making sense. "Nothing about that is simple!"

"I don't have a bug detector," he went on, as if she hadn't spoken. "And seeing as it's Friday night, I don't think I can get one before Monday."

"Why not?" Because she couldn't imagine this oh-so-simple situation didn't justify a damned bug detector.

A muscle in his jaw twitched. "I'm off duty for the next four days. I'd have to make a special case to get one, and Carlson and I like to keep our investigations off the record as much as possible."

She couldn't help it—she laughed. She sounded horrible, even to her own ears, but it was either that or cry. This entire situation was so far beyond the realm of normal that she briefly considered she might've fallen asleep in her office this afternoon.

"The way I see it," he went on, again ignoring her outburst, "you have two choices. You can go about your business as normal and I'll come back on Monday and sweep the house."

It was, hands-down, the most reasonable suggestion she was probably going to hear. So why did it make her stomach turn with an anxious sort of dread? "Okay. What's my other choice?"

That muscle in his jaw ticked again, and she realized that he looked hard—like a stone, no emotions at all. The playful grin was nowhere to be seen. "You come with me."

"Like, to your home?" That was it. She was definitely dreaming. It wasn't like her to nod off in her chambers, but what other reasonable explanation was there?

"In a professional capacity," he said in what was probably supposed to be a reassuring tone.

Caroline was not reassured. "If they bugged my house and I'm new here, why would your home be any less susceptible to surveillance?"

And just like that, his stony expression was gone. He cracked a grin and again, she thought of a wolf—dangerous but playful. And she had no idea if she was the prey or not.

"Trust me," he said, pushing off the car and coming to stand directly in front of her. "Nothing gets past me."

Four

They had been in the car for an hour and fifteen minutes. Seventy-five *silent* minutes. Any attempt at conversation was met with—at best—a grunt. Mostly, Tom just ignored her, so she stopped trying.

Pierre was a distant memory and Tom was, true to his word, breaking every speed limit known to mankind and the state of South Dakota. She'd be willing to bet they were topping out well past one hundred, so she chose not to look at the speedometer, lest she start thinking of fiery crashes along the side of the road.

There was no avoiding Tom Yellow Bird. This muscle car was aggressive—just like him. He filled the driver's seat effortlessly, seemingly becoming one with his machine. She didn't know much about cars, but she could tell this was a nice one. The seats were a supple leather and the dashboard had all sorts of connected gadgets that were a mystery to her.

Just like the man next to her.

The landscape outside the car hadn't changed since they'd hit the open plains, so she turned her attention to Tom. They were driving west and he still had his sunglasses on. She couldn't read him. The only thing that gave her a clue to his mental state was how he kept tapping his fingers on the steering wheel. At least, she thought it was a clue. He might just be bored out of his mind.

It wasn't fair. She hadn't thought of the Verango case in, what—ten years? Twelve? But that was exactly the sort of thing a bad guy would be looking for, because she didn't have anything kinky hiding in her closet. And a vibrator didn't count. At least she hoped it didn't.

She liked sex. She'd like to have more of it, preferably with someone like Tom—but only if it were the kind that couldn't come back to bite her. No messy relationships, no birth control slipups, no strings attached.

Not that she wanted to have sex with *him*. But the man had inspired weeks of wet dreams, all because he had an intense look and an air of invulnerability about him. And that body. Who could forget that body?

She wished like hell she didn't have this primal reaction to him. Even riding next to him was torture. She was aware of him in a way she couldn't ignore, no matter how hard she tried. She felt it when he shifted in his seat, as if there were invisible threads binding them together. And that wasn't even the worst of it. Although he had the AC blasting on high, she was the kind of hot that had nothing to do with the temperature outside. Her bra was too tight and she wanted out of this top.

She'd love to go for a swim. She needed to do something to cool down before she did something ridiculous, like parading around his home in nothing but her panties.

And the fact that her brain was even suggesting that as a

viable way to kill a weekend was a freaking *huge* problem. Because getting naked anywhere near Tom Yellow Bird would be a mistake. Yes, it might very well be a mistake she enjoyed making—but that wouldn't change the fact that it would still be a gross error in judgment, one that might compromise a case or—worse—get her blackmailed. A mistake like that could derail her entire career—and for what? For a man who wasn't even talking to her? No. She couldn't make another mistake like that.

Rationally, she knew her perfectionism wasn't healthy. Her parents had never treated her like a mistake, and besides, they were dead. And she couldn't take responsibility for the fact that Trent had been a whiny, entitled kid who'd grown into a bitter, hateful man. She didn't have to do everything just right in a doomed effort to keep the peace in the family.

Yes, rationally, she knew all of that. But her objective knowledge didn't do anything to put her at ease as Tom drove like the devil himself was gaining on them.

Finally, Caroline couldn't take it anymore. She had expected a fifteen-minute car trip to a different side of town. Not this mad dash across the Great Plains. It was beginning to feel little bit like a kidnapping—one that she had been complicit in. "Where, exactly, do you live?"

"Not too much farther," he said, answering the wrong question.

But he'd actually responded, and she couldn't pass up this chance to get more out of him. "If you're spiriting me away to the middle of nowhere just to do me in, it's not going to go well for you." She didn't harbor any illusions that she could make an impact on him. He was armed and dangerous, and for all she knew, he was a black belt or something. She was good at jogging. She had taken a few self-defense classes. She wasn't going to think about how long ago, though.

That got a laugh out of him, which only made her madder. "I have no intention of killing you. Or harming you," he added as an afterthought.

"You'll forgive me if I don't find that terribly reassuring."

"Then why did you get in the car with me?"

She shook her head, not caring if he could see it or not. "I just realized that when I said something felt off at my house, you trusted me. Anyone else would've told me I was imagining things. I'm returning the favor." She leaned her head back and closed her eyes. "Don't let it go to your head."

"I doubt you'll let that happen."

The car slowed as he took an exit. But he was going so fast that she didn't get her eyes open to see the name or number of the exit. They were literally in the middle of nowhere. She hadn't seen so much as a cow for the last—what, ten or twenty miles? It was hard to tell at the speeds they'd been traveling.

"Dare I ask how you define 'not too much farther'?"

"Are you hungry?"

She was starving, but that didn't stop her from glancing at the clock in the dashboard. The sun was low over the horizon.

"Do you always do that?" He tilted his head in her direction without making eye contact. At least, she assumed. She was beginning to hate those sunglasses. "Answer a question with an unrelated statement?"

She saw his lips twitch. "Dinner will be waiting for us. I hope pizza is all right?"

See, that was the sort of statement that made her wonder about him. He'd clearly said he was taking her to his house. Was he the kind of guy who had a personal chef? That didn't fit with the salary of an FBI agent.

But she couldn't figure out how to phrase that particular question without it sounding like an accusation. Instead, she said, "So that's a yes. And," she added before he could start laughing, "pizza is fine. Better if it has sausage and peppers on it. Mushrooms are also acceptable. Do you have any ice cream? Wine?"

"I can take care of you."

Perhaps it was supposed to be an innocent statement—a reflection of his preparedness for emergency guests. But that's not how Caroline took it.

Maybe her defenses were lower because she was tired and worried. But the moment his words filled the small space between them, her body reacted—hard. Her nipples tightened almost to the point of pain as heat flooded her stomach and pooled lower. Her toes curled, and she had to grip the handle on the passenger door to keep from moaning with raw need.

Heavens, what was with her? It had been a long day. That was all. There was no other explanation as to why a simple phrase, spoken in a particularly deep tone of voice, would have such an impact on her.

She locked the whole system down. No moaning, no shivering, and absolutely no heated glances at Tom. Besides, how would she know if his glances were heated or not? He still had on those damn sunglasses.

Instead, in a perfectly level voice, she said, "That remains to be seen, doesn't it?" She took it as a personal victory when he gripped the steering wheel with both hands.

Silence descended in the car again. If she'd had no idea where she was before, she had less now. They'd left the highway behind. The good news was that Tom was probably only doing sixty instead of breaking the sound barrier. With each turn, the roads bore less and less resemblance to an actual paved surface. But she didn't start to panic until he turned where there didn't seem to be any road at all, just a row of ragged shrubs. He opened the glove box and fished out a…remote?

"What are you doing?" she demanded.

He didn't answer. Of course he didn't. Instead, he aimed the remote at the shrubs and clicked the button.

The whole thing rolled smoothly to the side. She blinked and then blinked again. Really, her head was a mess. She was going to need a whole bottle of wine after this. "Be honest—are you Batman?"

He cracked a grin that did terrible, wonderful things to her body. Her mouth went dry and the heat that she had refused to feel before came rushing back, a hot summer wind that carried the promise of a storm. Because there was something electric in the air when he turned to face her. She wanted to lick his neck to taste the salt of his skin.

Maybe she would strip down. Her clothing was becoming unbearable. "Would you believe me if I said I was?"

She thought about that. Well, at least she tried to. Thinking was becoming hard. She was so hot. "Only if you've got an elderly British butler waiting for you."

His grin deepened and, curse her body, it responded, leaning toward him of its own volition. "I don't. Turns out elderly British butlers don't like to work off the grid in the middle of nowhere."

That got her attention. "I thought you said you had a home?" She looked around, feeling the weight of the phrase *wide-open spaces* for the first time. There was nothing around here except the highly mobile fake shrubbery. "I don't see…"

Then she saw it—in the direction where the ruts disappeared down the drive, there were trees off in the distance. "This is a real house, right? If you live in a van down by the river, I'm going to be pissed. A real house with pizza," she added. "And a real bed. I will walk back to Pierre before I crash in a sleeping bag."

It wasn't fair, that grin. His muscles weren't fair, his jaw wasn't fair and the way he had of looking at her—that, most of all, wasn't fair. Especially right now, when it was pretty obvious to everyone—all two of them—that her filters were failing her.

"I do have a housekeeper of sorts," he added, glancing at the clock in the dash. "She should have dinner underway. And in the meantime, if you'd like to swim..."

He had her at a complete disadvantage, and the hell of it was, she wasn't sure it was a bad thing. There was a part of her that desperately wanted to believe it was a good thing. At least, the part about being here with him was a good thing. There was no way to put a positive spin on someone breaking into her house and planting bugs.

"You have a pool out here?" She stared at the trees again.

"Not exactly," he said, sounding almost regretful about it. "But I have a pond—spring fed, nice and cool. If you need to cool off."

Somehow, she'd gotten close enough to him that he could cup her cheek with the palm of his hand. Her eyelashes fluttered and she couldn't help leaning into his touch. Even though this had been one of the stranger afternoons in her life, she still felt safe with him. Maybe she shouldn't. They were a million miles from nowhere. But she did.

"Let me take you home."

A pond? She didn't love mud squishing between her toes, but at this point she wasn't sure she cared. "Promise me we'll get there soon. I don't know how much longer I can wait."

She meant for the food and wine. For the cool pond. But

she felt his body tense and realized that she hadn't been talking about dinner at all.

She didn't know how much longer she could wait for this man. This confusing, confounding man who cared what happened to her.

"Ten minutes. You won't regret this."

"I better not."

Neither of them moved for a second. Then, so slowly that she could feel the electricity between them crackle, he stroked his thumbs over her cheekbones. His hands were rough, but his touch was gentle and she was too tired to fight the shiver of attraction anymore.

Damn his sunglasses. Damn her exhaustion. Damn the fact that they were parked in the middle of nowhere instead of at some romantic restaurant or, even better, a bedroom. Any bedroom. Damn this corruption case she was unwillingly a part of because, better than a glass of wine and a pint of ice cream, falling into Tom Yellow Bird's arms would definitely relieve some of her stress.

He held her there, stroking her cheeks, and she thought he was going to kiss her. She wanted him to. She also didn't—what she really wanted was for the world to go back to making sense—but that wasn't going to happen. So she'd settle for a kiss.

"We need to get going," he said, pulling away from her with what she chose to believe was reluctance. Because that way, it didn't sting as much.

"Of course," she said, staring at the trees in the distance. "Let's just go."

It almost didn't even matter where anymore.

Five

In his life, Tom had made mistakes. Beyond being unable to rescue Maggie and overlooking the fact that he should have been behind the wheel instead of Stephanie in the car accident—he had screwed up.

He'd lost the notoriously violent pimp Leonard Low Dog not once but twice and, as a result, the man had nearly killed Maggie. He'd lost the trail on Tanner Donnelly's killer until Tanner's sister, Rosebud, and her now-husband, Dan Armstrong, had cracked the case open. And Tom hadn't yet been able to uncover who was paying off judges in South Dakota.

All of those were epic errors in judgment, ones that he'd tried hard to rectify. Leonard Low Dog was serving twenty without parole. Shane Thrasher was doing forty for killing Tanner. Tom had put three judges in prison and had a hand in forcing others to retire from the bench.

But none of those mistakes were in the same category as bringing Caroline Jennings home with him.

She gasped when he finally rounded the last bend and his cabin came into view.

Aside from the Armstrongs and the Carlsons, Lilly and Joe White Thunder—people he trusted beyond the pale—he'd never brought anyone else back here. This was his sanctuary. This was where he could be close to the memories of Stephanie.

"Good God," Caroline exhaled. "Where the hell did this come from?"

"I built it." It was the summer home he and Stephanie had planned, once their careers had been established. Once they would've been able to take a month off in the summer.

And now Caroline was here. It was a mistake, but if there was one thing life had taught him, it was that there was no going back. Own up to what you did and keep moving forward. She was here, and he was sworn to protect her.

"You built it? Like, by yourself?"

"I had a few contractors, but only ones I could trust." He didn't see Lilly's pickup truck anywhere—good.

The low-slung building practically glowed in the fading sunset, the solar panels on the roofs of the house and garage glinting in the light. The panels had been a compromise. Someone could easily see his house from the air, but he was off the grid.

He hadn't exactly sworn to protect Caroline. He'd promised to take care of her. And when he'd made that promise, he'd felt the shiver pass through her body.

This was fine. Yes, he had to be in DC Monday evening, but she wouldn't be with him that long. He'd keep an eye on her this weekend until he could sweep her house. Early Monday morning, Tom would take her to work, and she'd go home Monday evening as if nothing had happened.

"This is amazing." Her voice was breathy—and that was

before she turned those beautiful eyes toward him. "You live here full-time? In the middle of nowhere?"

He shrugged. "I needed a place to think. I have an apartment in Pierre, but it's not as secure."

Right. That was why he'd brought her here. Security. He would do anything to keep her safe. Even break the rules—his own rules.

Bringing her to his house? That broke every rule he'd ever set for himself. That was him putting his selfish wants ahead of his job, and that was a risk not just for him, not just for her, but for all the years he and Carlson had spent on this case. That was an unacceptable level of risk.

But what was he supposed to do? He couldn't leave her. The pull he felt to take care of her wouldn't let him. But it was more than that.

Caroline hadn't cut him a single bit of slack. Except when he'd touched her, her soft skin warm in his hands.

He pulled into the garage. It wasn't until she gasped again that he looked at her. "Who the hell are you?" she asked, staring at his vehicles.

There were a couple of nondescript cars that he used for surveillance, his motorcycle, the old pickup truck he used when he went to the reservation and the new one he used when he was hauling supplies—not to mention his fire engine–red Corvette Stingray, which he only took out when he needed to give off an aura of wealth. "I know you may not believe this, but I don't make a habit of lying."

Based on her expression, if he thought that was going to fly, he had another thing coming. "You must not be including lying by omission in the definition."

He snorted as he got out of the car, pleased that she followed. He snagged her bags out of the trunk. "This way."

He led her to the wide porch that wrapped around three of the four sides of his house. "I have a few things I need to see to, so if you'd like to take a dip in the pond, now would be a great time." That would give him a chance to contact Carlson and see about getting her house swept for bugs.

But it'd also give him a chance to get his head back in the game. Lilly White Thunder should have gotten dinner started, and hopefully she'd had enough time to put fresh sheets on the beds.

But the thought of Caroline curled up in his bed, her hair mussed and the sheet slung low around her waist—

"Come on," he said, dropping her duffel just inside the door. The scent of pizza baking in the oven filled the cabin, but the windows were open and the house smelled fresh and clean.

As much as he loved Lilly, he was glad the older woman wasn't here. He didn't want to introduce Caroline to her, didn't want to risk the chance that Caroline's presence would slip out and make the rounds on the res.

Because that kept Caroline safer. Not because he didn't want Lilly looking at him with her warm eyes and getting any funny ideas.

Unable to help himself, he took Caroline by the hand. She was too hot and tired to meet new people, anyway. The sooner she got out of those clothes and cooled down, the better she'd be.

And her being nude had nothing to do with him. Not a damn thing.

He was rock hard as he led her through the patio doors and down a small flagstone path to where he had dammed the natural spring to create a small pool.

Caroline stumbled to a stop when she saw it. "It's...red. The water's red?"

"It is. Higher iron content. It flows into the Red Creek River," he said, stepping in close to her and pointing down the riverbanks. "That's where the name comes from. Don't worry, it won't dye your skin."

The next thing Tom knew, she whacked him on the arm. "Why didn't you tell me about this?" she demanded, her voice sounding unnaturally high. "If you had just told me you had a luxury log cabin complete with stone fireplaces and leather furniture and…" Her voice cracked. "And a little pond that isn't even a pond." She sniffed. "You lined the bottom with stones, didn't you?"

It was the most accusatory statement he'd heard—and it wasn't about a crime or a case. It was about his little pool. "If I want to feel mud squishing in between my toes, I'll swim in the river."

She slapped him on the arm again and he let her. "You could've told me. I didn't even bring a swimsuit."

"I didn't know you needed to cool down until we were in the car." He turned his gaze out to the trees, where his spring flowed into the river. He specifically did not look at her. "If you want to soak, it's about three feet deep," he added. "Not enough to do laps."

She sighed and he glanced back at her. She was staring at that water like it was a long-lost lover that she'd never thought she'd see again. And Tom knew he was crazy, because he was suddenly jealous of the pool. "If you look, I'll gut you in your sleep," she said, sounding so tired that Tom felt like a cad.

He knew he was not an easy man to get along with. Never had been—that's why Stephanie had been so good for him. She had never let him get away with anything. She'd challenged him and pushed him and held him to a higher standard. She had met him on the playing field as an equal, and Tom had loved her for it, completely and wholly.

But even Stephanie had never threatened to gut him like a fish.

Grinning, he said, "Then I best not look."

Caroline turned away from him and grabbed the hem of her shirt, slowly lifting and revealing the pale skin of her lower back. She had the shirt halfway off and she looked at him over her shoulder and if he hadn't been lost before then, he sure as hell was now. "Shouldn't you be hiding the knives?"

"You know I'm used to sleeping with one eye open, right?" She started to lower the shirt, so he quickly took a step back. "I'm going. I won't look. I'll let you know when dinner's ready."

"At the rate we're going, it's going to be breakfast," she said with a sigh.

He turned on his heel before he did something stupid, like give in to the urge to pull her into his arms. He'd been battling that urge since he'd pulled up in front of her house that afternoon, stomach churning with dread. She'd sounded so scared on the phone—she'd been trying to laugh it off, but Tom had heard the truth in her voice. All he'd wanted to do was hold her then and make sure she knew she was safe with him.

Instead, he'd gone into her house, ready to shoot any intruder who'd stolen her peace of mind. He'd told her to pack for a weekend away and driven her way out here. She was well within her right to gut him.

And now he had to make it through the next forty-eight hours alone with her. The only things to do out here were hike and hunt, soak in the pool, and sleep. There was no television, no internet, and the only cell service was his satellite phone.

She was safe now, and he was pretty sure she knew it. After all, wasn't she actively stripping out of her clothes? Wasn't she, at this very moment, stepping into the shallow pool he'd built, seemingly just for her? Wasn't she lowering her nude body into the water, feeling it lap at her inner thighs, her stomach, her breasts?

Jesus, how was he going to make it until Monday morning?

The water was deliciously, blissfully cold. It shocked Caroline awake and kept right on shocking her. Which was good. It was so much easier to sit and think about goose bumps than to let her mind wander over the events of the last four hours. Had it really only been four danged hours? Sheesh, what a day.

Her stomach grumbled. She would kill for a glass of wine but, bathed in the last light of dusk and letting this not-pool wash the day's sweat and anxiety away, she was content.

However, no matter how cold the water was, it couldn't erase all the heat from her body. Safely submerged beneath the waterline, her nipples were so puckered they were painful, and the heat between her legs? This water would have to be a whole lot colder before it knocked *that* down. Even though her skin was chilled, she was warm from the inside out.

She was lying naked in a pond that Tom Yellow Bird had built. She could almost pretend he'd built it for her, but she knew that was ridiculous.

Still, it was a nice fantasy. Why hadn't that man told her about this place? She could see leaving out detailed directions. He was more than a little paranoid, but maybe in his line of work, he had to be.

She floated sideways so she could get a better look at the house. She hadn't seen any sign of a maid or a housekeeper—or a British butler, for that matter. The only sign that anyone else knew where this house was had been the scent of pizza in the oven.

The house had also been spotless, as if this supposed housekeeper came in regularly to dust and air it out. Tom had hurried her through the house pretty quickly, but she'd gotten glimpses of the rough-hewn logs, a massive fireplace done in stone with a chimney that rose up to the ceiling. It was rough and overwhelming—much like Tom himself.

The whole house was a long structure, but not tall. It probably didn't even have a second story. It rode low to the ground like it didn't want to be noticed—except for the solar panels that covered the entire roof. There were trees close enough to the building to throw some shade on the porch, but otherwise, all they did was block the view from the road, however distant that was.

The logs were great behemoths of wood, and she let her imagination play over the image of Tom cutting and fitting them together like life-size Lincoln logs. Undoubtedly, he would've worked shirtless, sweat running down his neck and over his chest. Of course he would know how to use tools. And then he would lift each log into place, his muscles straining and—

"I'm coming down." His voice rang out over the plains, breaking up her reverie. "Are you decent?"

"I'm still in the water," she called back. "I...I don't have a towel or anything." And she had stripped a good six feet away from the pool because she had been so anxious to get out of her clothes. And her shoes—they weren't waterproof flip-flops. She couldn't just shove her feet back in them without ruining the leather ballerina flats, and she wasn't sure she could make it up the flagstone walk without slipping. "I may be trapped in here forever."

His laughter, deep and rich, was another pleasant surprise. She hadn't heard him laugh like that yet. "I would be a terrible host if I left you in there to turn into one giant prune. I brought you a towel."

"I haven't yet decided if you're terrible host or not. It better be a fluffy towel."

"The fluffiest. I'm not looking."

"You better not be," she said, standing slowly to let the water sheet off her body. But when she turned for the towel, she saw that he was standing by the pool, holding out the unfolded towel, his head ducked and his eyes closed. "What are you doing?" she demanded, sinking back into the water.

"The rocks are slick. I'm making sure you don't slip." He said it as if this were just an everyday occurrence instead of a giant leap of faith on her behalf.

Oh, hell—what was she talking about? How was the risk of him catching a glimpse of her nude somehow a bigger leap of faith than getting into a car with him and letting him whisk her away to the middle of nowhere?

She had already leaped. Now she just had to trust that he would catch her before she fell.

So she stood again, her skin tingling as the water rushed off it.

Moving carefully so she didn't do something embarrassing like face-plant, she stepped into the towel. His arms came around her, but he didn't step back. And he didn't open his eyes. She was so glad those damn sunglasses were gone. "You never lie?"

He shook his head. "I didn't look."

She shifted so that the towel was secured under her arms. It was a *very* fluffy towel. Then she took a deep breath and rested her hand against his cheek. His eyelashes fluttered, but they stayed closed. "Why did you bring me out here? And I don't want to hear that line about how you were keeping me safe."

"That line is the truth."

"There were a hundred ways to keep me safe inside city limits, Tom. Stop lying by omission. Why did you bring me out here?"

His hands settled around her waist, holding the towel to her body. She shivered, but it had nothing to do with the temperature of the water or the air. "I can take you back. If you want, we can leave after we eat."

She wanted to throttle him and kiss him and slap him and drop the towel. She wanted to drag him into that pool of water with her and spend time exploring. She wanted to go home and she never wanted to leave. "What if I don't want to go?"

His fingers dug into her waist, pulling her close. They were chest to chest now, her sensitive nipples scraping against the towel. Against his chest. Unconsciously, her back arched, pushing her even closer to him. "What if I want to stay?" she asked him, pushing up on her tiptoes.

"You feel it, too, don't you?" His voice was so soft she had to tilt her head to catch the words. "I never thought I'd feel this again."

Again? What the hell did that mean, *again*? He'd brought her here on the pretense of protecting her!

She pulled away from him—but she didn't get far. Her feet slid out from under her and she started to fall—but the impact never came. Instead, she found herself swept into Tom's arms as if she were something precious.

"Whoa," she said, impressed despite herself. It was ridiculous because this entire situation was ridiculous. Tom Yellow Bird was literally sweeping her off her feet. "You can put me down now."

"I didn't bring you all the way out here for you to crack your head on the stone pavers," he said, his voice the very picture of cool, calm and collected. And he did not put her down.

She had no choice but to lock her arms around his neck. "Why did you bring me out here?"

It took a lot to rattle Tom. He'd stared down cold-blooded killers and talked his way out of more than a few bad situations.

But catching a damp Caroline in his arms? Cradling her to his chest? Carrying her all the way inside and then setting her down and turning his back instead of heading straight into the bedroom and spending the rest of the night feasting on her body instead of dinner?

His hands shook—*shook*, damn it—as he stoked the fire in the pit. Then, when he judged that she'd had enough time to get dressed, he opened the wine and carried it down to where he'd arranged the patio chairs around the little table close enough to the fire that the worst of the bugs would stay away. It was better to focus on these tiny details than what was happening inside his bedroom.

Or what he wanted to happen in his bedroom.

Finally, he couldn't take it anymore. He took a healthy pull of his wine. Normally he didn't drink much. He didn't like having his senses dulled.

Right now? Yeah, he needed to be significantly less aware. Less aware of Caroline's scent combined with the fresh smell of the spring. Or of her weight in his arms or the bare skin at the back of her knees where he'd held her. He wanted to lick her there and see if she was ticklish—but he didn't dare.

Damn it all. He was failing at thinking about Caroline with any sense of rationality. So he did the only thing he could—he thought of the one person who could always hold his attention, who got him through the worst of the stakeouts and helped him sleep after the bad days.

Stephanie. His wife.

God, she had been too perfect for this world. The first time he'd seen her in that formfitting white dress, her jet-black hair and vivid blue eyes turning every head in the room...

Oh, he could still see the way her whole face lit up when they made eye contract. He could still feel that spark that had lit in his chest as he'd cut through the crowd to get to her—the spark that had told him she was *it*. That woman, whoever she was, was his forever and ever, until death did them part.

But for the first time in a long time—years, even—that memory of Stephanie didn't hold his attention. Instead of lingering in the past, he couldn't escape the present.

He heard the patio door swish open, then closed. He heard the sound of tentative footsteps crossing the porch and moving down the two stairs. He heard the evening breeze sigh through the grasses and the gentle burbling of his spring as it flowed out of his pool and made its way down to the river.

And when Caroline took her seat, he turned, and damn it, there was that spark again, threatening to jump the barriers he'd tried to erect around it, threatening to catch in the prairie grass, burning everything in its path. Including him.

Caroline wasn't Stephanie. Stephanie wouldn't have been caught dead in a pair of old cutoff shorts and a faded gray T-shirt. Flip-flops would have never crossed Stephanie's toes. Stephanie wouldn't have been seen with her hair curling damply around her shoulders. And Stephanie never would have picked up the empty glass and said, "There better be some of that left for me."

"I told you," he replied, filling her glass, "I'm not a terrible host. I'll be right back with the pizza."

He plated up the pizza and snagged some napkins. God bless Lilly for pulling something together on such short notice.

Caroline hadn't moved from her spot, except to draw up her feet. She wasn't perfect. But by God, the woman looked like she fit out here. "Sausage," he said, handing over her plate.

She took the pizza, and for a while, neither of them spoke. Tom was used to ignoring hunger when he was on a stakeout and delivery would have blown his cover, but Lilly had, once again, made just what he wanted, almost by magic.

He knew it was coming, though. Caroline was not going to sit quietly over there for long. Finally, she set her plate aside and turned to face him. "So?"

"So?" he agreed, refilling both their glasses. "You have questions?"

"You're damn right I do." It could have come out snappish—but it didn't. Her voice took on a languid tone, one that matched the hazy quality of the fire. "Explain this house to me."

"Like I said—I built it."

"By yourself."

"That's correct." He waited, but he knew he wouldn't have to wait long.

He didn't. She was sharp, his Caroline. "With what money? Because that was one of the nicest bathrooms I've ever been in—and it's not like Minneapolis has a lack of decent bathrooms. And the kitchen—it's a chef's wet dream."

He laughed and she laughed with him, but he knew he wasn't off the hook. "Quality is often worth the price."

There was something sharp about her eyes, and he wished he could see her in action in the courtroom as a lawyer. Not from behind the bench, but in front of it. "But that's just it. Who's paying for it? An FBI agent doesn't make this kind of money—no matter how special you are. You have a top-of-the-line cabin on what I can only assume is a pretty big spread of land."

"Eighty acres from the road to the edge of the Red Creek Reservation. I grew up about thirty miles from here." He met her gaze. "I enjoy my privacy."

He could see her thinking over that information. "You maintain an apartment in Pierre."

"And one in Rapid City." Her eyes got wide. "I have a lot of territory to cover. Plus, I have a safe house in Pierre where I can hide people for a while." Only after he said it did he realize what he'd just admitted.

He could have put her in the safe house. Sure, it might have been uncomfortable for a judge to suddenly find herself bunking with former prostitutes and recovering drug addicts, but she would have been perfectly secure.

Instead, he'd brought her out here.

"In the interest of full disclosure," he added with a wave of his hand.

"About damn time," she murmured. But again, she didn't sound angry about it. She was looking at him with those beautiful eyes and suddenly he couldn't figure out why he hadn't told her all this up front. "You own all these various and sundry properties?"

"Yup." He stretched his legs out toward the fire and, amazingly, felt some of the tension of the afternoon begin to drift away, like embers in the wind.

He was not a man who relaxed. There were too many criminals to track and arrest. He'd made so many enemies just doing his job that he rarely let his guard down.

But here? Sitting by a fire with a pretty woman on a clear summer night, a bottle of wine to share?

"Who paid for it?" she asked, her voice curious without being accusatory.

"My wife."

Six

She hadn't just heard that, had she?

"Your *wife*?" Well, that certainly made sense with the "again" comment from earlier. He was married. Of course he was. So what had happened down by the pool? "Where is she?"

He dropped his gaze to his wineglass. "Buried next to her grandparents in Washington, DC."

The air whooshed out of Caroline's lungs. "I'm sorry." Could she be any bigger of an idiot? She might as well have accused him of adultery.

He shrugged, but his face was carefully blank—just like it'd been on the stand when that defense lawyer had tried to trick him. "She died nine years ago in a car accident—hit by a drunk driver. I should have been behind the wheel—but I'd stayed at the party. I had some business to deal with."

The way he said *business* sent a shiver down Caroline's

back. She had the distinctive feeling that he hadn't been getting stock tips.

"In DC?"

He nodded and leaned back, his eyes on the stars. Caroline followed his gaze, and what she saw took her breath away. The night sky was unbelievably gorgeous, not a single star dimmed by city lights.

"The FBI was my way off the res," he began. "But I wasn't alone. Rosebud, the little sister of my best friend, Tanner, got a scholarship to Georgetown and we stuck together—two Lakota fish way out of water."

Caroline had some questions but decided that, since Tom was actually talking, she'd best not interrupt him.

"She and Carlson were in class together and started dating—she's the lawyer for the Red Creek tribe now. James and I got along, and he made sure I went with them to all the fancy parties that his parents made him attend. It always struck me as an odd way to rebel, but…" He shrugged. "That's how I met Stephanie."

He spoke with such tenderness that, once again, Caroline felt like an idiot. He'd loved his wife. Was it wrong to be jealous of a dead woman? Because she couldn't help but be envious of the woman who could hold Tom Yellow Bird's heart.

"She and Carlson were childhood friends—I think their mothers wanted them to marry, but they both settled on two dirt-poor Indians with no money and no family names." He laughed, as if that were funny. "Carlson came west because Rosebud and I needed his help with this case, and he met Maggie—it's quite a story. Ask Maggie about it sometime." A melancholy silence settled over him. "He treats her well, which is good."

The way he said it made it clear that if Tom didn't think Carlson was treating his wife well, there'd be bloodshed. "So you've been working with Carlson for...how long?"

Belatedly, she realized what else he'd said. He'd just assumed that she would meet one of his oldest friends. Maggie probably knew all his embarrassing childhood stories, every dumb and brilliant thing he'd ever done. Carlson was Tom's most trusted friend.

And Tom had just made the assumption that Caroline would meet them. More than that, that she'd meet his friends in a social setting instead of in a law office or a courtroom.

Almost as if Tom expected to be doing a lot more of this—sitting out under the stars, having wine and pizza, and talking—with Caroline.

"We've known each other for over fourteen years now."

Nine years since Stephanie died—Caroline did the quick math.

Tom looked at her. "I was married for almost four years. Since I know you're trying to figure it out."

"That's not the only thing I'm trying to figure out," she murmured. "She was well-off?"

"Her mother was an heiress and her father was a senator." He exhaled heavily. "We tried not to talk politics. They did their best to accept me, which is more than a lot of people in their place might have done. But I was from a different world." He was quiet for a moment, and Caroline couldn't figure out if he was done or if he was just thinking. "I still am."

"I'll give you that—this place is different." She looked back at the stars, galaxies spread out before her, their depths undimmed by something as innocuous as fluorescent lighting.

A little like the man next to her. She topped off her glass and his when he held it out. "I'm sorry about your wife," she said again, because it seemed like the thing to say—even though it wasn't enough. He'd lost someone he cared for, and that was painful no matter what. She reached over and gave his hand a squeeze. He squeezed back, lacing his fingers with hers.

Neither of them pulled away.

"So this was all because of her money?"

"I invested wisely. She ran a charity. Her mother still runs it." He opened his mouth, as if he were going to expand upon that statement, but then he shook his head and changed the subject. "How about you?" He lolled his head to the side, and for a moment, he looked younger. The faint lines of strain were gone from around his eyes and his mouth was relaxed. He looked ten years younger. "Any dead husbands—or other bodies—in your closet?"

She kept her face even. As much as she didn't want to turn the spotlight back onto her occasionally questionable choices, she was relieved that they weren't going to keep talking about his late wife. "Nope. I always figured that once my career was established, I'd settle down, start a family. I've got time."

A look of pure sadness swept over his features before he went back to staring at the sky. "I used to think the same thing."

She didn't like that sadness. "I was almost engaged once, in college," she heard herself say, which surprised her. She never told anyone about Robby. "We were young and stupid and thought we could make it work, us against the world. But we couldn't even make it through senior year." That was glossing over things quite a bit.

The truth of the matter was that she and Robby couldn't make it past a pregnancy scare. She hated making mistakes, and that particular one had nearly altered the entire course of her life.

She and Robby had talked about getting married in that wishful-thinking way all kids did when they were crazy in lust, but when her period had been three days late...

She shuddered at the memory and once again gave thanks that it had been stress, not pregnancy, that had thrown her cycle off.

"Things didn't go as planned," she admitted, which was a nice way of saying that when she'd told Robby she was late, he'd all but turned tail and bolted for the door. The fantasy of living happily ever after with him had crumbled before her eyes, and she'd known then that she'd made the biggest mistake of her life—up to that point, anyway.

Which was ironic, considering that Trent's nickname for her when she'd been growing up had been "the mistake." Not that her parents had ever treated her like that, but Trent had. He would have loved it if Caroline had made the exact same mistake in her own life. "I thought it was going to be perfect, but all it turned out to be was heartbreak."

"You didn't marry him, though?"

"Nope."

Tom shrugged. "No one's perfect—especially not in relationships."

Oh, if only it were that simple. "Regardless, I don't tell people about that. It reflects poorly on my judgment, you understand."

"Of course. I imagine he couldn't keep up with you."

She chuckled at that. "If I agree with you, it'll make me sound egotistical."

His laughter was warm and deep, and it made her want to curl into him. "Perish the thought."

Long moments passed. She sipped her wine, feeling the stress of the day float away on a pleasant buzz. He didn't think less of her because she'd almost tied herself to the wrong man.

Maybe he wouldn't think less of her because she'd made a mistake trusting the wrong man.

"Tom?"

"Yeah?"

"You still haven't answered my question."

Why was she here? What was going on between them? Because she couldn't imagine that he brought other potential witnesses out here and let them skinny-dip in the pond and hold his hand under the stars.

She wanted to think this was different, that he was different with her. Not like he was with his socialite wife in the rarefied air of DC politics and power—but not like he was when he was stalking bad guys and saving the world.

It wasn't egotistical—it was *selfish* to want a little bit of Tom Yellow Bird all to herself. But she did. In this time, this place—hidden away from the rest of the world—she wanted him. Not as a protector and not as a law-enforcement colleague—but as something else. Something *more*.

It was worse than selfish. It was stupid, a risk she shouldn't even contemplate taking.

So why was she contemplating it so damn hard? God, it'd been such a long time since she'd risked letting off a little steam with some good sex. And out here, so far removed from neighbors and courtrooms...

It felt like they'd left reality behind and she and Tom were in a bubble, insulated from the real world and any real consequences.

Would it be so bad to let herself relax for a little bit? Tom would be amazing, she knew. And now that she'd seen where he lived—how he lived—she trusted that no one would ever know what happened between them. No nefarious stalkers planting bugs here. Tom simply wouldn't allow it.

Surely, she thought, staring at his profile, she could

enjoy a little consensual pleasure with him without ruining everything, couldn't she? Take the necessary precautions, not let her heart get involved—not compromise the case?

He didn't answer for a long time. Then, suddenly he stood. "It's late," he said, his voice gruff as he pulled her to her feet. "Let me show you your room."

Yes, she wanted more—but it was clear that, at least right now, she wasn't going to get it.

Tom had always liked this bed. This was a top-of-the-line memory-foam mattress—king size, with fifteen-hundred-thread-count sheets. The ceiling fan spun lazily overhead, making the temperature bearable. Dinner had been delicious and the wine excellent. This was as close to peace and quiet as he got.

So why couldn't he sleep?

Because. Caroline was at the other end of the hall.

He forced himself to be still and let his mind drift. Even if he couldn't sleep, he could rest, and that was all he needed. He didn't need to be on full alert. He had a lazy weekend ahead of him. He just needed enough to keep himself—and his dick—under control.

He let his mind go over his plans for Monday. A morning flight to Washington—it was the only flight, so he hadn't had much of a choice there. Then he'd have dinner with Senator and Mrs. Rutherford—his in-laws. From there, they'd go to the gala fund-raiser for the Rutherford Foundation, the charity Stephanie had founded with her trust fund money. Celine Rutherford, Stephanie's mother, ran the foundation in her daughter's name, but Tom liked to help out whenever he could. It was his way of honoring his late wife.

He didn't love gala fund-raisers, because he'd never quite gotten over the feeling that he was an interloper. He didn't love going back to DC for the same reason, although if he went for work, he was usually fine. And while he greatly respected the Rutherfords, seeing them was still painful. Celine strongly resembled her daughter, and it hurt Tom to look at her and know that was what Stephanie would have looked like if they'd gotten the chance to grow old together.

Usually, he didn't go back for these sorts of things. He had cases to solve, bad guys to catch—and the Rutherfords understood that. They never questioned Tom's work ethic. Instead, they all seemed content with chatty emails from Celine every month or so, plus cards at the holidays.

But once a year, he made the trip out East. He sat down with the Rutherfords and celebrated his wife's life and legacy. The Rutherford Foundation was dedicated to furthering education for girls and women around the world, and thanks to Tom's involvement, he'd gotten some of those funds allocated to Native American reservations around the US.

The timing *sucked*. When he'd made the executive decision to bring Caroline out here, he'd reasoned that he'd have plenty of time to get her back, get the equipment he needed and sweep her house. But in talking with Carlson while she'd soaked in his pool, Tom had realized he wouldn't be able to make his flight if he swept the house himself. As it was, they were going to have to get up before the crack of dawn on Monday so he'd have enough time to get back to his place in Pierre and grab his tuxedo.

At least Carlson could do the sweep on Monday. Tom would feel better if he checked every inch of Caroline's house himself, but he trusted Carlson implicitly. After this, Tom was getting his own sweeper. To hell with using the department's. The things he could buy on the internet were almost as good. Good enough to have checked Caroline's house, anyway.

All these plans buzzed through his head as he lay there, which was fine. It was much better to think of airport security lines and tuxedos than it was to dwell on the mental image of Caroline lying nude in his pool.

He'd left her out there for almost twenty minutes while he'd called Carlson and gotten the pizzas Lilly had made out of the oven. And the whole time, he hadn't been thinking about his late wife or about gala fund-raisers. In all actuality, he'd barely been thinking about corrupt judges or bugged houses.

All he'd been able to think about was Caroline. Lying nude in his pool.

Even now, he could see her out there, the hazy golden light of sunset glimmering around her hair, the reddish spring water dancing over her skin. God, she must have been gorgeous. But he hadn't looked. He'd promised.

At some point in the still of the night, he became aware of movement. Wild animals sometimes prowled around at night—the smell of pizza could've drawn them. Without moving, he woke up and listened.

The sound he heard—the regular if light sound of footsteps, the faint squeaking of the floorboards, the sound of a knob turning—weren't coming from outside. He didn't react as Caroline stepped into the room. Instead, all he could think was that he hoped she didn't gut him like a fish.

He waited until, nearly noiselessly, she'd made her way over to him. "I told you I was a light sleeper."

She made a little noise of surprise. "You're awake?"

"So are you."

"I…" He heard her take a deep breath. "I couldn't sleep."

That got his eyes open. "Yeah?"

But the sight of her in a short cotton gown that fell to just above her knees, her hair rumpled with sleep—God, he didn't know if he could be this strong. "Do you really think someone is going to try and blackmail me?"

"No guarantees in life, but probably. Do you have something to hide?" He desperately wanted her to say no. Maybe it was because it was late or maybe it was because he hadn't been able to stop thinking about her since he'd seen her in her courtroom, ferocious and beautiful.

Or maybe it was just because she was standing in his bedroom in the dead of night, looking for reassurance. And if there was one thing Tom could provide, it was reassurance. Hands-on, physical reassurances. A lot of them.

For years—*years*—he had put all his energy into doing the job, because what else did he have? Not his wife. Not the family they'd planned for.

All he had was the never-ending quest for truth, justice and the American way. He gave the FBI nearly everything he had, and what he held back, he gave to rescuing girls from prostitution.

No matter what, he wanted Caroline to be honest and true. And he wanted her all for himself, selfish bastard that he was. He wanted Caroline for himself, not because she was a new lead or a key component of this damnable case.

He wanted her. God, it felt so good to want again. Even better to be wanted.

There was a pause that made him wonder if maybe he'd read the situation wrong. Then she said, "I don't have any kinks." He heard her swallow. "At least, I don't think I do..."

Tom's body was instantly awake. "You're not sure?"

"Who can say if it's something that's going to be used against me?"

Moving slowly, he sat up, ignoring the way his body jumped to attention. "I could," he offered, not even bothering to convince himself that it was knowledge necessary to keep her safe. This had nothing to do with protecting her, and they both knew it. "You could tell me what you like and I'll let you know if it's a hazard to your reputation or not."

He heard her swallow again, the soft click of her throat muscles working. Would she turn and go back to her bedroom, shut the door and lock it? Or would she...

"I like men," she began, her voice so soft he almost couldn't hear the waver in it.

So far, so good. "Just men?"

He could see her head bob—thank God for the full moon tonight.

"Nothing illegal about that. I think it makes you normal. Unless..." He breathed deeply. He would not lose control. Simple as that. "Do you do anything with your partner that might be dangerous?"

He saw her chest rise and fall as she exhaled. "I...I like to be on top. I have been told that I have extremely sensitive breasts. I like it when my lover strokes them and sucks them. But not biting—they're too sensitive for that."

Adrenaline slammed through his system, his heart pounding and his dick throbbing. He could see it in his mind's eye, her riding him, his face buried in her breasts. "That doesn't seem unusual." His voice cracked.

He needed to have her over him. He needed to feel the warm wetness of her body surrounding him, holding him. He needed to pull one of her nipples into his mouth and suck on it until she screamed with pleasure.

God, he wasn't sure he had ever needed anything so much in his entire life.

He didn't dare move. He didn't want to break the spell that had her sharing her deepest desires. "Is there anything else that could be considered unusual?"

"I..." She took a step toward him. It wasn't a big movement, but he felt it down to his toes. That spark that had always existed between them—it was no longer an isolated flash of light in the darkness. It was burning hotter and brighter than anything he'd ever felt before. It lit him up. *She* lit him up. "I like it when a man bends me over and takes me from behind."

For all of his years keeping his emotions blank and unreadable, Tom could not fight back the groan that started low in his chest and burned its way out of his throat. "Yeah?" he choked out.

"That's not dangerous, is it?" Her voice shook again, but it didn't sound like nerves. It sounded like *want*. "I sometimes fantasize about a man coming into my chambers and bending me over my desk because he wants me so much that we can't wait. He—he might hold me by my hair or dig his fingers into my skin. He can't even wait to get undressed." She took a shuddering breath. "Is it wrong, do you think? It's so risky..."

"Wrong?" He laughed, a dry sound. "I've never heard anything so right in my entire life." Her face practically glowed with what looked a hell of a lot like relief. "I wouldn't try it until your office has been swept for bugs, though. And only with a man you trust completely."

She took another small step closer. His breath caught in his throat—he could see her legs now, long and bare. She had an unearthly glow where the moonlight kissed her skin. He'd never been jealous of the moon before. "That's the problem, you see? There aren't very many men I trust."

"There aren't?"

She shook her head. "Only you."

Tom was on his feet before he could think better of it. Then she was in his arms and he was kissing her.

No, *kissing* was too generic a word that covered too many things.

It didn't cover this—he was *consuming* her. He devoured her lips and sucked on her tongue while he ran his hands down her back and over her bottom, squeezing hard.

"Anything else," he whispered in her ear before he sucked her lobe in between his teeth and nipped, "that could be used against you?"

"I don't like prissy, cautious sex." Her body was vibrating in his arms, and he could feel her nipples, pointed and scraping against his chest. "I like it wild and rough. Loud and—"

He couldn't take another moment of this exquisite torture. He swept her legs out from under her for the second time in a few short hours and threw her onto the bed. "I wanted to do this earlier," he told her. "But I didn't know what you wanted."

"You." He grabbed at his T-shirt. Her hands went to the waistband of his shorts, shoving them and his briefs down. It wasn't gentle or patient. He grabbed the hem of her nightshirt and yanked it over her head, leaving her bare before him just as his erection sprang free. She gasped and then palmed him. Desire ran ragged through him.

When she looked up at him, her eyes luminous in the moonlight, she said, "I want you. Because I feel it, too."

Tom paused for just a second, a wild look of need in his eyes, and Caroline wondered if she'd said the wrong thing.

Please, she found herself praying as she clung to him, *please don't let this be a mistake.*

It wouldn't be, and that was final. She wasn't a naive college girl living in her own little world anymore. She and

Tom were consenting adults and it was perfectly reasonable to burn off a little excess energy doing consensual things. What happened in this room had nothing to do with corruption or cases or the errors of her ways.

But the next thing she knew, Tom had pulled free of her grasp and fallen to his knees. Her hands were empty and she felt oddly bereft.

He grabbed her by the hips and hauled her to the edge of the bed, his fingers digging into her skin. "Caroline," he groaned and then his teeth skimmed over her inner thigh. "Did you ever think of this?"

Then his mouth was upon her, licking and sucking her tender flesh. She sank her fingers into his hair and gave herself up to the sensation. Tom shifted, lifting her legs over his shoulders and spreading her wider for his attentions.

"Sometimes," she got out in a breathy voice. But not very often.

Oral sex was just…one of those things. Her previous lovers had either not been enthusiastic about it or hadn't been good—the worst was when it was both combined. They would go down on her for a few minutes and consider that an even exchange for fellatio.

But Tom? Not only was he enthusiastic—and that would've been more than enough—but he knew what he was doing. He found the bud of her sex and tormented it relentlessly with his tongue. One hand snaked up over her stomach until he was fondling her breast, rubbing his callused thumb over her nipple until it ached. His other hand? When he slipped a finger inside her, she almost came off the bed. She wanted to cry with satisfaction. She didn't. Instead, she just held on for the ride.

Jesus, her fantasies weren't this good. Tom found a rhythm and worked her body. He teased her nipple and licked her sex and thrust his fingers into her body. He gave her no quarter, no space for her mind to wander off and debate the wisdom of this. He kept her in the here and now, in this bedroom, with him. He pushed her body relentlessly as the orgasm built. He must've been able to tell she was close, because suddenly, he wasn't just flicking his thumb back and forth over her taut nipple—he pinched it between his thumb and finger and made a humming noise deep in the back of his throat.

Caroline came undone. Her thighs clenched around his fingers as she rode the waves of pleasure until they left her sated and limp. Slowly, Tom withdrew. He went from licking to pressing gentle kisses against her sex. Instead of pinching her nipple, he stroked his fingers all around her breast and then down over her stomach. Slowly, he pulled free of her body. She shivered at the loss.

She felt she needed to say something, show her appreciation somehow. She should be polite and reciprocate, at least.

But she found she couldn't do any of those things. She was boneless with satisfaction, able to do little more than smile at him. "Hopefully," she said, her voice sultry even to her own ears, "that wasn't a hazardous activity."

Tom got to his feet. The moonlight kissed his skin, giving him an otherworldly look. His erection jutted out from his body, and she lifted her foot to nudge at the tip. "No," he said, his voice deep and commanding, "I don't think there was anything damaging about that." He grabbed her foot when she nudged him again and lifted it, pressing a kiss to the sole.

It tickled and she laughed.

He leaned over her, holding his body above hers. The scent of sex hung between them as his erection brushed her hip. Unexpectedly, her eyes watered. This man—more than his dammed spring, more than his wine and pizza—she'd needed this from this man. "You decide."

She touched his face, letting her fingertips trace the map of his skin. "On what?"

Even in this dim light, she could see his eyes darken. "Do I flip you over or make you ride me?" She gasped at his words, her body arching into his. He'd paid attention, bless the man. He went on, "Should I suck your breasts or slap your ass?"

She pulled him down onto the bed, rolling as he went. "I'm on top."

"God," he muttered, shifting so they were in the middle of the bed, "I love a woman who knows what she wants."

Seven

"Condoms? Something?"

It took a second for Caroline's words to sink in, because Tom was having trouble getting past the way she straddled him, her breasts ripe for the plucking. His erection ached with need—and it only got worse when she settled her weight on him. He could feel the warmth of her sex against his dick—so close, yet so far away. He flexed his hips, dragging against her sensitive skin.

She made a noise high in the back of her throat as she shifted, bringing him against her entrance. But before he could thrust home, she leaned up, breaking the contact. "*Tom.* Condom?"

"Um…" Right, right. Birth control was the responsible thing here. As much as he hated to lift Caroline off him, he couldn't risk her health just because he couldn't think of a single thing beyond how her body would take his in. "One second."

He kept a fully stocked emergency cabinet in the storeroom that could help him survive a few months out here—and along with the necessities in the kit were unlubricated condoms. He just had to find them—which he had to do naked, while not looking at the pictures on the wall.

As he searched, Tom could almost feel Stephanie's eyes on him. Which was ridiculous. But he couldn't bring himself to glance at their wedding photos. He couldn't display them out in the open, but he also couldn't put them in an album on the shelf. So they lived here, in his storage room.

She would've wanted him to do this, he told himself, rifling through the emergency supplies. Stephanie had loved him beyond the point of reason, and she wouldn't have wanted him to spend the rest of his life alone. Not that having sex with Caroline had anything to do with the rest of his life. Those two things weren't directly connected.

Except…for that spark.

Stephanie would have wanted him to be happy. Polished, quiet Stephanie, who liked slow seductions and quiet submissions and sex in a bed. Only a bed. Never in an office or on a desk.

Finally, he found the condoms and a tube of all-purpose lube. It felt like he'd been looking for hours, but it'd probably been no more than five minutes. By the time he made it back to the bedroom, he was afraid the magic of the moment had been broken.

He paused at the bedroom door, trying to play out all possible outcomes. Would she have fallen back asleep? Changed her mind? Would he have to go sit in his spring-fed pool to keep himself under control?

He could take care of himself—he'd been doing it for years. But he didn't want to. He wanted to get back to that place where he and Caroline were two consenting adults about to get what they needed.

He needed her.

He had from the very beginning, when she'd been magnificent in her courtroom.

"Tom?" Her voice was soft, sultry. Not the voice of a judge, but the voice of a woman. A woman who needed to be satisfied.

For a fleeting second, he wished he were bringing a little more experience to the table. He didn't want to think he'd forgotten how to do this, but it'd been a long, long time since he'd had sex with another person.

But then he licked his lips, the taste of her sex still on his mouth, and he figured, what the hell. Sex was like riding a bike, only a lot more fun. "I'm here."

She was splayed out on her side, moonlight kissing her in the most intimate of places. Places he'd kissed. Places he was going to kiss again.

He watched as she slid a hand over her breast, cupping it and stroking her own nipple. He went painfully hard at the sight as her head lolled back. "Did you find a condom?" she asked in a breathy voice.

Instantly, he was hard all over again. His mind might have some performance anxiety, but his body was raring to go. "I found several."

"Oh, thank God." She pushed herself up and patted the bed next to her. "Come to bed, Tom."

He dropped the supplies on the sheets and crawled over to her. "You look good in my bed," he murmured, rolling onto his back. "I like you there."

He reached for the condom—but before he could, her mouth was on him. "Caroline," he groaned, trying to pull her up.

"You didn't tell me what you liked," she said, her voice throaty as she licked up his length.

He sank his fingers into her hair, trying to pull her up

and trying to hold her where she was at the same time. His brain short-circuited as the unfamiliar sensations rocketed through him. Her mouth was warm and wet and she was just as fierce as he'd hoped.

"This...this is good," he ground out, his hips moving on their own. She gripped him tightly as she licked at his tip. "God, Caroline."

Then he looked down at her. She was staring up at him as she licked and sucked, a huge grin on her face as she pleasured him. "This isn't a hazardous activity, is it?"

He wasn't going to make it. He sat up and pulled her away. He needed the barrier of the condom between them, because it was too much—she was too much. "I can't wait," he told her, rolling on the condom and applying the lube. "I need you right now."

"Yes," she hissed, straddling him again. This time, when his erection found her opening, she didn't pull away. Instead, she lowered her weight onto him, slowly at first, and then, with a moan that made his gaze snap to hers, she sank down the rest of the way, taking him in fully. "Oh, *yes*, Tom."

His mind blanked in the white-hot pleasure of it all. It'd been so long—but his body hadn't forgotten. The smell of sex hung heavy around them, and Caroline's body pinned him to the bed. He blinked, bringing her into focus. He let go of her hips only long enough to shove the pillows under his shoulders.

Because he hadn't forgotten what she'd whispered to him. "These are amazing," he told her, doing his best to focus on her needs, her body—and not how he was already straining to keep his climax in check. He stroked his fingertips over her breasts. "Simply amazing."

Her back arched as her hips began to rock. "Do you like them?"

"I do. But," he added, reaching around her waist with one hand and pushing her down to his mouth, "I like them more here."

With that, he sucked her right breast into his mouth and teased her left nipple with his fingers. He didn't bite—but he didn't have to. Caroline went wild as he lavished attention on her breasts. She moaned as her flesh filled his mouth, his hands. He wasn't gentle, either. She wanted loud? She wanted to feel like he couldn't hold back?

It wasn't a stretch, that. He lost himself in her body, her sounds, her taste. She grabbed onto the headboard and rode him wildly. It was all he could do to hang on long enough.

But he did. When she threw her head back and screamed out his name, he dug his fingers into the smooth skin of her hips and, thrusting madly, let go. God, it felt so good to let go again.

She collapsed onto his chest, panting heavily as he wrapped his arms around her and held on tight. In that moment, he felt like he'd come home again.

Who knew that by losing himself in her, he'd find himself again? But he was alive from head to toe, truly *alive*.

"Tom," she whispered against the crook of his neck.

"Yeah." He exhaled heavily and wished he were a younger man, one who had it in him to roll her onto her back and take her again. He shifted, lifting her off enough that he could get rid of the condom before settling her back against his chest. "Wow."

After a long time—Tom had begun to drift—she propped herself up on her elbows. "So," she said, the happiest smile he'd seen yet on her face. "What are the plans for the rest of the weekend?"

And then, because he wasn't as old as he thought, he did roll her onto her back and cover her with his body. "This," he said, flexing his hips and grinding against her. "Pizza and wine and the pool and *this*, Caroline."

"Finally," she murmured against his lips as she wrapped her legs around his waist. "A straight answer."

He was already thrusting inside her when he realized that the sensation was more intense than it'd been last time. He withdrew long enough to get another condom before he buried his body in hers again.

He'd finally come home, and he damn well intended to stay here.

Eight

This was a mistake, Tom thought as he stood next to the bed, staring down at Caroline's sleeping form. A rare tactical error. A series of errors, each compounding the other until what he was left with was a huge mess of his own making.

He shouldn't have brought her out here, knowing damn well he had to fly out of South Dakota first thing Monday morning. And he shouldn't have fallen into bed with her, either.

But he'd done both of those things, anyway. For once, he hadn't put the case first. And now he had to deal with the consequences.

She wasn't going to like this.

"Caroline."

She startled, blinking sleepily at him in the soft light from the bedside lamp. "What? Time to get up?"

"Yes."

Tom handed over the cup of coffee. She sat up to take

it, which made the sheet fall down around her waist. He almost groaned at the sight of her breasts. Damn it, this was not how he'd wanted to wake her up, either. But the die was cast.

She smiled sleepily at him, an invitation and a promise all rolled into one. "How much time do we have?"

He gritted his teeth. He'd indulged himself all weekend long. That was a luxury neither of them had right now. "Get dressed."

She blinked at him. At least this time, her eyes were almost moving at the same speed. "Are we back to this? You're not going to answer any question directly? Come on, babe."

Crap. It wasn't even five fifteen in the morning, and all he wanted to do was climb back into this bed with her and forget about the rest of the world, just like he'd dared to do for the last two days.

The rest of the world, however, wasn't about to be forgotten. He sat down on the bed. Which was a mistake, because when he did that, he reached over and cupped her cheek. "There's been a change of plans."

She leaned into his touch, looking worried. He didn't like that look. "How bad is it?"

There was probably a diplomatic way to inform her of the change in their travel plans. But he didn't have time to figure out what it was. "You're coming to Washington, DC, with me."

Her mouth fell open, and she jolted so hard she almost spilled her coffee. "But I'm supposed to be at work today…"

Tom forced himself to stand and move away from her. "There's been an emergency. Your house will not be secure by the time you get off work today, and I'm not willing to risk you going back there without having it swept. So you're coming with me."

She blinked again and then, in one long swallow, finished the coffee. When the mug was empty, she smiled widely. "Funny. Real funny, Tom. It's a little early for practical jokes, but it's good to see that you have a sense of humor at any hour." Her voice trailed off when he didn't return her easy grin. "Wait—you aren't joking?"

He shook his head. "This trip has been planned for months. I thought I'd be able to secure your house before my flight left this morning, but when I realized I wouldn't have time, Carlson was going to do it for me. But he's had an emergency and I don't trust anyone else to do it."

The ticket desk at the Pierre Airport wasn't open yet, so he'd have to buy her ticket when he got there. He hadn't once been on a full flight from Pierre to Minneapolis to Dulles, so it shouldn't be a problem.

"I have to go to DC because you have to go to DC," she repeated, as if she were trying to learn a foreign language.

He nodded. "Because the only other person you trust to sweep my house for bugs that may or may not exist is dealing with an emergency."

"That's correct."

She flung off the covers, and despite the early hour, despite the less-than-ideal circumstances, his pulse beat a little harder as she stomped around his bedroom wearing nothing.

"I have cases on the docket," she announced, her voice suddenly loud. The caffeine must have kicked in. "I can't just jet off with you. There has to be someone else—"

"No, there isn't. I told you—Carlson and I keep our activities quiet. That way no one can compromise our investigations. His wife is having pregnancy complications and I'm not about to mess with our operating procedures—procedures that have led to several successful convictions—just because—"

"You're being ridiculous," she snapped, throwing on her clothes.

Maybe he was. Maybe he shouldn't be taking her anywhere. After all, it hadn't taken more than a few hours out here, away from prying eyes and ears, before they'd wound up in bed together. It was one thing to indulge in a long, satisfying weekend with her at his isolated cabin—it was something completely different to take her to DC.

Then, before he could come up with any sort of witty retort to "ridiculous," she pulled up short. "Wait—Maggie's having complications?" She spun on him. "Is she okay?"

The fact that she was suddenly concerned for one of his oldest friends—whom she did not know—despite the fact that she was furious with him made something tighten in his chest. "She's got the very best watching over her. She's had some problems with high blood pressure, but they're controlling it." He hoped like hell Maggie would be okay. He couldn't bear the thought of losing another woman he cared for.

"That's good. I hope she's okay. But I can't fly to Washington, Tom."

"Take a sick day. Two," he corrected. "We'll fly back tomorrow."

She jammed her hands on her hips. She'd gotten her bra and shorts on, but she hadn't zipped them up. He knew what she was going to say before she said it, though. "No."

"*Yes*, Caroline." He began grabbing the rest of her things and shoving them into her bag. They could argue in the car. And, knowing Caroline, they would. "I don't know what kind of man you think I am, but after what's happened between us this weekend, you have to realize that I'm not about to do a damn thing that would put you at risk."

"Except drag me across time zones."

"I'm not leaving you behind, and that's final."

"I'll stay at a hotel," she announced, pulling her shirt over her head.

For a moment, he considered that. Hell, a hotel was where he should have put her in the first place. Anyone else, he would've done just that.

But could he trust that whoever had bugged her house hadn't also bugged her office? That they wouldn't be waiting to track her back to wherever she went—her home, a hotel, the safe house?

Bringing her out here hadn't been his tactical error. Not the big one, anyway.

No, where he'd really screwed up was thinking that he could separate this weekend with her from everything else—his work with the foundation, his job investigating the corruption case, his life. All of it.

He hadn't put the case first. He'd made an exception for Caroline because when he'd looked at her, he'd felt this spark—and the power of that pull had completely erased his professional distance.

She was his assignment. That was all that should be happening between them.

But now that he'd gotten in this deep with her, he couldn't walk away. Or fly away, as the case might be.

"No," he announced.

"Why the hell not?" It was easier to have this argument with her now that she was fully dressed. She grabbed the duffel from him and gave him the kind of look that most likely had wayward attorneys wetting their pants. She was ferocious, his Caroline. "Give me one good reason why, Tom. One really freakin' *good* reason."

He could run through the list of collateral damage this corruption case had left over the years. Lives destroyed, reputations ruined. Justice subverted.

Or he could argue about her personal safety. He could go into excruciating detail about how he'd seen other people's houses get bugged and that information had been used to wreck their lives. He could scare the hell out of her, because a scared witness was willing to do anything to stay safe.

He could also tell her what, up until sixty hours ago, had been the truth—that one person's inconvenience and discomfort meant nothing—not hers, not his. Breaking this case open was the only thing that mattered, and he would do whatever it took to finally get to the bottom of who was buying and blackmailing judges.

He did none of those things. Instead, he closed the distance between them, pulled her into his chest and kissed the holy hell out of her. She tasted of coffee and Caroline, a jolt to his system that he was already addicted to.

"Because," he said when he broke the kiss. Her eyes were closed and she was breathing hard, and if they weren't pushing deadlines, he'd lay her out on the bed and to hell with the rest of the world. "Come with me, Caroline. I..."

He almost said he needed her. Which was *not* true. He needed to know she was safe. He needed to know she was beyond the grasp of blackmailers and violent criminals.

It wasn't like she was someone he couldn't live without.

"Just come with me," he finished, which was not a good reason. It barely qualified as a bad reason, but damn it, it was early and he had to get her to the airport.

Her brow furrowed and her tongue traced the seam of her lips. It was physically painful, resisting the urge to lean down and replace her tongue with his own, but he managed to keep his distance. "Please," he added, way too late.

Her shoulders sagged. "I am *definitely* going to regret

this," she murmured as she shouldered her duffel. "What the hell. Let's go to DC. But," she added, jabbing him in the chest with her finger, "you better make it worth it."

"I will," he promised, trying not to grin and failing. "Trust me, I will."

Nine

"Celine. It's me. Listen, there's been a change of plans."

Caroline had no idea if she was supposed to be eavesdropping—but it was hard not to. Tom was pacing in a small circle about five feet away from her. That was all there was room for at the gate in Minneapolis, while they waited for their connecting flight.

But even that small space couldn't contain his energy. Caroline couldn't stop staring at him. Even though she was beyond irritated with the man, there was still something about him that called to her.

Tom's voice was pitched low, and she had to strain to hear him over the noise in the terminal.

She'd had no plans to be in Minneapolis today. Sure, it was always great to come home again, but being stuck at the airport for a ninety-minute layover wasn't exactly a homecoming.

"I'm bringing a guest," Tom went on.

Well. At least Caroline had been upgraded from security risk to guest. That had to count for something, right?

Tom's gaze cut over to her. "For a case… No. Don't worry—she'll be fine. But we might have to change dinner plans."

Caroline was tempted to point out that nothing about this situation was fine, but she didn't want to interrupt. Who was Celine? Not a girlfriend, she was pretty sure. But not a hundred percent sure, because she wasn't one hundred percent sure about any of this. Had she really been pulled onto a plane by the man of her dreams without luggage, toiletries, coffee…?

"We're traveling light, so if you could have something for her tonight?… Yeah. I'm sorry to be such a pain."

Wait. Had Tom Yellow Bird just apologized? Oh, she had to meet this Celine. Because Caroline was reasonably sure she'd never heard the man apologize for anything, and he'd quasi-kidnapped her twice now.

No, he hadn't kidnapped her. That wasn't fair to him. She had, after all, willingly gone along with him both times.

And why had she done that? There wasn't any rational reason for why she had thrown caution, common sense and her professional reputation to the wind. Sure, Tom would try to dress the last four days up as a matter of her safety. Yes, there'd been something off in her house.

But who were they kidding?

She'd come with him because she couldn't help herself. Tom Yellow Bird made her want to do things that she shouldn't—want things she shouldn't. And as ridiculous as this whole situation might be, she'd come with him because it'd meant another few days with him. It'd meant learning a little more about Tom Yellow Bird.

It'd meant another night in his arms and, apparently, that was worth the risk.

A sour feeling settled into her stomach. At this point, at ten fifteen on a Monday morning, when she was supposed to be in court, Caroline was completely out of rational reasons for any of the choices she'd made since calling Tom on Friday night.

It was hard to even remember how this had started—her house had felt wrong. Tom thought it was bugged. Someone was potentially planning to blackmail her.

So what had she done in response to a blackmail threat? Run away with the FBI agent assigned to the case and thrown herself at him. And now she was running away with him again, this time to Washington, DC.

For someone who prided herself on making the right choices ninety-nine out of a hundred times, Caroline was sure screwing things up.

"Hold on, I'll ask her." Tom turned to her. "What size do you wear?"

It wasn't like he hadn't seen her naked and didn't have a really good idea of her weight. So this was just another indignity. "Eight."

Tom repeated the number and then said, "What?... Oh. Yeah, okay." Then he handed the phone to her. "Be polite," he said in a low voice.

She scowled. When was she not polite? "Hello?"

"If you could just give me your dress size, shoe size, hair color, eye color, skin tone and body type, that would make this so much easier," a cultured woman's voice said with no other introduction.

Whoever this was, she certainly sounded like a Celine.

"Excuse me?" Maybe this was some sort of personal assistant? Frankly, at this point, nothing would surprise her.

"For tonight?" Celine said, as if she were speaking to

a child. "Thomas has indicated you will need something to wear."

Thomas? She looked up at him. He was frowning, but that could have just been his normal expression at this point. "What's happening tonight?"

Tom's frown deepened. If she hadn't spent the weekend wrapped around him, she might be intimidated.

"Why, the Rutherford Foundation's annual gala benefit," Celine announced, as if that were the most obvious thing in the world instead of a complete surprise. "Thomas is, as usual, the guest of honor. And if he thinks enough of you to bring you as his guest, we can't have you looking like you just walked off the plane, can we?"

The Rutherford Foundation? Later, she was going to strangle the man. Slowly. But she'd promised to be polite—and she had to admit, she desperately wanted to meet the woman Tom not only apologized to freely, but would let call him Thomas. "Oh. Yes. He mentioned something about that," she lied. "I'm a size eight and I wear a seven and a half in shoes."

"Hair color? Eye color? Bra size? Are you pear shaped or top-heavy?"

This was not awkward at all, she kept repeating to herself as she answered the questions. Her face felt like it was on fire with embarrassment, but she answered as honestly as she could.

"Thank you," Celine said, and oddly, she did sound genuinely grateful. "If I could speak with Thomas again? Oh—I didn't even get your name."

"Caroline. Caroline Jennings." Should she mention she was a judge? Or was that on a need-to-know basis? "Thank you for your help," she said, remembering her manners. "Will I have the chance to meet you tonight?"

Celine laughed, a delicate, tinkling sound. "Oh, I wouldn't miss it for the world."

With that vaguely ominous statement, Caroline handed the phone back over. What the hell had she gotten herself into?

This wasn't her world. Her world was predictable and safe. She lived her life to minimize the number of risks she took. Risks like running off with a man who was little more than a stranger, or falling into bed with said stranger.

Or jetting across the country to attend a gala benefit for a foundation with a dress code that required her body shape to be up for analysis, for God's sake.

She was skipping work. That was a hazard to her professional reputation. And Tom…

"We'll see you in a few hours," he told Celine, his gaze cutting over to Caroline.

Tom was definitely hazardous.

Tom ended the call and loomed over her. Unlike in Pierre, where they had been the only people in the airport besides a ticket clerk who'd also been the baggage handler, the Minneapolis Airport was crowded with people. Tom had only been able to snag one seat at their gate, and he had insisted Caroline sit in it.

It was sort of chivalrous. Thoughtful, even—which was quite a change of pace from him waking her up at the butt crack of dawn and informing her she was flying to the nation's capital with him, no discussion allowed. But that one small chivalrous act was barely a drop in an ocean of other things that were the complete opposite of thoughtful.

"We're going to a gala benefit for the Rutherford Foundation?" she asked, wondering if she should pinch herself—hard—to wake up from this strange dream. "You don't think you might have mentioned that before I had to give my body type to some woman named Celine?"

"I wanted to make sure you would be welcomed at the benefit," he said, choosing each word carefully.

She tried to be understanding. Really, she did. If she were to look at the situation objectively, Tom's behavior made perfect sense within a certain context. And that context was that he was a widowed officer of the law. He'd lived alone for years. He was used to giving orders and having them followed. He was used to being right, because who was going to contradict him? The criminals he arrested?

No, she had known from the very first moment Tom had walked into her courtroom that he did things his way, and honestly, that was part of his appeal. Or it had been, until this morning.

But damn it, she was not some common criminal he was shuffling from courthouse to jail. Hell, she wasn't even a witness that he was protecting at all costs. She didn't know what she was, except the woman who couldn't resist doing whatever he told her to.

She was definitely going to regret this.

"For the record," she began, standing so he wasn't staring down at her, "you should have told me first. Even better, you should've asked me to go as your date. It's a lot more effective than ordering me around and keeping me in the dark."

"I'm not—it wasn't—"

"You were and it was," she interrupted. "I like you, Tom. I hope you realize that. I wouldn't be here if I didn't."

He took a breath that looked shaky. "I am aware of that."

God save her from men who couldn't talk about their feelings. Caroline pressed on. "But if you keep treating me like…like a chess piece you can move around the board whenever the whim strikes you, this won't end well for either of us."

She wasn't ready for what happened next. His scowl slipped, and underneath, she saw... vulnerability. Worry. "You're not a chess piece, Caroline." He stepped in closer to her. She felt him all the way down to her toes. "Not to me."

Her whole body leaned toward him without her express permission. Something more—that's what he was to her. That's what she was to him, right?

No. Get a grip, she ordered herself. She'd rather be mad at him. There was nothing wrong with angry sex, after all. But tenderness was dangerous. For all she knew, affection could be deadly.

So she didn't allow herself to feel any of that. "Good," she said, making sure to keep her voice firm, "Now, why don't you tell me about this gala benefit I'm accompanying you to this evening?"

Celine had done as she'd promised. More than she'd promised, Tom realized when he and Caroline walked into the room at the Watergate Hotel. Celine and Mark always offered to put him up in their guest room, but he'd been staying at this hotel for years. It was better this way. The room was a small apartment, really, with an office, dining room, kitchen and a generous bedroom—with a generous bed.

There, right there in the middle of the room, were boxes from Bloomingdale's, stacked seven high on the coffee table. Hanging over the back of the bedroom door were two garment bags, one long and one shorter.

An unfamiliar twinge of nervousness took him by surprise. He couldn't be nervous. He did this every year. He'd attended enough formal events that he could push through feeling that he was an impostor. He belonged here now.

At first, coming back to DC, getting suited up in his

tuxedo and pressing the flesh with the political movers and shakers had almost been more than Tom could bear, but he'd done it to honor Stephanie's memory and pay his respects to her parents.

By now this trip was old hat to him. He was on a first-name basis with those movers and shakers. His custom-made tuxedo was cut to conceal his gun. He could chat with Mark and Celine without feeling like his heart was being ripped out of his chest. There was no reason to be nervous.

"Holy hell." Caroline's voice came from behind him. She sounded stunned. "Look at this place! And—whoa." She stepped around him and stared at the boxes. "How much clothing did she get for me?"

It was a fair question. In addition to the seven boxes on the coffee table, there were three more on the floor. "Knowing Celine, she probably got you a few options, just in case something didn't quite work." A huge clotheshorse, Celine would have enjoyed the opportunity to shop for someone else.

But he didn't say that. He felt out to sea here, because he hadn't had a date, as Caroline had started calling this evening, in…

Okay, he wasn't going to think about how long.

It wasn't a date, though. He was not dragging her around the country just so he could have sex with her whenever he wanted. This was a matter of safety. Of public interest. He couldn't compromise this case any more than he already had.

Yeah, he wasn't buying that, either.

Caroline reached over as if to pick up the top box and then pulled her hand back. "I don't think I can afford what she picked out."

"I'm paying for it." She turned and launched another

blistering glare at him. "I'm the one who dragged you out here," he reminded her. "The least I can do is foot the bill for the appropriate evening wear."

She chewed at her lip, and even though his head wasn't a mess and he wasn't nervous about tonight, he wanted to kiss her anxiety away. He wanted to do a lot more than kiss her. He wanted her back in his bed, where they should have been this morning.

"And her husband—that's Senator Rutherford, right?" She nervously twisted her hands together. "I can't believe that he was your father-in-law. And I really can't believe that I'm going to a party with them tonight." Her brow wrinkled as she stared at the boxes.

"You'll do fine," he said—not so much because it was what she needed to hear, although it might be. But it was because he needed to hear it, too.

He was just introducing the only woman he'd slept with since Stephanie to her parents. No big deal.

"We've got a few hours," he said, carrying his bag into the bedroom. He needed to hang his tux and make sure his shoes were shined. "I need to check in with the office."

The look on her face let him know loud and clear that he'd said the wrong thing. "Oh."

Damn it. He immediately saw his mistake. What kind of jerk was he to drag her to DC and then ignore her? "What I meant to say is, after I check in, if there's something you want to see, we could go do that."

She snorted in what he hoped was amusement, but her face softened and he got the distinctive sense that she knew he was trying. Mostly failing, but trying anyway. "Play tourist with you? Now you're getting the hang of this date thing. Sadly, I don't think we have time to wander the Mall. I need to see what I'm dealing with here—" she gestured to the boxes "—and I definitely need a shower." She looked again at all the boxes. "I hope there's some makeup in there or something."

The mention of a shower caught his attention. Shower sex was definitely one of his fantasies. Nothing in this day had gone according to plan. Yeah, he was rolling with the punches as best he could, but...

He wanted to relieve some of the tension that had started to build the moment she'd sat up in bed this morning, the sheet pooling at her waist.

He wanted to get her naked and wet, their bodies slick and then he wanted...

But he couldn't. He had ignored his responsibilities long enough. He had to do his job. Long after whatever this thing with Caroline was had ended, the job would still be there.

So instead of leading her to the shower and stripping her bare, he took a step back and said, "I'm sure there is. And if there isn't, I'll get you some." She notched an eyebrow at him. "I'll have someone who knows something about makeup get some for you," he corrected. "Deal?"

"Deal." She cracked her knuckles and made for the boxes. "Let's see what we've got."

Ten

What they had, Caroline concluded an hour later, was half a department store's worth of clothes. *Good* clothes. The kind of designer names that made her bank account weep with frustration.

Armani. Gucci. Halston, even. Celine Rutherford had exceptional taste and apparently an unlimited budget.

How on earth was she supposed to let anyone else pay for all of this? Four gowns—gowns!—plus two summery sundresses, a pair of Bermuda shorts, a pair of twill trousers, four different tops to pair with the pants, matching accessories and shoes for every outfit. For God's sake, there was even lingerie in here. Really nice lingerie. The kind a woman wore when she was intent upon seducing a man. Pale pink silk, delicate black lace—damn.

And of course there was makeup. Hell, the stuff in one of those bags wasn't even the brands she sometimes splurged on at the department stores. Tom Ford? Guerlain?

She was looking at a complete wardrobe that had probably set Tom back close to ten thousand dollars. More, if the stones in the necklaces and earrings were real diamonds and emeralds and not reasonable facsimiles. She hoped like hell they were fakes.

Her chest began to tighten as she surveyed the luxury goods. This wasn't right. This was like when she'd been a first-year prosecutor, drowning under the weight of her student loans, and had woken up one day to discover that, somehow, all of her debts had been mysteriously paid off.

It had been a mistake then not to undo that. It would be a mistake now to accept all of this finery.

What complicated things even more was that she was afraid she was falling for Tom. Some of him, anyway. She wasn't in love with the domineering parts of him that gave orders first and made requests second. But a part of her even found that appealing. He was just such a strong man, confident and capable, willing to run toward danger. But underneath that was a streak of vulnerability that tugged at her heartstrings.

Wrap that all up in his intense eyes and hard body and—well, was it any wonder she was in Washington, DC, willing to compromise her morals *again* just to be with him?

She glanced back at the doorway that led to a small office. Tom had disappeared in there when she'd started unpacking the boxes—he obviously wasn't the kind of guy who was heavily invested in women's fashion. Every so often, she could hear him talking—was he working or was he checking in on Maggie?

It almost didn't matter. Caroline strongly suspected that, when it came to his friends, his focus was just as intense as it was when he was working a case. He took his job seriously and she respected the hell out of him for it, even if she selfishly wanted him all to herself.

If this whole crazy weekend turned into something

more...what would they even look like as a couple? She couldn't ask him to stop working—it was clearly such a huge part of who he was, just like being a judge was fundamental to who she was. It wouldn't be selfish to ask him to pull him back from his duties to spend more time with her—it would be unconscionable.

A flare of guilt caught her by surprise. No, she couldn't compromise his ability to do his job—any more than she already had. And she couldn't compromise her reputation any more than she already had, either. Gifts as extravagant as this wardrobe looked bad, and when it came to conflicts of interest, appearance was everything.

Which meant she couldn't keep the clothes.

She'd have to wear one of the dresses and the shoes. But she wouldn't take the tags off anything else. The rest of it was all going back.

Now she just had to figure out how to tell Tom that. She didn't want to seem ungrateful, but she didn't want it to look like she could be bought for the price of designer formal wear.

She needed a shower to clear her head. "I'm going to start getting ready," she announced after she tapped on the office door. "Is it okay if I shower first?"

He shot her a look that kicked the temperature of the room up a solid five degrees, and Caroline found herself hoping that he'd offer to join her. Then he said, "Be my guest."

She was not disappointed by this. She needed to shave and exfoliate, and it was hard to do all those things with a man in the tub with her. So this was just fine. Really.

She was rinsing her hair when the door to the bathroom clicked open. She turned to find Tom leaning against the sink, watching her.

There was something about the way he was holding his

body that made her nipples tighten in anticipation. Maybe he had come to join her, after all. She shouldn't want him here. She shouldn't willfully keep making the same mistakes, over and over.

But here he was, and she was powerless to send him away.

"Are you waiting on the shower?" As she asked, she ran her fingers over her chest and down her stomach, rinsing the soap off.

Even at this distance—maybe six feet between them—she could see his eyes darken. He practically vibrated—but he didn't move.

"Or," she said, musing out loud, "you could join me. Plenty of room." She made a big show of scooting to one side.

He made a noise that echoed off the tiled walls. His clothes hit the floor, and the next thing she knew, he had her pinned against the wall, his erection nudging at her. "Did I mention that this is one of my fantasies?"

"Is it, now?" She dug her fingers into his hair, tilting his head back so the water sluiced over him. "I don't recall you mentioning your fantasies. Just mine." It felt dangerous to tease him like this, but God help her, it felt right, too. Somehow, she knew she was safe with him.

"Caroline," he groaned. He flipped her around—and none too gently, either. "I can't wait—I have to have you right now." He nudged her legs apart with his knee and tilted her bottom up. "Okay?"

"Yes," she hissed, arching her back to give him better access.

He was against her and then he thrust inside her in one smooth movement, filling her so effortlessly that she almost screamed from the pleasure of it. But she just managed to keep her noises restrained.

The he wound her hair around his fist and pulled her head back. "You have no idea," he whispered in her ear, his voice hoarse, "*no* idea how much I love hearing you scream." As he spoke, his other hand reached around and took possession of her breast, his fingers expertly finding her nipple and tormenting it mercilessly.

Caroline shimmered as she surrendered to the sensations. Her body adjusted to his and then he began to thrust, long, measured strokes timed with his fingers tugging on her nipple, his hand pulling gently but steadily on her hair and his mouth, his teeth on her neck and shoulders.

This weekend had been intense, a fantasy played out in real time. But this? She flattened her hands against the wall and gave herself up to him completely.

"Scream for me, Caroline," he whispered in her ear, his voice desperate, his hands on her body as he drove into her again and again.

It was all she could do, the only gift she could give him. And she gave it freely. "Tom—*Tom*!"

He growled and sank into her. Caroline's world exploded around her in a shimmering white light. Seconds later, Tom relinquished his hold on her hair and breast and dug his hands into her hips. He slammed into her with a ferocity that she knew she'd never find in another man. A second climax had her screaming his name again as he froze, her name a groan of pleasure on his lips.

They sagged against each other, the wall holding them up. Without warning, Caroline began to laugh. It came from deep inside—a release that she hadn't known she'd needed.

Tom spun her in his arms and tilted her head back. "Okay?" he asked, an amused smirk on his lips.

She was laughing so hard tears ran down her face. All these years and *this* was what she'd been chasing. She'd had a bunch of mediocre sex and occasionally some good sex, all because it was careful. Safe. But this?

She'd always known something was missing. And all it took was one cryptic FBI agent with an overprotective streak and the fantasies she'd nurtured quietly for years to show her how much she'd settled for.

And the hell of it was, she'd *known*. From the first moment she'd caught him staring at her across the courtroom, so caught up in her that he forgot to be seated—she'd known he was something special.

"I've never been better," she said when she finally had herself under control as she pulled him back into her arms. "Never."

"Good," he said against her lips. "Because I have a few more fantasies I want to try out."

She tried to look coy, which was something of a challenge, given that they were naked underneath a stream of water. "Don't we have to go to some gala?"

He cupped her face in his hands. "I'm not talking about just tonight, Caroline."

The full meaning of his words hit her. Dating. A relationship, even. *"Oh."*

His grin was wolfish. How could a man look so hungry when he'd just been sated so spectacularly?

"Let's get through tonight," he told her. "Then..."

"Right. Tonight." She had to put on a gown and what were probably real jewels and hobnob with heiresses and power brokers.

What else did he have in store for her?

She tried on the black dress, but, as expected, she couldn't wear either her serviceable beige bra or the silky strapless pink one Celine had provided. She decided to go with the plum gown. The color was deep and rich, not quite purple and not quite maroon. It wasn't bright enough that she'd stand out in a crowd, but it wasn't black, either.

Although the floor-length dress was sleeveless, it had two little straps that met at the center of the neckline, a V nestled between her breasts that provided just enough support that she wouldn't spend the evening tugging at the top. She paired it with a cuff bracelet that she hoped like hell was covered in rhinestones and not real diamonds. Along with that went sparkly chandelier earrings. She chose the kitten-heeled silver sandals.

She managed to get the dress zipped on her own and then turned to look at her reflection in the full-length mirror on the closet door. What she saw stunned her—was that really her?

Because the woman looking back at her was glamorous—gorgeous, even. That woman bore only a passing resemblance to Caroline.

Maybe she could do this—waltz into this world of power and wealth, and if not fit in, at least fake it for an evening.

"Caroline? We need to leave," Tom called out from the living room.

"Have you heard anything about Maggie?" she yelled back, touching up her lipstick. Not that her lipstick needed to be touched up. It was possible she was stalling.

None of this seemed real. The clothes, the jewelry, being in a DC hotel room with Tom—she was afraid to break the strange spell he'd cast over her.

"They managed to get the contractions stopped and everything is stabilized. They're still keeping her another night, but better safe than sorry at this point."

"Good. I'm glad to hear it." It was obvious Maggie was important to him, but more than that, Caroline didn't wish pregnancy complications on anyone.

Finally, she couldn't stall any longer. She wanted to make a good impression on his...were they still his in-laws? Former in-laws? She didn't know, but she did know it was bad form to keep them waiting.

She took a deep breath and opened the door. "How do I look?"

Tom looked up, and his mouth fell open. Then he dropped his phone and came to his feet.

Her pulse began to beat hard as he took in everything—and as she stared at him in return. Good Lord, he was wearing a tuxedo. Which shouldn't have been a surprise—she'd seen him unpack it, after all. And this was obviously the sort of event where tuxedos were de rigueur.

But the way the tuxedo fit him? Sweet merciful heavens. It was like a tall, dark, handsome James Bond had just walked off the screen and into her hotel room. Tom made a suit look amazing, a pair of jeans even better.

But Tom in a tux was something else entirely. Her nipples went rock hard at the sight, and suddenly, the dress seemed a half size too small.

As if she wasn't nervous enough, a creeping sense of doubt moved up her back. She'd pushed it aside earlier, in the shower. But now reality reared its head.

Tom was still staring, that unmistakable hunger in his eyes. There were so many things she didn't know about him. She knew he'd loved his wife, but had he moved on from her death?

This was not her world. It had been Stephanie's world, and Caroline knew that she could never compete.

He still hadn't said anything yet. She looked down at the dress and shot him a nervous smile. "Is this okay?" She did a little turn so he had full view of the dress in the back.

When she got turned around again, he was giving her

such a hard look she recoiled back a step. "Tom? Is it all right?"

"Good," he said, his voice tight.

She began to panic. She'd thought this gown was the best option, but maybe it didn't make her look as glamorous as she'd thought. "I've never been to a gala benefit for a foundation before. There were other dresses…"

"No," he cut her off. "That one's perfect. You look amazing."

She blinked at him. "Was that a compliment?"

The look of confusion on his face almost undid her right then and there. "Was it?"

This man. "No, the correct answer is, of course it was."

She gave him a long look and she'd swear the room brightened when the lightbulb went off over his head. "Of course it was. You look amazing, Caroline."

Even though she'd had to walk him up to the words, the sincerity in his voice made her cheeks warm. "Okay, good. Everything else can be returned—except for the makeup and…" She looked down at the dress. She didn't want to discuss the lingerie with him right now. That seemed like a bad idea because they had to be someplace very soon and she suspected that, if she brought panties into the discussion, she'd find herself removing them within seconds. "Everything I'm wearing right now. It's far too much money for me to casually accept the rest as a gift. I don't want to create the appearance of impropriety."

His eyes crinkled, and she got the feeling he was trying not to laugh at her, because there was nothing proper about any of this, appearances or otherwise, and they both knew it.

"Caroline," he said and suddenly he was looking at her with undisguised hunger, his voice the sound of sex on the wind, "try not to think like a lawyer tonight, all right? This is a date, not a court hearing. You look amazing."

She was many things—intelligent, competent, dedicated—but so very rarely was she *desirable*. Or glamorous. And right now, she was both.

She was keeping this dress.

He was the most dangerous man she had ever met. Not because he had the capacity to be deadly or because he filled out that tuxedo.

It was because of the way he made her feel. Glamorous and desirable—those were terrifying emotions. They made her do unpredictable things, like skip work and crash a gala. Worse, she was afraid of what would happen if they were combined with other emotions—tenderness, affection and who could forget sexual satisfaction? All those things swirled around inside her until they formed a superstorm of something that felt much stronger than infatuation, more potentially damaging than a hurricane.

She had once fancied herself in love. With Robby, of course. Looking back now, she couldn't remember what, exactly, she had loved about him. She didn't recall him being a particularly good student, nor was he exceptionally kind to small animals. He was just…there. He'd liked her, for whatever reason. She'd been young. Being liked was half the battle.

She liked to think she wasn't stupid anymore. And she definitely wasn't young.

So this wouldn't be the same thing she'd had with Robby. She was older and wiser. Tom had hinted that they'd have something more after this weekend—but there was no law that it had to be marriage. They could keep doing this—having a consensual, satisfying relationship that didn't involve messy emotions or the potential for heartache. She should keep some distance between them and cling to the safety it provided.

Yes, that's what she should do. But what she did instead was sashay toward him, her hips swaying seductively. "Tom…"

He looked at her with such longing that she wondered how late they could be. But then he said, "We should go."

She wasn't disappointed at that. Not even a little. "We should."

But after this little gala, they were coming back here. And in the morning, she wasn't leaving until she'd found out how far he was willing to take this.

Eleven

"Nervous?"

Caroline rolled her eyes at Tom. "No, why would I be nervous? I'm just wearing a gown and accessories worth thousands of dollars, after riding in a limo far nicer than the one I took to high school prom, next to an armed man wearing a tuxedo, on my way to meet your former in-laws, who happen to be insanely wealthy and also powerful, all while attending a gala benefit filled with the elite in honor of your late wife. Why would I be nervous?"

The corner of his mouth ticked up, but he didn't smile. He couldn't, not with her on his arm as they made their way into the crush of the annual Rutherford Foundation Gala Benefit and Ball. When she'd walked out of the bedroom in that dress, the fabric clinging to her every curve, he'd been stunned past the point of coherence, physically shaking with the effort it took to restrain himself from mussing up her hair and peeling that dress from her body.

He hadn't, because Mark and Celine Rutherford were waiting on them. He had to keep up appearances.

He freakin' hated appearances.

He didn't get nervous anymore—but at times like these, he couldn't help flashing back to the first time Carlson had dragged him along to one of these events. Or the second time. Hell, even the tenth time, he'd still been painfully aware that he didn't belong. It'd gotten better after he'd married Stephanie, but...

But Stephanie, God rest her soul, wasn't on his arm. He didn't have her social graces smoothing the way and making sure he fit in.

Instead, Caroline was with him.

And there was no turning back.

He remembered how, the first few times they'd attended a function together, Stephanie had kept up a steady stream of survival tips, designed to put him at ease. So he did the same for Caroline. "It's open bar. But I'd recommend going easy on champagne."

"If it's all the same to you, I'd like to avoid making a complete and total fool of myself in front of—how many members of Congress will be here?"

"Probably no more than thirty. Or did you want to include former senators and congressmen?"

She stumbled, but he steadied her. Once she had her balance back, she whispered, "I can't tell if you're being serious or if you're teasing."

He was definitely teasing her. "Don't panic. There probably won't be more than two Supreme Court justices in attendance."

She hit him with her clutch. Hard. "Later, I'm going to get even with you."

He damn near grabbed her and marched her right back out to the limo. They didn't even have to make it to the hotel—the limo was big and had an abundance of flat surfaces. He'd wrinkle her dress with wild abandon before he peeled it right off her luscious body.

But he didn't. Instead, he kissed her hand, his lips warm against her knuckles. "Caroline."

She took a deep breath that did some very interesting things to her cleavage, but then she turned her gaze up to his face. Her eyes were so full of hope and affection that suddenly his own breath caught in his chest. "Yes?"

Yeah, he'd been trying to convince himself he'd brought her here for noble reasons. But now? After he'd taken her in the shower? Moments before he introduced her to the Rutherfords?

He realized how damn wrong he'd been. The case wasn't the reason they were here. Her security wasn't why she was wearing that gown, nor why he was about to introduce her to the Rutherfords.

She was the reason. He hadn't been able to put her in a hotel and forget about her. He hadn't been able to leave her behind.

He wasn't sure he could.

"I'm glad you're here with me."

She gasped, a delicate blush on her cheeks, and he felt himself leaning toward her. The rest of the crowd fell away, and it was just him and her and this spark that had always existed between them.

Just then, he heard, "Thomas!" The sound of Celine Rutherford's voice snapped him out of his insanity.

Celine swanned toward him, glamorous as usual in a lacy evening gown that managed to make her look at least twenty years younger than she actually was.

"Celine," he said, bending over to kiss her cheek. "You look lovelier than ever."

She did. He braced himself for the pain of seeing her

again but it didn't come. Not in the almost overwhelming waves that usually left him dazed, anyway.

A dull ache radiated from his chest, but it wasn't as bad as it normally was. Manageable, even.

"You sweet talker, you." Celine beamed, playfully patting his arm.

Tom grinned good-naturedly. "My apologies for being late. I always forget there's traffic here."

She waved this away. "The important thing is that you're here now. You look wonderful, Thomas."

Beside him, Tom was pretty sure he heard Caroline snort in what he hoped was amusement. And he knew why, too. No one called him Thomas for very long.

Except for the Rutherfords. "Celine, may I present Judge Caroline Jennings? She's my guest this evening."

Caroline stepped forward, looking starstruck. "It's a pleasure to meet you, Mrs. Rutherford. I cannot thank you enough for going to all the trouble of pulling that wonderful selection of clothing for me. I hope this meets your specifications?" she asked in a rush, as if the dress Tom had not been able to stop staring at for the last forty minutes was a feed sack on her.

Celine laughed, a light sound. "I think you made the right choice. You look marvelous, dear. That color suits you perfectly."

For years, seeing Celine Rutherford had been the most painful thing Tom had to survive. Stakeouts and violent criminals and occasional shoot-outs—he'd take those any day of the week compared to the mental torture of his annual visit to the Rutherfords. It was easier now, because Stephanie was forever fixed in his mind at twenty-seven years old and Celine got a little older and a little grander every year.

But it still hurt. There was a small, selfish part of him

that wished the Rutherfords weren't so kind to him, that they could all let the relationship drift away and Tom wouldn't have to face these memories on a regular basis.

Normally, he would get through this evening by drinking more champagne than was healthy and finding a few other people from the FBI he could talk shop with.

This time? He didn't want to deal with questions about who Caroline was and why she was here. It was bad enough that he was introducing her to Celine.

What the hell was he doing here? There wasn't supposed to be anything between him and Caroline, beyond her role in an ongoing investigation.

But had that stopped him from bringing her to DC? Or introducing her to his in-laws? Or thinking about a relationship after this?

Nope. All those things he shouldn't be doing, he was doing them anyway. Just to keep her closer.

Celine went on, "And it was no trouble at all. I had so much fun putting the outfits together. I so miss shopping for Stephanie." Her voice trailed off and her eyes got suspiciously shiny. "But then, I suppose I always shall. I do try to keep her spirit alive. This was her foundation, you know. She started it with her trust fund money. Thomas and I keep it going to honor her memory."

"I've always admired what the Rutherford Foundation does," Caroline said, and oddly, she sounded serious about it. "I don't think Tom knows this, but I've actually donated a fair amount of money to the Rutherford Foundation over the years. I admire your objectives about educating girls and women around the world."

"You have?" Celine smiled broadly, any lingering remnants of grief vanished from her eyes. "Why, that's wonderful! It's always a pleasure to meet people who appreciate what we're doing—isn't it, Thomas?"

"It is," he said, staring at Caroline with curiosity. "Why didn't you tell me that?"

She lifted an eyebrow. "I prefer surprising you."

"Oh, I can see we're going to get along famously," Celine said, linking her arm with Caroline's and pulling her away from Tom. "Thomas needs someone who can keep him on his toes. Come, I must introduce you to everyone. Thomas?" she called over her shoulder. "Are you joining us?"

For a long second, he couldn't move. He couldn't talk, even. All he could do was look at Celine and Caroline fast becoming friends and trail along behind the two women, shadowing them like a bodyguard. He was fine. It was just the shock of seeing Celine give what looked a lot like a seal of approval to Caroline. That was throwing him for a loop. Every few feet they paused and greeted someone. Celine introduced Caroline as if they were the oldest of friends.

What would Stephanie think of this? Would she have laughed at him because, as usual, he was taking everything too seriously? Would she have been hurt that Tom was bringing another woman to Stephanie's event? It wasn't like Caroline was replacing anyone. She and Stephanie didn't look alike, didn't have the same sense of humor and definitely didn't have the same background.

All they had in common—besides the ability to fill out an evening gown—was that, for some inexplicable reason, they both cared for Tom.

And he cared for them.

Caroline laughed at something Celine said to Representative Jenkins, and Celine beamed at her. Celine liked Caroline.

Caroline kept him on his toes and didn't let him get away with anything. Even when he steamrolled her, she didn't simper or whine. She gave as good as she got, and he loved it when she did.

Stephanie would've loved Caroline. The realization made his chest tighten.

Mark Rutherford fell into step next to him. "Tom," he said, giving Tom a strong handshake. "Good to see you."

"Mark," Tom said. He nodded to where Celine was showing Caroline off. "I would introduce you, but Celine has already staked her territory."

Tom liked his in-laws—he always had. They had never made him feel like he was a dirt-poor Indian who didn't belong. Even if that's what he had been, once upon a time. Tom wondered if they'd approved of Stephanie marrying him, but he'd never know. They had always treated him with warmth and respect.

Mark had aged quite a bit since Stephanie's death. He and his daughter had always been close. His hair had gone almost white within the year, and he had not sought re-election after his term finished in the Senate. His appearance was just another reminder of how much time had actually passed.

"How have you been?" Tom asked.

"Getting by. I'll be glad when this fund-raiser is over. It consumes Celine for months on end. And you know how she is when she gets focused on something." They shared a laugh, but Tom couldn't help looking at Celine and Caroline, who were continuing to make new friends. He knew exactly how his mother-in-law was when she focused on something—and right now, Caroline was the beneficiary of that focus.

"I'm sorry this is awkward," he began, because it felt awkward to him. "But it was unavoidable."

Mark waved this away. "No need to explain. We're thrilled to meet her."

Tom was so focused on Celine and Caroline that he almost missed what Mark had said—and put it together with something Celine had said earlier—about how Tom needed her to keep him on his toes.

Oh, *no*. Yeah, he'd been thinking about keeping Caroline closer—but he didn't know what that meant right now. It didn't mean wedding bells and babies, that was for sure—and he couldn't have the Rutherfords jumping to that conclusion. He needed to nip this in the bud. "I'm not here *with* Caroline."

Mark gave him a look that Tom had seen many times over the years, one that always made Tom squirm. "Am I reading this wrong? You show up with a gorgeous woman you can't stop staring at and I'm supposed to believe you two aren't involved?"

"She's part of a case." To his own ears, Tom sounded defensive. "You know how important my work is," Tom went on. "The job's not done."

True, none of that had exactly stopped Tom from sleeping with Caroline. Nor had it prevented him from bringing her here. Or telling her he wanted to see her after this trip, too.

His stomach felt like a lead balloon. It'd been one thing when they'd been tucked away in his house or at the hotel, far from prying eyes. But he hadn't been able to leave their relationship there. He'd convinced himself that it was all right—no, vital—to bring Caroline to this party and introduce her to the Rutherfords. And it was a lie. A selfish, willful lie just because he couldn't bear to leave her at a damned hotel in South Dakota.

What had he done? Celine and now Mark were both taken with Caroline. They were welcoming her into their world with open arms. Tom realized he was setting the Rutherfords up for more heartbreak when this...*thing*, whatever it was with Caroline, ended. He couldn't bear to hurt his in-laws. They'd already lost their daughter.

But more than that, Tom had essentially announced to the whole world that she was important to him when he was supposed to be hiding her, keeping things quiet. He was supposed to be protecting her, and instead, he'd opened them both up to more scrutiny. If someone were looking for something to use against either of them, Tom had just handed it to them on a silver platter.

This was too much. He'd left himself exposed and that made Caroline vulnerable. Hell, it made Celine and Mark vulnerable, too.

What *had* he done?

Mark's eyes sparkled with humor. "I've known you a long time, Tom. I've watched you force yourself to attend these things year after year when it's obvious you'd rather be anywhere else. And I've watched women flirt shamelessly with you." He clapped Tom on the shoulder and chuckled. "You could've had your pick, but they've all been invisible to you. But her?" he said with a nod of his head to where Caroline was laughing at something the House minority whip was saying, "You *see* her. Tell me, is that more important than a job?" Sadness stole over his face again. "It's not. Trust me on this one."

Tom gaped at the man, fighting a rising tide of indignation. "I was married to your daughter, sir. I loved her."

Mark looked at him with a mixture of kindness and pity. "And she died. We'll never forget her—she's the reason we're all here. But we moved on." He leaned in close, kindness radiating from him. "Maybe you should, too."

Twelve

"I can't believe I met the Speaker of the House!" Caroline marveled as she collapsed back in the seat of the limo. The whole evening had an air of the unreal about it.

Celine Rutherford had—well, she'd worked miracles. Caroline had felt perfectly dressed—because Celine had gone shopping. Caroline had met seemingly every mover and shaker in Washington, DC—because Celine introduced her.

And then there was Tom—who was currently sitting silently on the other side of the limo, staring out the window as the lights of DC went zipping past. He seemed...lost.

If she'd thought she'd understood that he was the strong, silent alpha male—then this evening had blown that image out of the water. He'd made the rounds by her side, smiling broadly and making small talk like a pro.

Now that the high of hobnobbing with the rich and famous was wearing off, she was acutely aware that she'd been awake since before dawn, had taken two connecting flights and socialized in a high-stress situation.

Still, she reached over and laced her fingers with Tom's. This was not how she'd planned to spend her day, but she was glad she'd come. "I had a wonderful evening. Celine and Mark were a delight."

At one point, she'd seen Mark Rutherford put his arm around Tom's shoulder in a fatherly manner.

But more than that, he'd spoken warmly with his in-laws—it was obvious that he cared for the Rutherfords a great deal, and they obviously thought the world of him.

It was the sort of loving relationship she'd lost when her parents had passed.

Tom had lost so much. She was glad he had the Rutherfords. He needed more people who cared about him in his life. It bothered her to think of him feeling as alone as she sometimes had after her parents' death.

She was being maudlin—which was probably just due to the exhaustion. It had been a long day, after all.

Tom might suck at talking about his feelings, but his actions spoke for him. It was one more piece to the puzzle that made up Tom Yellow Bird.

Dangerous FBI agent. Reserved private citizen. Thoughtful former son-in-law.

Incredibly hot lover.

Somehow, it all came together into a man she couldn't help but be drawn to. Ever since she'd first seen him in her courtroom, she'd felt something between them, and that something was only getting stronger.

"I'm glad to hear this evening wasn't too hard for you."

There was something in his smile, in his tone that gave her pause. "Was it for you?"

He shrugged, as if his pain were no big deal. "No matter how many times I do this, I still don't belong."

She gaped at him in shock. He'd blended in seamlessly while she'd struggled not to be starstruck. How could he possibly think he hadn't belonged?

"But you do," she told him. "Celine and Mark—they adore you, and you obviously care for them, too. You fit in better than I did." If it hadn't been for Celine, Caroline would have been hiding in the corner with a glass of wine, too anxious to brave the crowd.

He pinned her with his gaze—one she'd seen before. It was the same look he'd given the defendant in the court case—the day she'd met him.

Her back automatically stiffened. Why was he glaring at her? But then, just underneath that stone-cold exterior, she glimpsed something else—something vulnerable.

Scared, she thought as he began to speak. "Do you know where I came from?" he demanded, his voice quiet. It still carried in the limo. "Do you have *any* idea?"

She blinked in confusion. "You said…I thought…the reservation that's less than thirty miles from your house?"

"Yes, but that doesn't tell you where I'm from. Because I *don't* belong here." His scowl deepened. If she didn't know him like she did, she might have been afraid.

But she wasn't. "The Red Creek tribe is pretty small—fewer than four thousand people. I grew up on the banks of the Red Creek curve in a little…" He looked out the window, but not before she caught a flash of pain on his face. "My town was about four hundred people. We didn't even have a gas station. We had electricity at my house, but we pulled our water from the river."

She could tell that admission had cost him something. He was such a proud man—but he'd grown up in what sounded like very poor circumstances.

How many people knew this about him? His late wife,

for sure—but did the Rutherfords know? Any of those people who had been so happy to shake his hand tonight?

She sure as hell wouldn't have guessed it—not from his slick suits and his muscle cars and that cabin that had the finest money could buy, because quality was always worth it.

Why was he telling her this? Was he trying to scare her off—or convince himself that he still didn't belong? "We were all scraping by on government surplus foods," he went on, as if being poor was somehow a character flaw. "The only way to change your fate was to get off the res—so that's what I did. I decided to be an FBI agent—don't ask why. I have no clue where I got the idea."

As he spoke, she could hear something different in his voice for the first time. There was an accent there, something new in the way he clipped his vowels. It was the prettiest thing she'd ever heard.

She smiled, trying to imagine Tom Yellow Bird as a kid. All she got was a shorter guy in a great suit. "But you actually did it," she said softly, hoping to draw him out.

"I did. I got a college scholarship, got my degree in criminal justice and headed for DC. It was this huge city," he added, sounding impossibly young. "I'd never been anywhere bigger than Rapid City, and suddenly there were cars everywhere and people and they were all wearing nice suits—it was *crazy*. If I hadn't had Rosebud and, through her, Carlson—I honestly don't know if I could've made it."

"It was that big of a culture shock?"

"Bigger. I was used to the way people on the reservation treated me—as someone to be proud of. I was an athlete and I was smart enough to get a scholarship. I was a big fish in a very small pond, but DC—that was the whole ocean and it was filled with sharks. And I…" He shook his head and she could feel some of his tension fading away.

"I was nothing to them. With this last name? Nothing but a curiosity."

She tried to picture it. After all, she was from Rochester, Minnesota, originally—and that was a lot smaller than Minneapolis. But she had been a girl moving from a mostly white town to an even larger mostly white town. People never looked at her as a curiosity, because she blended in.

No, she couldn't imagine what it would've been like to go from living on government surplus cheese to being invited to bigwigs' parties in DC because your friend thought it would be fun.

She thought about Tom's house, how it was off the grid but still in the lap of luxury. He squeezed her hand, which she took as a good sign.

Had something happened at the party to upset him? Or was it just seeing his in-laws? She didn't know.

"Is it still like that on the reservation?"

"A few years ago they built a hydroelectric dam. The tribe owns forty percent of it and they used a lot of local labor in the construction. The res still isn't a wealthy place, but it's better. Ask Rosebud about that when you meet her—it's her story to tell."

Caroline blushed from the tips of her toes to her hair, because he'd again, just casually, tossed off the fact that she *would* be meeting one of his oldest friends. That she'd be part of his life moving forward.

Which was what he'd said in the shower, too. But…

She wanted to spend time with him. But she couldn't keep doing what they'd been doing—running away together and ignoring the real world. The last three and a half days had been risky and dangerous and if she kept up this sort of behavior, it might well come back to haunt her.

Still, she wanted to meet his friends. She had the feeling it was another piece to the puzzle that was Tom Yellow

Bird. "I'll do that." She was trying to hear what he wasn't saying, because if she knew anything about Tom, it was that what he didn't say was almost as important as what he did. "Have *you* changed the reservation for the better?"

"I try," he went on. "I honor Stephanie by keeping most of her money in the Rutherford Foundation. I have the safe house I told you about. I also fund a bunch of college scholarships. If there's a kid who wants to work hard enough to get off the res, I'm going to help them do it. And no," he added before Caroline could ask the obvious question, "it's not all her money. I invested wisely. It's amazing how easy it is to make money when you already have it," he added in a faraway voice. "Simply *amazing*."

She knew how damned hard it was to start from nothing, to be buried under such debt that a person couldn't breathe, couldn't sleep. "I don't know many FBI agents who run charities. You could have retired, you know."

"The job wasn't done. It still isn't." Something about the way he said that sent a shiver down her spine. "Besides, I don't run the charities. I pay people to run them for me."

"Are any of those people members of the Red Creek tribe?"

His lips curved into a smile that was so very tempting. "Maybe."

And that, more than anything else, was why she was in this car with Tom Yellow Bird. He was just so damned honorable. Yes, he was gorgeous and financially independent—but there was more to him than that.

She had a momentary flash of guilt. He was protecting his people and fighting for what was right. Hell, he was protecting her. He was protecting her and sweeping her off her feet, and she wasn't worthy of him. Because she couldn't make the same claim to being honorable.

She had done her best to make up for her grand mistakes—

but a mistake was something you did accidentally. That was the definition of her pregnancy scare, sure. But more likely it was a mistake she'd made by being involved with Robby, by not taking the proper precautions. And after that scare, she'd buckled down. No more Robby; no more casual attitudes about birth control. From then on, she was careful, and it'd paid off. She hadn't experienced that kind of heart-stopping terror again.

But her pregnancy scare was a world of difference from what had happened with the Verango case. There had been nothing noble about her actions, and what she'd done was exactly the sort of thing someone might use against her.

She came *this* close to telling Tom about it. After all, he'd opened up to her. They were moving into uncharted territory here. How easy would it be to say, *I did a favor for a friend and my debts were paid off in full*? One sentence. Less than twenty words. It wasn't like she'd accepted a bribe intentionally—her law professor had manipulated her. But she hadn't returned the money because she hadn't known how.

Instead, she'd made donations—once she had a salary—to charitable causes, including the Rutherford Foundation. By her rough estimates, she'd given away slightly more than the original amount of the loans that had been paid off with dirty money.

"I don't talk about that. About any of that," Tom said, sounding more like himself. "It's…"

If he was trying to convince her that his hardscrabble life and his wife's death were things he should somehow be ashamed of, she was going to kick his butt. "It's brave and honest and true, Tom. To take something like losing your wife and turn it into something good? Not even good—amazing?" Tears pricked at her eyes, and she cupped his cheek. "You are the best man I've *ever* known."

He slid his arm around her shoulder and touched his forehead against hers and said, "It was different tonight. And that was because of you."

Her confession died on her lips. Whatever this was between them, it was good. She cared for him and he cared for her, and there was that something between them that neither of them could deny. This wasn't pretend. This was real.

If she told him about her one mistake, would he still look at her with that tenderness, with that hunger? Or would he see nothing but a criminal?

The most she could hope for was that no one would put her student loans and Vincent Verango's plea deal together. It was perfectly reasonable that a first-year prosecutor would offer a plea deal to a supposed first-time offender.

"Caroline..." His voice was barely a whisper. "I..."

Yes, she wanted to say. He'd taken her to his house, brought her to Washington. He'd taken her to a gala benefit and introduced her to his late wife's parents. He'd made crazy, passionate love to her. He'd said he wanted to see her after tonight. She'd cast aside common sense to follow him, because there was something between them that was real and true.

Whatever he wanted, the answer was *yes*.

Suddenly, he pulled back, all the way to the other side of the limo. It hurt worse than a slap to the face. "After we get back tomorrow, I'll sweep your house myself."

Maybe that was supposed to be a tender gesture from a man who had forgotten how to discuss emotions. *When you care enough to sweep the house yourself*, she mused.

But there was no missing the way Tom had pulled away—not just physically, but emotionally. Caroline swore she could feel a wall going up around him. "When will I see you again?"

The silence stretched until she was at her breaking point. "We have to be careful to avoid the appearance of impropriety," he finally said.

He wasn't so much throwing her words back at her as using them as laser-guided weapons, because they hit her with military precision. "Oh. Right."

Objectively, she knew this was true. She'd fallen into bed with him this weekend. She'd skipped work today—and tomorrow—by claiming she had the flu. She was wearing ungodly expensive clothing and jewelry that he'd paid for. She was taking stupid risks with her heart, her health and her career. She hadn't had this much sex in years.

If someone really were looking to blackmail her, this weekend would be a great place to start.

So, yes, she knew they needed to put some distance between them. It just made rational sense.

But there'd been that promise of something more in the shower today. She'd started to believe that this wasn't just a crazy weekend—that this was the start of a relationship.

That explained why Tom's mixed signals hurt so much.

"I have to put the job first," he went on, not making it any better. "My feelings for you…"

Hey, at least he had feelings he was admitting to. That had to count for something. "No, I understand. We both have jobs to do. I just…forgot about that for a little while."

Maybe it was just her, but she thought he visibly sagged in relief. "It's easy to forget everything when I'm with you. But when we're back in Pierre…"

Yeah. When she went back to being Judge Jennings and he went back to being Agent Yellow Bird, neither of them would forget.

Damn it all.

Thirteen

"Fourteen." Tom flung the small bag of recording devices onto James Carlson's desk. "Fourteen damn cameras in her home."

It took a lot to piss Tom off. He'd been doing this for a long time. He'd thought that his rage had burned out of him in the years after Stephanie's death.

Apparently, he'd been wrong.

Carlson looked up at him, eyebrows quirked. "That does seem a little excessive."

"A *little*? There were two cameras in her bathroom—one in the shower and one guaranteed to get an up-skirt shot on the toilet. And three in her bedroom! You and I both know the only reason you would need three separate angles of her bed was if someone was planning on mixing footage."

Several years ago, Rosebud Donnelly had been secretly filmed with her husband, Dan, and the tape had been used in an attempt to blackmail Rosebud into dropping a lawsuit against an energy company. She had come to Carlson and Tom for help.

One minute of Rosebud having her privacy violated and her dignity assaulted. It had been a trade-off then because Carlson and Tom had thought—after all these years—that they'd finally found the man behind the curtain, as Tom thought of him. Dan Armstrong's uncle Cecil was an evil man. For years he'd been blackmailing people and paying off judges—including the judge who had made a mockery of the judicial system by using Maggie so very wrongly.

That should have been the end of the case. If this were a movie, it would've been. But it wasn't. Fourteen cameras made it loud and clear—this wasn't over by a long shot.

Why wasn't it over?

Tom sat in the chair in front of James's desk, vibrating with anger. He was capable of violence, but he rarely resorted to it. However, right now? Yeah, right now he could shoot someone. Repeatedly.

What would've happened if he had let Caroline convince herself that she was imagining things? What would've happened if he had left her alone all weekend? If he'd dropped her off Monday morning and gone on his merry way to DC alone?

He'd been right to take her with him. Fourteen cameras proved that. But he'd also been so, so wrong to do so, because he'd still put her in a position of risk.

"You seem a little worked up about this," Carlson said casually, picking up the bag. "What did Judge Jennings say when you told her how many cameras you found?"

"I didn't. I mean, I haven't—yet." He wasn't sure he could bring himself to tell her, because he knew what it would do to her. It would destroy her sense of peace. She wouldn't be able to sleep, to shower—to do anything personal and intimate.

Like this weekend. When she'd stripped and floated in his spring-fed pool under the fading sunlight. Or when she had straddled him and ridden him hard, crying out his name. Or in DC, when he'd paid God only knew how much to outfit her in gowns and jewels so he could introduce her to his in-laws. Or when he'd taken her in the shower.

If he told her about the cameras, she wouldn't be able to be herself. He would take that freedom away from her.

He wasn't sure when he realized that Carlson wasn't talking. It could've been seconds later, it could've been minutes. He looked up to find one of his oldest friends staring at him. Anyone else and Tom might've been able to keep his cards close to his vest. But Carlson was no idiot, and they knew each other too well.

Tom dropped his head into his hands, struggling to find some equilibrium—or at least a little objectivity. But he didn't have any. He hadn't since he'd heard her voice on his phone on Friday, small and afraid.

Hell, who was he kidding? He hadn't had any objectivity when it came to Caroline Jennings since she had walked into that courtroom. And after the last four days, he couldn't even pretend there was distance between them. Because there wasn't. He had been inside her, for God's sake.

"Do you ever think about her?" he heard himself ask. "Stephanie?"

"I do. She was a good woman."

Silence.

Normally, silence would not work on Tom. Waiting was what he did best. In the grand scheme of things, what was a few minutes when someone was hoping to make him slip up?

What was almost ten years without his wife—without anyone?

"Do you think..." He swallowed, calling up the image

of Stephanie at that last party, her body wrapped in a silky blue cocktail dress and her mother's sapphires. Stephanie, telling him she was tired and ready to go. Stephanie, smiling indulgently when he said he had just a little more business to see to—he'd catch a cab. She should take the car. The car *her* money had paid for, not his.

Stephanie kissing him goodbye—not on the lips, but on the cheek. Stephanie, walking away from him for the very last time.

He had loved his wife with every bit of his heart and soul. But in the end, he'd only known her for four years. It hadn't been enough. It would never be enough.

In the end, he'd put the job ahead of her. He should have been with her and he hadn't been, because he'd been chasing a lead, hoping for someone to slip up under the influence of alcohol.

Had it been worth it? Tom couldn't even remember what that case had been. He hadn't finished it, he was sure. He'd been lost in burying his wife.

No. The job hadn't been worth it. Maybe it never would be. Wasn't that what Mark Rutherford had said?

"She would've wanted you to move on." Tom looked up and realized that Carlson was no longer sitting behind his desk. He was now leaning against the front of it, looking at Tom with undisguised worry in his eyes. "It's been almost ten years, Tom."

Mark's words, almost exactly. Tom let out a bitter laugh, because it was that or cry, and he didn't cry. Not ever. "It's not like I've been moping. I've been busy."

Carlson smiled indulgently. "That you have. But can you really do this forever?"

"I'll do it until it's finished." Yes, it was easier to think about the job—corruption, the people who were hurt by faceless men of evil.

"No one questions your commitment to this case."

Tom collapsed back into the chair, defeated. "I took her out to the cabin. And then I took her to DC with me. I introduced her to Celine and Mark. There. Happy now?"

It was difficult to shock Carlson, but in that moment, Tom was pretty sure he had succeeded. He knew for certain when Carlson said, "No shit."

"It might have been a mistake," he conceded—which was an understatement, to be sure. Because before Caroline had called him, fear in her voice, Tom had been content to watch her from a distance. But now?

No distance. None. Which was why he'd practically begged for distance that night in DC. It had hurt like hell to push her away, but it'd been the right thing to do. This proved it.

He glanced back at Carlson, and if he didn't know better, he would say his friend was trying not to laugh. And if Carlson laughed, Tom was going to punch him. It would feel good to punch someone right about now.

"I've got to meet this woman. Maggie will love her."

Tom groaned. This was only getting worse. "I might have compromised the case." Because he had definitely compromised Caroline Jennings. Repeatedly.

Carlson did burst out laughing. "Right, because I've never done anything—including sleeping with a witness—that might have compromised a case. Or do you not remember how I met my wife?" Carlson actually *hooted*, which was not a dignified noise. Tears streamed down his cheeks. "Damn, man—you've been an FBI agent for too long. There's more to life than arresting the next bad guy, Tom." He leaned over and picked up a picture of Maggie. He had several scattered around the office, but this one was newer—a soft-focus shot of her in the hazy afternoon sunlight, cradling her pregnant belly. "So much more."

Tom worked real hard not to be jealous of his friends' happiness, but he was having a moment of what could reasonably be described as weakness, and in that moment, he was green with envy. "Be that as it may, I'm not going to continually compromise this case. Someone sent her flowers. Someone bugged her house. I'm going to go sweep her office after this, but I'm not going to be shocked if it's bugged, too. Sooner or later, someone's going to reach out to her."

Carlson looked at him for a moment before silently agreeing to go along with the subject change. "Do they have anything on her?"

Tom shook his head. "She's so clean she squeaks. I think that's why they resorted to the cameras—there's nothing else to blackmail her with." Except for how he'd flown her across the country and showered her with gowns and jewels and…

"We need her," Carlson said, any friendliness gone from his voice. "If they reach out to her, I want her to play along and see how much information she can get before they become suspicious. This could be a game changer, Tom."

Carlson wasn't just stating an obvious fact—he was reminding Tom to keep his pants zipped from here on out.

He stood, knowing what he had to do and knowing how damned hard it was going to be.

He wanted her. But that need scared him—because it endangered her, of course. His wants and needs had nothing to do with this. Not a damn thing. The only thing that mattered was that he couldn't risk her. "I need to keep an eye on her, do regular sweeps of her house and office. But I'll do anything to keep her safe between now and then. Including not seeing her."

Carlson considered this. "Does she mean that much to you?"

If it were anyone else but Carlson, he'd lie. And Tom hated lying. But Carlson was one of his oldest friends, and he owed the man nothing less than the truth. "She does."

"Well, then," Carlson said, pushing off the desk and resting a hand on Tom's shoulder. "You do what you need to do."

Tom nodded and turned to go. But when his hand was on the doorknob, Carlson spoke again. "She would've wanted you to be happy, Tom. You know that, right?"

It was like a knife in the back. Tom opened the door and walked out without responding.

Fourteen

Caroline did her best to go back to normal, but it wasn't easy. The trip left her drained in ways she hadn't expected. Apparently getting up at crazy hours and jetting across the country was exhausting.

But that minor inconvenience wasn't the only problem.

Where the hell was Tom Yellow Bird? He was like a ghost in her life. She hadn't seen him in the weeks since they'd come back from DC, but she got regular text messages from him that included the date, time and location he'd swept for bugs. He apparently had checked her office and her house on alternating days—but never while she was there. And he didn't tell her if he'd found anything, just that her house was clean now.

Not that she needed a text to know he'd been in her home. Just like she'd felt it when someone had broken in several weeks ago, she could feel Tom's presence. It was unnerving how easily she could tell that he'd been in her home. Maybe it was the faint smell of him that lingered in the air. Whatever it was, it led to some of her wildest dreams yet.

But when she texted him back to thank him or ask how he was, she'd get one-word replies, if that. It was as if he were still barreling across the highway, inscrutable behind his sunglasses and avoiding any and all questions.

Where was the man who'd swept her away to DC? Who couldn't keep his hands off her? The one who helped her live out some of her favorite fantasies? The man who caught her in his arms when she slipped on wet rock rather than let her fall and couldn't bear to let her out of his sight? She missed *that* man.

Maybe she shouldn't be surprised that he hadn't come around. She didn't quite understand what had changed at the Rutherford Foundation gala, but clearly something had. The Rutherfords had been warm and welcoming—but there was no missing the fact that they were Tom's late wife's parents. Maybe it'd messed with his head to see them all together.

If she could talk to the man, she'd reassure him that she wasn't trying to replace his wife. How could she? She'd never be Stephanie—not in looks, not in family history and not in the way she loved Tom.

Because Stephanie had loved a different Tom than the one Caroline had entrusted with her safety—and quite possibly her heart. Stephanie had loved a younger, more insecure Tom, a man more desperate to prove he belonged in the rarefied DC air. Perhaps Stephanie's Tom hadn't been quite so dangerous, so inscrutable.

That wasn't Caroline's Tom. The man she missed more every single night was unreadable and playful, commanding and commandeering. He could blend seamlessly into a courtroom, a cabin on the high plains and a DC ballroom.

Caroline wanted more than a wild weekend with him and, despite the ghosting, she was sure he wanted more, too. She just had no idea when she might get it because, aside from the flowers she'd received almost two months ago—and the constant sweeps of her home and office—she had no other indication that there was any sort of nefarious activity happening. She got up, exercised and went to work. She came home and slept. Then she did it all again.

Which was fine. Being with Tom had been a whirlwind of impulse and attraction, one that had led her to take crazy risks. At least there hadn't been any lasting consequences from her time with Tom—except that she missed him.

All she could do was hope that he missed her, too.

Ironically enough, a few weeks after she called in sick to work, she started to get sick for real. She'd been feeling draggy, which she'd chalked up to the stress of, well, *everything*. She had no idea where she stood, both with the corruption case and with a certain FBI agent.

She slept more on the weekends, but she couldn't get caught up with her rest. Then she got sick to her stomach in court and barely called a recess in time to make it to the bathroom. Afterward, she felt fine. It must have been something she ate? She threw out the rest of the chicken salad she'd taken for lunch. It smelled funny.

Then the same thing happened the next day—she felt fine until right after lunch, when her stomach twisted. Again, it was a close call, but she made it to the bathroom in time. As she sat on the floor, waiting for her stomach to settle, she realized something.

It hadn't been the chicken salad.

She'd been tired. Now she was sick, but not with the flu or anything. Caroline did the math. It'd been three weeks since her whirlwind weekend with Tom. And her period…

Oh, *crap*.

She should have gotten her period last week.

Caroline was sick again. The whole time, she kept thinking, *No*.

No, no, no, *no*. This couldn't be happening, not again. She'd dodged this bullet once before. She'd missed a period due to stress and it'd made her see that she shouldn't marry Robby, that she couldn't prove her stupid brother right—she wasn't a mistake.

Oh, God. She'd lost her head and her heart to Tom Yellow Bird. For one amazing weekend, she'd thrown all caution to the wind and put her selfish wants and needs before rational thought and common sense.

Had she really been stupid enough to think she'd managed to avoid the consequences of her actions? *Idiot.* That's what she was. Hadn't she learned that anytime she stepped outside the safety of making the correct choices—*every* time—fate would smack her down?

Now she was most likely carrying Tom's child.

Oh, *God*.

She sat on the floor of the bathroom, the tile cool against her back, and tried to think. The first time her period had been late, all the way back in college, her life had flashed before her eyes. She'd been terrified of telling Robby, then her parents. They would have gotten married and she would've had to notify the law school that she'd have to defer a year—or withdraw completely. Her career prospects, all of her plans—all of it would have been wiped away by a positive test result. She'd been sick then, too—but with sheer dread as she waited on the pregnancy test results.

No. She'd known it then and she knew it even better now. Marrying Robby and having his baby would have been the biggest mistake of her life.

Now? Oh, she was still panicking. Unplanned potential pregnancies were an anxiety attack waiting to happen.

But instead of filling her with dread, this time when her life flashed before her eyes, she felt...hopeful. Which was ridiculous, but there it was.

She saw her body growing heavy with Tom's baby. Instead of ghosting through her life, she saw Tom coming home to her at the end of the day, cuddling a little baby with his dark hair and eyes. She saw nights in his arms and trips to visit both his friends on the reservation and the Rutherfords and...

Oh, no.

She wanted that life with Tom. She didn't want this to be a mistake.

She needed to talk to him immediately. Or, at the very least, as soon as she had peed on a stick.

Okay. She had a plan. After work, she'd go buy a pregnancy test. And then she was tracking down Tom Yellow Bird if it was the last thing she did.

"Judge Jennings."

The silky voice pulled her out of musing about baby names in the parking lot on her way home from work that day. She found herself standing a few feet away from a man in a good suit wearing mirrored sunglasses. But it wasn't Tom. This guy was white with light brown hair that he wore stylishly tousled. He was tall and lean—much taller than she was—but due to the cut of the suit, she could tell he had plenty of muscles.

He could've been attractive, but there was something in the way his mouth curved into a smirk that she didn't like. Actually, that wasn't strong enough. There was something about this guy that was physically repulsive.

"Yes?" she said, trying to gauge how far she was from

her car without actually looking at it. Too far. She'd have to go back into the courthouse. Which was fine. The security guards were still there and they were armed.

"I'm glad we've finally met," the stranger said, his smirk deepening. "I've been looking forward to getting acquainted with you for quite some time now."

Oh, crap. "If that was supposed to sound not creepy, I have to tell you, it didn't make it." She smiled sympathetically, as if he were socially awkward and doing the best he could instead of scaring her.

"Excellent," he said, the smirk widening into a true grin. "A sense of humor. It makes everything so much easier, don't you think?"

Oh, she didn't like that smile at all. She took a step back. If she kicked out of her heels, she could run a lot faster. And screaming was always a viable option.

The man straightened. "Relax, Judge Jennings. Did you enjoy the flowers?"

Double crap. She was starting to panic—but even in the middle of that, James Carlson's last email came back to her. *If they reach out to you, play along.* So she straightened and stood her ground, trying to look like she was the kind of woman who could be swayed by several hundred dollars' worth of cut flowers. "They were lovely, actually. Am I to thank you for that?"

He waved the suggestion away. "I must say you are a very difficult woman to get a handle on," he said, as if he had a right to get a handle on her at all. "I have been deeply impressed by your record on the bench."

How was she supposed to play along when he was making her skin crawl? She couldn't. "Still creepy," she said, backing up another step. "If you'd like to make an appointment to discuss something of merit, feel free to call my assistant and schedule a time. Other than that? I don't think we have anything to talk about here."

"Oh, but we do. We do, Judge Jennings," he repeated, because apparently annoying was just a way of life for this guy. "It would be such a shame to see a fine judicial career destroyed because of one naive mistake, don't you agree?"

The world stopped spinning. At least, that was how it felt to Caroline as she suddenly struggled to keep her balance. "What? I don't know what you're talking about." The protest sounded weak, even to her own ears. "I don't make mistakes."

He advanced on her, two quick steps. She tensed, but he didn't touch her. She couldn't run, though—she could barely hold herself upright.

"Excellent," he said again. He was overly fond of that word. "Then the Verango case was intentional, was it? Terrence Curtis was your mentor, after all. It's funny how these things work out, isn't it?" He said that last part so softly Caroline almost leaned forward to catch the last words.

She didn't dare. "I've had a lot of cases," she said, wondering if she sounded like she was on the verge of blacking out. "I can't say for certain which case you're talking about." It wasn't much of a lie, but it was all she had right now.

Tom had known this was coming. He had warned her, and she had willfully ignored his warning because...

Because she'd thought the shameful truth wouldn't get out. No one had ever drawn a connection between her and Verango, between Verango and Curtis. Because she had convinced herself that there was no connection beyond the mentor and mentee relationship.

"Yes," the man said in what might have been an understanding voice coming from anyone else. "I can see that you know exactly what I'm talking about. And won't our mutual friend, FBI Special Agent Tom Yellow Bird, be interested to know about this new development?" He snapped his fingers. "Better yet, I could call James Carlson up and inform him that, despite his hopes and prayers, he has yet another judge to prosecute, hmm?"

"What do you want?" she demanded, trying to sound mean and failing miserably.

"Not much," he said, his tone giving lie to his words. "Merely an exchange. I keep your unfortunate mistake between you and me—like friends do—and in exchange, when a case of interest to me comes before you, you'll give me a moment of your time to make my case." His mouth tightened, and Caroline was afraid that was the real guy, finally cracking through the too-perfect exterior. "Although I won't be scheduling an appointment with your assistant. I'm thinking more along the lines of...dinner?"

"You want me to throw a case?" On some level—the logical, rational level—she knew this was great. This was exactly the break that Tom and James Carlson had been waiting for. Whoever was buying off judges was actively trying to blackmail her!

But there was nothing great about this. Not a damned thing. "He can't watch you forever, no matter how hard he might try," the man said, leaning forward and finally letting the true menace in his voice bleed through. "Do you really want him to know how easily you can be bought?"

There was no need to ask who *he* was.

"No," she whispered, shame burning through her body. Because that was the truth. Tom would find out what she had done all those years ago and it would change things.

Even more than things had already changed. She might be carrying his child.

God, how she didn't want to regret what had happened between her and Tom. She didn't want to regret him. But he might damn well regret her.

Who would want to be saddled with a woman who'd lied by omission about her past, who'd gotten pregnant? She could ruin his career as well as her own. All because she'd lost her head for one weekend.

All because she couldn't say no to Tom Yellow Bird.

Her stomach lurched dangerously, and she fought the urge to cover her belly with her hand. "I don't."

"Excellent," he repeated yet again. "Judge Jennings, it has been a pleasure making your acquaintance." He pulled a business card out of his pocket and held it out to her. But when she went to reach for it, he held it just out of reach. "We understand each other, don't we? Because I would hate to see a promising career like yours destroyed over a little mistake like this."

Caroline swallowed down the bile in the back of her throat. "We understand each other," she agreed. Because she did. Her promising career had indeed been cut short.

She waited for this vile man to say "excellent" again, but he didn't. Instead, he reverted back to a smirk and handed the card over. "If you have any questions or need anything from me—anything at all—I can help you. But only if you help me."

She didn't even look at the card. She slid it into her purse and tried to smile. She didn't know how she would ever smile again. "Of course," she said, impressed that she managed to make it sound good.

With a nod of his head, he turned on his heel and walked off. He didn't get into a car. He merely walked away. When he rounded the corner of the courthouse, Caroline counted to five and then followed. If she could get a car, a license plate—something…

But by the time she could see around the corner, he was gone. Not a car in the street, not the back of his head—nothing.

Her stomach rolled. She was going to be sick.

And it was no one's fault but her own.

Fifteen

The only reason Tom didn't leave flowers for Caroline at her house after every time he swept it was because he didn't want to freak her out. After all, she didn't exactly have positive associations with random floral displays in South Dakota.

But he was tempted. After the initial sweep, he hadn't found any other bugs in her house or office. Which was good. He probably didn't need to be checking things on a regular basis. He should return her key to her. But he couldn't stop. He had to make sure she was safe.

But it was the only thing he could do while keeping his distance. In the meantime, he and Carlson waited for the other players to make their next moves. He knew from a career of waiting that counting each tick of the clock wouldn't make it move a damned bit faster.

He hated not having the ball in his court. Whoever had bugged her house knew that Tom had pulled the devices. They probably knew Tom was doing regular checks. And it was safe to assume that the bad guys had put two and two together and knew that Tom and Caroline had spent at least part of that weekend together. They were no doubt plotting their next move, and all Tom could do was wait to react defensively.

The wait was going to kill him. Slowly.

Because he *missed* Caroline. That, in and of itself, was new. He didn't miss people, not like this. The only other person he'd felt this consuming loneliness for was...

Well, Stephanie. But she'd been dead and he'd been grieving the loss. Caroline was pointedly not dead. In fact, she was within an easy drive. All he'd have to do was park in her driveway and knock on the door.

He couldn't. He was on a case—several cases.

As the days passed, he couldn't stop thinking about what Mark Rutherford and Carlson had both said—that maybe it was time to move on. Maybe Tom already had, but he hadn't realized it until the moment he'd seen Caroline across the crowded courtroom.

He'd spent an electric weekend with her. He'd kicked back and relaxed. He'd enjoyed the explosive sex. He'd taken her to meet the Rutherfords. All of those were things he didn't normally do. That was the only thing that was messing with him. He'd tried something new.

That was all it should have been.

But it wasn't. Because he missed her.

He'd wanted...he wasn't even sure what he'd wanted with Caroline. Sweeping her house and keeping his distance wasn't it, though.

If he were being honest, he'd wanted to see her more. A lot more. But doing that would jeopardize the case.

Spending more time with Caroline...

It had felt like a betrayal of Stephanie. But the thing that Tom couldn't get his head around was the fact that no one else seemed to think that. Not Stephanie's parents. Not Carlson—and they'd all known Stephanie for a much longer time than Tom had. Every single one of them had said the same thing—Stephanie would have wanted him to move on.

Was that what Caroline was? Was Tom finally moving on?

These were the thoughts that occupied Tom constantly as the days dragged on. Tom was tracking down a lead on a different case—sadly, crime waited for no man—when his phone buzzed and he answered it. "Yellow Bird."

"Tom." It was Carlson.

Tom felt a flare of hope. Had someone made a move on Caroline? He hoped like hell they had so this case could end—although he was irritated that she would have gone to Carlson instead of him.

Carlson went on, "There's been a development. You need to come in to the office."

"When?"

"Now."

The last of the lunch rush was thinning out, so it only took Tom twenty minutes to make it over to Carlson's office. He called Caroline to make sure she was all right, but she didn't answer.

He had a fleeting moment when he wished that he had called her at some point during the last few weeks or come up with some sort of excuse to stop by the courthouse and see her. Texting hadn't been enough. He knew there were solid reasons why he hadn't. He didn't want anyone to make a connection between them. He didn't want to compromise the case any more than he already had, so he'd kept his distance.

A growing sense of dread was building inside him and he wasn't sure why. A development should be exciting—

another step closer to finishing this case and finding out who was behind the corruption. This was what he lived for, right?

As he thought about what he lived for, though, it wasn't slapping cuffs on a dirty judge that came to mind. It was Caroline. The way she looked curled up next to the fire pit, wineglass in hand. The way she looked curled against his chest the next morning, a little smile on her face as she slept.

He could hear Mark Rutherford asking him if the job really was the most important thing. And suddenly he knew—it wasn't. He could give everything he'd ever had and ever would have to the job, but what could it give him in return? The promise of more criminals committing crimes. The certainty that the job would never be done.

The realization that he might have given up his dreams of living a long and happy life with Stephanie, but he hadn't given up those dreams of a home, a family.

A wife.

After this, he was going to take some time off, he decided as he walked into Carlson's office. He needed to start over with Caroline. She was probably furious with him—and she was well within her rights to be so, considering he hadn't seen her in much too long. But he knew now that he couldn't keep putting the job first, because it would never return the favor.

And then, as if he'd summoned her just by thinking about her, there she was, standing up from the chair in front of Carlson's desk. Carlson, sitting behind the desk, didn't move at all.

Tom blinked a couple of times, trying to make sense of what he was seeing. Caroline was here and his heart gave an excited little leap—but she wasn't happy. There was something wrong—her eyes were red and watery and her mouth was tight. Instinctively, he moved closer to her. "What's going on?"

Something bad had happened—he knew that much. It was physically painful when she turned her gaze to his. The way she was looking at him—it was like someone had killed her puppy. And she didn't have a puppy.

No one said anything. Tom went to her and put his arms around her shoulders. She sagged against him a little as she drew in a shuddering breath, and in that moment, Tom knew he would kill for this woman. Whoever had hurt her, they would pay.

Carlson's face was drawn and worried. He had arranged his features into a stern look, but Tom could tell he was concerned. "Is someone going to tell me what's going on or not?"

"I'm so sorry," Caroline whispered against his chest.

That didn't sound good. In fact, that sounded bad. He held her tighter and glared at Carlson. "Well?"

"As anticipated, someone reached out to Caroline. We have his name and contact number, as well as a description."

"Okay…" That was fine. They'd expected that. "I know they didn't have any bugs in your house and they didn't have anything on you. What were they trying to use for blackmail?"

Caroline shuddered again and then inexplicably pushed him away. She sank down into her chair, staring at the floor as if it held all the answers. "They do have something on me," she said in a voice so torn with anguish that Tom crouched down next to her to catch all of her words.

"What? I checked you out. You're completely clean."

She shook her head. "No. Not completely."

She wouldn't look at him. Why wouldn't she look at him? Anger flared. He'd really like to punch something.

"Caroline has explained the situation," Carlson began. Tom wanted to ignore him, but he was the only one talking and Tom still didn't know what was going on, so he had to pay attention. But he didn't look away from Caroline. Tears dripped down her cheeks, and each one was like a knife in his heart.

"When she was a first-year prosecutor in Minneapolis, her college mentor approached her. He had a friend of a friend who'd been arrested. It was the usual line—the charges were baseless, the friend was really innocent. He pressed Caroline to drop the charges. She wasn't able to do that, but she offered a plea agreement, which led to a suspended sentence and no time served. As a result, her student loans were paid off."

It all sounded so clinical coming of Carlson's mouth. There was a dinner, a conversation. A plea agreement. Loans were paid off.

"How much?"

Carlson didn't answer, and after a moment, Caroline replied, "Almost two hundred thousand dollars." She still wouldn't look at him.

He stood so suddenly that she recoiled in the chair. If he'd been a younger man, Tom would've put his fist through the wall. Maybe even the glass of the door. But he was older and wiser and he knew that breaking his hand wouldn't solve any of life's problems.

No matter how good it might feel.

"They're counting on her doing anything to keep that series of events quiet," Carlson went on. "The fact that she has come forward to voluntarily share this information before allowing it to compromise yet another case is to be commended. She also detailed how, over the years, she's donated a comparative amount to various charities—

including the Rutherford Foundation—in an attempt to make restitution."

Tom glared at his friend. Carlson was trying to make this sound good—but there was no way to put lipstick on this pig. Caroline had lied to him. He had asked her—repeatedly—if there was anything in her history that could be used against her. Okay, maybe most of that conversation had gotten distracted by sex—but he had asked. She had said no.

Not only had she lied to him, but...

She could be bought.

He didn't just want to punch something. He wanted to shoot something. Repeatedly.

Because they were supposed to be equals. One of the things that made them good together was the fact that they both took their jobs seriously and upheld the law. They didn't throw cases, they didn't accept bribes and they didn't subvert justice.

"Tom," Carlson said, his voice more severe this time, "it was a long time ago. And since that time, Judge Jennings has upheld the law with honor and dignity."

He knew what Carlson was trying to do. He knew what Carlson wanted—he wanted Caroline to play along. He wanted her to find out more information not just about the man who had approached her, but about who that man was working for. He wanted to use Caroline.

Tom's vision narrowed, growing into a murky red around the edges. "Is there anything else?" His voice sounded wrong even to his own ears.

Panic clawed at the edge of his awareness, because he knew this feeling. *Nothing.* He felt nothing.

It was the same horrifying numbness that had overtaken him as he'd stood next to his wife's bed in the hospital and watched life slip away from her broken body.

He couldn't afford to feel anything right now, because if he did, he would lose his mind, and there would be no coming back from that.

He'd thought he'd known Caroline. More than that, he'd taken her to his house. He'd introduced her to the Rutherfords. He'd...he'd trusted her. And he'd thought she'd trusted him. But had she, really?

"Actually, there is." Carlson came around the desk. Without further explanation, he walked out of the office and closed the door behind him.

Bad sign. Getting worse.

"Tom, sit. Please." Caroline's voice broke, but it didn't hurt him. It couldn't.

He sat and waited. How much worse could this get?

"You have to understand—I was so young. I was twenty-four, in my first job. I was drowning under the weight of my student loans. I was having trouble sleeping and was falling behind on my bills and..." She covered her mouth with her hand, but he wasn't going to be moved by it. "Terrence Curtis was my mentor. He always pushed me to be better, and I trusted him. He wrote me letters of recommendation and helped me get into law school..."

"Sure. You owed him."

"It wasn't like that," she snapped, sounding a little more like her old self. Good. He wanted her to fight him about this. He didn't want her to make a pitiful plea. "I should've known better. But he asked me out to dinner to talk about how things were going. I was struggling. We talked and then he mentioned the case that I had coming up—Vincent Verango. He said he knew Vincent personally and it was all a big misunderstanding and he would vouch for the man. And I had no reason not to trust him. I shouldn't have, but I did."

"There's a bit of a gap between trusting a mentor and taking that much cash."

"It wasn't like that," she protested. "He never said, 'If you let my friend off easy, I'll pay off your student loans.' He was too smart for that. I... I was too smart for that. He twisted everything around, and I didn't even know that the loans were going to be paid off until suddenly, they were gone. Vincent was gone, too. Out of state. He's since died, I heard. It was only then that I began to get suspicious. I dug a little deeper and discovered that Vincent had a long list of plea deals and dropped charges—racketeering, money laundering—he was in deep with so much and...and Curtis was in bed with him. Curtis protected him. He used me," she said, sounding angrier by the second. "He knew I trusted him and he used that, and for what?

"God, I was such an idiot but I couldn't see how to undo it without ruining my career. So..." Her anger faded as quickly as it had come on. "I didn't do anything."

"It's a great story, Caroline. I'm not sure any of it's the truth, but it's a great story. You make a very convincing innocent bystander." The color drained out of her face, but Tom didn't care. "Was there something else you needed to tell me? Because if not, I have things to do."

She looked terrible. Not that he cared anymore, because he didn't. But if he had, he would've been legitimately worried about her. She looked on the verge of passing out. Maybe he would ask Carlson to track down something for her to drink—he couldn't leave her like this.

She didn't answer, which unfortunately gave Tom time to think.

He'd spent years coping with the fact that there would be no happy endings for him, not after Stephanie. And then Caroline Jennings had shown up and given him a glimpse of a different life—of the different man he could be with her.

That was the cruelest thing of all, Tom decided. Just

a glimpse at what could've been, and now it was being snatched away.

If she'd never come here and he'd never laid eyes on her, he wouldn't know what he was missing. But now he would. From here on out, every time he went out to his cabin and lay in his bed, he'd think of her, probably for the rest of his life. His miserable, lonely life.

He could definitely shoot something. He'd start with her mentor, work his way through this Vincent guy and then finish off with whoever had confronted her today.

"I'm so sorry," she whispered again.

For some reason, that made him feel like he was the bad guy here when he most definitely wasn't. He had done nothing wrong. Was he yelling? Was he flipping the desk? Was he threatening bodily harm—at least, was he doing it out loud? No. He was doing none of those things. He was politely listening to her tale of woe.

Damn it, he wanted to reassure her that it would be all right. He wasn't going to, but he wanted to. "About the bribe you took, or is this particular apology in regards to something else?"

She moved then, reaching down and pulling her purse into her lap. Her hands were shaking so violently that it took her a few tries to get it unzipped. Tom watched her curiously.

Then she held something out to him. It was a white stick, maybe four inches. One end of it was purple and there was a small digital screen on it.

He blinked. Desperately, he wanted to believe that was a digital thermometer, but he knew better. Jesus, he knew better. Because sometimes, when a girl wanted to get off the streets, it wasn't for her—but for the baby she was carrying. He kept a supply of pregnancy tests in the safe house.

"I..." she said, holding the pregnancy test out to him. "We..."

This wasn't happening. He was hallucinating. Or having a nightmare. Did it matter at this point? No. What mattered was that he had left reality behind and was stuck in some alternative universe, one where his second chance at happiness betrayed his trust and got pregnant with his child at the same time.

He was tempted to laugh because this was crazy. Simply insane. The only reason he didn't was because Caroline was crying and it hurt him. Damn it all to hell.

"We used protection," he said out loud, more to himself than to her. He tried to think, but his brain wouldn't function. Nothing was functioning.

She nodded, wrapping her arms around her waist and curling into a ball. "That's what I thought, too. Then I was tired and then I got nauseous. And I thought...the shower? In DC?"

Jesus, she was pregnant. With his baby, no less. All those dreams of fatherhood that he had put away years ago—they tried to break free and run rampant around his head. He wouldn't let them. He couldn't afford to.

She was right. He'd been so swept up in living out his fantasy of shower sex that he hadn't taken the most basic of precautions. "That's..." He swallowed and then swallowed again. "That's my fault."

She nodded. "Mistakes happen."

He closed his eyes, but that was when all of those hopes broke free. Caroline, in his bed every night. Caroline, her belly rounded with his child. Caroline, nursing their baby while Tom made her dinner. A thousand visions from an everyday, ordinary life flashed before his eyes—a life that, until twenty minutes ago, he had wanted.

But now?

"Why didn't you tell me about the bribe?"

"I put it behind me. No one ever connected Curtis to Verango, much less to me and my student loans." She sighed, looking more like the judge he knew. "I knew it was wrong, but I couldn't go back and undo it. How was I going to unpay the loans? Who would I give the money to, even if I could come up with that much cash?" She shook her head. "It's not a good excuse, and I know it. But I figured that, since no one had made the connection, no one ever would. I didn't…" She sniffed and Tom got a glimpse of the younger woman she'd been, trying so hard to be an adult and not quite making it. "I didn't want to own up to my poor judgment. But more than that, I didn't want you to think less of me.

"But now that it's out in the open, I wanted to tell you, because I knew that if you could just see that I'd been young and stupid, you would do what you always do."

"And what do I always do, Caroline?" It came out more gently than he'd intended.

She looked up at him, her eyes wide and trusting. "You protect me, Tom. You keep me safe."

He stood and turned away, because he couldn't be sure what expression was on his face right now. Damn it all. He wasn't supposed to care about her at all. She was a part of an ongoing investigation. That should have been the extent of it.

Except now she was pregnant. With his child. Because he hadn't done his goddamn job and put the case first.

He'd put *her* first.

"I didn't…I mean…" She made a hiccuping noise that about broke his heart. "I understand if this is a deal breaker, of course. But it was never malicious. And I *never* meant to hurt you."

She was making this worse. "How long ago was this?"

"Almost thirteen years ago."

He dropped his head in his hands. Thirteen years ago, Stephanie had still been alive. He hadn't yet let her walk out of that party alone. He had desperately been trying to prove that he was good enough for her and wondering if he would ever feel like he belonged.

He turned to face Caroline. God, even now, meeting her gaze was a punch to the gut. "Anything else I should know?"

She nodded tearfully. "I had a pregnancy scare in college. With the guy I almost got engaged to. I was…I was terrified. I hadn't been careful enough. I'd made a serious mistake, and I realized when it happened that I didn't love the guy. And I was going to have to marry him and it was going to kill my career aspirations and my parents were going to be so disappointed in me. They'd finally see what my stupid brother had been saying for years, that I was a mistake."

He was going to shoot her brother if he ever got the chance.

But more than that, each word was like a knife to his chest. Yeah, he could see how an unplanned pregnancy would have changed the course of her life back then.

Just like it could do right now.

"What happened?" he asked in a strangled voice.

"I was just late. It was the stress of senior year." She tried to smile, as if she wanted to display how relieved she was. "I didn't want anyone to know, because it was a serious lapse in judgment and if I couldn't make the right choices to avoid something entirely preventable, like an unplanned pregnancy, then why should anyone take me seriously as a professional?"

"Right, right." He looked down at the little stick. "This isn't just stress, is it?"

She shook her head. "I'm so sorry."

Yeah, he was sorry, too. It would be easy to blame her for this, but hell—she didn't get pregnant by herself. "I'm almost afraid to ask—but anything else?"

"No. I made a serious error in judgment my first year as prosecutor and I'm pregnant. I think that's enough for one day." She paused and looked at him, still nervous. "Tom, this guy—he said you couldn't protect me forever."

Tom moved without being conscious of what he was doing. He hauled Caroline out of her seat and crushed her to his chest.

He was mad, yeah—but he couldn't walk away from her. "He doesn't know me very well, then, does he?"

She wept against his chest, and he held her tight. He couldn't help himself.

His trust in her had been misplaced. And maybe he wouldn't get that second chance. But he'd be damned to hell and back before he threw her to the wolves. He protected people.

He was going to protect her.

He stroked the tears away from her cheeks with his thumbs. "I've ruined everything, haven't I?"

She was going to have his baby. She was in real danger. He'd compromised the case. He'd compromised her.

She hadn't ruined anything. He, on the other hand, might have destroyed everything he'd dedicated his life to.

Oh, if only Stephanie could see him now. What would she say? Would she laugh and tell him to relax, like she used to when he got uptight about some fancy shindig in DC? Would she give him that gentle look and tell him he was being an ass?

Or would she tell him that there was more to life than work? That he, more than anyone else, should know not to let life slip through his fingers, because it could all go away tomorrow?

He and Stephanie had always wanted a family. Would she tell him he'd be insane to let this second chance with Caroline pass him by?

A light tap cut off his jumbled thoughts. The door swung open, revealing a very worried Carlson. "Is everything okay in here?"

Tom glared at the man, but he knew he couldn't get rid of him. Not only were they in Carlson's office, they were friends. "Now what?" It came out more of a growl than a question.

"You aren't going to like this," Carlson warned.

Tom tensed, because he knew how far Carlson would go to root out this corruption. Carlson would want Caroline to get closer to her contact and get as much information as she could without endangering herself. He'd want her to wear a wire, maybe flirt—anything to get the information the case needed.

He stared down into Caroline's eyes. How was he supposed protect her—and their child—if she did any of that?

"No," he said, turning his body so that he stood between Caroline and Carlson. "We do this my way or we don't do it at all."

Sixteen

Suddenly, after a career of waiting, Tom didn't have patience for a single damn thing.

This Todd Moffat scum had contacted Caroline and threatened to ruin her career if she didn't go along with what he wanted.

Caroline had withheld the truth from Tom.

She was also carrying his child.

How was he supposed to do anything but spirit Caroline as far away from the likes of Moffat as possible? Worse, how was he supposed to trust her?

The wheels of justice turned mighty slowly. Tracing Moffat took time, as did getting the appropriate warrants. Neither Tom nor Carlson wanted to get a case dismissed on a technicality—especially not about something as important as this. They couldn't rush this just because Tom couldn't sleep, couldn't eat—couldn't breathe.

He'd compromised the case. He'd compromised Caroline.

God, he hoped like hell he hadn't ruined everything.

Yes, it was important, what he was doing. This yearslong investigation was connected not only to judicial corruption, but also to environmental rights and tribal sovereignty—all of it was very, *very* important. Damned important, even. Lives hung in the balance.

But he couldn't let what Caroline had said about her so-called mentor go. She'd lied to Tom about her past—but had she lied about what had actually happened? Had she glossed over her real role or had her mentor used her like she'd said he had?

Tom needed to know. He couldn't let it go. It took a few days because he moved through nonofficial channels, but eventually he tracked down the telephone number for one Terrence Curtis.

When Curtis said, "Hello?" in a voice that shook with age, he sounded ancient.

Tom announced himself. When Curtis spoke again, he sounded more confident. "Agent Yellow Bird, how can I help you today?" He did not sound like a suspect trying to hide his guilt.

"I need to ask you a few questions about one of your former students—Caroline Jennings? Do you remember her?" Tom kept his voice level, almost bored.

"Oh, yes—Caroline. One of my best students—and I say that as someone who taught for decades. We've fallen out of touch, but I've kept up with her career. She's done great things, and I know she'll go on to do even better things."

He sounded like a proud father, not a man who had hoodwinked his best student into abetting a criminal. But the fact that Curtis remembered her fondly made Tom feel a little more kindly toward him. "So you remember her."

"I just said that, Agent Yellow Bird," Curtis said, sounding exactly like a teacher scolding a student. "Is everything all right with Caroline?"

"What can you tell me about the Verango case?" Tom said, hoping to catch Curtis off guard.

"The...I'm sorry," he said quickly. "I'm not sure what you're talking about."

"You're not? That's a shame. Because Caroline, one of your best students, remembers the conversation very clearly. The one where you convinced her to settle for a plea agreement that would let your friend Vincent Verango go free?"

There was a stunned silence on the line, and for a second, Tom thought the old man had hung up on him. He didn't want that to happen. Curtis still lived in Minneapolis and it was a hell of a long drive.

"That's..." Curtis said flatly. "That's not how it happened. Verango and I were not friends. I never—"

"Oh, but you did, didn't you, Mr. Curtis?" Tom cut him off. "It's not a point of contention up for debate. I'm just trying to corroborate her story. Because Caroline, your best student, has done great things, and as you say, she could conceivably continue to do great things from the bench—if her entire career isn't derailed by a corruption scandal. One that traces directly back to *you*."

Curtis made a strangled noise, somewhere between a choke and a gasp. "What—who?"

"All very good questions. Here's what I think, Mr. Curtis. You were her mentor. She looked up to you. She trusted you—maybe she was a little naive about that, but you were both working for the good guys, right?" Silence. "She says that, when she was struggling during her first year as a prosecutor, you took her out to dinner to offer her some moral support. A pep talk. And while you were there, you mentioned you had a friend, Vincent, who had been unfairly arrested. You vouched for him, and as a result of your conversation, Caroline did not throw the book at him. She pulled her punches and Vincent walked." More silence. Man, he really hoped Curtis hadn't hung up on him. "Shortly thereafter, all her student loans were paid off in full. Am I leaving anything out?"

"I..." Curtis sounded older—and definitely more scared.

"And that's why you fell out of touch, isn't it? Because when she figured out that you had abused her trust—it was gone, wasn't it? She kept her distance because it was the only way to protect herself."

"I needed the money," he said, his voice shaking. "I made sure she got a good cut—"

"I don't give a shit what your reasons were. I just need to know whether or not Caroline Jennings was your dupe or if she was an active participant in the miscarriage of justice."

"Of course she didn't know!" Curtis erupted. "I didn't think she'd mind—I was trying to help her out. I should've known better. She always was one of the smartest students I've ever had."

Tom had what he needed—proof that Caroline had not intentionally broken the law. She'd just put her faith in the wrong man.

That pregnancy scare in college, this thing with the Verango case—each time Caroline had slipped up, it was because she'd trusted the wrong man.

And now she was pregnant with Tom's child because she'd believed him. When he'd told her he needed to take her out to his cabin to keep her safe, she'd gone. Same for the trip to Washington. She'd questioned him, sure, but in the end, she'd put her faith in him.

They'd both trusted that what happened at the cabin and then in DC was somehow separate from their jobs.

Well, it wasn't separate anymore.

Tom looked up to where Carlson was listening on another receiver. "Anything else?" He was asking both Curtis and Carlson. Carlson shook his head.

"If you talk to her," Curtis said, sounding tired, "tell her I'm sorry. She was one of my best students, you know."

"I'm sure she was." Tom hung up, feeling almost lightheaded. Caroline wasn't a dirty judge. Yeah, she still should have told him about this, way back when he'd asked if there was anything that could be used against her.

But damn it all, he understood that impulse to bury a past mistake. Hadn't he been doing the exact same thing? Ten years of his life focusing on the job so he could justify living while Stephanie had died.

"Well?"

"I think I have everything I need," Carlson said, making some notes. "I wasn't going to charge her—you know that, right?"

"She wouldn't expect any special favors. Neither would I." Tom knew that about her. Justice was blind.

Technically speaking, the job wasn't done. The department was closing in on Moffat, but no arrests had been made yet. There was a part of Tom that wanted to be the one to slap the cuffs on his wrists, to look him in the eye and make sure he knew that Tom Yellow Bird had been the one to serve justice. Finally, after all this time.

That was still important to him. But it wasn't the most important thing. Not anymore.

Caroline was his second chance.

He wasn't going to let the job ruin that for him.

Tom stood. "Do you need me for anything else?"

Carlson smiled knowingly. "No. In fact, if I see you in the office in the next five days, I'll have you arrested. Show your face within the next two days, you'll be shot on sight."

Tom was already heading out the door. He paused only long enough to look back over his shoulder. "Go home to your family. Trust me on this, James—you don't want to miss a single moment."

Because everything could change in a moment.

No one knew that better than he did.

Seventeen

Really, not that much had changed over the last several weeks—at least, not on the surface, Caroline thought as she packed up at the end of yet another ordinary day.

She got up, she walked—instead of jogging, which was her only concession to being pregnant and even then, it had more to do with the crippling summer heat than her physical state. She went to work, she came home and she did it all over again.

She did not run away with Tom. In fact, after their confrontation in Carlson's office, he had all but disappeared off the face of the planet. She couldn't blame him. After all, she'd screwed up. She'd made a series of unfortunate mistakes that had compounded upon each other. She'd done serious damage to both of their careers, and if she knew one thing about Tom, it was that his career was everything to him.

She hadn't talked to her brother, Trent, in years. They'd

managed a semi-civil nod across the aisle at Mom's funeral several years ago, but Caroline chalked that up more to the influence of his wife than any sentimentality on Trent's part.

Even though she'd cut him out of her life—and vice versa—his hateful words from when she was just a little girl had never left Caroline. She was a mistake and she ruined everything.

She'd heard it so often, in so many ways, that she'd completely internalized Trent's hatred.

Okay, so—yes. She had screwed up. She'd made mistakes. But that didn't make *her* a mistake any more than her parents having her late in life made her a mistake. She might not have been a planned child, but she knew in her heart that she'd made her parents happy.

Yes, Caroline was now pregnant and it could reasonably be described as a mistake.

But that's not what this child was. No, this child was a gift.

Her brother was a hateful man who had blinded her to the truth—far from being a mistake, Caroline had been a gift to her parents. They'd loved her, even if Trent couldn't.

She hadn't planned for this—not for any of it. She hadn't planned to make love with FBI Special Agent Thomas Yellow Bird. She hadn't planned to have her errors in judgment thrown back in her face when she'd least expected it. She had absolutely not planned to get pregnant.

But, yes—unplanned or not, this child was a gift. That didn't mean she and Tom were going to raise this baby together. Even though she was wishing for exactly that.

Because just like it took two to make a baby, it took two to raise one. Oh, sure, Caroline could do the single-mom thing. Women had been successfully raising babies on their own for millennia. But she didn't want to.

She wanted long drives into the sunset and long weekends at a cabin in the middle of nowhere. She wanted to meet the people Tom had grown up with, and she wanted her child to know his roots. She wanted to spend time with Celine and Mark Rutherford and do what she could for the Rutherford Foundation.

She wanted Tom. All of him, not just the parts that looked good in a suit. She wanted the insecure young man carving out a place for himself where none had previously existed and she wanted the overconfident agent who did what he thought was best, come hell or high water. She wanted the fantastic lover and the man who made sure she had the right clothes for events so she wouldn't be nervous.

And if she couldn't have him—all of him—then...

Then he couldn't have her. She wasn't going to settle for anything less than everything. They'd have to share custody or something.

Frankly, the very idea pissed her off. As did the fact that he still hadn't called. Was that just it, then? She'd lied by omission and he was done with her? If that wasn't the pot calling the kettle black, she didn't know what was. Getting a straight answer out of that man about anything was only accomplished by magic, apparently. He hadn't told her he was taking her to his luxury cabin. He hadn't told her she was going to the Rutherford Foundation gala. He hadn't told her anything until the information became vital.

Was that because she wasn't important enough to trust with the information? Or was it just that the job would always come first?

Deep down, she was afraid she was on her own, because in all honesty, she wasn't sure if Tom would ever be able to put her and the baby before his job. She couldn't replace his late wife, and he lived and breathed being an agent. She might be up against forces beyond her control.

When she finally did see him again, she didn't know if she'd kiss him or strangle him, frankly. It depended heavily upon the hormones.

Caroline was staring at her refrigerator, battling yet another wave of not-morning sickness and trying to decide if there was anything that was going to settle her stomach when someone pounded on her front door.

"Caroline!"

Adrenaline dumped into her system as the fight-or-flight response tried to take hold, because who on earth could be banging on her door at six thirty in the evening? Was it a good guy or a bad guy? She couldn't handle any more bad news.

"Caroline! Are you in there?"

Wait, she knew that voice. She sagged—actually sagged—in relief. *Tom*. He was here. Oh, please, let it be good news. Please let it be that they had arrested all the bad guys in the entire state of South Dakota and—and—

Please let him have come for her.

She peeked through the peephole, just to be sure—but it was him. Alone. She threw open the door and said, "Tom! What are you—" but that was as far as she got because then she was in his arms. He was kissing her and kicking the door shut and walking her into the living room and she knew she needed to push back, find out why he was here. But she couldn't. She had missed him *so* much.

But that wasn't her fault. A flash of anger gave her the strength she needed to shove him back. "What are you doing here?" she demanded, gaping at him. He had a wild light in his eyes she could only pray was a good thing. "The case—"

"Screw the case," he said, pulling her back into his arms. "It doesn't matter."

"How can you say that? Of course it matters. What if someone followed you here? What if someone puts us together?"

He was grinning at her. Grinning! He was in the middle of her living room, cupping her face in his hands and looking down at her like she was telling a joke instead of having a panic attack about what the future held. "They better put us together," he said, touching his forehead to hers. "Babe, I am so sorry."

"For what?" She pulled completely out of his grasp, because she couldn't think while he was touching her, couldn't formulate words when he was holding her so tenderly. She stomped to the other side of the living room and crossed her arms over her chest. "I'm the one who screwed up, remember? I'm the one who compromised the case because I lied about my past. I'm the one who threw a case all those years ago. I'm the one who lied to you, Tom. Why are *you* apologizing to *me*?"

She was yelling, but she didn't care. He was here. She was happy and furious and saddened all at once. Stupid hormones.

And he was still smiling at her, the jerk! "Why are you smiling at me?" she shouted.

"Have I ever told you that you're beautiful when you're furious?"

That did it. She threw a pillow at him—which, of course, he caught easily. "You're not making any sense!" Her voice cracked and her throat tightened and she was afraid she would start crying, which would be terrible. She might have ruined her career and she might be unexpectedly pregnant, but that didn't mean she wanted to break down in front of him.

"I'm just so glad to see you. But," he added, before she could launch another throw pillow at him, "I actually came to tell you something." He held up his hands in the sign of surrender. "Okay, you screwed up. But you're acting as if no one else has ever made a mistake in the history of the world, and you're wrong. I've screwed up more times than I can count, Caroline. Including with you. I got it into my head if I just kept my distance from you, that would keep you safe. That would also keep me safe. And all it did was make us both miserable. I miss you. I need you."

He fished something out of his pocket and held out his palm to her. "I want to be with you. Not just now, not just for the weekend—for the rest of my life. Because I feel it. I've felt it since the very first second I saw you."

"What—what are you doing?" Was that a ring?

"I'd given up on a happy ending, Caroline. I'd fallen in love once before and had it ripped away from me, and I figured that was it. No happy endings. No family. Just my job. And then you showed up." His eyes looked suspiciously bright as he took a few steps across the room. "I saw you and I felt it again—hope. Desire. *Love*. I hadn't been with a woman since the night before my wife died and then you came along, and suddenly, I couldn't keep my hands off you. And that led to *my* mistake. I had no intention of getting you pregnant, and I had no intention of leaving you alone to deal with it by yourself. I'm sorry that I haven't been here. But if you'll have me, if you'll forgive me, I will always be here for you."

Okay, so she was crying. It didn't mean anything. She wiped the tears out of her eyes and looked down at his hand, which was now before her. It *was* a ring. Of course it was. A perfect ring with a really big round diamond and a bunch of smaller diamonds on the band. It was the kind people wore when they got engaged. When they meant to spend the rest of their lives together.

She looked back up at him, trying to keep it together and failing miserably. "But the case—the job—"

Tom shook his head. "For so long, it was personal. I had to prove I belonged by being better than everyone else, and then, when Stephanie died, I...I didn't have anything left. Everyone in my family had passed. I was a long way from home. All I had was the job, and I gave it everything because it was the only way to make things right."

She didn't like the image of him all alone. "Is that why you've been radio silent for so long? You're making things right?"

Tom pulled her into his arms. He looked tired. Was that because of the job or because of her? "I'm not going to let anyone intimidate or threaten you, Caroline. That's a promise. But I don't have to give everything to the job. Not if it keeps me from you." He rested his free hand on her belly. "Not if it keeps me from *this*. I've missed you so much, Caroline. You mean everything to me and I've let you down. If you give me another chance, I won't let you down again."

She swiped madly at the tears rolling down her cheeks, but they were replaced too quickly. "I missed you, too," she sobbed. "I've missed you so much."

Unexpectedly, he fell to his knees. "Caroline Jennings, will you marry me? Because you will always be more to me than a case or a job. I love you. I have from the very first. And I want to spend the rest of my life proving it to you."

She tried to look stern, but it wasn't happening. "I don't want this to happen again," she told him, starting to hiccup. "I don't want you to disappear for days and weeks on end. I don't want you to leave me alone, wondering..."

"I won't. It was a mistake to do so. But," he went on, climbing to his feet and holding her hands in his, "I have one thing I need to tell you."

She groaned. "What now?"

"I spoke with Terrence Curtis." She gasped, but he just kept going. "He admitted that he convinced you to amend the charges and that you had no idea he had an ulterior motive. He also told me to tell you that he's proud of everything you've accomplished since then. You were one of his best students."

"You tracked down Mr. Curtis for me?"

Tom had said he would protect her. She'd always assumed he meant physically—safe from bad guys and evildoers.

But this? This was her reputation. Her career. And he'd protected it.

"I wanted it on the record that you hadn't intentionally or maliciously broken the law. Carlson won't be pressing charges, either."

"What about…"

"Moffat? We're building the case. We know who he is and who he's working for. We've got him—thanks to you."

She stared at him, because that was all she could do. There weren't any words.

He was back to grinning wildly at her. "Say yes, Caroline. Be my wife, my family. Our family," he added, stroking her stomach. Instantly, the air between them heated, and she felt that spark catching fire again as his hand drifted lower and then higher. She burned for his touch—but with fewer clothes. A lot fewer clothes.

"I took a couple of days off," he murmured. "Let me show you how much I love you."

"Yes." Yes to it all—to his touches, to his proposal,

to his love. "I love you, too. But I'm going to hold you to your promises, okay?"

"I'm counting on it."

She couldn't stop the tears, but she smiled anyway as she pulled him into her. "Good. Because I feel it, too. And I'm never letting you go."

Epilogue

Once upon a time, Tom had considered tracking down criminals and arresting them to be difficult but rewarding work. It involved a lot of sleepless nights and hours of patiently waiting for a few moments of intense activity—the arrest—and then, much later, the payoff, a guilty verdict.

All in all, it had been remarkably good training for being a parent.

"Never thought I'd see the day," James Carlson said. Carlson was speaking to Tom, but his gaze was fastened on his wife.

Maggie sat next to the fire pit with Rosebud Armstrong, Celine Rutherford and Caroline. The women were laughing and chatting, all while Maggie rubbed her pregnant belly. Everyone was hoping to make it through this Memorial Day barbecue without the untimely arrival of the second Carlson child.

"See what?" Tom kept an eye on Margaret as she picked up leaves and handed them to Caroline. Tom knew his thirteen-month-old daughter could sit in one place for a while sometimes—but not when Carlson's two-year-old, Adam, was chasing the Armstrong boys around. The twins, Tanner and Lewis, were almost seven and didn't have time for a two-year-old. Instead, Rosebud and Dan's kids were splashing in the spring-fed pool. Poor Adam kept getting soaked, but instead of fussing, he was giving as good as he got, giggling the whole time. Dan Armstrong was nearby, keeping the kids safe in the shallow water.

Margaret watched the whole scene with fascination, and Tom knew it wouldn't be much longer before she tried to follow the older boys into the water. It didn't matter that she could barely walk, much less run. She'd be after them in moments, shrieking with joy. She was such a happy baby. Just looking at her made Tom's heart swell with joy.

"You," Carlson laughed, taking a long pull on his beer as he flipped a buffalo burger.

Tom gave his old friend a dull look. "You see me all the time." Margaret pushed herself to her feet, almost falling into Caroline's legs. Although Caroline kept her attention focused on Rosebud—who appeared to be telling a story about the twins' most recent exploits—she easily caught her daughter and cuddled the baby to her chest.

For years, Tom had waited. He and Stephanie had wanted to make sure they had their careers set before they took time off to have a family, and then...it'd been too late. He'd figured that he missed his window and fatherhood wasn't in the cards for him.

He had never been more thrilled to be wrong as he was right now.

"No," Mark Rutherford said, watching all the children, "I know what he means. We never thought we'd see you this *happy* again."

Caroline looked up and caught him watching her. And,

just like he always had, Tom felt that spark between them jump to life. Every time he saw her, he fell in love with her all over again.

"Yes," Carlson laughed, flipping another burger. "Just like that."

Tom didn't know how to respond to that. He was in uncharted territory here. In addition to being a Memorial Day party, this barbecue at his cabin also marked the end of the corruption investigation that he and Carlson had pursued for years. It also potentially marked the end of Tom's full-time commitment with the FBI. The job was finally done, hopefully permanently.

Todd Moffat had been arrested, tried and convicted. His employer had been revealed to be Black Hills Mines, a mining company that had been locked in several protracted legal battles with the various tribes over uranium rights. Uranium mining was a dirty business, but there were huge deposits underneath the land that made up many of the reservations in South Dakota. Black Hills Mines wanted the right to strip the uranium out of the ground. Understandably, the tribes preferred not to have their reservations destroyed and contaminated. Moffat had turned in favor of a lighter sentence and everything had fallen into place.

The job was over—for Tom, anyway. He was taking a leave of absence from the agency. He'd continue to be available as a consultant—he was still the best agent to deal with cases that involved tribal issues. But he was turning his attention to the Rutherford Foundation.

They were building a new school on the Red Creek Reservation. Tom was going to make sure it was everything his tribe needed.

So this wasn't a farewell party. The agency had gotten him a cake for that at the office. This?

This was a welcome home party. Margaret was at a really amazing age, and he couldn't bring himself to spend his nights sitting in a surveillance vehicle in the hopes that the bad guy did something when he could be at home with his wife and his daughter.

However, no matter how perfect this moment or any of the moments in the previous twenty-three months had been, he knew he didn't have all the time in the world. Maybe he was jaded, but he knew better than anyone else that it could all end tomorrow and he wouldn't waste another moment on something as impersonal as a career. His career would never love him back. It would never give him a family or those thousands of small moments every day that made up a good life.

Margaret was going to start running and talking soon. And Tom was going to be there to see it with his own eyes. He was going to show his little girl the world—powwows and parties and everything that made him who he was, everything that would make her who she was, too.

For years, he'd made his own family—finding members of his tribe and others who were lost and needed a way home. And he hadn't given that up. He might have stepped aside from his job, but he would never turn his back on those who needed him. He had a charity to run, scholarships to fund and people to help. But he didn't need a badge to do that. Not anymore.

He just needed to know that, at the end of a long day, Caroline was coming home to him. She'd returned to her seat on the bench once her maternity leave had ended, and Tom was proud of what she'd accomplished.

Margaret looked up at him and smiled, her fingers in her mouth. She'd probably be up late tonight, fussing at her sore teeth. But right now, she grinned at him and all Tom could think was, there she was—the most perfect little girl in the world.

It was different, the love he felt when he looked at his daughter. It was full of hope and protection and sweetness, whereas when he looked at his wife, it was full of longing and heat and want. But it was love all the same.

"She would have been happy for you," Carlson said, shaking Tom out of his thoughts. "This was what she'd have wanted for you. You know that, right?"

Tom looked at his wife and daughter and fell in love again, just like he did a hundred times a day. Some days—like right now—he thought his heart might burst from it.

When he'd first fallen for Caroline, he'd struggled to give his heart to her completely. But he knew now—loving Caroline and Margaret didn't take away from the love he'd felt for Stephanie. It didn't make him less. It only made him more. So much more.

"Yeah," he said, staring at the loves of his life. "Yeah, I do."

"We should get a picture," Rosebud called out. "Something to mark the retirement of one of the best special agents the FBI has ever seen."

Everyone agreed, even though it felt like overkill to Tom. He was still adjusting to this new reality, where he wanted people to take pictures of him and his family—wedding pictures and baby pictures he didn't hide in a storage closet, but displayed on the walls of his cabin. He'd paved the road down to the cabin and done away with the shrubbery hiding the turnoff. He didn't have to hide who he was anymore. He belonged, just as he was.

It took time to wrangle all of the kids. Dan had a new tripod for his phone, so he was able to set it up to take a photo of all of them.

Tom's throat tightened as he watched his family and friends arrange themselves around him. Caroline leaned into him, her touch a reassurance. "Okay?" she asked in a quiet voice meant just for his ears.

He stared down at his wife and knew that later, after everyone had left and Margaret had fallen asleep—at least for a few hours—he'd take the spark that had always existed between them and fan it into a white-hot flame. Because he had known from the very beginning—there she was, the woman he was going to spend the rest of his life with.

He kissed her, a promise of things to come, because he would never be done falling in love with her. "I've never been better."

* * * * *

COMING SOON!

We really hope you enjoyed reading this book.
If you're looking for more romance
be sure to head to the shops when
new books are available on

Thursday 19th June

To see which titles are coming soon, please visit
millsandboon.co.uk/nextmonth

MILLS & BOON

FOUR BRAND NEW BOOKS FROM
MILLS & BOON MODERN

The same great stories you love, a stylish new look!

Conveniently ARRANGED
LYNNE GRAHAM   LORRAINE HALL

WANTED: HIS HEIR
MAYA BLAKE   DANI COLLINS

DEFIANT Brides
Tara Pammi   Michelle Smart

THE BILLIONAIRE'S LEGACY
ABBY GREEN   NATALIE ANDERSON

OUT NOW

Eight Modern stories published every month, find them all at:
millsandboon.co.uk

LET'S TALK
Romance

For exclusive extracts, competitions and special offers, find us online:

- **f** MillsandBoon
- **X** @MillsandBoon
- **◯** @MillsandBoonUK
- **♪** @MillsandBoonUK

Get in touch on 01413 063 232

> For all the latest titles coming soon, visit
> millsandboon.co.uk/nextmonth

afterglow BOOKS

Afterglow Books is a trend-led, trope-filled list of books with diverse, authentic and relatable characters, a wide array of voices and representations, plus real world trials and tribulations. Featuring all the tropes you could possibly want (think small-town settings, fake relationships, grumpy vs sunshine, enemies to lovers) and all with a generous dose of spice in every story.

@millsandboonuk
@millsandboonuk
afterglowbooks.co.uk
#AfterglowBooks

For all the latest book news, exclusive content and giveaways scan the QR code below to sign up to the Afterglow newsletter:

SCAN ME

afterglow BOOKS

- Sports romance
- Enemies to lovers
- Spicy

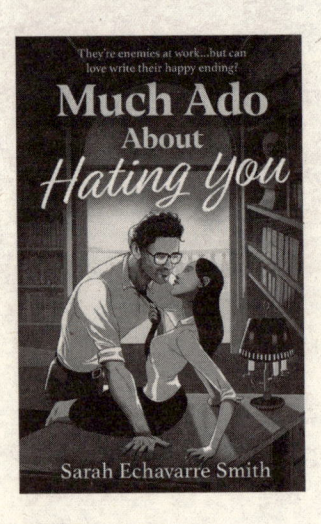

- Workplace romance
- Forbidden love
- Opposites attract

OUT NOW

Two stories published every month. Discover more at:
Afterglowbooks.co.uk

MILLS & BOON

THE HEART OF ROMANCE

A ROMANCE FOR EVERY READER

MODERN — Prepare to be swept off your feet by sophisticated, sexy and seductive heroes, in some of the world's most glamourous and romantic locations, where power and passion collide.

HISTORICAL — Escape with historical heroes from time gone by. Whether your passion is for wicked Regency Rakes, muscled Vikings or rugged Highlanders, awaken the romance of the past.

MEDICAL — Set your pulse racing with dedicated, delectable doctors in the high-pressure world of medicine, where emotions run high and passion, comfort and love are the best medicine.

True Love — Celebrate true love with tender stories of heartfelt romance, from the rush of falling in love to the joy a new baby can bring, and a focus on the emotional heart of a relationship.

HEROES — The excitement of a gripping thriller, with intense romance at its heart. Resourceful, true-to-life women and strong, fearless men face danger and desire - a killer combination!

afterglow BOOKS — From showing up to glowing up, these characters are on the path to leading their best lives and finding romance along the way – with plenty of sizzling spice!

To see which titles are coming soon, please visit

millsandboon.co.uk/nextmonth

OUT NOW!

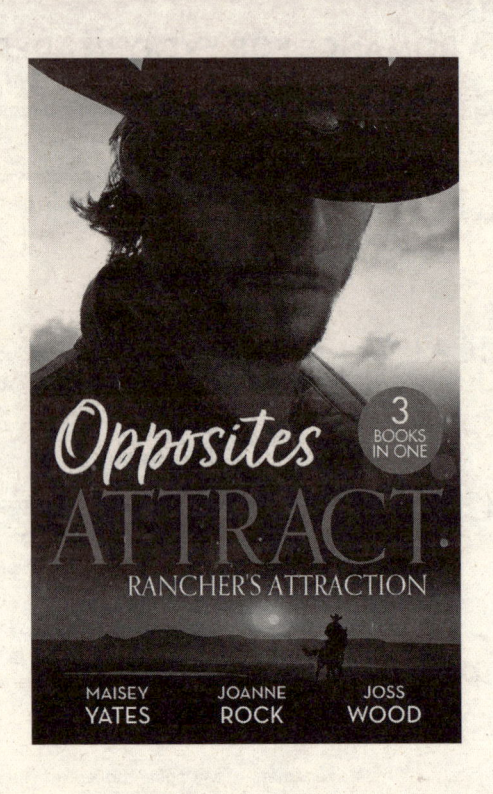

Opposites ATTRACT: RANCHER'S ATTRACTION

3 BOOKS IN ONE

MAISEY YATES · JOANNE ROCK · JOSS WOOD

Available at
millsandboon.co.uk

MILLS & BOON

OUT NOW!

Princess Brides: A Royal Baby

Amy Ruttan · Catherine Mann · Jennie Lucas

3 Books in One

Available at
millsandboon.co.uk

MILLS & BOON

OUT NOW!

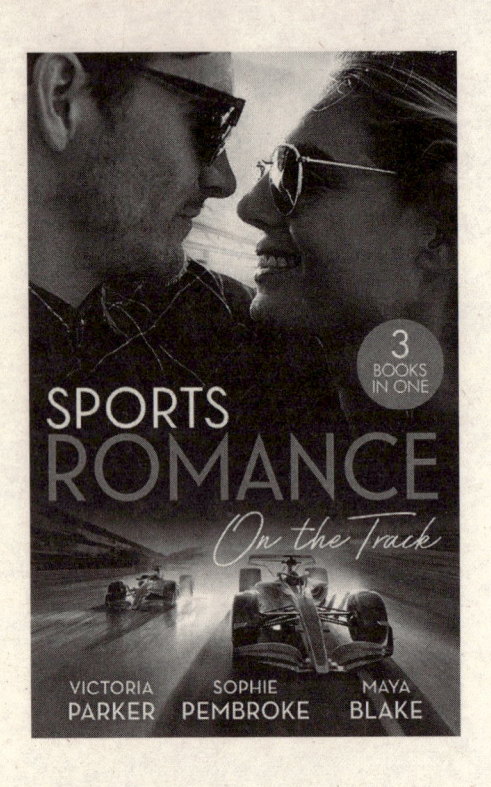

SPORTS ROMANCE
On the Track

VICTORIA PARKER
SOPHIE PEMBROKE
MAYA BLAKE

3 BOOKS IN ONE

Available at
millsandboon.co.uk

MILLS & BOON